GOOD HOPE

GOOD HOPE

MALCOLM KOHLL

THAMES RIVER PRESS

Good Hope

THAMES RIVER PRESS
An imprint of Wimbledon Publishing Company Limited (WPC)
Another imprint of WPC is Anthem Press (www.anthempress.com)
First published in the United Kingdom in 2014 by
THAMES RIVER PRESS
75–76 Blackfriars Road
London SE1 8HA

www.thamesriverpress.com

© Malcolm Kohll 2014

All rights reserved. No part of this publication may be reproduced
in any form or by any means without written permission of the publisher.

The moral rights of the author have been asserted in accordance
with the Copyright, Designs and Patents Act 1988.

All the characters and events described in this novel are imaginary
and any similarity with real people or events is purely coincidental.

A CIP record for this book is available from the British Library.

ISBN 978-1-78308-203-2

This title is also available as an eBook

To Rafaela and Harlan
My Alpha and Omega

Prologue

'The problem with 9/11 was that that the day after, the very next day, they started cleaning up. After *we* are finished the land will be poisoned for a thousand years. Nobody will come near the place – we will have made a wasteland for the infidel like they have made for us.' Sayeed Dhatri looked at the three faces around the table. His hooded blue eyes contrasted starkly with his coffee skin and shock of black hair. The others nodded as he rolled out a large scale map onto the oilskin tablecloth. 'There will be two attacks – one from the sea, and one from the land. Once we have penetrated the reactor core then the pressurised water vessel will explode and blow the roof off!'

The stocky man raised a hand. 'I've been to the plant and the outer walls must be two metres thick, reinforced concrete. How do we breach that?'

Sayeed smiled and pointed to the map. 'See here – this dotted line. A narrow gauge railway line - it's where they bring the fuel into the reactor.'

'But it must have security doors?'

'It has. Two sets of steel blast doors. But we will be driving a small diesel engine loaded with a ton of explosive straight into the doors. We will knock – Allah will open for us!'

They all laughed.

'And from the sea?'

'A Zodiac with RPG may not get right through the walls but will weaken them so that when the water container blows, the whole side will shear off. Cape Town will become uninhabitable.'

Chapter 1

Observatory, Cape Town. A mixed suburb near the University of Cape Town, consisting of small Victorian houses let out to students, artists and those of modest income. Like policemen. Which is why Gerry Viljoen and, until very recently, his girlfriend Aletta lived there.

But after the fight, he had just let her go. She slammed the door and he heard her footsteps clicking on the slasto *stoep* then crunching the gravel in the driveway. He tracked her footfalls past the loquat tree where the mouse birds lived, then the screech of the iron gate and the loud clang as it relocked itself. The car door slammed and finally her Yaris started and she drove off into the night. 'Bitch,' muttered Gerry as he poured himself a stiff brandy and stared at the ashes of his life. 'Bitch!' he yelled into the darkness.

It had all started innocently enough. Aletta had said that she had bumped into her ex-fiancé, Louis Eskteen, and gone for coffee with him.

'Where? Where'd you bump into him?' demanded Gerry. His tone caused her to frown. 'In Greenpoint. He's got a flat nearby.'

'Nice place, is it?'

'What? Christ Gerry, I don't know. We went for coffee. To Café Neo. Louis made me an intriguing offer…'

'I'll bet,' muttered Gerry.

'Excuse me?' said Aletta, her cheeks burning. 'What the hell's that supposed to mean?'

'Nothing.'

'No, you meant something. Come on! What?'

'It's fine. You go have coffee with your ex.'

'Gerry! I can't believe you're saying this! He made me a job offer! Partner in a new pharmacy in George.'

'George? That's fucking great! So you want to go and live in George now?'

'For Christ's sake stop being so ridiculous! I wanted to discuss it with you!'

'I can't live in George!' Yelled Gerry. 'You want to go and be with your old flame, fine!'

'I can't believe you!' said Aletta, tears in her eyes as she grabbed her handbag and stamped out.

Gerry squinted at his watch. It was past midnight and a full hour and four fingers of Klipdrift brandy since Aletta had left and since then, silence. Gerry had spent his time ruminating, and eventually what started out as a dim and slightly crazy notion had coalesced into something ineffable in his woozy brain. One way or the other, he had to know.

He climbed into his blue Impreza and blipped the throttle a couple of times before pulling a tight U-turn and zig-zagging through the quiet back streets of Observatory towards the highway leading to the City bowl, then out to Mouille Point. There was virtually no traffic at that time of night and Gerry flew along De Waal Drive, flanking the Mountain, feeling a shove in his back as the turbo kicked in. Then down through the gears as he swooped off the flyover back to street level. He buzzed through the robot on amber and swung right towards Sea Point, hitting nearly 160KPH as he stormed towards Greenpoint Stadium.

He knew that Eksteen lived in a three bedroom flat on the beachfront, within spitting distance of Café Neo, where the rich and beautiful would congregate for skinny lattes after jogging to the lighthouse or walking their Schnauzers. The café was shut, and Gerry was cruising slowly along the line of cars parked against the curb in Beach Road. He suddenly slowed – there was Aletta's Yaris, within five hundred metres of the porticoed entrance of Mirabelle, the five storey block of Art

Deco flats, recently renovated in cream and burnished chrome. Gerry found a parking space around the corner and was immediately accosted by a Cameroonian with a pock-marked face in a fluorescent vest who guided him into the opening and promised to keep his car safe. Gerry scowled at him and crossed the road, the better to observe the flats from the nubby salt grass verges leading up to the sea wall. A mist had risen off the steely South Atlantic swell, frosting his eyelashes as he looked up at the top floor to the only lit flat. As he watched, the lights went out.

'Fuck!' said Gerry and glared at the dark block, then turned and walked back to his car. Moments later the Cameroonian emerged from the darkness with his hand outstretched 'Sharp-sharp, boss.' Gerry was about to argue but slapped two Rands into the man's hand and shut the car door. His hands were trembling slightly as he opened the cubby hole and took out a matchbox. Inside was a white and gold wafer the size of his thumbnail. He slid open the back of his phone and inserted the new SIM card and dialled.

'There's gunshots and screams coming from a flat…Mouille Point, Beach Road. The block is called Mirabelle…You spell it like it sounds, *Jissis*… Top floor, number 513.'

Gerry rung off and replaced the SIM with the original one, slid the untraceable one back into its matchbox and pulled away from the curb, chuckling to himself. 'Coitus interruptus, my friend. Big time.'

Heading back towards De Waal Drive he passed two Police cars driving fast the opposite way, sirens keening and lights flashing.

By the time Gerry got home the effects of the Klipdrift had largely worn off. While taking a handful of Advil he glanced in bathroom mirror and saw a man in his mid 30's, rings around his eyes, stubble on his chin and a stain on his shirt staring out at him. 'Arsehole,' he said, shaking his head. He fell onto his bed and waited for insensibility to overwhelm his hurt.

Six thirty in the morning isn't a time, it's an insult. And Gerry felt truly disrespected when the doorbell jangled his fried neurons and he staggered to the front door in his underpants and yanked it open, hoping to see a contrite Aletta standing there. Instead he saw a tall muscular black man in combat trousers and a tight olive vest, New Balance running shoes on his feet. He pushed past Gerry into the small bungalow.

'You were supposed to be ready! Six thirty – ding-dong! It's gonna be hot today and we're going up the long way.'

Gerry groaned. The idea of climbing Table Mountain with an elephantine hangover and awash in self-pity and remorse made no sense. Having his colleague and friend Tau Molepe in boundless good humour and enthusiasm only made matters worse.

'Letta not here?' asked Tau.

'No,' said Gerry. 'Put on some coffee, I need a shower.'

'Really? That rank sweat is kinda fetching,' said Tau wrinkling his nose. 'I thought you guys were in last night?'

'We were, but she's not here now, okay? Just get the coffee on!'

Gerry went up the short passage to the bathroom and entered the shower cubicle. It smelled of Aletta's soap and shampoo. Gerry muttered darkly and turned on the hot tap. He stood out of the stream until the water was steaming, then plunged, feeling the heat scalding his skin. Then he flipped the lever to Cold, and let the icy blast snap him back into consciousness. Two minutes later he walked into the kitchen, tugging up his black rugby shorts over which hung a Springbok green and gold striped rugby shirt. Tau was watching the coffee drip through the filter cone and didn't glance up.

'You were yelping in there,' he said. 'Hangover?'

'I don't yelp. And only girls and students get hangovers,' growled Gerry.

Tau poured two mugs of coffee and set one silently before Gerry.

'You want to tell me about it?'

'No,' said Gerry.

Tau sniffed the air.

'Mmm. Nice. Is that Lily of the Valley or White Lavender?'

Gerry went to his bedroom and emerged moments later with his Sig Sauer P250, loaded with 9mm hollow-points.

'I might have to shoot you today. I'm just letting you know,' he said, tucking the gun into his waistband.

Tau nodded and started opening cupboards. 'Touchy,' he said. 'You have issues with your manhood. Look, Lily of the Fields doesn't make you homosexual. You haven't started listening to Barbara Streisand have you? Where are the biscuits?'

Gerry waved his gun vaguely at the cupboards. Tau grabbed his wrist and seized the gun and flipped out the magazine and laid it on the counter.

'Don't EVER point a fucken gun at me! Now find me some of your *ouma's* rusks before I have to kick your sorry arse.'

'Now who's touchy?' grumbled Gerry. '*Jissis*. Top shelf.'

Ten minutes later they were driving towards the Constantia end of Table Mountain, and within twenty minutes were striding through the *fynbos* of the lower slopes of Skeleton Gorge. The sun had burned away the last trails of mist and the rock hyraxes were sunning themselves on flat boulders. Gerry stopped for a pull on his water bottle and squinted at the narrow stony path stretching up towards the summit – it was going to be a long hard climb. Tau, about 50 metres ahead of him, turned round with a wave. 'Feels good!' He called. Gerry ground his teeth and carried on.

After the first hour Gerry had sweated most of the toxins out of his system, and was in more familiar territory of burning muscles and pounding heart. The snatchiness of his stride had given way to smoother and more regular footfalls, but he was still struggling to keep sight of Tau who seemed to power effortlessly ahead.

A bright green snake skittered across the path just in front of Gerry and he leaped back with a cry. Tau came bounding down the track towards him.

'OK?'

'Ja. Looked like a mamba! Just there!'

Tau glanced quickly around.

'Probably more scared of you than you are of it,' he said.

'Right. Till the bastard bites you. Then you're plenty scared.'

They took a drink from their canteens and rested on a smooth grey rock etched with patches of green and orange lichen. The ancient forests were spread below them on one side, on the other the city bowl. And above, the looming presence of the Mountain. A table cloth of white cloud was pouring over the summit.

Tau turned and squinted. 'Not much visibility up top,' he said.

'Bout two more hours,' said Gerry. 'Might clear.'

'We shouldn't sit too long,' said Tau. 'Don't want the muscles seizing up.'

'You missed your calling,' said Gerry. 'Should have been a nanny.'

The path grew steeper and in some places disappeared entirely, but as they approached the summit the sun burned through the low cloud and slowly the vista opened below them.

'If I have a heart attack you must promise me one thing…' gasped Gerry, hauling off his rucksack and falling flat on his back. He lay staring up at a porcelain sky braided with cloud, his heart hammering, lungs searing in the crisp air. The sun was now directly overhead, an unseasonal 32 degrees.

'What?' Tau fell onto the earth beside him, also gulping lung-fulls of oxygen.

'No mouth-to-mouth. If I'm gonna die then take a big rock and smack me across the head with it.'

'Be my pleasure,' said Tau.

After a few moments Gerry managed to raise his wristwatch to his face.

'Three hours forty. Not bad,' he said.

'It's not record-breaking, but we did come up the hard way.'

'You got any water?' Asked Gerry. 'I finished mine even before the halfway marker.'

Tau shook his empty water bottle.

'Sheesh. Not even a Coke?'

Tau laughed and sat up. Gerry sat up as well, groaning from the exertion. From the top of Table Mountain they could see the entire Cape Peninsula laid out below them, the bottommost tip of Africa jutting out into the ocean. The clear confluence of the Atlantic and Indian Oceans was visible, and beyond that a distant haze stretching uninterrupted all the way to Antarctica.

'So?' said Tau. 'How did you screw up the only good relationship you ever had?'

Gerry was about to argue but saw it was futile. 'I think she's seeing another bloke,' said Gerry.

'THINK? You know thinking's not your strong suit. Do you have proof?'

'I saw her go into his flat late last night and all the lights went off!'

'And?'

'Do you want a fucken road map?

'So what did you do?'

'Busted,' muttered Gerry.

'Come again.'

'I had them busted. I called in a 515. Suspected homicide.'

'Anonymously?'

'I'm not a total cunt, you know.'

'Jury's still out. So did she call you from the cells? Say *Gerry honey, having me arrested was the best thing you ever did for me*?'

'No,' said Gerry miserably. 'But if she was innocent, why was she there? And what happened after lights out?'

'Well, short of throwing yourself on her mercy and begging forgiveness, I doubt you'll ever know.'

'You don't think she'll suss that it was me who called it in?'

'Oh, I reckon it would take her about five seconds on a slow day.'

'Fuck.' Said Gerry. 'Fuck. Fuck. Fuck.'

'On reflection,' said Tau, leaning back on his backpack. 'You know what you said earlier about being a cunt..?'

'Thanks, pal,' said Gerry.

'Nothing you can do now but wait and see how she reacts. But don't get your hopes up.'

'If she is seeing another guy then it's over, right?'

'Knowing Aletta, I'd say that in the remote chance she was seeing someone else, she'd admit it.'

'That's what's bugging me. She was steaming because I wouldn't believe her.'

'You've got trust issues.'

'Maybe I *should* have shot you,' muttered Gerry as he pulled a grass stalk out of its sheath and nibbled the soft tip.

They sat in silence for a few minutes.

'It's so peaceful up here,' said Tau, feeling the sweat cooling.

'Why did you have to say that? Huh?' Yelled Gerry. 'What an arse!'

'You're very superstitious for a white man,' said Tau.

'That's rich from someone who thinks his *oupa* is a chameleon!' said Gerry, fumbling in his backpack. He held out a stick of biltong. Tau snapped it in half and handed one piece back to Gerry.

'I'll discuss animism and its role in traditional beliefs any time, but the reason I don't like chameleons is because… I just don't like the way they change colour all the time,' said Tau.

'Like the Chinese,' said Gerry. Tau gave him a sideways look then turned to stare out at the vista. They chewed their biltong in silence. The singing of the cicadas presaged a breeze, cooling the sweat on their bodies. Minutes ticked by. Gerry hummed a soft tune, waiting him out. Finally Tau could take it no longer.

'What do you mean, "Like the Chinese?"'

'In the bad old days under apartheid they were made "honorary whites" – now they've asked to be classified as "blacks" to take advantage of Black Economic Empowerment.'

'Ja, exactly like a chameleon,' growled Tau.

Which was when a tinny version of *The Ride of the Valkyries* trilled in the bottom of Gerry's rucksack. Gerry glared at Tau.

'Superstitious? Prescient!' said Gerry, fishing for the Blackberry. He glanced at the Caller ID and braced himself.

'Sir?'

'I want you and Molepe in my office within the hour.' The bass rumble came from Jonas Chitepo, Head of the NIA, the National Intelligence Agency.

'Uh…We're actually on top of Table Mountain…' said Gerry, mentally working out the quickest way down.

'One hour,' said Chitepo and the line went dead.

'Did he say why?' asked Tau.

'*Jissis*,' grumbled Gerry. 'Doesn't he know it's Sunday?'

'What does that tell you?!' Said Tau, hauling himself to his feet.

'That he needs to get a life,' said Gerry. 'Last one to the cable car station is a sissy.'

'I hope it's running,' said Tau, striding out across the rocky tussocks. A family of *dassies* skittered away, and overhead a hawk soared on a thermal, wingtips trimming flight, tail balancing.

They managed to reach the cable car station in just under 20 minutes, as a car arrived at the dock. A queue of tourists was waiting for the car to settle before the doors opened when Gerry walked up to the attendant and flashed him his identity card, which showed a grim-faced Gerrit Hermanus Viljoen, 32 years old, staring straight into camera and identifying him as an Officer in the National Intelligence Agency. The attendant nodded and waved Gerry and Tau into the car ahead of a couple of Japanese tourists who grumbled loudly until Tau silenced them with a glare.

The ride down the mountain was spectacular, with the car slowly revolving to give a full panoramic view of Cape Town and its harbour before coming gently to a halt at the docking station at the foot of the mountain.

Gerry and Tau stepped into the blinding sunshine of the parking lot.

'How are we supposed to get to our car? It's round the other bladdy side,' muttered Gerry just as an unmarked Corolla pulled up beside them.

Leaning out of the window was Ramalao, one of the cheerful pool drivers in a garish T Shirt with straw hat perched jauntily on the side of his head. He flung open the passenger door.

'Hop in, gents. The bossman wants you like yesterday!'

'I'm liking this less and less,' muttered Gerry.

'Since when did "like" feature?' said Tau as they clambered in.

'Buckle up or die,' said Ramalao.

'You aren't wearing your seatbelt,' said Gerry.

'Ah, that's because I know I won't crash. But you don't know that.'

Ramalao put a flashing light on the roof and hit the siren and grinned at Tau who was sitting in the front beside him.

'Great, huh,' he said with a wink. 'The chicks love it.'

'I hope you don't pull this stuff when you're off duty,' muttered Tau trying to look reproving. Ramalao laughed and bore down on an old woman who leaped out of the way in the nick of time.

Ten minutes later the car swooped into the cool underground car park of an anonymous city block, distinguished from the outside only by a plethora of aerials on the roof. Concrete bollards defined where the cars could move, watched over by a bank of CCTV cameras, with two guards slowly patrolling in flack jackets with Uzis held across their chests. Ramalao gave them a cheery wave and they ignored him.

'See you later, gents,' he cried, and spun the car around and roared towards the exit.

Tau and Gerry jogged across to the lift and punched in a security code. Both stared into the camera mounted above the lift and moments later the door opened and whisked them to the top floor. They walked along a corridor and stopped at a solid oak door and knocked twice and entered.

They found themselves in a large ante-chamber with several government-issue chairs arranged against the wall, a coffee table containing some of the more lurid popular magazines in English, Afrikaans and Xhosa, a glossy rubber plant and a desk behind which an attractive young Indian woman, Soraya Naidoo, sat. She smiled at them. On the wall a picture of the President beamed down at everyone.

'So, Miss Naidoo, what brings us all in on a Sunday?'

'I couldn't possibly say, Agent Viljoen,' she said sweetly.

Tau leaned forward over her desk.

'Perhaps there's something you could tell *me*, Miss Naidoo,' he said giving his brightest smile.

'Yes, Agent Molepe, there is. You and your good friend Agent Viljoen could both benefit from a shower. Why don't you take a seat and wait for the Director.'

Gerry and Tau sat down, suddenly self-conscious. Both men were sweat-stained and dusty, exuding a sun-ripened miasma.

'Hurry up and wait,' muttered Tau through clenched teeth.

'SNAFU' said Gerry. 'Are we the only clowns on call today?'

'There's an American in with him,' said Miss Naidoo in a stage whisper.

Just then the door to the inner sanctum flew open and the imposing figure of Jonas Chitepo filled the space. He was over six feet tall with a prosperous belly and black-rimmed glasses that gave definition to his large jowly face. Peering through the glasses were shrewd eyes, now examining his two best field agents who looked less than impressive as they scrambled to their feet. In turn, Gerry and Tau were regarding their chief in stunned silence – Chitepo had obviously arrived from the golf course and was wearing powder blue golf pants and a yellow knit shirt, giving the impression of an over-inflated beach ball.

'Gentlemen. Come in.' He left the door open and walked back into his air-conditioned office with a panoramic view over the port on one side, the Mountain on the other.

Gerry and Tau entered the office as a slim man in well-cut suit got to his feet. He had a silver-streaked brush cut and a face weathered by outdoor life and large workman's hands with manicured nails that gleamed as though varnished. They already knew Stanton Fitzwarren, the Africa Station Chief of the CIA who had spent a week the previous summer in Cape Town, briefing the local personnel about the twin threats of Islamic Militancy and Pan African Socialism that were sweeping down through Africa.

Fitzwarren grinned, hand extended.

'Tom'n'Jerry. How're you boys doing?'

'It's Tau, and it means Lion,' said Tau squeezing the American's hand harder than necessary.

'And it's Gerry with a 'G' and it means 'don't come to my house and pee on the rug. Sir.'

'Good to see you fellas are all still piss and vinegar. We're gonna need it. Jonas?' Said Fitzwarren, turning to Chitepo.

'Stanton here was just lecturing me on the evils of African Socialism,' said Chitepo with a deep chuckle. 'He thinks it might be catching.'

'Not so much lecturing as having a free and frank exchange of ideas,' said Fitzwarren with a wink. 'I still don't get it – where in the world has it worked? Look North, my friends – there are failed states across Africa. Russia. Even in Cuba they are now introducing a private sector'.

'I believe that Cuba has 100% literacy and free health care,' said Gerry, deadpan. 'How does that compare with the USA, sir?'

Fitzwarren held up his hands in mock-surrender.

'OK, but they still drive 1954 Chevvies and when Fidel hung up his cigar it was brother Raoul who stepped into his shoes. We don't do dynasties in the States,' said Fitzwarren.

'Aside from the Bushes and Kennedys,' said Chitepo.

'Going back to your earlier point,' said Tau, 'when the ANC was fighting to free this country it was only the socialist regimes who supported the struggle. Margaret Thatcher and your own President called us "terrorists", and Nelson Mandela was the terrorist-in-chief.'

'I do find these discussions bracing – kinda like a douche with an icepack. Well now, putting aside all the power-crazed oligarchs, we've got some real bad boys to deal with,' said Fitzwarren. 'Here's the situation - the world AIDS conference will take place in Cape Town March 26 through 28 this year.'

'I thought it was all happening in Rome,' said Tau, frowning.

'We have a developing situation,' said Fitzwarren. 'Yesterday afternoon a plumber was called to a fifth floor bathroom in the hotel complex where all the world leaders were to be billeted. The bath was leaking and when they removed the panels they found a couple of pounds of plastic explosive rigged to a timer, ready to blow at the height of the conference.'

'They only discovered this NOW?' said Gerry, incredulous. 'I thought they would have been sweeping the hotel for months.'

'They were. And in fact had used dogs to check for explosives that very morning. But here's the thing – the explosive and timer were shrink-wrapped in plastic and gave off no odour. Nothing. So the security boys did a full sweep of the hotel and dismantled all the bathrooms and found other four devices, all rigged and primed to go off at the same time. But what's worrying is that the timers were on a 12 month clock. Our initial estimate is that they were put in place nearly eight months ago.'

Chitepo peered over his glasses at them. He spoke slowly in a voice like thunder rolling across the veldt. 'Right after the venue for the conference was announced,' said Chitepo. 'Which brings us to the present. The national security heads agree that the site was violated because of the advance notice, and decided to switch not only hotels but country as well to remain one step ahead of the terrorists. Hence Cape Town.'

Fitzwarren said, 'We're all in favour of this initiative, but our big concern, starting today, is security.'

'The end of March is less than a month away!' blurted Gerry.

'Correct. And you're gonna need every single day to make this place tighter than a ducks' ass.'

'Where will the conference be staged?' asked Tau.

'The Mount Nelson,' said Chitepo. 'The guests will be billeted there as well.'

'How many?' said Tau.

'Including all key personnel, 350.' said Fitzwarren. 'And the special guest who will be flying in for the final day of the conference is the President of the United States.'

Gerry looked at Tau who sucked on his teeth.

'There will also be the other G8 leaders, and your own president has been asked to preside at the closing ceremony.'

'Is there any indication of possible trouble at this stage?' asked Gerry.

'Well,' said Fitzwarren, 'we took the decision yesterday evening and since then the electronic chatter has gone up considerably.'

'Where?' asked Tau.

'Mostly from Iran.'

'Iran? What's this got to do with the Iranians?,' said Gerry.

'PAGAD,' growled Chitepo.

'I have a dossier,' said Fitzwarren. 'And any help you boys need, we're only a phone call away. Thank you, Jonas, for enabling this briefing to take place at such short notice. And gentlemen, there will be an aircraft carrier berthed at Simonstown with a full complement of my people, plus a circling AWAC for 24 x 7 airborne surveillance during the conference. Just to give you guys a bit of extra juice.'

Fitzwarren stood and shook hands all round and exited. The others looked at each other. Chitepo slid them each a thick file.

'We'll have to get hold of Achmad Karriem,' said Gerry.

'You had better call your significant others and tell them that you're going to be late tonight,' said Chitepo.

'Very good, sir,' said Tau. 'Will our American colleagues be calling the shots on this one?'

'It's our area of influence, but the security services for each of the Heads of State will be conducting their own operations.'

'Great,' said Gerry. 'So we could have our own people shot by one of our trigger-happy American buddies.'

'That's why they call it friendly fire,' said Chitepo. 'Seriously, you will have to put in place a system which ensures nothing like that happens. While these players are delighted to come and shake our hands and drink our wine, if anything goes wrong they will only be too happy to have their worst prejudices confirmed about Africans being only one step away from chimpanzees. And I don't intend giving them that opportunity. Understood? Now get to it.' Chitepo was already working on a sheaf of papers before they reached the door.

In the outer office Gerry smiled at Miss Naidoo. 'Can you get us a pool car, Soraya?'

'I'll check,' she said, frowning. She picked up the phone and dialled a number. Moments later she looked up with a smile.

'Ramalao's on his way. Two minutes.'

'Thanks,' said Gerry. Tau was saying nothing. He stalked out of the office, followed by Gerry who punched the lift button.

'You look happy,' said Gerry.

'Joyce is gonna kill me,' muttered Tau. 'We were due at her brother's engagement *braai* tonight.'

'You're right. She is gonna kill you,' said Gerry, then immediately realized with a pang that he would not have to tell Aletta that he would be late because he didn't know where she was, nor if she even cared what Gerry was doing. Tau hunted for a signal on his phone while they waited in the car park but the area was electronically shielded to prevent remote control car bombs. Moments later Ramalao screeched to a halt beside them and sped out onto the street where Tau tried to get a signal to speak to his wife of 18 months.

At 28, Joyce Matabane was a senior lecturer in Sociology at the University of the Western Cape. She was destined to be a high-flier and Tau always felt somewhat overshadowed by the professors and visiting academics tripping over themselves to spend time with the beautiful Joyce. He sensed that she wished he were something other than a 'bloody policeman' which is what she had once called him during a heated row.

She retracted the statement immediately, but the words had cut deep and Tau wondered whether or not their small house near the University would become their permanent residence, or merely prove to be a stepping-stone to separate lives like so many others of their friends whose marriages had collapsed. Tau was determined that theirs wouldn't go the same way, but he could only influence events so far – if Joyce didn't want the same things then the inevitable slide would start.

He didn't relish discussing his personal affairs in front of Gerry or Ramalao, but he owed it to Joyce to let her know as soon as possible. He sighed and hit speed dial.

'Hi sweetheart,' he said, trying for a light tone.

'Hi. Did you boys have a good climb?' she asked.

'Great. We did it in three forty,' said Tau. 'But we were called in to see the boss. I'm speaking from the pool car right now,' he said, hoping that by alerting her to the fact that the call was not private he could avoid any embarrassing scenes.

'Uh-huh,' she said, 'so when will you be home?'

'That's just the thing,' said Tau, 'I might be a bit late…'

The silence lengthened. Finally Joyce said, 'But you will make it for Sandile's party, won't you?'

'I will do my best, sweetheart, but you should go ahead and I will come just as soon as I'm done.'

'I hope so,' said Joyce frostily. 'You've known about this for months.'

'I'm sorry, Joyce, but there is a major security alert. This is what I do,' said Tau softly. 'Give Sandile my best.'

Tau hung up and looked defiantly at Gerry for some smartarse comeback.

'I bet if we were doctors on call nobody would bat an eyelid,' said Gerry, trying to be helpful. 'Probably be pleased with all the overtime we'd be earning.'

'You're not letting Aletta know?' demanded Tau.

'Aletta who spends the night with another man?' said Gerry, looking out the window.

'Or maybe in jail,' said Tau looking grim. 'And we don't get overtime.'

The traffic was starting to build. Ramalao attached a flashing blue light to the roof and roared up the emergency lane.

They retrieved Tau's car from the side street near The Gardens. 'Mrs Vee?' asked Tau. 'Nobody better,' said Gerry. 'This is gonna be fun,' he growled. Tau swung the car around, looking grim. Twenty minutes later they pulled up outside an old colonial building at the top end of Roeland Street, within sight of Parliament. Despite the parquet flooring and elaborate carvings and plaster gingerbread, the library serving the National Intelligence Agency was equipped with the latest computers and operated one of the few ultra-high-speed broadband links in the country. At the desk was old Mrs Van Der Westhuysen whom it was rumoured had been a librarian when Lord Charles Somerset had presided in the Cape in the 1820s.

'Oh it's you two,' she said sniffily.

'Hello *Tannie*,' said Gerry affably, 'what are you doing here on a Sunday?'

'Where else am I going to be?'

'We want everything you've got on PAGAD.'

She looked hard at him. 'Everything? Do you know what you're asking, young man,' she said.

'Yes,' said Tau testily. 'From soup to nuts. Past, present and future.'

'Just so you know,' said Mrs Van Der Westhuysen. 'And I'm not your bloody auntie either.'

Tau and Gerry exchanged a grin and followed her down one aisle of books, then another. Finally she turned a corner where two computers sat facing each other across a desk. Reaching from floor to ceiling were filing cabinets, open shelves of reference books and a bank of CDs and DVDs. Gerry groaned.

'PAGAD,' said Mrs Van Der Westhuysen gesturing at the stacks. 'Enjoy.'

'Hang on, Mrs Vee. Look, we don't have half a lifetime to trawl through all of this – can you give us a potted version? *Asseblief tog.*'

'We'd appreciate it,' said Tau. 'General aims, history, that kind of thing.'

She looked shrewdly at them. 'It'll cost you,' she said. Tau slid a glance at Gerry who nodded. 'A bottle of Klippies?'

'Make that two,' she said. Gerry was just about to protest when she gave a 'be my guest' gesture at the huge amount of raw data.

'No problem,' said Tau.

Mrs Van Der Westhuysen drew up a bentwood chair.

'Sitting comfortably are we? Right, I'll begin…' She took off her spectacles and pinched the bridge of her nose. She shut her eyes tightly and started speaking in a slow fluid monotone.

'PAGAD – acronym for People Against Gangsterism And Drugs, was started by a Muslim organization in the slums of the Western Cape. In its conception it was a benign organization designed to address the issues of young people who were sucked into the spiral of drug dependency and easy money, which inevitably led to shootings and stabbings.' She opened one eye. 'Are you keeping up?' she asked. Gerry nodded irritably and carried on jotting notes. She shut her eye and resumed.

'The movement sprung from an organization called Qibla which had started in the 1980's, modelling itself on the Iranian revolution and funded covertly by Iran. The aim was to promote Islamic interests in apartheid South Africa. After independence in 1994 the organization shifted shape and spawned PAGAD, which in turn produced several offshoots. In its most benevolent form, the community-based activities took the form of vigilantism targeted against gangsters and drug lords within the black and 'coloured' community. Generally, the police were lax in following up these kangaroo courts because they were effective in helping to clean up certain high crime areas, and this crude form of self-policing at least enjoyed a degree of community support which the national police did not.'

She paused and poured herself a drink of water from a plastic bottle. Tau nodded encouragingly. 'Give me a second,' she said, and took a deep breath.

'The police were more interested in the G-Force or Gun Force splinter group of PAGAD. These were armed men who would kill their opponents, and worked in close-knit cells that were extremely difficult to penetrate. In 1998 PAGAD attacked a special police unit and thereafter the gloves were off. The leaders were detained and many sentenced to lengthy jail terms, and after that the overt face of the organization largely disappeared.

What happened was they went underground, now linked closely to the Iranian regime and targeting not the South African government directly, but foreign interests such as tourists and American businesses operating within the country. And as the wars in Iraq and other Muslim countries continued, so the organization found an endless stream of new recruits. These men did not need to go to foreign lands to secure their jihadi training but could remain in Africa where a host of regional wars were being played out – Somalia, Aden, the Horn of Africa, the Yemen. More recently Mali and the Sahara.'

She opened both her eyes and put on her spectacles. 'In the past few years Al Queda in the Maghreb has been ramping up its operations and spreading into Nigeria through Boko Haram and various other local offshoots – same ingredients, different flavours. Here endeth the lesson,' she said.

'And locally here? Any sign of Militant Islam?' Asked Tau.

'Small. There are rumours of four possibly five cells but these guys are very tight knit and it's hard to get definite insider information.'

Gerry and Tau shared a look.

'Of course,' said Mrs Van Der Westhuizen. 'Our people are trying to infiltrate, but you gentlemen would probably know more about that then me. But I'm only a humble librarian, what do I know?'

'Right,' said Tau. 'You know more than the bloody Joint Chiefs.'

She smiled humbly. 'I am here to serve. Now if you would kindly remember my brandy when you're passing a bottle store…'

'A pleasure,' said Tau. She nodded and shuffled back to her desk.

'Kiss-arse,' said Gerry.

'She saved us six hours of tedious work. I reckon it's worth it.'

'We need to speak to the inside man,' said Gerry dialling a number on his cellphone. After a brief hiatus of atmospheric clicks and whirs, it defaulted to message. 'Achmad, Gerry speaking. Give us a call, pal. A-bladdy-Sap.'

'Now we wait,' said Tau.

Chapter 2

Achmad Karriem, a young "coloured" man of Malay extraction, had been at the Police College with Tau and Gerry and then been singled out with them for further advanced training within the security forces. Achmad was the class clown, a happy-go-lucky figure who always had a snappy comeback and witty retort, but in recent days he had found his reserves of humour dwindling fast.

After two years of trying, the NIA had managed to infiltrate Achmad into one of the most hard-line PAGAD cells, a tight unit of four men who called themselves Scimitar. Achmad had moved into a two-roomed bungalow in the poorer part of District Six with the cover story of having come from up the West Coast where he had worked in a fish cannery.

He found a job at Pep Stores and started attending the local mosque, and after a few months of asking questions was pointed in the direction of a surly young man known only as Moosa. Achmad indicated that he was bored by the tame sermons of the local Imam, and wanted to hear something with a bit more bite. He had heard that in a private back room Moosa and some friends periodically screened DVDs of firebrand foreign Imams. Moosa was initially suspicious of inviting Achmad into the group until one day Achmad arrived with a DVD of Abu Hamza, the hook-handed Imam who had spent years in detention in Britain before being extradited to the USA. Thereafter Achmad became a regular at the private screenings, often arriving with new DVDs to share with group, having obtained them from his colleagues in the NIA hours before.

There was always an intense debate after the screenings about what the role of a Muslim was in a world where his beliefs were under attack. One day Moosa silently pushed a DVD into the player and they watched as flickering images of a jihadi training camp lit up the screen. Further videos of the 'struggle' followed, with footage of actual 'martyrdom' operations of car bombings in Iraq and Afghanistan. After one of these sessions Achmad approached Moosa and explained that he felt passionately about the cause of oppressed Muslims and wanted to involve himself further.

It took another four months before he was finally inducted into a secretive unit comprising three G Force men, led by Hakim. They were thugs who had previously spent time in jail on drugs and weapons charges and boasted of recently busting a major cocaine dealer and then selling his stash and keeping the profits, while at the same time letting it be known that PAGAD had taken another dealer off the streets. The younger man, Ibrahim, had killed a man when he was 14 years old. The other, Ravi, had spent time in jail for selling guns.

For them the Islamist umbrella was a convenient cover for their other activities, but being street smart and highly suspicious of any newcomers, they gave Achmad a task – he had to rob at gunpoint some wealthy tourists at the Waterfront. Achmad had stuck his pistol into the gut of a heavyset 'German tourist' – in reality a National Intelligence Agency weapons instructor from Pretoria named Goosen - who handed over his wad of traveller's cheques, and Achmad had escaped through the busy crowds and jumped into the waiting car belonging to his newfound comrades. He had passed the test.

That night they sat around the kitchen table in a small bungalow in Salt River. Hakim, the leader of the group, produced a crudely drawn map that he laid out on the oilskin table cloth. He jabbed a stubby finger at the map. 'Here. Tomorrow night.'

Achmad squinted at the drawing – where Hakim was pointing was a six pointed star. 'The Gardens Synagogue. Firebombs. We burn the fucking place to the ground!'

The others yelped with laughter. 'See here...Only one guard at night between midnight and six AM. He's got a little hut here by the corner. We take him out and then smash into the place and set the fires and gone. Five minutes top!'

'Sounds like a plan,' said Achmad. 'What time do we go?'

'Four thirty in the morning. We meet here tomorrow night at ten to prepare. Clear?' They all nodded.

Achmad placed a call to his boss as soon as he got home, explaining that he wanted the best men possible because Hakim's team would have to be taken down, but that he would need to be able to escape. He didn't want some trigger-happy clown shooting him in the belief that he was the enemy.

When he arrived at Hakim's house the next night the first thing Hakim did was ask for the cell phones of all the members. 'There's been a change of plan,' he said. 'We are going in at three AM.' Achmad nodded. 'Can't be too safe,' he said, fervently hoping that the NIA counter-terrorist team would be in place by the time they arrived.

'Let's get busy,' said Hakim. He produced a couple of boxes of washing powder and a milk bottle crate filled with empty bottles. He carried in a jerry can from outside and used a funnel to half-fill all of the bottles with petrol. The washing powder was added to each bottle to make a thick viscous jelly, then rag strips were torn and stoppered into the necks of the bottles and doused in fuel.

The bombers sat back to admire their handiwork. 'Can I make some coffee?' asked Achmad. 'Coffee?' barked Hakim. 'Sure. I have my own muti.' He produced a couple of Mandrax tablets that he washed down with a slug of whisky. The other two grinned and opened a small paper envelope and emptied a gram of cocaine onto the table top and started chopping out lines. 'Come,' said Ibrahim, 'this stuff will give you courage to fight.' Achmad waved his hand. 'I don't do that shit,' he said. 'I stick with coffee.'

An hour later they staggered out to Hakim's car, each man carrying a rucksack in which nestled four of the glass firebombs. Achmad, the only sober one amongst them, muttered a silent prayer that his team would be in place.

Hakim's eyes were glittering as he pulled up in Wandel Street, a quiet avenue lit only by Victorian street lamps, spread far apart. The four men hopped quickly out of the bakkie and picked up their rucksacks from the back. 'Check your guns,' said Hakim. Achmad glanced nervously around, hoping that they were already under surveillance. Hakim walked quickly along the street, followed by the others, dipping into the inky shadows and avoiding the pools of yellow light.

When they turned into the square where the synagogue was located, Hakim pointed at a small wooden hut, inside of which a figure was huddled deep in a greatcoat, head rolled forward onto his chest.

'There! Bastard's asleep. We take him – two shots to the head, then break into the place and throw the bombs. We outta there inside five minutes, neh. We got that?'

'Shoot him?' asked Achmad, his mouth suddenly dry.

'Ja. You got a problem with that?'

'You said "take him out." I didn't know you meant permanent, like.'

'It's permanent,' said Hakim. The others nodded. 'Now we do it.'

He chambered a round in his pistol and walked quickly towards the sleeping security guard, sitting on a three-legged stool inside the peaked wooden doorway of his watchman's hut, his cap pulled low over his eyes. As he raised his Star pistol, Hakim was caught in the blaze of a spotlight.

'STOP! Throw down your weapons!' Half a dozen armed police emerged from the shadows, guns drawn. The 'security guard' threw aside his coat and produced an H&K sub-machinegun pointed straight at Hakim. 'Allahu Akbar!' cried Hakim, firing wildly at the searchlight, only to be cut down in seconds in a welter of gunfire. Ibrahim had his gun in his hand and was firing wildly at the darkness when he was struck by a burst of automatic gunfire and whipped around in a jerky dance before falling in a bloody heap. Ravi started to run and was thrown onto his face as five bullets tore into his back and spine.

Achmad turned and fled as the bullets whined around him, whacking chunks off the tarmac. He managed to reach his own car, parked two streets away, and was already a kilometre away when the sirens converged on the blood-splashed open ground in front of the temple.

Achmad arrived at Moosa's house in a quiet street in Fishoek, speckled with the blood of his slain comrades. The house was in darkness and it took a few minutes of urgent knocking to produce a light. Moosa appeared in a short robe, a surly look on his face.

'What the fuck?' he demanded.

Achmad pushed past him and shut the door.

'Ambush! The cops were waiting for us!'

'Were you followed?'

'No, I wasn't followed. But someone tipped them off.'

'Where are the others?'

'Dead. The cops were waiting. Like a fucken shooting gallery! They'll be after me now too. You got to hide me.'

Moosa was furious but realised that he had to get Achmad out of the house as soon as possible. He opened the door to the adjoining garage and put Achmad on the floor of his *bakkie* and covered him with some hessian sacking and drove off into the night. The watching police saw only one man in the car and decided that Achmad was still inside Moosa's house, and so remained in position although they alerted HQ that Moosa's pickup was on the move.

After ten minutes bumpy drive Moosa stopped the car and threw back the sacking to reveal that they were outside a small house perched on a dark hillside. Achmad took a moment to orientate himself then recognised the arc of Kalk Bay below. The night was dark with a herringone sky, a sliver of moon breaking through the clouds and splintering off the waves in the harbour. The air smelled of salt and seaweed, and the green navigation beacon blinked slowly on the end of the jetty. Moosa led Achmad into the house and told him to stay put and drove swiftly away. Twenty minutes later the Highway Patrol had stopped Moosa on a supposed traffic violation and conducted a search of the *bakkie* and found it to be empty. Moosa was sent on his way and the watchers remained in place, confident that their man was still inside the Fishoek house.

Achmad sat in a bare living room with the cheap curtains drawn, waiting. He felt secure that his watchers would have followed him from Moosa's house and knew that as long as the security police knew his whereabouts he was relatively safe. A few minutes later he heard a motorbike pull up outside the house and a tall young Asian man entered. He had hooded blue eyes which contrasted startlingly with his coffee skin and black hair, carrying a crash helmet in one hand, a rucksack in the other. He stared hard at Achmad for some time before speaking, then put his hand inside the rucksack and kept it there. Achmad felt the hairs on his neck tingle, aware that he was in the presence of someone with power.

'How is it,' said the Indian, 'that your comrades all died and yet you came through without a scratch?'

'Allah saved me for further work. Perhaps it was not my time for martyrdom,' said Achmad.

'Clever answer,' said the other man, 'also very convenient.'

'Do you presume to question Allah?' asked Achmad. 'With respect, my friend, it is you who is glib.'

The Indian held Achmad's eye for a long moment then laughed. Achmad decided to press the issue.

'This is also about ability,' said Achmad. 'They were idiots. Thugs. They didn't have strategy or planning. All they had was simple plans and big guns. Unfortunately, the cops had bigger guns. Someone informed.'

The Asian man nodded. 'You seem to have strong opinions for a shelf stacker from Pep Stores.'

'We all need to earn a living,' said Achmad. 'I find that physical work lets me concentrate on more important things.'

'Such as?'

'Jihad,' said Achmad.

'There's something about you that doesn't quite ring true,' said the Indian. 'Tell me, where did you come from?'

Achmad picked at a hangnail for a moment before answering.

'You know already. Why are you asking me? I just nearly had my head blown off!'

The blue eyes became icy as the Indian withdrew his hand from the rucksack holding a 9mm parabellum Star that he put gently on the table, its barrel facing Achmad.

'Why don't you tell me again?' he said softly.

Achmad licked his lips. 'My Pa was an alky who worked on the railways till he disappeared. A wheel-tapper…'

'Disappeared? Where?'

'If I know that he wouldn't be disappeared, would he? Ma says he ran off with this cherry from Bellville. We never saw him again. My Ma brought us up. She took in sewing, did house cleaning for some rich whities there up in Rondebosch by the name of Carter. Posh – very larny. More English than the English.'

Achmad was speaking easily and fluently, because what had said so far was true. 'When I was 15 she told me to *voetsek* and get a job. I heard there was good work at the fish cannery up the coast and found work there. I was nearly seven years with those stinking fucken fish, man. Finally I had enough and decided to come to Cape Town.'

'Have you always been devout?'

'Not so much, bra. When I was younger I was a bit of a *skelm*. Busting pipes, taking Mandrax, chasing all the cherries. Did a bit of house robbery and nearly got caught. But then just before my Ma died I went to see the old lady and I was *vrot* on *Tassies* and she just looked at me and said 'You gonna be a rubbish just like your Pa if you carry on like this.'

Ahmad sighed deeply. 'Next day she died and at the funeral I started speaking to the Imam and he told me to come to see him at the mosque. To be honest, I hated it at first, but then you know, something got to me and I started reading seriously. That's what brought me to the struggle.' Achmad looked straight at the Indian. 'And what about you?' he asked.

The Indian's eyes darkened. 'It's not your place to ask me questions,' he said softly.

'My place? No-one tells me what my place is anymore, *boet*. OK? I respect Allah, not some bloke I just met.' Achmad smiled mirthlessly. 'How do I know you're not fucken Special Branch?'

The Asian looked at Achmad for a long moment, then slid back his Star's slide, cocking the pistol, and shoved it against Achmad's head. Achmad did not dare breathe.

'If I was Special Branch I'd blow your brains all over the lino,' he said. 'And if I find out that you're not the man you say you are, believe me, friend, you will die.' After a moment he un-cocked the weapon and put it back into his pocket.

'Listen, I've got nothing to lose. The cops won't rest until they've got me. Please, let me involve myself in something worthwhile.'

'So you think you're capable of being something other than a wild dog? Let's see. I will put you together with some more experienced men. We are planning a big operation that will put our cause on the map. Not just in South Africa but all the way to Washington. But any sign of police like tonight, and you will be the first to go. Do you understand?'

'I expect nothing less,' said Achmad, 'I welcome the chance to prove myself. I'm worth more than sticking up some fat tourist for a few Rands.'

'You will stay here. This evening you will be met and taken to a safe house where you will be briefed. Understood?'

'Yes,' said Achmad. 'What is your name, brother?'

There was a pause while the Indian considered. 'I am not afraid to tell you because your path is now the same as mine, the path of Holy War. I am Sayeed Dhatri. If you ever mention my name to anyone outside of this room I will kill you like that!' said Sayeed, snapping his fingers. 'Go into the bathroom and remain there until you are let out.'

Achmad nodded and entered the bathroom. Moments later he heard the key turn in the lock and shortly after that Sayeed's footsteps walking across the floor and exiting the door. A few seconds later Achmad heard a motorbike start up and roar away down the hill. He tried to open the frosted panes but the window was screwed shut. Achmad sat on the chequered tile floor, breathing deeply. He wanted to phone HQ and report in but he felt that he was not alone, so he turned off his phone and sat with his head cradled on his arms, thinking.

Suddenly Achmad woke up, momentarily disorientated. The room was dark, with only the pale yellow light from a distant sodium street lamp filtering through the square window panes of bubble glass. His watch showed 3.40 - it would soon start getting light. Something had disturbed him and he stretched his stiff limbs, trying to get the circulation going in his hands and feet. An instant later the key rattled and light flooded into the bathroom.

Achmad held his hand to his eyes as he stood. A squat, curly-haired man with a broad barrel chest and long arms and a wide face like a catfish stared at him. He held a snub-nosed .32 in his hand, pointing at Achmad's stomach. Achmad blinked at him.

'You're disturbing my beauty sleep,' said Achmad. 'Who are you?'

'Kasim. You like pickled fish?' said the fireplug.

'Sure,' said Achmad. 'Provided there's enough onions. People always skimp on the onions.'

'Don't worry about onions,' said Kasim. 'Come.'

'If you're inviting me for dinner you won't need a gun,' said Achmad.

Kasim put his gun away and led Achmad outside to his waiting car.

'Where are we going?' asked Achmad.

'To eat,' said Kasim.

Kasim drove across the peninsula to a quiet backstreet in Table View, adjacent to the industrial area of Paarden Island. He let Achmad into his modest bungalow with a green corrugated iron roof, where they were assailed by the overpowering smell of curried fish. Kasim led him through to the kitchen where a huge enamel saucepan stood on the stove. Kasim produced a couple of chipped plates and ladled out big chunks of yellow pickled fish onto the plate and slopped an additional layer of onions on Achmad's portion. Kasim pulled up a chair and he and Achmad attacked their fish in silence. Achmad started humming to himself then looked up.

'Good,' said Achmad. 'Bloody good.'

'*Kabeljou*' he said. 'And not too much *borrie*.' Kasim passed Achmad a chunk of white bread to mop up the gravy and the men sat back in relaxed contemplation.

'Now what?' asked Achmad.

'Now we catch some rest. You sleep here in the kitchen. I'll bring you a mattress.'

'How long will I be here?' Asked Achmad.

'Until you're needed,' said Kasim. 'Relax.'

'What do I do about my job?'

'They'll find another shelf stacker. You're with us now.'

Chapter 3

Tau left Gerry at the Library at eight o'clock and had rushed back to his house to change his clothes and freshen up. He called Joyce en route to let her know that he was on his way and would be with them within the hour. When he arrived back at their yellow brick bungalow with the old jacaranda tree in the garden, he found that Joyce had left out some freshly ironed clothes. Tau smiled and stepped into the shower. He started humming to himself as he soaped his aching muscles, glad that his little spat with Joyce had been resolved and thinking about how much he wanted to be with her. And how little he wanted to be at the engagement party.

He found her brother, Sandile, a pain in the arse. Sandile was what Tau thought of as a coconut – brown on the outside, white on the inside. He was the personification of the black yuppie, a lawyer who had made a fortune from property speculation, and played a constant game of one-upmanship with Joyce and Tau. Not that it was any competition – Sandile earned more in a month than Joyce and Tau combined a year, and fully indulged in the splashy extravagance of the *nouveau riches*. It was rumoured that part of Sandile's success came from his close ties to a government minister who issued planning permits, and Tau would from time to time make a casual enquiry to see how Sandile's portfolio was related to recent government land acquisitions and developments.

Tau didn't resent him his success, but found it hard to forget his own roots. Tau and his baby sister Lindiwe had grown up on a wine farm in the Western Cape where his parents worked on the vines. Tau was precocious from an early age and came top of his class at the small school that the farmer, Neels Koornhof, had built for his farm labourers' children. Tau was 11 when his father had taken him to see Boss Koornhof one Saturday after work. Tau had been scrubbed and his feet forced into some new *takkies* and he shifted uneasily from foot to foot as he stood on the *stoep* of the grand Cape Dutch house.

Finally Koornhof appeared.

'Is this the boy?' he asked of Tau's father.

'Yes, sir. We think that he can do very well at the Christian Mission school.'

'What do *you* think?' said Koornhof looking Tau in the eye.

'I want a chance,' said Tau. 'I read all the books in the school and know my times tables.'

'That's a good start,' said Koornhof. 'And what do you want to be when you grow up? A farmer like your Pa?'

'No sir. A policeman.'

Koornhof studied the youngster to see if he was being mocked, but the child's sincerity was blatant.

'Well,' said Koornhof, 'The way this place is changing, we're going to need police, that's for sure. And you need to be qualified.' Koornhof looked at Tau's father. 'This is what I propose,' he said. 'Theunis Le Roux across the valley goes past the Mission School each day on his way into Malmesbury. I'll arrange for him to give Tau a ride to school.'

Tau's face was alight with enthusiasm. 'Thank you, sir!' he cried.

Tau's father shushed him with a look. 'Thank you, Boss Koornhof, but I will need to make a loan from you to pay for his uniform and books.'

'Here's what I'll do,' said Koornhof. 'I will cover his uniform and books. In exchange Tau will work every Saturday here in the gardens, and if he ever slips from top of the class, he's out.' Koornhof held out his hand. 'Have we got a deal, young man?'

Tau shook his hand solemnly, and never looked back. He matriculated at the top of his class and won a scholarship to the police academy. At college he had again achieved top marks, beating Gerry into second place by three points. Gerry was a better marksman and said that field craft always won out over academic work, but the two had become fast friends and had been partners for their entire professional lives.

Tau still sent back a portion of his monthly salary to his widowed mother, his father having died some years before. He also sent a small stipend to Lindiwe who had made a bad marriage and brought up two unruly boys on her own, still living on the same farm where she had grown up.

Twenty minutes later Tau pulled up outside a new ranch-style house in Bishops Court. There was a clutch of Mercs in the drive and Sandile's girlfriend's MX5. Tau slid in beside Joyce's lime green Nissan, drew a deep breath, pasted a grin on his face and walked up to the house. There were half a dozen driver/bodyguards lounging against their owners' cars. One of them instinctively reached for the bulge under his arm as Tau approached but Tau raised a finger and air-shot the man who suddenly smiled as he recognized Tau. Tau noted that there was a ministerial black Merc with a government plate, and wondered which MP was freeloading tonight.

He could hear laughter and music rippling around the back of the property. He pushed open the steel security gate and found about 50 people standing around the pool. Coloured fairy lights were strung in the trees and the pool lights carved an azure square out of the dark lawn. Overhead loomed the bulk of the Mountain. A three-man band was blowing up a storm, and people danced with drunken abandon. A woman was holding a broken heel in one hand while wandering around aimlessly, her shoulder strap slipping down to reveal a frothy bra top. A sheep was turning on a spit and the chef, Tau noted, was a young white man with a goatee and checked trousers who was carving platters of meat while two other white girls, dressed in French Maid outfits, circulated amongst the guests distributing food and drinks.

Joyce was leaning against a tree, chatting with a prosperous-looking man in a suit and tie. He was laughing loudly at her jokes while dropping occasional glances at her cleavage. Tau slid an arm around her waist and leant in for a kiss.

'At last!' said Joyce. 'They put off the toast until you got here.'

'They didn't have to,' said Tau, sticking out his hand and crushing the other fellow's, smiling like a shark eyeing up its prey.

'Tau Molepe,' he said. 'I see you've already met my wife.' The other man gave a small whimper and slunk away.

'He was very interesting,' said Joyce. 'He's a merchant banker.'

'He was ogling your breasts,' growled Tau. 'Talking of tits…' He gave a crooked smile as Sandile approached, his over-filled plate splattering food all around.

'TAU!' he roared. 'Good to see you, old pally! You still saving the nation, eh?' He roared with laughter, his huge belly shaking with mirth.

'Congratulations,' said Tau. 'Where's the lucky lady?'

Sandile looked around, trying to focus through a haze of brandy fumes. Finally he saw a pretty, young woman dressed like an expensive hooker, Cynthia, , standing chatting at the poolside with a short fat man with jet black skin wearing a chalk stripe suit. Tau recognized the Minister of Lands, Tito Badusa. Cynthia tottered over on precarious high heels clutching a glass of champagne. She air-kissed Joyce and Tau.

'Howzit sissie,' she said to Joyce. Joyce strained a smile.

Sandile tapped his glass for silence.

'Friends. Family. Welcome! Thank you for being here tonight to celebrate the engagement of the lovely Cynthia and myself. I have known this wonderful woman for over a year, and we finally decided to do the right thing. As an engagement present, I bought her the lease on a new shop at Century City, to be called Cynthia Fashions! Four thousand square feet at top dollar!'

Cynthia squealed in delight and clapped her hands and smothered Sandile in kisses.

'Thanks so much, big man,' she said to whistles and applause. 'I'll make it the best damn boutique in the whole Cape! And I've got something for you!'

She handed Sandile a box wrapped in gold foil and tied with a pink bow. He opened it and took out a Rolex Submariner to 'Oohs' and 'Aaahs' from the assembled guests. He hugged Cynthia and swung her around.

Minister Badusa stepped forward.

'A toast, to the happy couple!' he cried.

'THE HAPPY COUPLE!' chorused everyone. Moments later the music started and Sandile seized Cynthia for a dance. Tau exhaled slowly and caught Joyce's eye just as Badusa waddled up.

'Hello Tau,' he said. 'I hear you're doing great things in the NIA. You don't mind if I whisk your lovely wife off for a dance, do you?'

'Not if she doesn't mind,' said Tau through clenched teeth.

Joyce rolled her eyes but Badusa whirled her away and danced energetically while the music swirled. One of the 'French Maids' appeared at Tau's elbow.

'Champagne, sir,' she said sweetly.

'Thanks,' said Tau downing it in a swoop. 'I'll have another.'

He glared at the rotund minister trying to fit his hands around Joyce's waist as she swatted him off. Tau had heard rumours of Badusa awarding government contracts to developers in exchange for generous backhanders, but they were too shrewd to be caught with their fingers in the till. So far. But Tau knew that sooner or later he would have a quiet word with his friend in the new governmental anti-corruption unit, and that Minister Badusa and his wealthy friends, including, no doubt Sandile, would be rushing forward to cut deals with the State Prosecutor. The music ended and Joyce came back to Tau, fuming.

'Let's go!' she said.

'So soon?' asked Tau innocently. 'I was just starting to enjoy myself.'

Chapter 4

At nine o'clock Mrs Van Der Westhysen emerged from behind a stack of documents.

'Haven't you got a home to go to?' she said. 'Your pal left nearly two hours ago.'

Gerry looked up. His muscles were starting seize up and his brain was exhausted. He nodded and packed away his files.

'Good night, *tannie,*' he called as he exited the building and suddenly realized that his car was where it had been all day, safely tucked away in his garage. Cursing, he flagged down a taxi and drove around the flank of the Mountain back to Obz, getting dropped off at the local Steers a couple of blocks from his house.

Sitting over a rack of Karoo lamb ribs and salad, he sipped a frosted Windhoek lager and picked up his phone to dial Aletta. He suddenly realised that he had not heard from her for nearly 24 hours – he wondered if he should ring Sea Point CID and ask if she had been brought in for questioning, then realised he could not do so without exposing his own prior knowledge. He set the phone down on the table, thinking back to when they had first met.

It was during a half-marathon, when she had suddenly appeared beside him and loped along, easily keeping step with his long strides, her blonde ponytail flying out behind her. Gerry had winked at her and cranked up the pace and was startled to see that she kept up with him. It was only in the final sprint for the finish that Gerry was able to stretch out and put a couple of metres between them, but had then collapsed with such a stitch that he couldn't move for ten minutes while Aletta stood nearby, head bowed, hands on knees, puffing. She finally walked over to Gerry and held out her hand and pulled him to his feet.

'Long legs,' she panted, 'otherwise I would've had you.'

'You can still have me,' gasped Gerry. 'Gerry Viljoen.'

'Aletta Du Plessis,' she said.

'Pleased to meet you,' said Gerry, meaning it. 'Can I see you later?' He said, startling himself.

'That's a bit forward,' she said. 'How do I know your intentions are honourable?'

'I can assure you they are entirely dishonourable,' said Gerry, glancing surreptitiously at her long slim legs.

She laughed. 'You're a bit of a slick operator, Mister Viljoen,' she said. 'Are you always such a smartarse?'

'I'm just trying to hide my excitement beneath a veneer of sophistication. Hell, I come from Somerset West, what can you expect?'

'See you at the Buddha Bar at nine,' she said.

Gerry nodded and grinned. She smiled at him and got into her car and drove away. As soon as she was out of sight Gerry threw up behind a tree, his muscles screaming in pain.

Gerry was unusually nervous that night when he set off for the bar. He changed clothes a few times and eventually decided that she would have to accept him as he was – khaki chinos, a new white T-shirt, tan boat shoes and soft suede jacket and he was ready to go. He'd never been to the Buddha Bar in Green Point although he'd often driven past and glimpsed the rich tourists and locals hard at play. He entered between the heavy wooden gates topped with flaming torches, and made his way into the smaller of the two bars and glanced around, not seeing Aletta. He was halfway through his first beer when he felt a gentle touch on his elbow.

Aletta had the clean-scrubbed looks of an athlete, with her complexion exuding a healthy glow and her hair swinging on her shoulders. She wore no makeup but looked very sexy in a buttery muslin dress that contrasted with her tan. Her only ornamentation was an African necklace of small cowrie shells and lucky beans.

'Hi,' she said. 'I didn't know if you'd come.'

'Snap,' said Gerry. 'But I'm glad you did. You look great. What are you drinking?

'Thanks,' she said. 'A white wine will be good.'

They enjoyed an immediate rapport. Both were sports mad and both had come from small town, Afrikaans families, although as Gerry explained he was now 'slightly detribalized.' Gerry's journey had been a long one. Born in Somerset West, Gerry's father had been the *predikant* at the local Dutch Reformed Church - the 'Much Deformed Church' as Tau had described it.

When Gerry was nine years old, his younger brother, Samuel, nicknamed Ampie, had drowned while swimming in a nearby dam. Gerry was supposed to be looking after him but had gone to buy them ice creams when Ampie had decided to go into the water. Etched in his memory was the picture of his father, ever-more frantic, diving into the murky water as his mother ran hysterically along the bank, screaming. Finally, Reverend Viljoen had surfaced with the pale limp body of Ampie in his arms. Adults had tried to shield Gerry from the view but he saw his brother's open mouth leaking muddy green water, and his sightless blue eyes staring into the sun. Nobody ever blamed Gerry for having lost sight of his brother for that critical minute, but Gerry still carried the guilt, an acid that ate into him every day of his life, a familiar homunculus growing in his breast, bitter and shrivelled, always lurking. After the tragedy something in his mother had withered and she became withdrawn, and although she remained dutiful in her attention to Gerry, he always felt that he was somehow second best.

Gerry suddenly became aware that his voice was trembling and he looked up fiercely to find Aletta leaning forward, hanging on his every word. She gently squeezed his hand.

'Jeez, I haven't ever told that to anyone else,' said Gerry. 'That's a hell of a way to make a first impression. Sorry.'

'No,' said Aletta. 'I'm honoured that you felt comfortable enough to talk about it. How did your poor parents cope?'

Gerry felt a weight lifting as he spoke to her, a sense of growing relief as the words tumbled out. He explained that although his father was a staunch believer, Reverend Viljoen's faith had been deeply shaken and he had taken time from his pastoral work to spend a few months in a seminary in Holland.

It was there that he was introduced to the notion of liberation theology and, while never fully embracing it, had come to realise that the artificial construct of apartheid was doomed. He recognised that Gerry needed to be equipped to cope with the rapidly changing world, a million miles from the insular enclave of an Afrikaans parish in a small *dorp* in the middle of nowhere.

Consequently, when he returned to the Cape, he sent Gerry to the local English-speaking school where, being the only Afrikaner, he experienced fights on a daily basis. Thereafter, Gerry always spoke English except when at home, and when later found that the language of instruction at police college was English. In Cape Town he found that the international language was English and so he spoke less and less Afrikaans, although when he had given the oration at his father's funeral, he made a point of making the address in Afrikaans.

Aletta had learned English from an early age too and, although she and Gerry spoke English most of the time, they would sometimes lapse into Afrikaans when looking for a particularly apt expression or when in a hurry. After a while the language between them became an intimate argot reflecting the marriage of the two cultures. When at Police College Gerry had also learned to speak rudimentary Zulu, and now felt as he was truly a part of the new 'Rainbow Nation' envisaged by Nelson Mandela at independence.

Their first date had lasted longer than either had anticipated and their discussion had covered a spectrum of subjects. Aletta revealed that she was 26 years old, a pharmacist working in a chemist shop in Gardens, had just put down a deposit on her own flat, had two brothers who were still in her home town of Darling, and had never been married. She admitted that she had been engaged to a guy while she was still a student but the proposed date for the wedding kept being set further and further back until they realised that it was something that neither had really wanted. Aletta had broken it off, rather than continue in a tepid relationship just because there was nothing better to replace it with.

Gerry took a long pull on his beer and decided to jump in at the deep end. 'I'm divorced,' he said and took a long pull at his beer, watching her carefully. 'Kids?' she asked. 'No,' said Gerry. 'What happened?' Gerry explained that when he was 19 years old and still at college he had been dating a girl for a couple of months when she announced that she was pregnant. Gerry took her at her word and hurriedly married her only to discover that she was not pregnant at all but was instead slightly crazy, and had determined to be married by the time she was 18. Nonetheless Gerry had tried to honour his commitment to making the marriage work, but finally came to the conclusion that he could not survive another 40 or 50 years with this delusional woman and so had divorced her. Gerry shrugged apologetically and took another pull at his beer.

'Did she remarry?' asked Aletta.

'Yup. A sheep farmer from the Karoo. He was also a bit crazy so they got on like a house on fire. Five kids and counting,' said Gerry.

'Uh-huh,' said Aletta. 'Did she put you off commitment?'

'She put me off marrying another lunatic,' said Gerry. 'But you do things when you're 19 which you wouldn't consider as an adult. I was a kid then – what the hell did I know?'

'And your work?'

'Ah,' said Gerry, 'now that's more interesting.'

He spoke for a long time about the passion that drove him to be part of an organization keeping the enemies of the state at bay. As he spoke she saw the young boy behind the man, the fierce idealist who had taken a message from his father's pulpit speeches about the need for justice and equality, and felt herself drawn to him.

But of course the dance is never that simple. They had dated for nearly a year before Gerry had suggested that they move in together. Aletta had resisted at first and when pressed said that it was a proven fact that people who cohabited and then got married tended to get divorced at a much higher rate than those whose experience of joint living started with marriage. Gerry had opened his mouth to say something about the underlying presumption of the statement, but caught himself just in time and his mouth snapped shut.

So although they spent most nights together, sometimes in Aletta's flat, sometimes in Gerry's little house, they both knew that sooner or later the question of long-time commitment would arise, and they also both knew that they would make the leap, but Aletta was shrewd enough to wait until Gerry felt that the idea was his.

And now Gerry was staring at his cellphone, hoping that his fit of drunken pique had not destroyed their chances forever. However, the anger flared briefly at the memory of seeing the light go out in Eksteen's flat and he gritted his teeth, determined not to call her. He paid his bill and stepped out into the cool night air, realising that the moment of truth lay ahead – if Aletta had cleaned out her stuff then it was over.

He walked deliberately slowly the half kilometre back home. As he turned into his road he saw that his house lights were on and Aletta's Yaris was parked outside. Gerry clanged the gate loudly to let her know that he was back and walked up to the front door, unsure whether it was going to be a happy reunion or a bitter farewell. He unlocked it and went inside.

Aletta was sitting on the sofa, her face wan.

'Hi,' said Gerry.

'Hi,' she replied. There was a moment of silence, then Aletta said the words that struck ice into Gerry's heart. 'We need to talk.'

He nodded and sat down in his leather chair.

'I've had an interesting time,' she said.

'Me too,' said Gerry, hoping to deflect her. 'We're on maximum alert!'

'I went to see Louis last night…'

Gerry's breath faltered. If there was anything he had learned in the past 24 hours it was when to keep his mouth shut. He gave a brief nod.

'Aren't you going to ask why?'

Gerry had been outfoxed again. He thought he was doing the smart thing by saying nothing, but that too was wrong. 'Okay,' he said. 'Why?'

'To ask him to come and tell you to your stupid bladdy face that his only interest in me was as a reliable business partner. That's why!'

Gerry was thinking fast. 'So..Uh…why didn't he come?'

'Because I'd just pitched up unannounced in the middle of the night and woken his wife and their three month old baby!'

'Wife? …Uh…Baby? But I thought…'

'Yes. You thought. Those kind people offered me their pull-out sofa because they saw I was so upset. We hadn't been asleep ten minutes when guess what?'

'Baby woke?' Said Gerry, shrugging. 'How the hell should I know?'

She fixed him with a piercing glance.

'No, that would be normal. This was highly unusual.'

'Are you going to keep me bladdy guessing?' growled Gerry, his heart thumping. She was regarding him with deep suspicion.

'The cops had a tipoff of gunshots and screams. From Louis' flat.'

Gerry toyed with the tasselled fringe of a cushion.

'Shots, huh? Who was shooting?'

'Nobody. That was the point. But someone had called in a false alarm. Very specific.'

'But you weren't arrested or anything?'

'No. The cops saw in five minutes it was a hoax.'

Gerry exhaled slowly. 'So that's all okay then! This kind of stuff happens…'

'They're trying to trace the caller.'

'Good luck!' He said, looking relieved. She fixed him with a steely glare. Gerry faltered. 'I mean, these hoax guys don't leave their names, do they?'

'No. He didn't leave his name. Funny that.'

'Ja well – some crazy hoaxer. What can you expect? But like I said, we're on major alert. I was at the archives working late.'

'You're deflecting,' she said. 'This is all about trust, Gerry. If you and I are going to make it, we have to have trust. You behaved like a prick.'

'That's a bit harsh.'

'HARSH?'

'Ja, well I'm a jealous guy."

'Jealous? We're talking psychopathic here.'

'Okay! Jeez, I'm sorry. I shouldn't have assumed the bladdy worst.'

She held his eye for a long moment, then softened. 'It's late,' she said. 'Let's go to bed.'

Gerry nodded and sprang to his feet. Too soon. 'But if I ever hear anything, even the most remote hint that you were in any whatsoever involved with that call to Louis, we're finished. *Verstaan?*'

'Me?' said Gerry, summoning up what he imagined wounded pride would look like. 'Me?'

'One teensy word,' she said.

Gerry hugged her tight.

'Don't be so bladdy stupid,' he said, kissing her on top of her head.

Chapter 5

Sayeed Dhatri was 28 years old. He came from a large, affluent Indian family that owned a chain of furniture shops, Dhatri Brothers, around Cape Town. Sayeed was the eldest of four brothers and had been expected to take over the business from his father, now in his seventies, but after a promising start had incurred his father's contempt by abruptly passing control to his younger brother, Iqbal.

Sayeed remained working at the store as it gave him the financial freedom and legitimacy that he needed to pursue his other activities as a vigilante killer. When he was 15 years old, he had seen the street in which he had grown up descend into a maelstrom of violence that followed the growth of illicit drugs trade. There was always some *dagga* in the area which had never caused any major problems, but Mandrax and speed had started to come into the township, and then the Nigerians had moved in bringing cocaine, heroin and inevitably crack cocaine and the crystal meth called *tik*, that was now rampaging through the townships.

One night a car pulled up loaded with three drunken students from the Free State. They scored an arm of *dagga* and some speed and then raced away. The driver momentarily lost control of the car which mounted the pavement and ran over four-year-old Reena Chowdury then sped away into the night – neither car nor students were ever found - but the Chowdury family never recovered from the loss of their daughter.

Two nights later Sayeed was sitting on the step of his father's house, watching as one car after another would draw up outside the Nigerians' house and a figure would come to the car window and exchange a wrap of drugs before melting back into the shadows until the next car arrived.

A nondescript car with three men inside went past Sayeed. He noticed them pulling bandanas over their lower faces and watched with interest as they slowed down outside the Nigerians' house. The shadowy figure approached the car and suddenly there were a couple of flashes followed moments later by two distant bangs. Then the car doors flew open, and the men burst into the Nigerians' house. Several rapid shots accompanied by a long, drawn-out wail followed and the three men charged out of the house and jumped back into their car and raced off at high speed. Sayeed and half a dozen other neighbours cautiously approached the drugs house.

A tall Nigerian with a tribal scars cut into his face lay twisted at the side of the road, his chest punctured by two bullet wounds. A woman burst from the house, howling in fear, drenched in blood. Behind her there was another man sprawled on the floor, blood seeping from a massive head wound. Sirens could be heard in the distance, but not before Sayeed heard a word whispered from mouth to mouth – PAGAD!

His family, devout Muslims and pillars of the local community, had worked hard and kept their heads down. As non-whites in the segregated world of apartheid South Africa, this policy of invisibility was necessary to enable the family to run their own business and send their children to university.

But Sayeed viewed the acceptance of their lot as cringing before white authority, and saw on the night of the PAGAD attack how people could stand up with pride and defend themselves. Thereafter he worked hard to insinuate himself into the organization, first as a low-level spotter used to locate the drug dens in the township and point them out to an older boy who would in turn pass on the information to the notorious G-Force.

Sayeed's father was furious when he learned that his son was associating with the radical Muslims who were already attracting the attention of the police. The old man effectively grounded his son until he had completed his Matriculation exams. Sayeed achieved excellent grades and his father was pushing him to attend university but Sayeed said that he wanted to enter the family business, and became a trainee at his father's store in Deep River.

Sayeed had taken a small flat near the store and rejoined his comrades in PAGAD. He was introduced to a man with the melodramatic *nom de guerre* of Zapata. He was of Malay extraction and wore a droopy moustache and had sleepy eyes, but he was ex-Special Forces, and was an expert on every sort of hand-held weaponry. He taught Sayeed and two other youngsters about handgun use and maintenance in a kloof that was a hard hour's walk through the bush near Melkbosstrand.

The two young men were keen students and showed some proficiency, but Sayeed was the best marksman. Zapata singled him for advanced training and spent some time showing him how to fire a semi-automatic AK-47, and how to strip and reassemble the weapon within minutes. He said that if Sayeed had the nerve and stomach for serious weapons work, then he would show him how to make explosives from fertilizer and how to detonate remote control bombs.

Zapata had explained to the young zealots that it was one thing to shoot at monkey apples and see their pulpy insides explode; it was an entirely different thing to shoot at living flesh and blood. The youngest of the recruits had been unable to pull the trigger when he went out on a night raid with two more seasoned G-Force colleagues. Thereafter he was quietly dropped from the team, although they kept a close eye on him to make sure he told nobody. The other young man had shown some fear on his first raid, but had shot a street dealer through the head, and elation and a feeling of invulnerability meant that he was now eager to kill again.

Finally it was Sayeed's turn to venture out into the townships at night. He and two of the older G-Force men had cruised past a street corner where a couple of dealers operated openly. The plan was to drive slowly by and shoot one and be gone, but Sayeed asked his comrades to let him off halfway down the block. He got out of the car, his pistol at his side, and walked calmly up to one dealer, shot him through the eye, then turned and shot the other man in the chest and walked back to the waiting car, showing neither fear nor panic. He had tasted the power of death and through it the intoxication of life, and knew that nothing could ever stand in his way again.

After two years and 19 targeted killings, Sayeed approached his 21st birthday as one of South Africa's most prolific serial killers. And nobody knew about him, save the two other G-Force men who comprised his team. One of the men – Zakkie - told his girlfriend about some of their activities and the police ambushed him one night on his way home and he was killed in the shootout. The second man fled to Jo'burg and disappeared amongst the millions of migrants, shadow people and criminals who lived in Hillbrow. Sayeed went into deep cover, hiding in plain sight.

He spent the next six months working hard in his father's business and moved to the flagship store in Sea Point. He became a model manager: courteous, attentive, and a strict enforcer of best business practise. His steely resolve when disciplining errant employees troubled his father but he could not argue with the results.

Sayeed recognised that being an urban vigilante was limited. He needed to be involved on a planning level within PAGAD, helping to develop strategies to cope with the changing world and to further the cause of militant Islam across the globe. Then one cataclysmic event had drawn all the strands together - on 9/11 he had watched open-mouthed as the planes crashed into the Twin Towers, felling them in a massive column of smoke and flame, killing thousands and creating a shockwave throughout the world that still rumbled on.

He realised that he too could create an iconic event of similar status in South Africa, something that would rock the world. The Madrid and London bombings had crated an immediate and local impact, but Sayeed thought about a target that would create an international impact with effects lasting long after the actual attack had subsided. His name would be mentioned in the same breath as Osama Bin Laden and he would have fulfilled his destiny as a *shaheed*. One day while driving up the West Coast to fetch some *perlemoen* from his cousin he saw the signs for Koeberg Nuclear Plant, and knew that he had found his target.

By this time he had access to the upper levels of PAGAD, and after a police crackdown had netted the three most senior players, Sayeed rose rapidly through the ranks. He used his business acumen to help launder funds as they trickled in from the wealthy Gulf Arabs who supported the struggle, and from Iran, which had supported PAGAD from its inception. Sayeed also gained access to a raft of other illegal endeavours to fund further operations – false passports, guns and drugs that were wholesaled to street dealers. The irony was not lost on Sayeed and he admired its daring.

Sayeed planned his operation in secret, but knew that he could not execute it by himself. He brought one of his most trusted men, Kasim, into the operation and a third man, Hamidullah. This closed cell would be the nucleus of the operation, recruiting others only on a strict operational basis. But Sayeed needed two things – experience in the planning and logistical phase, and finances. Sayeed set up a visit by a Pakistani imam, Mullah Mohammed, ostensibly to preach at the 11th Street Mosque, but it was the time that they spent together after the prayer meetings that had yielded the greatest benefits.

Mullah Mohammed presided over a *madrassa* in the border area of Peshawar in Pakistan, and was famed not only for his fierce denunciation of all things Western, but for his connections within the shadowy world of militant Islam. It was rumoured that he had spent time with Sheikh Osama during his years as a fighter with the Taliban, and that he had recruited hundreds of young men from around the world to the cause of Jihad. He also had strong links to an Iranian who was close to the top of Al-Qaeda, a man named Tariq Dar. Dar was something of an anachronism – a Sunni in a predominantly Shia country, who somehow managed to overcome the natural antipathy of the two groups and while not overtly embraced by the regime, was nonethtless allowed space in which to operate. Mullah Mohammed had promised to introduce Sayeed to Tariq Dar, and a few months later a carefully encoded message came through.

Sayeed told his father that in order to expand his business, he should be looking into the markets beyond South Africa's borders. Sayeed arranged to visit Kenya armed with a camera and his laptop computer, filled with images of sofas and dining sets, an electronic catalogue of all of Dhatri Brothers' products.

On his arrival in Kenya, Sayeed was met by a tall morose African who put him onto a rickety, six-seater plane and flew him to a remote grass strip in the northeast corner of the country. With the engine still running, Sayeed was bundled out of the plane and into an old Land Rover and driven through the bush for five hours, finally coming to a stop at a tented camp of about 100 armed men. The terrain was semi-jungle, permeated by the rank stench of burned meat from a fire where two women turned an antelope on a spit. There were half a dozen Toyota pickup trucks with heavy machine-guns mounted on the flatbeds, and fierce-looking young men draped with bandoliers carrying AK47s.

He noted that they all wore loosely wrapped scarves like turbans on their heads, making them look more Arabic than the Africans in the South. Sayeed suddenly realised that he had crossed the border and was now in Somalia. Sayeed, dressed in a lightweight suit and carrying a leather holdall and laptop, felt their hostile glares and heard ominous muttering. He suddenly realised that he could be stripped bare and murdered in moments and no-one would ever know what happened to him. Just then a short rotund man with a large moustache emerged from the largest tent in the company of a Somali warlord, Aydid. The short man held out his hand.

'Tariq Dar,' he said. 'Salam.'

'Salam Alaikum,' said Sayeed, feeling at that instant an electric tingle as he became aware of his own destiny.

Sayeed spent three days with Dar, becoming inspired with a fervour that would carry him through flames. Dar was enthusiastic about attacking Koeberg, and he and Sayeed devised a plan entailing an attack on the reactor by a crop duster aircraft loaded with C4 plastic explosive. They worked out a method to communicate when Sayeed was back in South Africa and Dar assured him that all matériel would be put at his disposal as and when he needed it. Finally, he gave Sayeed a film canister half-filled with diamonds to fund the next step of their operation. Sayeed had embraced him tightly, tears seeping from his eyes, and had managed to croak out 'Allahu Akbar' before getting back into his Land Rover for the long journey back to Nairobi.

On returning to Cape Town, Sayeed curtly told his father that the Kenyans were thieves and that the company should first expand across South Africa before embracing pan-African ambitions. Sayeed had then found a small flight school outside Cape Town where he enrolled as a trainee pilot under the name of Farouk Parveen. The instructor, Leon Wessels, had been suspicious and explained that he needed to notify the government of each new trainee pilot. Sayeed had shrugged and handed over an ID that identified him as Farouk Parveen and gave a false address.

Wessels had duly copied the document and sent it to the appropriate authorities and then got on with what he knew best, flight instruction. Although he was somewhat surly and withdrawn, Sayeed proved an adept pupil and gave as his cover story that he wanted to learn how to fly a crop duster as his uncle had extensive cotton fields in Gauteng Province where there was a lot of work to be had. Sayeed had only one hour of training left before he qualified in the little yellow Piper Pawnee, and then he would be allowed to fly solo.

Everything was falling into place. Then came the unauthorised attack on the synagogue.

Chapter 6

Achmad woke early and threw off the scratchy blanket that Kasim had given him. The cushions that he had pushed together to make a mattress had slid apart during the night and he had slept for the most part on the cold cement floor, smelling of dust and Cobra Polish. He got stiffly to his feet and yawned. Moments later Kasim entered the kitchen.

'You sleep all right?'

'Fine. Can I take a shower?'

'Sure,' said Kasim. 'There's a towel behind the bathroom door.' Although it was bare, the bathroom was clean and Achmad managed to get a stream of water directed onto his head. He showered and washed his hair with a thin sliver of Palmolive soap and towelled himself dry. He brushed his teeth with his finger and finally emerged from the bathroom feeling more human.

Kasim had a pot of coffee on the stove and was frying some fat cakes when Achmad returned to the kitchen.

'Sit,' said Kasim. 'I've had some news. We're going on a recce.'

Achmad sat forward. 'What's the target?'

'You ask a lot of questions,' said Kasim. 'We aren't like those other guys throwing petrol bombs. This is serious.'

'Okay,' said Achmad. 'Ready when you are.'

'Maybe, maybe not,' said Kasim. 'You know how to use this?'

Kasim reached into a cupboard and produced a Nikon with a digital back and a 500 mm telephoto lens. Achmad took the camera from him and quickly checked it over. He nodded.

'Five hundred mil. Nice.'

'They teach you a lot in Pep Stores, huh?' said Kasim with a chuckle. Achmad felt his insides go cold but laughed loudly.

'My uncle Ibrahim had a small photographic studio at the bottom of Plein Street. I used to help out when I was a kid.'

'Digital only came in recently,' said Kasim.

'That's why I bought myself a little Sureshot so I wouldn't be left behind. Are we going to spend all day talking cameras or are we actually going to do something?'

'Finish up and let's get going,' said Kasim.

At the end of the street was a café and newsagent. The Cape Argus headline yelled 'Three Die in Synagogue Massacre.' Kasim glanced at Achmad.

'I saw the TV news. They're looking for the fourth gunman but the identity kit picture looks more like my *Ouma* than you.'

'Lucky,' said Achmad, knowing that his colleagues had intentionally issued a misleading E-fit picture so that he could continue his undercover work without some zealous member of the public either calling the cops or shooting him on sight. Achmad glanced in the wing mirror to see if his plainclothes watchers had managed to keep up with him, but saw no following vehicles. Either they were very good, or they had screwed up and lost him. He would need to call HQ as soon as possible.

'Have you got your gun?' asked Kasim.

Achmad patted his pocket. 'Still here.'

'Did you get off some shots?'

'Five, then I split.' Said Achmad.

They drove in silence through the outer suburbs, past the docks and onto the coast road, heading northwest. As the environs of Cape Town slowly fell away, the land became more barren. On the Atlantic Coast side of the road were tussocks and dunes, on the other side scrubby bush and low hills. Achmad was starting to doze - there was nothing much of interest this far from the city, just a few small satellite *dorps*, some scattered farms, and a sign for the Koeberg Nuclear Power station, the only nuclear facility on the African continent.

Achmad swallowed hard. 'It's Koeberg, isn't it?'

'They said you were a clever one,' said Kasim, smiling broadly.

The power station was about 30 kilometres from Cape Town, a couple of kilometres from the road, venting into the sea. The approach to the station was through low flat scrubland, giving excellent visibility to the security staff that manned the base.

At the 25 kilometre marker Kasim swung his car off the road. It seemed like they were going straight into the bush, but it was just possible to make out a faint track. Kasim drove a little further then stopped the car out of sight of the main road.

'This is the plan. You go straight ahead for a couple of kilometres keeping the sea to your left. Don't go to the shore or you'll be visible. Circle around the power station and shoot off as many strategic photos as you can. We need to use this data to plan our approach, so make sure you do it properly.'

Achmad nodded. 'Aren't you coming?'

'They have patrols every twenty minutes. If they pick up my car they'll sweep the bush until they find us. I will return to this spot in exactly four hours. You will be waiting.'

'And if I'm seen?'

'Then you cannot be taken. Understood?' said Kasim, handing him the Nikon.

Achmad nodded. 'Allahu Akbar,' he said.

'Allahu Akbar,' said Kasim. Achmad got out of the car and set off at a jog through the bush. A moment later he saw the car turning around and bumping away towards the main road.

Achmad continued into the bush for about half a kilometre then stopped, panting in the heat, his head buzzing. He sat down on a rock and rested against the trunk of a thick tree, sweat pooling in the small of his back. He slowly caught his breath, listening to the chirrup of the cicadas and the barking of a distant dog while in the background was a faint hum of traffic from the main road. He drew his cell phone from his pocket and was relieved to find that the signal was strong and he dialled HQ. He saw that there was a message and recognized

Gerry's phone number, but he had more pressing matters to report.

'Soraya, it's me. Can I speak to the chief?'

He waited for a moment as she connected him to Chitepo.

'Sir? It's Achmad Karriem…'

'Where the hell are you?' Barked Chitepo. 'Those idiots who were supposed to be watching lost you at Moosa's house!'

'I'm near Koeberg, sir. I've just met…'

Just then he heard something snap behind him. He threw down his phone and reached for his Smith & Wesson just as Kasim emerged from behind the tree with a silencer screwed into the end of a black pistol. Achmad felt detached from reality as he noted the technical details of the weapon pointed at him. It was a Glock with an 18 shot magazine sticking out of the grip, the 9mm version favoured by law enforcement officers worldwide.

'What's up, bra?' asked Achmad, looking into Kasim's eyes.

Chitepo's voice sounded tinny as he yelled for Achmad to answer him.

'Pick up the phone,' said Kasim softly.

'No problem,' said Achmad. As he leant forward he threw himself into a break-fall roll and spun halfway around, snapping off a shot at Kasim while still tumbling. Achmad never heard the shots that killed him. The first shot punched a hole the size of a hen's egg through his skull, the other two tore through his heart and viscera. Achmad was dead before he hit the ground.

Achmad's wild shot had taken Kasim low in the wall of muscle beneath his navel. Cursing in agony, Kasim picked up the cell phone, the blood bubbling through his fingers as they pushed at his waistband, struggling to keep his guts in.

'Your filthy little informer is dead!' he said and cut the connection. He dropped the phone in the dirt beside Achmad's body. He kicked the dead man a couple of times, picked up his Nikon and set off through the bush to his waiting *bakkie,* stumbling in pain.

By the time Kasim reached his vehicle he was drenched with sweat. His trousers and shirt were soaked in blood and he knew that his wound was serious. He pulled out his own phone and dialled a number that he had committed to memory.

'Listen,' he gasped. 'The new man...Achmad...NIA. He's been cancelled...I'm hurt. I'm coming in now...'

'Where's the body?' asked Sayeed.

Kasim felt his anger growing.

'Fuck him! He's dead! In the bush! The wild dogs will get him!'

'The operation's been compromised,' said Sayeed. 'From now on no further contact.'

The line went dead. Kasim cursed several times and then started the engine. Each bump of the track shot fire through his bowels until he finally reached the tarred road and swung the *bakkie* back towards Cape Town. Sweat was running down his face and he was having trouble seeing clearly and several cars hooted as he strayed over the central line, but he knew that if he could make it back to his own house then he could get hold of a doctor who would patch him up with no questions asked.

Kasim was starting to feel light-headed. The pain was now a deep ache and he had trouble moving his legs. He tore round a bend on the wrong side of the road only to see a temporary sign ahead – POLICE STOP - and a young officer advancing into the road, his hand raised. Kasim pushed his right foot down hard on the accelerator and aimed straight for the cop. Police at either side of the roadblock scrambled to get out of the way and Kasim saw a cop raise a handgun as he cried 'Allah Akubar!' and swerved straight at the fleeing policemen at over 150 kph. The final thing he saw was the startled expression of the young cop squashed against the windscreen as it crazed, then blackness.

Chapter 7

Moosa was wrapping a fillet of yellowtail and chips in his fish shop when his cell phone rang. He frowned when he saw the 'Caller Witheld' message flash up on his screen.

'Don't speak,' said Sayeed. 'That guy you brought to us was an informer. He's dead. Kasim's also dead. Clean everything and meet me at the usual place in an hour and a half.'

The connection was broken. Moosa hurriedly shut up the shop and jumped in his *bakkie* and went home. The two watchers followed at a leisurely pace and drew up some distance from his house. Inside, Moosa quickly destroyed any evidence linking him to anyone else in the organization. He felt apprehensive because Sayeed's tone implied that Moosa had compromised their operation whereas Moosa believed that he had acted as a good Muslim by helping his brother in the holy war. Nonetheless, Moosa put his .38 revolver into his pocket as he hopped into his *bakkie* and set off for the rendezvous.

In the earliest days of PAGAD he and Sayeed had determined on a meeting spot on Boyes Drive, the scenic route that clung to the cliffs as it traced the path from Simonstown to Muizenberg. The small lay-by where they pulled off offered an excellent vantage point, with visitors constantly stopping to admire the view, so that two people standing and chatting while watching the rollers at Muizenberg would not draw any attention and be immune from eavesdropping.

Sayeed parked his bike off the road behind a thick stand of *fynbos*. He scrambled up the rocky side of the mountain until he found a good vantage point, then hunkered down. He took the gun case from his backpack and assembled the sniper rifle, extended the bipod legs and sighted in the 'scope, screwed the silencer into the end of the barrel and snapped the clip of steel-jacketed bullets into the breech, then settled down to wait. He had chosen his position well because there was a steep hairpin bend just below his vantage point and cars would emerge from the tight curve quite slowly but would start accelerating towards the crest. He checked his watch. Moosa was usually punctual.

Ten minutes later he was rewarded by seeing Moosa's *bakkie* emerge from the bend, picking up speed. Sayeed was able to read his tight expression through the scope. The gun popped and suddenly Moosa's eyes flew open as the windscreen shattered and the bullet smashed into his jaw, tearing off the lower half of his face The *bakkie* swerved towards the mountain and bounced against the embankment, then spun across the road and flew over the edge. It rolled end-over-end down the steep mountainside and burst into flames halfway down. Moments later Sayeed saw a plain Toyota pull up on the shoulder where the *bakkie* had gone over and two men get out and start marshalling the traffic. One of the men was speaking into a walkie-talkie.

Sayeed smiled to himself. The two plainclothes cops were an unexpected bonus. He snapped off one shot, lifting Mister Walkie-Talkie off his feet and hurtling him back over the edge. It took his stunned colleague a moment to realise what happened, then he drew a handgun and crouched down behind the car, anxiously scanning the bush for signs of the shooter.

A BMW was coming along the road at high speed from the Muizenberg side. As the driver started to slow down Sayeed slammed a shot through his window and he ploughed straight into the Toyota behind which the plainclothes cop had hunkered down. Sayeed saw the officer fly up into the air then crash down onto the road where he lay unmoving. The driver of the BMW was slumped across his steering wheel, horn blaring.

Sayeed grinned to himself – the road was now blocked in both directions with people rushing to help the victims, but nobody was sure about what had provoked the pile-up. He swiftly broke down his weapon and put it into his rucksack then got onto his bike and rode slowly away, threading through the stationary traffic until the road opened up.

Chapter 8

Tau and Gerry sat silently before Jonas Chitepo as he outlined the last 24 hours. After Achmad's call the police had triangulated the area where the signal came from and 20 minutes later a helicopter landed near the spot where Achmad's body lay. In keeping with Muslim tradition Achmad would be buried the next day.

'I heard him die,' said Shablala grimly. 'He was surveilling Koeberg for Scimitar and they somehow got onto him.'

'Why weren't we aware of what he was up to?' asked Tau. 'I thought he was under 24/7-watch ever since he left the scene of the synagogue attack.'

'They followed him to Moosa's house. But Moosa evidently spirited him away under their noses and our boys missed it!'

'Where's Moosa now?' asked Gerry.

'Dead. That accident on Boyes Drive yesterday was no accident. The news people don't know that Moosa was shot, then one of his watchers, Van Staden, took a hit and the other one, Welby, is in hospital with every major bone broken. So counting Achmad, the cop at the roadblock and those connected with Moosa, we are looking at three confirmed dead, with another two likely to go the same way. I want these bastards!'

'Leads?' asked Tau grimly.

'Achmad and his killer, Kasim Bey, were recceing the power plant. We need to get to the bottom of that, and then everything else will become clear.'

'Terrorists have been talking about attacking a nuclear facility for years. A radioactive leak would poison the entire Cape.' Said Tau.

'Chernobyl,' said Gerry. 'Farms thousands of kilometres away were affected and that whole region is now a dead zone.'

'Koeberg is pretty secure. You can't get near the place by road,' said Chitepo.

'Actually,' said Tau, 'if you had a bulldozer you could drive straight through the outer wall and pierce the reactor itself.'

'There are numerous security measures in place,' said Chitepo.

'What about a tank? If those guys got hold of a light tank from the army they could drive through everything and blast their way in.'

'How are they going to steal a damn tank?' demanded Chitepo.

'Not steal. Drive out the front gates of the camp. You don't think they have fanatics in the army?' said Gerry.

'OK,' said Chitepo, 'I will institute an immediate review of security. Those bastards aren't going to breach Koeberg on my watch.'

'I keep thinking about the Twin Towers,' said Tau. They looked at each other.

'We'll check out the flight schools,' said Gerry.

'I thought that was routine after 9/11,' said Tau.

'A seaborne attack is also possible,' said Chitepo. 'A high-speed boat and a couple of SAMs could blow a hole in one of the reactors.'

'If these bastards have got SAMs we're pretty much screwed anyway,' muttered Gerry. 'They could launch from 20 kilometres away and the first we'd know about it is when our skin started dropping off.'

'But they were recceing the land side so I think it'll either be by plane or land.' Said Tau.

'If they're smart they'll recognise that they've been compromised and find another target. But we know they're serious.' Said Chitepo.

'Outside of this room, who else knows about the AIDS conference?'

'Only the Americans and the various heads of state,' growled Chitepo. 'We were looking to go public in March.'

'Have we got anyone else inside PAGAD?' Asked Tau.

'Nobody. Achmad had to work for months to get in and now they'll be shut down so tight not even a fly could get in there. We have to watch and wait,' said Chitepo. 'Sooner or later they've got to show themselves.'

'I can't sit on my arse and do nothing, sir. We'll carry on combing the PAGAD files,' said Gerry.

'There might be one lead,' said Chitepo, 'it seems Kasim Bey made a call just before he died. His cell phone was destroyed in the crash but the bits have been flown to Pretoria where the specialist electronic boys are trying to work out the last call details and extract all of the numbers on Bey's phone memory.'

'We need to find out where Achmad went between Moosa's house and Kasim Bey,' said Tau.

'We also need to find out who shot Moosa,' said Gerry. Tau nodded and stood, itchy to be doing something.

'I need an honour guard for the funeral tomorrow,' said Chitepo. 'Can I count on you two?'

'We'd be offended if you didn't' said Tau.

Chapter 9

Sayeed was furious. He knew that Kasim's loss would be hard felt, but his real rage was directed towards the NIA who had so convincingly managed to infiltrate his cell. He was relieved that Kasim had followed his intuition and that Achmad had been dealt with so swiftly, but nonetheless the cops would be all over Koeberg, and for the time being at least, the plan was put on hold. He also knew that they would be searching through every bit of forensic evidence they could find.

He had immediately called Hamidullah and gave him the pre-arranged codeword to run, then called Moosa and set him up. It was not that he thought Moosa was a liability; on the contrary, he was exactly the sort of stalwart foot soldier that every movement needed – tough, loyal and obedient. But Sayeed also knew that, sooner or later, everyone cracks under interrogation. And so Sayeed had to protect the movement, and himself, by martyring his old comrade.

After the phone calls, Sayeed removed the SIM card from his phone and threw it into a storm drain. Then he replaced it with another SIM card from a batch of stolen cards, so that the calls couldn't be traced. Sayeed knew that his best cover was to carry on working at the furniture store and bide his time. He carefully reviewed his activities over the past few months and felt increasingly secure that nothing had been overlooked. Even his flight training had been under another name, and he would need to turn up for his final lesson as usual if he wanted to avoid doing anything that may draw attention to him.

He would remain unobtrusive until the heat passed, and use this enforced hiatus to try and find another target. He cursed once more — Koeberg would have been the best thing since the Twin Towers.

He was showing a family a *kiaat* dining table with six chairs when he saw on TV a picture of Moosa's mangled *bakkie* halfway down the mountain, with a couple of paramedics carrying away a body under a black rubber sheet. Then the scene cut to a shot of Moosa's house. Shocked neighbours were crowding into the frame and Moosa's old mother was wailing and screaming, while two other old women were trying to comfort her. Sayeed turned off the TV in disgust — didn't she realise that her son died for a holy Jihad? That he should be honoured, not vilified. He turned to his customers and saw that they were scared, and realised that he had been shouting. He put on an apologetic smile and knocked 200 Rands off the asking price for the dining suite and clinched the deal. The customers left happy and Sayeed told his father that he wasn't feeling well and was going home to lie down.

He did indeed go home, but it wasn't to rest. He fished around in the hollowed out space above the doorjamb until his hand closed on a soft muslin bag. He carefully unwrapped his Taurus PT92 and checked the action and that the magazine was full of 9mm hollow point rounds. He favoured the hollow points because they would fragment on impact, and their heavy load could stop a buffalo. The heft of the gun gave him confidence and he knew that it would help to restore the balance of justice on the street. When dusk came he showered, said a quick prayer, and prepared for battle.

He tucked the pistol into his jacket, pulled on his full-face helmet and went into the garage at the side of his house. He backed his 1000cc Suzuki V Strom through the garage doors and out into the street.

He fired up the engine and let it warm up until it reached a slow idle, then snicked it into gear and headed for town.

The urge to kill was on him, hot and passionate, but this time the victim would not be some drug dealing scum, but the real enemy.

He swooped over Kloof Nek and felt the exhilaration as he saw the moon reflected in a sea of hammered pewter below. He focussed on the bike's speed and handling as he laid the Suzuki down in the series of switchback bends that took him down to Camps Bay where the tourists and revellers were sitting at the sidewalk cafes and bars. The air was warmer at the beach, and the salt tang permeated everything. He cruised slowly along the strip, checking out a likely target. At the end of the road he turned around and cocked the gun and tucked it back into his jacket pocket.

He drove up to an open-air tequila bar, filled with young men and women, red-faced from the sun and the booze, flirting and laughing. A samba tune was playing from a speaker lashed to rafters clustered with vines, adding to the carnival gaiety. Sayeed pulled up and rested a foot on the curb, attracting no attention as he reached into his jacket. A large man was standing with legs splayed, his shirt open to the waist revealing the swell of a beer belly. He was guffawing loudly and just raising a beer bottle to his lips when Sayeed shot him twice through the gut and sped off. The man's beer flew into the air as he grabbed at his belly. Then he fell heavily onto a table, splintering it and ending up face down on the floor in a frothy soup of beer suds and blood, glittering from the shards of broken glass. People were screaming and rushing to get away, climbing over each other in their desperation to escape the carnage.

Sayeed raced away up the hairpin curves towards Sea Point, but as soon as he had left the restaurant strip behind he slowed down and pulled his bike into the deserted car park at Bantry Bay. He slipped off his crash helmet and sat on the low wall, watching the sea and listening to the ticking of his engine as it cooled. He thought he could hear screaming in the distance, but a couple of minutes later he heard what he had been waiting for – sirens. Two cop cars sped by on the beach road, followed by an ambulance with its lights flashing.

Sayeed got slowly to his feet and pulled on his helmet and started the bike. His heart leaped when he rounded the curve in the beach road that let him look down onto Camps Bay. Four cop cars were raked into the kerb at the tequila bar, their blue strobe lights bouncing off the bar's façade. He realised that the other two police cars must have come from the Hout Bay force. A crowd of shocked and distraught people was gathered on the grass across the road from the bar, speaking to four uniformed police. The doors of the ambulance closed and it started up the hill, siren blaring.

Sayeed took the road slowly until he reached the level at the start of the strip. He put the gun into his hand and sped up to the knot of people assembled opposite the bar. A cop half-turned as he approached and Sayeed shot him first, then snapped off three other quick shots towards the uniforms. Sayeed nailed the throttle, the bike shot forward and he was snaking up the back roads behind Camps Bay before anyone could comprehend what had just happened. He heard the sounds of distant pursuit and saw a cop car go wailing past on the coast road, its lights flashing and siren screaming. Sayeed stopped his bike at the roadside, waited for the sirens to fade, then took a sedate ride home, avoiding all the major roads and keeping within the speed limit.

He was just in time for late night news which carried a breaking story about how a New Zealand tourist had been gunned down while he he was having drinks at a bar in Camps Bay, then the gunman had returned and killed two police officers and wounded a woman who was in critical condition. The vox pops with shocked drinkers gave wildly differing descriptions of the two events and Sayeed chuckled to himself as he cleaned his pistol, refilled the magazine,wrapped it in its bag and went to bed.

Chapter 10

Tau and Gerry had spent a frustrating morning at the forensics laboratory. Doctor Schneider, the Senior Pathologist, was an elderly woman with firm opinions and an acute mind. They met in her office, hoping that she could shed some light on the bullets that blew Achmad's body apart.

'Standard issue copper jacketed bullets,' she said. 'The rifling marks didn't trigger a match on our database. Sorry,' she said. Gerry tutted irritably and Tau got to his feet.

'Thanks,' said Tau.

'There is one thing which may be of interest,' said Schneider. 'It's still early days but we managed to recover one of the bullets from the Camps Bay drive-by last night. It's a match with a bullet we dug out of a street dealer about a year ago. Soft nose hollow point.'

'I thought they opened up like flower petals,' said Gerry.

'They do. But there are still some distinctive grooves at the base of the bullet where it was crimped into the case.'

'The dealer killing - was it a gang shoot-out? Some turf war thing?' asked Tau.

'No. It was more like a hit.'

Gerry and Tau exchanged a look.

'Thanks Doc.' Said Gerry.

They exited her office and went down to the basement where, amid a number of wire mesh cages, a small team of people worked with computers and a battery of electronic equipment.

The head of the lab, Charlie Brits, lead them aside. Charlie was a somewhat eccentric figure – a PhD in Forensic Science but in common with a number of the super-bright, lacked many of the social skills that less cerebral people exhibit. He was of medium height with his thinning brown hair worn down to his shoulders. He also favoured baggy shorts and sandals, regardless of weather and occasion, and the stubble that clung to his cheeks was more a function of absent-mindedness than a major fashion statement.

'What have you got for us?' asked Tau.

'We are pursuing three lines of enquiry,' said Charlie. 'You see? Down here we don't just do stuff – we 'pursue lines of enquiry' we 'further our investigations.' That's why we're the fucken 'A' Team and the rest of you are the wannabes.'

'Charlie, here's the thing,' said Gerry looming over him, 'If you want to talk like a pompous *poes* that's all very well, but it's time to start giving.

Charlie sighed loudly. 'Just trying to raise your game. First, we are trying to work out who Kasim Bey called. Second, trying to get whatever forensics we can from the Moosa shooting, and third, there is the Camps Bay massacre. Now look around, I've got five full-time people and one jackass who's only fit to make coffee. Each line of enquiry on its own would take us a month, not to mention the normal roster of shootings, stabbings and murders. So I need to hear from you which one to prioritise.'

'Doc Schneider says that the Camps Bay hits were from the same gun that was used in a dealer killing 12 months ago. There's something there.' Said Tau.

'But what's the link between some scabby dealer and a tourist from New Zealand? It doesn't compute,' said Charlie.

'He was a magnet,' sighed Gerry. 'The killer shot the guy at random, knowing that the cops would come. Then he went for the cops.'

'Jesus,' muttered Charlie sucking his teeth. 'Was that what happened with this Moosa character?'

'I think Moosa was killed because he knew the high-ups and they were scared he would talk. I think the plainclothes followers were taken out because they were there.'

'So what is this – a cop killer?' Asked Charlie.

'I think it's political,' said Tau. 'I think PAGAD are sending us a message.'

'Have they dug out the bullets from the Boyes Drive hit?' asked Gerry.

'It's just come through. Standard NATO issue 7.62 mill. From that range, could be a sniper's rifle.'

'That's specialist kit,' said Tau. 'That could give us some leads.'

'Sadly, it's a common gauge. But there is a very slight chance we'll be able to work out from the rifling what weapon it came from.'

'How long will that take?'

'It's in the electron microscope right now,' said Charlie gesturing at a huge machine humming quietly in the corner. Katja, an attractive young female lab technician in a white coat, was peering at a screen.

'Did they find where the shooter was hiding,' asked Gerry.

'Yup. Range was roughly two hundred metres from the target. No shell casings or anything. He was behind some rocks, about 20 metres off the road. Pro job – one helluva shot.'

'Where was his car parked?' said Tau.

'No car. We found some wheel tracks indicating a motorbike.'

'Have you analysed the treads?' asked Gerry.

'Whoa!' said Charlie holding up his hands. 'Hold on a minute there, Tonto - our guys are doing what they can, but too much work and not enough hands.'

'The Camps Bay hits were done by a guy on a bike,' said Tau. 'Try and drag down any CCTV footage from the area. And if you want a priority, work out the tyre tracks.'

'We've got to go,' said Gerry tapping his watch.

Tau nodded and scribbled down some numbers. 'Call us any time,' he said.

Tau and Gerry drove back to HQ in Tau's little Mazda.

'I hate fucken funerals,' said Gerry.

'Me too,' growled Tau.

'No question,' said Gerry. 'Do you know who's going to be there?'

Tau shook his head and swung the car into the underground car park at HQ.

They showered silently and put on their drill uniforms, then drove to the Muslim cemetery in Mitchell's Plain where about 40 cars were already waiting. They entered the cool dark building where Achmad's body was wrapped in a white shroud and laid on a bier. An attractive young woman wearing black with a chador wrapped around her head and a child riding on her hip was standing staring down at the corpse, utterly distraught. A bearded Imam faced away from the body, muttering prayers. Two other officers, Matabane and Griggs, were already there, standing against one wall. Tau and Gerry nodded briefly at them.

'Is the Chief here?' whispered Tau.

Just then Chitepo emerged from the far door at that moment in a dark suit.

'Gentlemen,' he said.

The four pallbearers picked up the handles of the stretcher and eased it onto their shoulders. Gerry thought to himself how light Achmad felt and wondered if there was any vestige of sentience left, or whether he was simply dead meat and fit only for a hole in the ground.

On emerging into the bright sunlight Gerry noticed that all the women had remained behind. They had reached a dais set up beside the grave. The four pallbearers let the stretcher down gently and then Chitepo unrolled a South African flag over the corpse and two uniformed Marines stepped out and fired a salute over the body. When the smoke and the echo of the detonations had died away, Chitepo stepped forward.

'It's been a bad week,' he said. 'Our forces have come under the most savage and vicious attacks from terrorists who are hell-bent on destroying our way of life. Achmad was one of our bravest men, who ventured deep into the enemy camp and paid the ultimate price. His presence will be sorely missed, not only by his colleagues but by his young wife and son...'

Tau glanced up at Gerry – neither had known that Achmad was even married, let alone had a child.

Chitepo was still speaking…'Ours is not a mission of vengeance, but rest assured Achmad's sacrifice will not be in vain. The security laws proscribe me from telling you what he achieved, but Achmad thwarted what would have been the biggest-ever calamity to befall our country. Your time is now over, Achmad, but our struggle goes on. *A luta continua. Amandla!*'

The Imam stepped forward and continued with the Muslim rites, until finally four bearded men gently picked up the shrouded figure of Achmad and lowered it into the ground, lying on his side, facing Mecca. They started filling in the hole, the dry red earth standing out against the white shroud.

Driving back to Cape Town the unspoken thoughts of mortality hung between them. Finally Tau said, 'Do you think that's how we'll end up?'

Gerry shrugged, thinking of a flip retort to banish the darkness, but he knew that Tau's question demanded a serious answer. He sighed heavily.

'On a bad day I think some druggie or psycho or terrorist will punch my ticket and then – who knows. I just hope it's quick.'

'And the hereafter?'

Gerry laughed. 'I have enough trouble living in the here and now, mate. If I ever get to the hereafter I'll handle it at the time. Honestly? I think you become worm food, whether or not you're facing Mecca, saying your Hail Marys or praying to Jehovah. When the darkness comes, it's time to say goodnight.'

Tau shook his head. 'You are something else. And on a good day?'

'On a good day it's dying of heart failure from a blowjob while driving my Cobra at 200 kph around De Waal Drive.'

'You forgot "while eating a hamburger."'

'Goes without saying,' said Gerry. 'I know you've got something deeply spiritual planned.'

'I think matter has no start or end. We change, mutate, go into another space. It's not like Heaven or anything, it's just energy.'

'Reincarnation? Balls,' said Gerry. 'Once around is just fine for this boy, thank you.'

Tau snorted. 'And Letta? After you're gone?'

'She'll take up with some rich bastard and move to Toronto!' said Gerry savagely.

'Whoa!' said Tau. 'Sorry if I trod on a corn.'

Gerry glared at him. Tau smiled sadly, 'My worry is that Joyce will find a gifted Professor and bugger off while I'm still alive – that's what scares the shit out of me.'

'Ja, nothing like a good funeral for putting the world to rights,' said Gerry, lapsing into silence.

Two minutes later Tau's cell phone rang.

'It's Charlie Brits. I've got something.'

Chapter 11

Tau and Gerry were squinting at an HD TV screen, trying to see clearly what Charlie was showing them.

'I got this CCTV footage from the car park at Bantry Bay. I've enhanced it as much as possible – after this it breaks down into pixel soup.'

They watched the grainy image of a motorcycle enter the deserted car park and make a slow turn before stopping, maddeningly out of frame. Then they saw a figure with a full-face helmet enter frame and sit down on the wall. He took off his helmet but they couldn't make out his face. He sat still for a few moments then lifted his head, listening. Then he pulled on his helmet and exited frame only to speed through the frame a moment later, heading for the exit.

'Stop!' said Gerry.

Charlie hit the stop button and the image froze as the bike was exiting the parking area. The number plate was deep in shadow.

'Fuck!' said Tau. 'Can't you sweeten the picture?'

'Here we only do the impossible,' said Charlie. 'For miracles you need to go to church.'

'It's a Suzki V Strom,' said Gerry. 'I can't make out if it's a 1000 or a 650.'

'Where are the witness statements?' asked Tau.

Charlie reached for a batch of files.

'Did you match the tyre marks from Boyes Drive?' asked Gerry.

'Yup. It's a Dunlop Sportmax, 180 section…'

'Then it's probably the 1000cc bike,' said Gerry, flipping through the witness statements. 'Here! A blue and white bike, going really fast.'

Tau was looking mystified.

'We need to run down all of the one litre Suzuki V Stroms bought in the past two years.'

'Laidlaw!' bawled Charlie. A nervous-looking young man jumped up from his desk spilling his coffee into his lap.

'Get onto vehicle registry,' said Charlie. 'We need some info. And don't piss your pants again.'

When Tau and Gerry left an hour later they had a list of 43 Suzukis sold in the Cape in the past 24 months. Seven had been written off in accidents and five had been taken off the road, leaving 31 rideable bikes.

'It's a start,' said Gerry.

'Do we have to follow up every single one of these?' grumbled Tau.

'No. Only the guilty one,' said Gerry.

'I haven't eaten since breakfast. Strategy meeting?'

Gerry nodded. They went to their boardroom, The Hungry Heifer beachfront burger stand set on a small promontory in Sea Point overlooking the ocean. The menu was strictly limited but good, the secret being that all of the burgers were a mixture of beef and lamb, and cooked over a charcoal bed. They sat on a slatted bench in the dazzling sunshine, while a fitful wind gusted in off the ocean, blowing spindrift from the whitecaps as they ate in silence. Finally Tau sighed.

'I never knew he was married,' he said.

'Me neither,' muttered Gerry. 'Poor bastard had a kid as well.'

'Nice looking wife and boy,' said Tau.

'Yup,' said Gerry. 'We can't make it right again.'

'I know that, but we can at least nail the fuckers that did it.'

They chewed their burgers in silence and got back into Tau's car.

'What's the first one?'

'Here. Kokkie Terblanche, 87 Mooi Street. Parow.'

'Sounds like a good Muslim name,' said Tau, hitting the siren and peeling across two lanes of traffic.

They arrived forty minutes later at a small whitewashed house with a chain link fence and a scabby white lawn of dead Kikuyu grass out front and a pit bull straining at his chain. Moments later a pot-bellied sunburned man covered in tattoos and wearing only tight black shorts emerged from the house and stared at them. He was wearing flip-flops and limped, one ankle crazed with a zigzag of ugly purple stitches.

'What the fuck do you want?' he demanded, breathing beer all over them.

'First,' said Tau affably, 'get your dog away before I shoot him, second, are you Kokkie Terblanche?'

'Who's asking?' he said stepping forward belligerently.

'We are,' said Gerry flicking his ID at him. 'Please listen Kokkie, we've not had a nice day and between us we would really enjoy kicking the shit out of some lardy bastard, so I suggest you co-operate and you'll sleep tight in your bed tonight, with all your teeth. OK, *my bra?*'

Kokkie squinted at them, then exhaled like a punctured lilo.

'What have I done now?' he asked.

'Have you got a V Strom?' asked Gerry.

'Ja?' Suspicious.

'Where is it?'

Kokkie turned around and trudged away. Tau and Gerry exchanged a glance and followed him round the side of his house. Kokkie pulled back a tarpaulin to reveal a motorcycle with its forks twisted back, its headlight smashed and a ding in the fuel tank. A filigree of rust crawled over the dented bike.

'What happened?'

'Hit a fucken Alsatian. Busted my ankle in the process. But you should've seen the dog.'

'When was this?'

'Seven weeks ago. Why?'

'Thanks,' said Gerry. 'If we need anything else we'll be in touch.'

'Is this about compensation?' Yelled Kokkie. 'That dog should've been chained up!'

Back in the car Gerry said, 'One down, only 30 left to go.'

'I tell you what we're going to do,' said Tau, looking grim. 'We are going to get hold of the Criminal Division and get them to do all the scut work and if they throw up anyone who looks remotely suspicious then we'll do the follow-up. How does that sound?'

'O-kay,' shrugged Gerry.

'But?'

'But those uniformed clowns wouldn't know a terrorist from a shoplifter if he jumped up and bit them in the arse.'

'Well then why don't we feed the names into the computer and do a cross-reference with militant Islamists and see if we get a hit.'

'I don't get it. Why don't you like motorbikes?' demanded Gerry.

'It's not about lumps of bloody iron! We're looking up stinking exhaust pipes for the next six weeks while our boy is perhaps shooting a few more cops. That's why!'

They glared at each other.

'At the moment it's all we've got,' said Gerry.

Just then Tau's cell rang.

'Molepe!' he snarled.

'It's Charlie. Listen, a CCTV camera outside The Codfather got a glimpse of the shooter as he drove off. We got the last digit on his number plate. There's only five bikes which have number plates ending in a seven.'

'Thank you, Lord,' said Tau. 'Shoot.'

They wrote down the names then set off to check out the possibilities with a fresh enthusiasm.

Their first call was at the Protem site of the University of Cape Town, the Graca Machel Halls of Residence. The bike was registered to Jonathan Steinberg, a fourth year medical student and trainee cardiologist. They found him just as he was leaving his room, crash helmet in hand.

'Jonathan Steinberg?' enquired Tau holding up his ID.

'Yes.' He replied anxiously. 'What's up?'

'Have you still got your Suzuki?' asked Gerry. Steinberg relaxed somewhat and held up his helmet.

'Last time I looked. Why? Has it been pinched?'

'Please show it to us.'

Steinberg hurriedly led them to the car park at the back of the residence. He slowed down as he saw his bike still chained to the post where he had left it the previous night. It was painted a bright banana yellow.

'How long's it been yellow?' asked Gerry.

'A mate sprayed it for me last year. Why, is it a crime?'

'Only against good taste,' said Gerry.

'Where were you two nights ago, between 7 and 9PM?' demanded Tau.

Steinberg though for a moment then brightened.

'I was on call at Groote Schuur. We had a PUTCO bus crash. I tell you, there was all sorts of mayhem. What's this about?'

'No problem,' said Gerry. 'Thanks for your time.'

Back in the car Tau drew a line through the first name on the list. The sun was starting to set and the traffic was clogging in the evening rush hour.

'We do the guy on Buitenkant Street then grab a bite?' asked Gerry.

'Sure,' said Tau. 'Make a left at the next off ramp.'

They sat in traffic for the next ten minutes.

'So how was the brother-in-law's bash?' asked Gerry.

'Tito Badusa was there. One day I'll kick his fat arse all the way to jail…' growled Tau darkly.

'Great. So now you want to nail a cabinet minister. And the party itself?'

'He's a pimp, my brother-in-law.'

'Nice. And the fiancée?'

'A hooker.'

'Cool,' said Gerry. 'Sounds like you had a ball.'

'And we've got cocktails tomorrow night with some visiting academic from Boston who will slobber all over Joyce and treat me like I'm the gardener.'

Gerry slid a sidelong glance at his friend and put on the blue light onto the roof and turned on the siren and carved a path up the emergency slip road.

Nico Steinhof lived above a funky little gallery called Afrikanus exhibiting local sculpture. He was a tall German with a shaven head and numerous piercings, wearing black leather trousers and cut off T-shirt. He opened the door of his flat with a frown. A blast of Salsa music and marijuana smoke followed him out.

'Ja?'

'Hi,' said Gerry. 'National Intelligence Agency. May we come in?'

'This is not a good time,' said Nico, blocking the door.

'You're right,' said Tau, 'this is not a good time. We're looking for a cop killer and if we find him here it will become a very bad time.'

Nico took a step back.

'Killer? But what has this got to do with me?'

'Do you own a Suzuki?' asked Gerry.

'Yes. It's in the basement.'

'Who're they, Nico?' asked another shaven head which popped out of the flat, belonging to a young man who appeared to be wearing nothing at all. 'Oooh, she's handsome,' cried the young man, pointing at Tau.

'Get back inside,' said Nico. 'Come, I show you my bike.'

He led them down into the basement where a gleaming blue and white V Strom was secured.

'Where were you two nights ago, between 7 and 9?' asked Tau looking Nico straight in the eye.

'The gallery. We had an opening for this wonderful young artist from the Cameroon. Works primarily in wood but does some outstanding sculpture in green soapstone.'

'Any witnesses?' said Gerry.

'About 60 people, including the reporter from the Argus. Got a good review, for once.'

Tau and Gerry exchanged a glance.

'Let's go,' said Tau.

Tau sat in silence as Gerry headed up the hill towards a Cuban bar/restaurant. Gerry sniggered to himself. Tau glared. Gerry sniggered again.

'What?!' barked Tau.

'Ooohhh! She's not so handsome when she's cross,' lisped Gerry.

'Arsehole,' said Tau.

At Little Havana they ordered light lagers and two platters of yellow-tail *ceviche*, while munching on peri-peri cashew nuts.

'It's not *echt* Cuban, but not bad for a local approximation,' muttered Tau.

'What do you want – Fidel Castro and cigars?' growled Gerry, snaffling a couple more cashews.

It was still early in the evening and the place had only one other couple, a young pair holding hands across the table and staring soulfully into each others' eyes.

'Aren't you glad you aren't young any more?' said Gerry.

Tau cocked an eyebrow. 'What am I? Methuselah?'

'Relax,' muttered Gerry popping another cashew. 'You've got a hair up your arse. I just mean, thank God we aren't at that dopey stage…' he said, jutting his chin towards the young lovers.

'It's kinda nice,' said Tau, softening. 'At that age it's all promise.'

'Hmmm,' said Gerry.

Just then the bar's owner pointed the remote control at the TV mounted on a corner bracket. The TV had been on all the time, but muted. Now it suddenly barked into life. The news anchor cut away to a picture of a beaming African with gold-rimmed glasses and a wide smile, Silas Maponya, the Deputy President. Tau half-turned to see what was going on.

'In another development today, Deputy President Silas Maponya announced that Cape Town is to be the venue for the next World AIDS conference in March. This is the first time that South Africa will be hosting this conference and will be welcoming the leaders of the G8. Minister Maponya has special responsibility for HIV in South Africa, and was recently acquitted of rape charges. In another story, there was a crash between a car and a train at an unmarked level crossing in Limpopo Province…'

Tau turned to Gerry with a look of stunned disbelief on his face.

'Why did he have to make the announcement NOW?'

'I thought we had a few weeks' head-start,' said Gerry, 'but this really screws us!'

Moments later Gerry's cell phone rang.

'Yes boss. We just saw. Okay, 8AM sharp.'

Gerry snapped his phone off.

'He wants us first thing tomorrow morning. He was really pissed off!'

'I wonder who leaked it.'

'Doesn't matter,' said Gerry. 'The tiger's out of his cage. Now we have to grab his tail and try and hold on.'

In a bare living room in another part of town, Sayeed was staring open-mouthed at the television set. He had prayed for another chance to strike a blow for his faith, and now Allah the all-powerful had answered his prayers.

This time the team would be tight. Hand picked, trusted men. No strangers, no newcomers, just soldiers who would follow every order to the death. The scale of the operation would be huge, but would have to be accomplished with only a few men and limited resources. It would require the assistance of a master planner.

Chapter 12

This time, when Gerry and Tau arrived at HQ, Miss Naidoo showed them straight into the boss' office. Chitepo was behind his desk, a stack of files in front of him. Across the yellow wood table from him sat the Minister for Intelligence, Zak De Bruyn. He wore a black suit and glasses with brown lenses, giving him the air of a Spanish Fascist from the 30's.

Tau and Gerry went straight across to De Bruyn and shook hands.

'Minister,' said Gerry.

'Viljoen. Molepe. Jonas has been bringing me up to speed on the Internal Security situation, but said that your information was even more current. Proceed.'

In a few brief sentences Tau outlined the investigation as far as it had run.

Gerry said that straight after the meeting they were going to see another three possible suspects who were related to the Boyes Drive and Camps Bay shootings, the common thread being PAGAD and the links to Koeberg.

'Do you still think Koeberg will be on their hit list?' asked the Minister.

'If it was me, sir, I'd feel that the target had been compromised and would most likely choose another one.'

'My feelings exactly,' rumbled Chitepo. 'And our good Deputy President offered one up to them last night.'

'What the hell was he playing at?!' demanded Gerry.

'He had his reasons, no doubt,' said the Minister.

'Like trying to regain some moral authority after his court appearances! Now he's imperilled the whole summit!' Growled Tau.

'I appreciate your feelings,' said Chitepo, 'but understanding our political masters is not within the remit. Our job is to deal with the issues affecting national security as and when they arise. Now, from what you know of PAGAD, are they capable of organizing an attack on the G8 by themselves?'

Tau looked at Gerry. 'In my opinion, sir, no. They would need outside help.'

'All of PAGAD's high-ups are in detention,' said Gerry.

'But someone was obviously running the Koeberg operation - who?' Asked the Minister.

'As near as we can work out, and this is all speculative, sir, there is a cell of perhaps five hardcore radical Islamists who have so far managed to slip below the radar.'

'Are five sufficient to mount a feasible attack on the summit?' demanded Chitepo.

'It only took four men to fly a plane into the World Trade Center,' said Tau.

'Well, it's time to flush them out,' said the Minister. 'I have indicated my displeasure to our Vice President but the damage is already done. Gentlemen.'

He stood and picked up his slim briefcase and was just about to exit when Gerry half-raised his hand.

'If I can say, sir, although it might only be five fanatics who actually want to martyr themselves, there's got to be a whole infrastructure behind them. Armourers, financiers, and ... informers.'

'Do you know something?' growled Chitepo darkly.

Gerry took a deep breath. 'Tau and me, we were discussing things last night, sir, and came to the conclusion that someone must have leaked the details of the G8 summit to the Vice President in the first place. I thought that nothing had gone beyond these four walls.'

'Everything was on a strictly need-to-know basis. And as far as this office is concerned, our Vice President had no such need.

Obviously in the fullness of time, blah blah blah. But at this early stage, definitely not!'

They all looked at each other.

'I think he's right. I will have a word with the VP and see who told him,' said De Bruyn.

'And if he's not co-operative?' said Chitepo.

'We are a democracy, Jonas. Nobody is above the law. If necessary, we subpoena the bastard, this time with his pants up.'

The Minister was as good as his word. Two hours later he was being ushered into the office of the Deputy President, Silas Maponya. The office was cool and air conditioned, with smoked glass windows and blonde wood. Maponya sat behind his large desk in an Aeron chair, making marks on a document with a luminous highlighter pen. He adjusted his spectacles and put a smile on his face as De Bruyn entered, and he gestured the Minister to a seat.

'To what do I owe this pleasure, Zakkie?' he asked, ever the avuncular populist.

'Mister Deputy President,' said the Minister popping open his briefcase. 'Your announcement on the AIDS conference – where did you get the information?'

Maponya sat back, frowning.

'With respect, what business is it of yours?'

'You've undermined the secrecy attendant on building a viable security operation. We believe that the information came to you from an unauthorised source. Now where did you get it?'

'This is most irregular,' huffed Maponya. 'I should remind you that I am the Deputy President and not some underling to be treated like a naughty schoolboy!'

'And I should remind you, Mister Deputy President, that I can issue a subpoena at any stage to get the information I require, and with the greatest respect, sir, your tenure might not survive another court appearance.'

'You cannot talk to me like this!' yelled Maponya, slapping his desk.

The Minister sighed and drew a brown envelope from his briefcase and passed it silently to Maponya. Maponya reached inside and pulled out a grainy photo showing himself on top of a woman, both naked. Her face was clearly visible.

'I believe that this lady isn't your wife,' said the Minister quietly. 'In fact, she's a well known prostitute and I think that the public would like to know that on the various occasions that you have used her services you never use a condom. As the minister in charge of the AIDS project, I don't think this would play very well with either your constituents or the party.'

Maponya glared at him and opened a drawer and handed him a single flimsy sheet of paper. It had a single sentence printed on it ' WORLD AIDS CONFERENCE TO BE HELD IN CAPE TOWN MARCH 26–28.' Nothing more.

'And on the basis of this unsubstantiated story you went public?'

'I'm not a fool,' said Maponya. 'I had to check it out.'

'So why didn't you come to us?'

Maponya laughed. 'You guys were the ones who were keeping me in the dark! Making me look like an idiot.'

'So how did you confirm the facts?'

Maponya played with an executive desk toy for a few moments.

'Come along, sir,' said the Minister.

'You're not the only one with friends,' said Maponya. 'I called the CIA Africa Desk and they confirmed it. Stanton Fitzwarren and I go way back.'

The Minister nodded and slipped the sheet of paper between two clear plastic leaves. Maponya reached out for the photo but the Minister shook his head and put it back into his briefcase.

'Thank you for seeing me, Mister Deputy President,' he said and slipped out. Silas Maponya opened his desk and took a swig of Pepto Bismol. He determined that when he became President he would summon De Bruyn for a meeting that would have a very different outcome from this last one. Until that time, he would watch his back.

Meanwhile Gerry and Tau were on their way to the cracked tarmac and razor wire industrial sites of Paarden Island. They drove around the various plots until they found a long low factory block with a sign of an igloo saying 'Eskimo Refrigeration.' They went into the reception where a young 'Coloured' woman sat at desk. She had her hair piled up on her head, held in check with a pink plastic Alice Band, and the fading signs of a recent black eye. Her two front teeth were missing - although it was falling out of fashion, the so-called 'Passion Gap' was still deemed sexy in some parts of the 'Coloured' community.

Tau showed his badge and she sat up a bit straighter and put aside her Fairlady magazine.

'Ja?' she demanded, snapping her bubble gum.

'Is Martin Spence here?'

'Martin? He's through the back there.' She indicated somewhere vaguely behind her and resumed reading her magazine. Gerry gently took it out of her hands. She looked startled.

'What's your name, sweetie?' he said.

'Oscarina.' Snap.

'Now you listen nicely, Oscarina. You get off your lazy backside and go and fetch Martin right now so that we can have a chat with him. OK?'

'Who's gonna mind the front office, you tell me that,' she asked, defiantly jutting out her chin. Snap.

'Tell you what,' said Gerry leaning forward conspiratorially, 'If someone tries to steal one of your fucken fridges I'll personally tear off his arms and beat him with the bloody stump. How does that sound?'

She got sullenly to her feet and snapped another bubble then walked through some double doors and disappeared from sight.

'You've just got to be more charming,' said Gerry to Tau.

A few moments later she reappeared and did not glance at the policemen but plumped straight down at her table and resumed reading. The double doors opened and a squat man in a brown dust jacket emerged. He squinted at the cops.

'I'm Martin Spence,' he said.

'Have you got a Suzuki Storm?' asked Tau.

'No,' said Martin. 'I've got a V *Strom*. Bloody stupid name, I admit. But is that it? I'm like a bit busy.'

'No,' said Gerry. 'That isn't it.'

'Where is the bike?' asked Tau.

'Come,' said Martin.

He led the way through a busy small factory where industrial refrigeration units were being put together. Inside a booth a man in a chemical suit was spraying steel fridge carcasses white. Martin opened the rear doors to where a small private car park held four cars and several motorbikes. Martin led them over to his bike.

'There she is,' he said. 'Now will you mind telling me what this is all about?'

Gerry bent down and looked at the rear tyre – it was Bridgestone, fairly well worn.

'Where were you on the night of the third between seven and nine PM?'

'The third?' Martin went red and mumbled something.

'I didn't catch that,' said Gerry.

'I was downtown. Pussy Galore.' said Martin.

'The whole time?' enquired Tau.

'You think if I pay a hundred bucks just to get in that I'm going to leave after three dances? No ways. They chucked me out at one-thirty.'

'Can anyone verify that you were there?'

'Tiffany and Sissie and Twinks and Blaze. Oh yes, there was also Ebony. She was hot, that one!'

'Do you own a gun?' asked Tau.

'Ja. Little Smith & Wesson belonged to my old man. Shit, I don't know if you can still get bullets for the thing.'

Gerry nodded to Tau that they should go.

'Thanks,' said Gerry.

Back in the car Tau said, 'There's something about that guy I didn't quite like.'

'He's not the shooter,' said Gerry.

'Why are you so confident?'

'His tyres are Bridgestones, not Dunlops. It's possible that he could've changed tyres after the hit, but unlikely. Also, he had a sound alibi.'

'You ever go to those sort of clubs?' asked Tau.

'Titty bars? Not these days. Aletta would kill me. But when I was a young buck I had been known to visit a strip club on occasion. What of it? I suppose you never went?'

'Never had to,' said Tau with a grin.

'*Big bok*,' muttered Gerry. 'Listen I need your help this weekend. I found this guy in Kleinmond who's got a mint condition Piranha from 1977.'

'You're into old fish now?'

Gerry sighed, recognizing that with Tau he had as much of a mountain to climb as with Aletta. He started slowly. Patiently.

'A Piranha is a Ford Capri into which they shoehorn a fuck-off Boss Mustang 5 litre engine. Of course you have to up-rate the suspension and brakes and everything else, but it goes like shit off a shovel.'

'And that's what you want? Shit off a shovel?'

'Look, I need a driver, not a bladdy lecture. Are you in or out?'

'While it's tempting to waste my Sunday driving halfway to the Transkei and then back again, I will have to pass. Joyce and I are busy. Can't you get Aletta?'

'She's about as enthusiastic as you,' muttered Gerry. 'Okay, I'll have to use my charms on her. What are you and Joyce doing?'

Tau stared hard at the map.

'This next guy is way out in Muizenberg.'

'I'm on my way. But you aren't answering. What are you doing?'

'Lounge suite,' muttered Tau.

'Come again?'

'We are going to the mall to buy a three piece fucken lounge suite, all right?'

'Jeez, you don't have to shout,' said Gerry with a smirk. 'I think all that talk about Pussy Galore has upset your equilibrium. It's a long way from hot passion to fucken lounge suites. Sounds to me like Little Tau's not getting out as much as he used to.'

Tau wagged a warning finger at Gerry.

'One, Little Tau is not so little, and two, when you grow up you need somewhere to sit. Hence the lounge suite.'

Gerry nodded, not entirely convinced.

'Domestic, huh,' said Gerry, 'so here's the thing – I've been thinking about popping the question to Aletta. Is marriage something you can recommend?'

Tau thought about the previous night. He had rushed home from work and helped Joyce prepare the canapés and drinks, and then had been bored catatonic by Professor Brown from Harvard as he and Joyce made jokes about semiology and semiotics that were semihumorous. Tau was contemplating throwing himself on the *braai* when the Professor's wife arrived, an hour late.

Only she wasn't his wife, she was his 'partner,' and she was slightly tipsy and found Tau a hell of a lot more interesting than the Prof. The unwonted attention lifted Tau from his stupor and he found himself warming to Clarisse as she matched him drink for drink and started regaling him with stories about skinny dipping off Catalina Island. By the time the party ended Tau and Clarisse were dancing to the Inkspots while the Prof and Joyce were still locked in earnest debate. After their guests had left Joyce accused Tau of embarrassing her and being a shameless flirt, and he passed a bad night sleeping on the sofa. It was this, amongst other things, that had helped decide him on the need for a new lounge suite.

'Yes,' he said to Gerry. 'Best thing that ever happened to me.'

They drove in silence for a couple of kilometres then turned off to Muizenberg. They stopped outside a four-storey block of flats called La Mer and rang the buzzer of 7C. After a moment a woman's voice came to them on the tinny intercom. She said that she was Jacko Smit's wife and that Jacko was at work. Fortunately, his work was nearby and Tau headed out along the coast road towards Simonstown. Set back from the beach they found a surf shop called 'Jacko's Boards' and went inside.

A couple of tanned surfers with sun-bleached hair were leaning over the counter watching Jacko Smit lay fibre glass mesh on the surfboard he was fabricating. Loud kwaito music blared from a CD player. The surfers gradually became of aware of Tau and Gerry standing there.

'Jacko Smit?' asked Tau.

Jacko looked up, frowning. He was of average height with long brown hair and bright blue eyes. He was wearing baggy shorts and a striped T-shirt, revealing a massive scar on his arm running from his shoulder to just below the elbow. Visible at the edge of the scar like jagged saw marks were shark teeth punctures.

'That's me.' He said.

'You have a V Strom?' asked Gerry.

'Nah, pal. Sold it maybe six months back.'

'The Vehicle Registry shows that you are still the recorded owner.'

'Those arseholes must have screwed up again then,' said Jacko with a shrug. 'Look, I've got to keep laying this glass before the resin sets or this board'll be scrap.'

'Talk while you work then,' said Gerry. 'Who did you sell the bike to?'

'Some Indian bloke. Paid cash money too,' said Jacko, mounting the tailfin and quickly overlapping some glass mesh around the base.

'You get a bill of sale?' asked Tau.

'Sure. All straight up.' Said Jacko.

'Where is it?' said Gerry.

'You need to give me a bit of time,' said Jacko. 'It's at home.'

'Call your wife and tell her to bring it,' said Tau.

'You guys are interfering with my business. It's like bad karma,' grumbled Jacko.

'How's this for bad karma?' Tau stepped forward and snapped some handcuffs on Jacko who looked at his wrists in disbelief.

'Jesus! What's your fucken problem, china?'

'My problem is I have a job to do and I haven't got time to messed around. So either you call your wife and tell her to bring the receipt down now, or we go to town and I book you in and then you can wait in the cells until we have the documents we need. Which is it to be, *china*?'

Jacko held out his hands for the cuffs to be released. Tau unlocked them and Jacko rubbed his chafed wrists. The other two surfers banged fists against Jacko's and slunk away. Jacko dialled a number and waited.

'Listen Cooks, I need to you go the shoebox at the bottom of my cupboard and bring it to me. Now. Listen, I don't care, the cops are here and I need that box!'

He banged down the phone and resumed applying resin to the glass mesh. His hands were shaking.

'Why did you sell it?' asked Gerry.

'The missus was up the duff. Had to get ourselves a car,' he said with a shrug.

'How did the buyer find you?' asked Tau.

'I put in ad in the Argus. He was the second caller.'

'What did he look like?'

Jacko shrugged. 'It was six months ago, man. Like I said, an Indian or maybe a Malay, but I remember now his name sounded like something from Curry Paradise.'

Tau counted slowly to five while Gerry made a calming gesture with his hands.

'Any distinguishing marks? Height. Age? Scars? Anything?' said Gerry.

Jacko sighed at the mental effort. 'Dude was taller than me. Coffee skin. No scars. Black hair. Short. Oh ja, and these eyes. Blue. I mean, you don't get many blue eyes on them, do you?'

Just then a *bakkie* skidded to a stop outside the shop and a harried looking young woman, about 19 years old in a cheap cotton print dress with a stud in her nose, entered the shop carrying a cardboard box.

'I was in the middle of making baby lunch!' she yelled at Jacko. 'What's so important about a bladdy shoe box?'

Jacko gestured at Tau and Gerry who showed her his badge. The little spitfire flew at Jacko, beating his chest with her small fists.

'What have you done?!' she cried.

Jacko calmly took her fists and forced her hands to her sides.

'Nothing. Now don't make a scene, hey. Where's baby?'

She looked distrustful and gestured at the *bakkie*. 'Outside there.'

'Go!' said Jacko. She went. Jacko shook his head and opened the shoebox. He leafed through the pile of chaotic receipts until he finally found what he was seeking. Written on blue airmail paper, crumpled in one corner, he smoothed it out and handed it to Tau.

Tau looked at the handwritten name: Farouk Parveen, and an address in Green Point. He passed it to Gerry who nodded.

'Thanks,' said Gerry dropping the sheet of paper into a plastic evidence bag.

'Hey, that's my receipt!' said Jacko.

'It's evidence,' said Tau. 'Here's a docket.'

Tau scribbled something on official paper and passed it to Jacko who looked suspicious.

'What's going on?' he demanded.

'National security,' said Tau. 'Don't tell anyone about this enquiry or you'll be in trouble. And if you remember anything else about this guy, get in touch. OK?'

He handed Jacko a card. Jacko read it carefully and nodded.

'What tyres did you run?' asked Gerry.

'I beg yours?' Said Jacko, frowning.

'Tyres. On the Suzi,' said Gerry.

'Dunlop Sportmax,' said Jacko.

Gerry nodded, his instincts tingling.

Outside in the car Gerry looked at Tau.

'He's our boy,' he said.

Tau nodded. 'Kiss your arse goodbye, Mister Parveen,' said he said. 'Where to?'

Gerry didn't need to look up the address.

'Green Point,' he said. 'Flat 23, Montclair House, 365 Beach Road.'

Tau put the blue light on the roof and hit the siren. Things were happening at last.

Chapter 13

Sayeed awoke with a sense of purpose. During the night the plan had coalesced in his mind and he was anxious to start work. The first call was to his father to say that he wasn't feeling well and would not be in. He then sent an SMS message saying 'CALL' to Hamidullah, his comrade in arms who had fled to an undisclosed location. He showered and dressed then turned on the TV and had just prepared his first cup of coffee and was running through the final aspects of his flight manual, when he happened to glance up at the news.

'…The police have released the following image of the motorbike seen speeding away from the Camps Bay massacre. It is a blue and white Suzuki V Strom and you can see that the last number in the number plate is a 7. If you have seen this bike please contact your local police station…'

Sayeed struggled to regain his breath. He would have to get rid of the motorcycle. The local kids knew the bike and had asked him how fast it went and all the other stuff that young boys enjoyed. He would have to resolve the situation, but first, he had his final flying lesson. He tucked his flight manual under his arm and got into his Mazda and set off.

He was heading for the N7 motorway when his phone rang. He pulled over at the side of the road.

'Yes?' he said.

Hamidullah's voice was faint.

'You must come back,' said Sayeed. 'There is a party to arrange.'

'Is this the March event?' asked Hamidullah.

'Yes. A big celebration. Have you got far to come?'

'I will be there by the weekend.'

And the line went dead. Sayeed put the car in gear and joined the traffic. Five minutes later he was on the motorway, heading for the countryside.

He arrived just before 11 at the Bluebird Flying School some 50 kilometres from Cape Town, the single hangar and clapboard office rimmed by blue mountains and vineyards. The trim yellow Piper Pawnee was waiting on the grass runway as Leon Wessels tinkered with something under the cowling. Sayeed parked his car under a tree beside the office and walked over to Leon.

'Hi Farouk,' said Leon. 'So today's the big day, hey. You feeling confident?'

'It'll be great,' said Sayeed, feeling a surge of excitement.

'Just changing the plugs,' said Leon. 'We don't want you falling out of the sky on your first solo, do we?'

Sayeed managed a grin and shook his head. Leon shut the cowling with a clang and secured the latches. He squinted at the windsock, hanging limp, lifted by the occasional gust of wind like a flaccid old man fitfully recalling his wild youth.

'Perfect conditions – the wind is from the South East about four knots,' he said. 'We'll do the written and oral test in the office then you'll take her up. Take off, circle the field twice, climb to five thousand metres, do a stall, left recover then circuit the field once more then a 15 metre pass along the runway, up, round and bring her in. OK?'

Sayeed nodded and he and Leon went back to the office. Sayeed had studied hard and after an hour he and Leon were ready.

'That was excellent,' said Leon. 'Ninety-eight percent. If you fly as well as your theory you'll be an ace.'

Sayeed nodded. He expected nothing less. Leon was slightly irritated because he felt that he was a good instructor and it was rare to have such a diligent student, but he found the man he knew as Farouk Parveen to be something of a cold fish. He shrugged to himself – he didn't have to like the guy, he just had to do his job and put another pilot through flight school. He held out the keys to the Piper.

'We ready?'

'Yes,' said Sayeed taking the keys. 'I just need the toilet.'

Leon laughed. 'They all do before their first solo,' he said. Sayeed looked hard at him then disappeared into the tiny stall at the back of the office. Once inside he produced a flat tobacco tin filled with Plasticine. He pressed the Piper's key into the modelling clay and took a careful impression, then screwed back the lid of the tin and popped it into his pocket, flushed the toilet, and emerged.

Leon was already at the plane. Sayeed stood on the reinforced wing and swung easily into the cockpit. He put on his helmet and earphones and fitted the key into the ignition, and closed the Perspex hood.

'Ready?' yelled Leon.

Sayeed nodded, gave a thumb's up and flicked the ignition switch causing the red light on the dash to glow. Leon turned the prop by hand until he reached compression point then swung it hard. The engine barked once, emitted a puff of blue exhaust smoke, then settled into a steady thrum. Leon pulled the chocks from the wheels and stood back, waving Sayeed ahead. Sayeed eased the throttle forwards and the plane started to move. He swung it around into the wind, and then revved the engine, engulfing Leon in warm prop wash as the plane taxied along the bumpy strip, gathered speed and lifted gracefully into the air.

Sayeed was grinning to himself as the plane climbed steadily then he banked it around and circled twice around the airfield. Leon stood rooted to the spot, shielding his eyes against the sun as he followed the plane as it started its climb. Sayeed emitted a wild whoop of delight as the plane rose steadily, the altimeter clicking up the altitude as it ascended.

When he reached his ceiling he pulled back on the stick forcing the plane's nose upwards. It slowed until it could not climb any further, and suddenly dropped one wing towards the ground in a steep spiral. Sayeed used opposite flaps and ailerons and at 2000 metres the craft suddenly steadied and levelled out. Sayeed slowly exhaled and realised that he had been grasping the stick for dear life. He silently thanked Allah for giving him the courage to master the skills that would ultimately deal a deadly blow to the enemy and propel him to Paradise.

Down below Leon was sweating. He was always anxious when a novice pilot did his first solo stall – he remembered some years ago seeing a young man freeze at the controls as the plane cart-wheeled out of the sky and crashed in a fireball in a vineyard five kilometres away. Leon had kept the plane's bent propeller at the back of the hangar, a grisly reminder of the dangers of flying. Since then, touch wood, he hadn't lost anyone, and he had to admit that this young Indian guy had talent.

Sayeed did the low level run along the landing strip, peeled off into the sky and brought the plane down in a perfect three point landing. He taxied up to Leon and cut the engine. Leon stepped forward with his clipboard while Sayeed scrambled out of the cockpit and handed Leon the key. Leon made a final notation on his clip board.

'Congratulations Farouk. You are now a qualified pilot. I'll send the papers off to Cape Town and you should receive your documents in a month or so. Oh yes, there's an additional two hundred Rands processing fee.'

Sayeed smiled and shook hands, and counted out the final payment and the additional levy.

'If you ever want a job crop-dusting, give me a call, hey,' said Leon.

'I'll see you around,' said Sayeed as he walked back to his car and drove away.

Leon watched him go, frowning. The Indian had initially come to him saying that he wanted work as a crop duster, but showed no interest when Leon had raised the possibility. 'Fuck him,' thought Leon. He wouldn't rush to send in the paperwork. He was quite happy to let the bastard sweat.

Sayeed had turned onto the main road back to Cape Town and was playing some raga music on the car's CD. He took the

Milnerton off-ramp and went to a locksmith in the main street called Deepak Security.

Ravi, a tall young Asian man with a fringed beard was serving a customer. Sayeed waited patiently until they were alone.

'Salaam,' said Sayeed.

'Salaam Alaikum,' replied the younger man.

Sayeed handed him the tobacco tin and the young man carefully lifted the lid and examined the impression.

'Unusual key,' he said. 'What's it from?'

'Can you do it or not?' said Sayeed.

The young man shrugged eloquently as if nothing was beyond him.

'Take me a couple of days,' he said.

'Excellent,' said Sayeed. 'I'll drop in next time I'm passing.'

Ravi nodded, glad to be of service to such an important man.

'One thing,' he said. Sayeed turned. 'The cops are looking for a guy on a blue and white Suzuki...' Sayeed held his eye and said nothing. 'I just thought you should know,' said the young man.

Sayeed nodded and exited the shop. He knew what he had to do.

Chapter 14

Gerry was starting to get angry.
'Slow down, man,' he snapped. 'It must be around here somewhere.'
'It's a false address,' growled Tau.
They were driving up and down Beach Road in Green Point, looking for a block of flats called The Montclair. They followed the street numbers and stopped outside number 365, a small Spar supermarket.
'Maybe it's his workplace,' said Gerry lamely. Tau gave him a look and cut the engine. He and Gerry walked into the cool supermarket that was empty apart from one old man who was comparing prices on tins of pilchards. There were three checkouts but only one was open, and Gerry marched straight up to the grey-haired woman working the cash register.
'Is this The Montclair?' he barked. She looked puzzled, trying to work out what he was saying.
'Does Farouk Parveen work here?' asked Tau. By this time the woman's mouth was hanging open and her lower plate had shifted to one side. Her one eye was watering and twitching with a life of its own. She nosily sucked her plate back into her mouth and blinked at them several times.
'What?' she finally said.
'Is the manager here?' asked Gerry, forcing himself to be calm.
'Manager? That's Mister Opperman,' she said.
'Yes,' said Tau, fighting the urge to leap across the counter and throttle the aged crone. 'Mister Opperman. Is he here?'

'I'll just check,' she said and shuffled slowly to the back of the shop and entered a small office, carefully shutting the door behind her. The minutes crawled by.

'Jesus, how long can it take? Either he's there or he isn't. Does she think he's hiding in the bladdy *koeksusters*?' growled Gerry.

Finally a portly man emerged from the back room followed by the old woman who was peering fearfully at Tau and Gerry from under Opperman's pendulous dewlap.

Tau showed him ID. 'Are you Opperman?'

'Yes sir. Tertius Opperman. What's the trouble, constable?'

Tau drew a hand over his eyes and breathed deep.

'For starters, I'm not a constable. Do you have anyone working here by the name of Farouk Parveen?'

'Parveen, you say?' said Opperman turning his head to one side like a bird, trying to apprehend an elusive worm. 'Parveen?... Parveen! No. I don't think so'

'Think hard,' said Gerry. 'Nobody of that name work here in the past 12 months?'

'Twelve months? Parveen? I would say not.'

'You're definite?' said Tau.

'Well, Mrs Blatch and I are the only ones who work here, isn't that so, Mrs Blatch?'

'What's that, Mister Opperman?'

'We're the only ones who work here, aren't we, dear?' Yelled Opperman.

'Oh yes. I'd know if there was someone else.'

'And was this shop ever a block of flats called The Montclair?'

'Montclair, you say? No constable, before this shop was here there was just a vacant lot. This was built in 1984, wasn't it, Mrs Blatch?'

'Just veldt here,' she said. 'The old Crown bioscope wasn't far away. I saw Douglas Fairbanks there, you know.'

Tau looked at Gerry who was scowling. 'Let's go.'

'You don't want anything else?' Asked Opperman hopefully. 'We're doing a special on litre bottles of Sparletta.'

'Ginger beer?' asked Gerry hopefully.

'Crème soda,' said Opperman. 'Buy two get one free.'

Like a *stompie* flicked into a muddy puddle, the one small bright spark in Gerry's day was extinguished. He hated crème soda. They sat in the car for a long time saying nothing. Finally Gerry spoke.

'OK, so it was a false name and address. At least it tells us that we're onto the right guy.'

'Maybe he's just a plain old crook. Shouldn't we check out the last bike with the 7 tag?'

'It's registered to Daryl Els who lives in Pinelands. I wouldn't say off the top of my head that he's a likely suspect.'

'Why? Just because he hasn't got a Muslim name?'

'No. Because he's my bladdy dentist,' said Gerry.

'Are you serious?'

'What? A dentist can't ride a motorbike? He also has a BMW trail bike. Big deal.'

'Then where to?' said Tau.

'Let's get back to the lab and see if they've dug up anything else.'

The staff had all left and Charlie was about to shut up for the day when Tau and Gerry walked in.

'I was just leaving,' groaned Charlie. 'Catch the last wave of the day.'

'Wrong again,' said Gerry. Charlie sighed and turned on all the lights.

'You guys get anywhere with the number plate lead?'

'Yes and no,' said Tau. 'We think we ID'd the shooter but he gave a false name and address for the bike registration, so as of now, nothing.'

'I saw that the cops put our little bit of CCTV onto the box, so that may yield something.'

'Mmmm,' said Gerry. 'What about forensics? Anything on the guns or ammo?'

'Something quite interesting came up on the Boyes Drives shooting,' said Charlie opening his desk drawer and taking out some ghostly grey prints. 'The electron microscope picked up these little grooves just here…' he said, pointing to what looked like shallow valleys on a smoothly curving grey landscape.

'And?' said Tau.

'These were made by a silencer,' said Charlie.

'Since nobody heard anything I thought that was bladdy obvious,' grunted Gerry.

'Sheesh, who's Mister Angry?'

'Get on with it!' said Tau.

'This is the unusual part – normally you can't tell one suppressor from another, but this one used a new gas blowback baffle which leaves a unique footprint. These marks were made by a suppressor developed specifically for a Russian sniper rifle called the SV-98. There aren't many in the country. The army had a dozen for evaluation purposes and there are some collectors who have them, but as for the rest they will have crossed the border illegally from Angola or Mozambique. The Soviets used them extensively in Angolan War. Shot seven sorts of shit out of our boys up near the border, I can tell you. It's a top piece of kit.'

'Great. So our murdering son-of-a-bitch is also buying illegal arms,' said Gerry.

'Say it ain't so,' said Charlie.

'Any news on the phone traces?'

'The SIM card in Kasim's phone was pretty much destroyed. But the phone company was able to work out who he called just before he tanked. It's here somewhere…'

Charlie rummaged among a whirlwind of papers on his desk. Finally he found it.

'Ja, there's a number but unfortunately the recipient's SIM card was untraceable.'

Tau was now looking murderous. 'How can that be? I thought all SIM cards were listed. How else do you use the damn things?'

'Stolen,' said Charlie smugly. 'A batch disappeared last month from Durban docks while awaiting collection. Right there in the bonded warehouse. What happens is the *skollies* buy up the SIM cards, use them until they're starting to get hot, then ditch them and use another. No trace.'

'Can't you at least work out where the caller was?' said Gerry.

'In urban areas it's relatively simple to triangulate the whereabouts of the call by using land relay stations, but in the countryside it becomes a lot more vague. We're working on it.' said Charlie.

'Is there any way of telling if this guy is still using the same SIM card?' asked Tau. 'Maybe you can put out a trace marker on it so that if it's ever used again it alerts someone?'

'Already done, old pal. And we got a hit earlier in the day.'

'Why the fuck didn't you tell us?' demanded Tau.

'I'm telling you now,' said Charlie. 'Don't bust my balls here, guys. I'm stretched so thin you can wrap me around your dick and call me a condom.'

'Horrible thought,' said Gerry. 'What did you find?'

Charlie snuffled to himself for a few moments as he rummaged through more papers and finally held something aloft.

'Here we go. Eight-fifty four this morning an SMS message to another unregistered SIM card phone.'

'Did you get a fix?'

Charlie chewed his lip. 'Well, it's not quite so simple. There's a heavy storm coming in off the Atlantic hitting the Namibian Coast and bringing with it a huge cloud of ionised air.'

'And why,' said Gerry, a vein pulsing in his forehead, 'should I give a puckered rat's arse about the Namibian ionosphere?'

'Because,' said Charlie holding up a finger, 'for long distance radio transmissions we use a communications satellite. The ions are affecting the magnetic resonances which the geosat uses to fix locations.'

'In other words,' said Tau, 'you don't have a fix?'

'Correct,' said Charlie. 'But the guy he messaged is in Namibia.'

'Well that narrows it down,' said Gerry sourly.

'And the sender?'

'Somewhere in the Cape.'

'Hi-tech bullshit,' growled Tau.

'Not quite, said Charlie. 'Our boy received an incoming call an hour later. This time we got a fix.'

Gerry was tingling. 'Do we have to beg or just beat the shit out of you?'

'You're not going to like it. It seems he stopped at nine-thirty two on the roadside to take the call. A trunk road leading to the N7 near Stellenbosch. Spoke for 37 seconds then he cut it off.'

'And the caller?'

'The caller was in Swakopmund. Near the railway station.'

'We're going to need all the motorway cameras checked for an hour each side of the timed call,' said Gerry.

'You must be fucking joking!' Said Charlie hotly.

'No joke,' said Tau.

'Then you need to go to your big boss and get some extra bucks to throw at this. With my staff levels it would take two months to review that footage.'

'We'll get the extra bodies,' said Gerry.

'And listen,' said Tau, 'if this guy picks up his phone again then let us know immediately. Day or night. OK?'

'Got it,' said Charlie. 'Now if you don't mind, I've got a life.'

Tau and Gerry decamped to The Hungry Heifer where Tau had a Noo Yawk Dawg with all the trimmings while Gerry assaulted a Heiferlump with blue cheese dressing washed down with a Coke Float.

'It looks like our boy's running,' said Gerry through a mouthful of food.

'We should look at the Namibian angle,' said Tau. 'Swakomund is a pretty small place. Let's give the local Special Branch a call.'

'Do you have any juice with the Namibian service?' asked Gerry. 'I've got nothing. Never even been there. Sand flies and heat rash – you can keep it thanks.'

'Joyce and I honeymooned in the Okavango. What a wonderful place! But that's about it.'

'You honeymooned in a swamp? Jeez. If Aletta and me get hitched we'll go to the Seychelles or somewhere cool – cocktails, skiing, scuba, surfing. You can keep your elephants and crocodiles, mate.'

Tau shook his head. 'We'll speak to the boss. He went to that regional security summit last year. He must be able to cut through the red tape.'

'There is one other thought,' said Gerry slurping the remains of his Coke, 'we might have to bring in our pal Stanton Fitzwarren.'

Tau groaned. 'If we involve the CIA then we kiss the investigation goodbye, and end up looking like clowns who can't do anything. I say no.'

'Listen,' said Gerry, 'they have massive computing power and guys who can analyse images way quicker than our boys. Perhaps we can feed them the motorway footage and get them to do a quick analysis. Charlie and his boys will take forever and bellyache all the time.'

'Maybe,' said Tau. 'But it has to be ring-fenced. Just the data analysis.'

'Quite frankly,' said Gerry. 'I don't give a damn who does the number crunching. I just want the information.'

'Well, the next time he uses his phone, we'll nail the bastard,' said Tau, more in hope than certainty.

Chapter 15

Sayeed parked in the street behind the mosque and let himself into the grounds via the gate on 11th Street. The whitewashed building had a single tall minaret for the calling of faithful to prayer, and its shady courtyard with date palms and a cracked mosaic fountain was more reminiscent of Arabia than the Southernmost tip of Africa. Sayeed checked that nobody was watching and approached a low, whitewashed brick building attached to the back of the mosque. Mynah birds were chattering in the trees and the building looked pink in the fading light of day. Sayeed unlocked a door and let himself in.

The place was cool and quiet. It consisted of a large open plan office with four desks in it, used for administration during the day, and a bare room at one end which was used for community activities two nights a week. Sayeed went through this room and unlocked a door at the back, marked 'EQUIPMENT'. He pushed past some ratty exercise mats and an old vaulting horse and a wire basket filled with basketballs for when the young faithful came to play. A threadbare rug, on one corner of which stood a battered green filing cabinet, covered the floor. Sayeed swung the cabinet aside and threw back the rug revealing a trapdoor set into the floor, with a lock recessed into the thick wood just below the grab ring. Sayeed opened the door and climbed inside, shutting and locking the trapdoor behind him.

The simple cellar was lit by a row of fluorescent tubes, with dangling wires leading to a gang of plugs attached to the wall.

Water stains permeated the brickwork, and the place always smelled of damp earth. There was a long steel case, also heavily padlocked, at one end of the room. At the other stood a simple wooden desk with a computer.

Sayeed opened the metal box. Inside were 17 pistols of differing makes, but all shooting the same 9mm load. There were four AK-47s, the Russian sniper rifle, an ancient bolt-action .303 and a couple of Belgian FN assault rifles. Plus two green steel Claymore landmines, half a dozen Denel hand grenades and six sticks of demolition dynamite and detonators. Neatly stacked at one end were box after box of ammunition for the weapons. There were also six sets of walkie-talkies, and right at the back a small box of SIM cards. Sayeed popped the old one from his phone into his pocket and slid in a new one, committing the number to memory. He took out one of Claymores and a grenade, and locked the box and started the computer.

When he had met Tariq Dar in Somalia, they had established a system of communicating in cyberspace designed to evade interception. The system was fairly simple to operate. Sayeed would send a coded message to an email address in England. Tariq assured Sayeed that the Bradford-based brother was a computer genius who had in turn set up a system of onward transmission that went to France, then Greece, then a detour via the Dutch Antilles, Paraguay, Turkey and finally Iran. The reply would come back via the same route and was as safe from interception as possible.

Sayeed wrote. 'Greetings Brother. We are throwing a large party for our uncle and his important guests in March. I need your help to plan a wonderful surprise for him.' Sayeed smiled to himself and hit the 'send' button. He did not expect an immediate reply but left the computer on while he made a rough sketch of his house and garage. A few minutes later the computer pinged and Sayeed looked in the inbox. The message read 'Good news, brother. We need to meet soon.'

Sayeed typed back, 'Where? Same as before?'

The answer when it came gave him a rare thrill. 'No. I will come to your house. Details later.'

Sayeed smiled to himself and shut down the computer, erasing every trace that he had ever been there. He put the Claymore and grenade in a nylon sports bag, turned off the lights and headed for home.

Sayeed was feeling elated that the great Tariq Dar had felt him important enough to risk visiting in South Africa. Sayeed would have to be meticulous in his planning to protect the safety and security of his esteemed guest. He carefully locked the office and set off across the dusty square towards his car, carrying the nylon holdall bag. He stopped briefly and felt in his pocket, then flipped the old SIM card into the dusk and went on his way.

Night had fallen by the time he turned into the quiet residential street where he lived. His recent elation turned to ashes in his mouth as he saw a police car drawn up outside his house. One uniformed cop was knocking at the door while a second was on his tiptoes trying to see into the garage window. They were standing with one of the local youths who had 'ooh'd' and aah'd' when Sayeed had blipped the throttle on the Suzuki and peeled off at speed.

Sayeed turned his car around and drove slowly away, feeling the adrenaline pumping. He parked two blocks away and cautiously returned to his street. Ten minutes later the cops became bored and left. Sayeed rushed back to his car and parked it some distance from the house and slipped inside, clutching the nylon sports bag.

He worked in the dark, swiftly throwing his clothes into a suitcase, checking the bathroom and bedroom one last time. He dragged the mattress into the small living room and slit it open, exposing the wadding. He entered the garage through a side door and took a jerry can of petrol back into the house. He extended the Claymore's scissor feet, facing the door, two feet above the ground, rigged to detonate when the door was opened. He checked it one last time then poured the petrol into the mattress wadding. Then he tore a bed sheet into strips knotted together and made into a rope that he soaked in fuel and ran from the mattress into the garage where the end dipped into the Suzuki's fuel tank.

Sayeed took a deep breath, slid open the side door of the garage and tossed a match inside then shut the door and walked nonchalantly away. He saw the orange flames flickering through the garage window then suddenly there was a 'WHUMP' as the windows blew out. A ribbon of flame leaped inside the house and the last thing Sayeed saw as he slipped into his car was the neighbours running into the street as his house burst into flame, lighting up the night sky. As he drove slowly away he heard the approach of distant sirens and smiled.

Chapter 16

Just as Sayeed was knocking at the door of Ravi's house in Milnerton, Gerry and Aletta were sitting down to dinner at '*Ouma's Kombuis*,' a chic new restaurant overlooking the sea at Kalk Bay. The place was all cool cream interiors with Mediterranean tiles on the floors and olive trees in large zinc cubes dotted around the room. A tall lemon tree hung with yellow fruit grew through the floor and scented the air with a lemony tang.

Gerry had put on a jacket and tie and Aletta was as usual looking lovely in that relaxed way of fit, tanned people comfortable in their own skin and without the need for artifice. Gerry had come to a snap decision. Nestling in his pocket was a ring box containing a diamond ring set on either side with emeralds, Aletta's favourite stone. Gerry did not believe in coincidence, precognition or predestination, yet he nonetheless felt that the string of events that had brought him to the brink of proposing to his sweetheart was somehow pre-ordained.

In fact, marriage was the last thing on his mind when he had pushed his three wheeled Morgan onto the drive the previous day. He was checking the magneto on the JAP engine because the spark had been somewhat erratic, when he became aware that another car had stopped a few feet away, a British racing green XK - 140 Jaguar. The owner got out of the car and strolled over. He was a serious collector, a Brit with a holiday home in Constantia, the type of person Gerry normally loathed. But he knew his stuff and attended the Goodwood classic races each year and had raced his Aston Martin DB4 the previous season.

Despite himself, Gerry found that he was warming to Mac Macpherson, a feeling reinforced when Macpherson attacked the Morgan's magneto and pulled out the carbon contacts and sanded them down in the street, oblivious to the black dust that coated hands and face. The Morgan started like a dream and after half an hour's haggling they shook hands and the Morgan was sold. Gerry had winced several times on selling his beloved Morgan, but Mac had paid well, in cash, and with the imminent arrival of the Piranha, space was at a premium.

It was the cash in his hand that had led him back to the jeweller's store in Green Point where Aletta had 'oohd' and 'aaahd' over the ring in the window. Gerry hated hire purchase and the cost of the ring was so far out of his reach that he put it out of his mind, until, unbidden and unwanted, Mac Macpherson had come into his life and suddenly provided the wherewithal to make it happen.

Aletta had intuited that something important was going on inside Gerry's head because he was more distracted than usual and had even forgotten to tape the All Blacks/Springbok game the previous night. He was now staring at the wine list, wishing that he could rip off his tie and jacket and be more relaxed. He wondered if he should go down on one knee to pop the question, but dismissed this idea as soon as it occurred because he wasn't prepared to look like a bloody fool for anyone. He glanced up and saw her looking at him through lowered lids.

'Hi Letty,' he said.

'Hi Gerry,' she said. He growled something incomprehensible and went back to looking at the wine list, trying to keep his eye on the left side of the page rather than the right.

'Uh…Did you decide what you're having?' he said to her. 'It helps with choosing the wine.'

'It's a lovely menu,' said Aletta. 'I've wanted to come here for ages. Is there a special occasion?' She asked with a half-smile.

Gerry looked uncomfortable. 'Can't a guy bring his girlfriend somewhere nice without there being a reason?' he asked.

She was about to answer truthfully but instead said 'That's just the kind of sweet gesture I love you for.'

Gerry sighed and relaxed. 'Fish or meat?' He asked.

'I can't decide. Sometimes these menus are so up themselves you don't actually know what the food is like.'

'Ja,' said Gerry. 'Maybe we should get a bottle of each, just to make sure.'

'I've never tried Springbok,' she said. 'What's it like?'

'Last time I had Springbok I was 11. My Dad and I were near Christiana. We'd been camping, just the two of us, and Dad bagged a buck at about 300 metres. We cleaned it and roasted the filet over a fire. I have to say it was the best thing I've ever eaten.'

'Mmmm,' she said. 'I don't know. The fish looks pretty good. Maybe the *perlemoen*. My brother once got some *perlemoen* but it was like a rubber hockey puck.'

'You need to beat it first,' said Gerry. 'Then it's fantastic. You could try the Atlantic lobster.'

They shared their starters of *bredie* and red onion tart then Gerry opted for the Springbok while Aletta finally settled on a Dover Sole. The food was excellent and the service quiet and unobtrusive, although there was a sticky moment when Eduardo turned up at their table and announced himself as their server for the night. Eduardo was camp as Christmas and managed to irritate Gerry by complimenting Aletta on her earrings and fabulous sandals. In Gerry's entire life he had never thought of sandals, not even his all-terrain lightweight hiking sandals, as 'fabulous' and became increasingly irate as they chatted about strappy sandals and the new season's colours.

'He wouldn't have lasted long in MY Ouma's kitchen,' growled Gerry. Aletta's laughter had diffused the moment and as the wine flowed their mood became more intimate.

Gerry had resolved to pop the question after the *melktert* and before the coffees – Aletta favoured Kahlua in her Don Pedro – whereas Gerry liked a straight-up Irish Coffee. Gerry considered himself a man of resolve, and once his mind was made up there was little to deflect him from his course. Which is why he was even more irritated by his current paralysis. His mouth was dry and his one foot tapped a nervous tattoo underneath the table, waiting for the right moment.

He realised that he wasn't procrastinating because he was scared of the asking the question, but was suddenly seized by fear of a rebuff. What if she turned him down? He would have to kill her, no question. No, that would be inappropriate, thought Gerry, he would have to deal with it like a man. Yes, he would kill her. No, in fact, he wouldn't harm a hair on her head, but realized that he would rather kill himself. Even that was rash. No, he would go on a massive bender, drink Cape Town dry, find some cute young thing, and her twin sister, and…

'Are you feeling all right, Ger? You look like you're having a stroke,' Aletta said, looking concerned.

'I'm fine, just this bladdy collar's strangling me,' he muttered, fingering the box in his pocket.

'Good *melktert*,' she said. 'I haven't had this since I was a kid.'

'Me too,' said Gerry, watching with exquisite anticipation as she forked the last crumbs into her mouth. The moment had arrived. Gerry took a firm grip on the ring box.

Just then a trendy young couple entered, talking animatedly.

'A bomb!' Said the young woman. 'In Deep River. Who the hell would put a bomb there?'

'The radio said that there was a fire and when the firemen came the place blew up,' said her partner.

'Probably a gas bottle,' said the man. 'Come, let's sit down.'

Gerry froze. When he arrived at the restaurant he had switched off his phone because he didn't want to be interrupted.

'What's it?' asked Aletta, anxious.

'Sorry,' said Gerry. 'I've just got to check in. I'll be back in a second, sweetheart. Order me an Irish, please.'

Gerry got up and walked out to the small balcony where he blipped on his phone. There were three messages. Two from Tau, sounding pissed, and one from his boss, equally irritated. Gerry dialled Tau first.

'Where the hell have you been!?' yelled Tau.

'Go boil your bladdy head,' said Gerry. 'I was out of range. I heard there was a bomb.'

'Not a bomb - a fucking Claymore! The place had been torched and the mine was rigged so when the firemen opened the door three of them were cut to pieces by shrapnel. Gone. Finished. Red Mist. And one other guy is in Groote Schuur right now fighting for his life. It was a trap.'

'Similar MO to the Camps Bay shooting?'

'You'd better believe it. In the garage was the burned-out Suzuki.'

'I'm on my way,' said Gerry.

Gerry shut the clamshell and stared out at the sea. Phosphorescence was undulating off the gentle swell giving the water ghostly green aura. In the troughs between the waves the water looked black and unfathomable. He turned and went inside. He sat down at the table and gently took Aletta's hand.

'Let's finish up and go, sweetie,' he said, looking sad.

'What's wrong?' she asked.

'Oh, just about everything. I have to go into the office.'

'Wake me up when you get in,' she said, squeezing his hand. At that moment he felt that he truly loved her. But he wouldn't rush the proposal now. He would wait. He leaned over the table and kissed her gently.

'Gerry! Are you crying?'

'Don't be so bladdy stupid,' he said. 'Just got a *miggie* in my eye.'

Chapter 17

Miss Naidoo had made several jugs of coffee and when Tau and Gerry entered the office Chitepo was on the phone. He waved them to chairs while he nodded and made non-committal grunts and finally hung up. Tau was in a tracksuit, having coming from the gym, whereas Gerry was still in his jacket but had yanked off his tie as soon as he left the restaurant.

'The house was rented out to an Indian man, late 20's, blue eyes, called Farouk Parveen. The vehicle registration and national tax office people are trying to track him down. We're also sifting through the bank records.' Said Chitepo.

'Waste of time,' said Tau.

'Why?' demanded Chitepo.

'It's a false name,' said Gerry.

Chitepo glared at them. 'What else do we know about this guy?'

'He did the hit on the Camps Bay officers and we suspect that he was also the guy behind the shooting of Moosa Ibrahim.'

'In other words, he's a high-up in PAGAD. And he's connected with Koeberg and the death of our agent.'

Tau and Gerry nodded.

'So how do we get hold of him?'

'The techies in Charlie's unit are trying to trace the calls from his cell phone. Yesterday he rang someone in Swakopmund.'

'We need you to use your leverage to get the Namibian security people to help out here,' said Tau. 'The guy may still be in Swakopmund – it's much easier to find someone there than here.'

'I saw the file,' said Chitepo. 'I already put in a call to Titus Mpho, who runs things out there.'

'Is he any good?' asked Gerry.

'Well, they normally deal with cattle rustling or the occasional drunken murder, but he seemed competent.'

'Going back to the Deep River house – was it possible to find any prints?'

'That's why he torched it. Not a damn thing.'

'Someone somewhere must know this guy. And the blue eyes thing makes it pretty distinctive. Why don't we flash an Efit on the TV?' asked Gerry.

'That's very much a last resort,' said Chitepo. 'We need this to be intelligence-led. We need to close down the whole operation, not just one man. There are people behind him – look at his weaponry. Claymore mines! Sniper rifles! This bastard has more weaponry than the fucking Army! And if he's using fake ID there must forgers out there, print men, guys who can get hold of passports. And he needs money. We need to explore every avenue!' said Chitepo slapping his fat hand on the desk so hard that his coffee cup leaped in its saucer.

'I think we should go to Pollsmoor and shake down some of the PAGAD big shots,' said Tau.

'You think they'll speak to us?' said Gerry.

'I doubt it, but it can't hurt,' said Chitepo.

'We need to get someone inside there,' said Tau. 'Set him up and have him thrown into Pollsmoor with the hard men.'

'It will take some time,' muttered Chitepo. 'Besides, are they still pulling the strings or are the cells working autonomously?'

'Even if they are independent, the guys inside will still be able to help with armourers, forgers, bag men etc. I think it's worth a shot.' Said Tau.

'There's a bright young guy coming up through the ranks right now, Chris Pieterse. Meet with him tomorrow and work something out. In the meantime try and use our forensics to get a lead on our man, or his Namibian connexion.'

'What's your pal Mpho doing?' asked Gerry.

'He's checking car hire and trains, and movements to and from the town. He's put up roadblocks on all the major roads along the coast and to Windhoek.'

'I'm no expert, but if we know this guy's phone number why can't we call him and when he picks up we zero in on the call?'

Tau and Chitepo looked at Gerry for a long moment.

'Sounds too simple,' said Tau. 'We should ask Charlie.'

'Get going,' said Chitepo. 'There's a mountain of stuff you have to get through.'

'One thing, sir,' said Gerry. 'Charlie's guys are working at full stretch. I wonder if we could use the Yanks to help with data analysis, like going through the motorway camera tapes.'

'I want to try and avoid it,' said Chitepo. 'There's no free lunch.'

'Then you have to give Charlie some extra hands,' said Gerry, 'or we'll still be here at Christmas.'

'Well you'd better find this guy or one thing you can be sure of, you won't be here at Christmas,' said Chitepo.

Just then his phone rang.

'Yes? Thanks.'

He jotted something down on a pad and tore off the sheet of paper and passed it to Tau.

'The pilot's registry have a hit. It seems like our friend Parveen has just completed his pilot's training. Here's the address of the flight school.'

'That's all we need - some bastard flying a plane into Koeberg. Better alert the airport guys as well,' said Tau.

It was close to midnight when Tau and Gerry exited Headquarters. They had tried calling Charlie, to no avail. The flight school was also on answer phone and there was not much new to be gleaned. They decided to go home and start early in the morning.

Chapter 18

Sayeed had spent the night at a safe house, run by the young Muslim locksmith. Sayeed woke early and watched the breakfast news with Ravi, who was so nervous that he dropped a pot of coffee. Sayeed said that he would soon be going and that there was no need to be concerned, but he shouldn't mention to anyone that he had come. Ravi nodded, grateful that he had been able to help an important man like Sayeed, but even more grateful that he would not be called on again.

Sayeed drove to Paarden Island and made his way to Raj Printers, a small commercial printing works on a dusty backstreet. The reception area was piled high with brightly coloured leaflets awaiting pickup, and the chemical smell of printing ink permeated the building. From the back of the premises Sayeed could hear the rhythmic crash of the old press as it churned out its work. There was nobody on the front desk and Sayeed pushed through the little half-gate and entered the main printing area. The brass and cast-iron press was in the middle of the room while around the walls four young men seated at Mac workstations were doing the layout and compositing electronically. Rajit Patel, a man in his 50's with a grey stubble beard and half-moon glasses, was peering at some proofs against the light. He turned when he saw Sayeed and nodded towards his office.

The cinder block office was as chaotic as the work area but after Raj closed the door it became marginally quieter. He swept a pile of brochures from a chair and gestured for Sayeed to sit.

'So' said Raj. 'What brings you here?'
'I need some documents,' said Sayeed.
'The whole pack? Passport, ID, Driver Licence?'
'Yes,' said Sayeed.
'You got photos?'

Sayeed slid across an envelope which Raj opened and extracted a sheet of four passport-sized colour photos. Raj looked at them for a few moments then took out a magnifying glass and scrutinised them hard.

'You want some advice? Get coloured contacts. With those baby blues the cops will pick you to of a line-up in five seconds. With dark brown eyes you look just like any other coolie.'

Sayeed bristled but realised that Raj was correct.

'How quickly can you deliver?'
'Take me two days.'
'And what will it cost?'
'Twenty thousand.'
Sayeed whistled. 'That's robbery!'
'Then go somewhere else,' said Raj getting up.
'Wait,' said Sayeed. 'Half now and half on delivery?'
'Fine,' said Raj. 'But change your eyes, neh.'
'Do you know someone? An optician?'
Raj scribbled a note. 'Say I sent you.'
Sayeed looked at the name. 'Goldman? A Jew?'
Raj shrugged. 'A businessman. He'll keep his mouth shut, don't you worry. We've done too much business.'

Sayeed nodded and opened a money pouch. He counted out ten thousand Rand and handed it to Raj who smiled and shook his hand.

'Salaam,' he said.
'Salaam Alaikum.'

Sayeed drove to Sea Point and found the optician's shop in a strip mall on the main road. An old Jewish woman with blue hair and a Pekingese dog in a plaid overcoat was choosing some diamante spectacle frames from a rack at the front of the shop. A pretty young woman with large breasts and thick black hair smiled somewhat uncertainly at Sayeed.

'What can we do for you today, sir?' she said.

'Mister Goldman – is he in?' asked Sayeed.

'Do you have an appointment?'

'No. A friend recommended him to me.'

'I'll just check if he can see you.'

She disappeared into a back office and emerged a moment later.

'Take a seat please. Milton will be with you shortly.' She turned her smile and cleavage to the old woman.

'Find anything you like, Mrs Perlmutter?'

The old lady handed over a heavy lilac frame studded with fake diamonds along the arms.

'Lovely,' said the young woman. 'Milton will make them up for you. Come in tomorrow morning?'

The old woman nodded and exited, dragging her dog behind her, scrabbling sideways against its lead, its toenails clicking on the tiled floor. The receptionist looked up brightly at Sayeed.

'You can go through now.'

Sayeed entered a cool office with an eye chart and eye testing equipment. Everything was black leather and blonde wood. Milton Goldman was a young man in his 30s, already balding and slightly paunchy. He wore heavy, black-framed oblong designer glasses and smiled perfunctorily at Sayeed.

'A friend recommended you. Who?'

'Raj Patel,' said Sayeed.

'Ah. Very well, what can we do for you?'

'I need to change the colour of my eyes,' said Sayeed. 'Can you do anything?'

'Hmmm,' said Goldman. 'Please, put your chin in this cup and look straight into the light.'

He positioned Sayeed's chin in a plastic support and aligned two eyepieces with his eyes, then went around to the other side of the machine and turned on a light and examined each eye briefly, then turned off the light and resumed his seat behind the desk.

'Your eyes are good. I would recommend a set of coloured contacts. What colour do you have in mind?'

'Dark brown,' said Sayeed.

'That's easy,' said Goldman taking out a colour chart. 'Which of these?'

Sayeed chose the second darkest, almost black. 'They won't affect my sight will they?'

'Not a bit of it. The iris is perfectly clear – it just changes the look of the cornea.'

'And how do you wear them?'

'It feels strange at first but most people get used to them within a couple of days. I'll get some sent over from the depot and you can come back this afternoon and I'll show you how to fit them and take care of them. How many sets do you want?'

'How many sets? I've only got two eyes,' said Sayeed, mistrustful.

'You might only have two eyes, but if you let a lens dry out or get scratched or lost then you would look a little strange with one blue eye and one brown eye. But don't let me sell you anything you don't want, OK? If you're happy, I'm happy.'

'I'll have two sets,' growled Sayeed, determined that when the Muslim theocracy gained control of South Africa, Milton Goldman and his ilk would be driven into the sea.

'Fine. I'll have them ready by four. And I presume this is cash?'

Sayeed pursed his lips and exited. He went out through the front of the shop, ignoring the receptionist, and stepping into the traffic and bustle of Main Road.

'Rachel,' said Goldman through the open door. 'Did we get him on tape?'

She checked the CCTV recorder.

'All fine, why?'

'Let me have that tape, will you. Put in a new one, OK, doll?'

Sayeed determined that he would not find new accommodation until he had his new identity, and so went to his father's store. His father was somewhat surprised to see him.

'I thought you were sick,' he said. 'Better?'

'I'm fine, Dad,' said Sayeed. 'I'm going away for a while.'

'Away? What kind of nonsense is this?'

'It's not nonsense, Dad. I'm doing it.'

'Where? Where are you going?'

'I've got some business to attend to. In Jo'burg.'

'Jo'burg? Who do you know in Jo'burg? Jo'burg's no place for you.'

'That's it, Dad. I'm not changing my mind. Give Mom my love.'

'You aren't even going to say goodbye to your mother!?'

'I'll call. 'Bye.'

Sayeed hugged his father tight, then turned and walked quickly away.

Chapter 19

Tau and Gerry were waiting outside the Forensics Lab when Charlie appeared.

'Oh no. It's bad cop and bad cop,' he said. 'Can't one of you be good cop, even for a bit?'

'How come the rest of us manage to be at our desks by 8.30 but you haven't even opened up by nine?' asked Gerry.

'It's because we need to keep our faculties acute,' said Charlie opening the doors to the lab and flipping the light switch. 'Shorter hours but more productive.'

Tau and Gerry outlined their idea of calling the relevant numbers and trying to triangulate the position of the users, and Charlie agreed to give it a try, all the while complaining about lack of resources. By this time the rest of his staff had trickled in bearing Styrofoam coffees, hangovers and in the case of Laidlaw, the remains of an Egg McMuffin on his shirt.

'Listen up, people!' roared Charlie. 'We're going for an intercept on the Namibian number and the Cape Town number of the recent police murders. Laidlaw!' The young man jumped. 'I want you onto Police HQ telling them to stand by for some intercept or arrest information. Mbalo – a studious-looking man with round glasses looked sleepily at Charlie – you set up a line to the Nambian Special Branch, same info. Petrus, you set up monitoring with the cell phone operators and do the idents on the relay stations. You can do the actual dialling.'

Petrus stuck up his hand like a schoolboy. 'What if he answers?'

'Then you bladdy speak to him, *poephol!* Pretend you're Koos Van Der Merwe and you're looking to buy his tractor.'

'Uh. Who's Koos Van Der Merwe?' asked Petrus.

'Jesus,' groaned Charlie turning to Tau, 'you see what I have to put up with!'

Katja half-raised her hand. 'What do you want me to do, Charlie?' she asked.

'Make the bladdy coffee, of course!' said Charlie, yelping at his own joke. 'Seriously, I need you to co-ordinate these jokers – if we get a hit when some guy is off scratching his arse then I will be displeased. Severely unhappy, and you don't want that. You are in charge, and reporting to me.'

'Why her?' grumbled Petrus. 'It's always her.'

'Because she's got great tits!' Charlie yelped again at his own fine wit. *'Why her?'* he repeated, looming over Petrus. 'Why do you think? She's the only one here who can read without moving her lips. Now get to it, people!'

Tau gently took Katja's elbow. 'You must have great patience working with Charlie,' he said.

She shrugged and smiled, 'He's a freak of nature – an arsehole with a heart of gold,' she said.

'When will you be set up?' asked Gerry.

'We should be ready to cook in a couple of hours if we can get the Namib boys on line,' said Katja. 'It's outside our jurisdiction – do we have any friends there?'

'Yes,' said Tau. 'Chitepo spoke to a guy called Titus Mpho, head of Special Branch in Swakopmund – use Chitepo's name.'

'Great,' said Katja flashing him a smile.

'Great,' said Tau.

'Great,' said Gerry. 'I'm going to grab a coffee before I drown in all this greatness.'

'We'll be back in two hours,' said Tau.

In the car Tau said 'I put in a call this morning to Chris Pieterse.' 'Who?'

'That young hotshot whom Chitepo said we could use. Why don't we meet the guy and see if there's any way he can help.'

Gerry shrugged. 'Fine. Give him a bell. Tell him to come to Carluccio's. I need some caffeine to jump-start the day.'

Twenty minutes later they were sitting on a small terrace on the side of the mountain drinking coffee when a tall young man with light brown skin and grey eyes approached.

'Molepe and Viljoen?' he asked. Gerry's eyes flicked to Tau. 'Ja,' said Gerry. 'If you're Chris, pull up a chair. If you're from Internal Affairs, you can stick your muffin up your arse and fuck right off.'

'I have to say that I'm honoured to be working with you,' said Chris.

'Good attitude,' said Tau, 'but we aren't working together. Not just yet. Wait till you hear what we have to say first, then see if you're still so keen to share the glory.'

'We need to get a man inside Pollsmoor Prison. To infiltrate the PAGAD hard core…' said Gerry.

'I was brought up Muslim,' said Chris.

'Don't be so eager,' said Tau. 'The last insider was shot dead when he was discovered.'

'Achmad Karriem. I was at his funeral.'

'Just so you understand. If we can set up your cover story you will go to court, be sentenced and serve hard time with the other Muslim brothers. You could be there for two, three months before we get you out again. And after that, your card will be marked. These guys have got a very long reach and very long memories. You must understand all of this completely,' said Tau.

'If a job's worth doing it's worth doing properly,' said Chris. 'If being inside means we might catch the bastard who killed Achmad and those other officers, it'll be time well spent.'

'If the boys inside get any sniff that you might be an informer, they'll kill you. And it won't be as quick as a bullet, believe me,' said Gerry.

'I'm not scared,' said Chris.

'Well you bloody well should be!' Barked Tau.

They talked for another hour straight and agreed to meet up the next day. The seeds of a plan had been formulated and Tau and Gerry would need authorization from their chief before it could be implemented. Also, they wanted to give Chris 24 hours to reconsider, but they knew that he wouldn't waver. Nonetheless, they owed it to him.

Gerry put his bisocotti into his pocket for a rainy day and they made their way back to the Forensics Lab.

'Are you guys ready?' he asked.

'We're all standing by wetting ourselves with excitement,' said Charlie, indicating his staff who looked bored witless. 'Who are we going for first?'

'I say Cape Town. Gerry?'

'Ja. Let's do it.'

Katja fiddled with a knob on the amplified phone circuit. They all listened intently as the numbers were dialled. After 10 seconds they heard 'The number you are calling is switched off. Try again later. The number you…'

'Dammit,' said Gerry. 'Try the other one.'

Katja spoke into a stenographer's headset. 'Commander Mpho, are you standing by while we attempt a trace? Thank you for your help sir….'

She signalled for Petrus to dial the number. They heard the pips then a moment later they heard the phone ring.

At that moment Hamidullah was sitting beside his cousin, Zakes, driving into the outskirts of Windhoek. They had driven through the night along the ribbon of tarred road arrowing through the Nambian wilderness, and had finally reached the capital city. They had encountered two police roadblocks but Zakes had been smart enough to load the *bakkie* with a couple of fine Merino sheep, and he and his cousin looked like farm hands taking the sheep to market. Zakes had done all the speaking and after a perfunctory check the cops had waved them through. They were looking for an ATM so that Hamidullah could give his cousin some money, if not an explanation, for his sudden appearance at a bar in Swakopmund in the middle of the night.

Hamidullah frowned at the phone screen that said 'caller withheld.' The phone rang a couple more times.

'Aren't you going to pick it up?' asked Zakes.

Hamidullah pressed the green button. 'Yes?'

A voice he didn't know with a heavy Afrikaans accent came on this line.

'Hullo. This is Jurgen De Wet. Is your tractor still for sale?'

'What?'

'That Massey Ferguson that you were advertising in Farmer's Weekly. Is it still available?'

Hamidullah cut the line, suddenly sweating.

'Stop!' he said. Zakes looked puzzled. 'There. By that *bakkie*.'

Zakes pulled over to where a *bakkie* was being loaded with sacks of mealie meal outside the Farmer's Co-Op. Hamidullah stepped out of his vehicle and waited until the coast was clear then slipped his phone between two sacks of meal and walked quickly back to Zakes.

'What the fuck's going on, cuz?' he asked.

'Nothing,' said Hamidullah. 'Let's find an ATM then you can drop me at the airport.'

'Nothing? Am I gonna see your face all over the TV in Ten Most Wanted?'

Hamidullah laughed. 'If you see me I won't be Ten, I'll be number One!'

Zakes laughed but noted that his cousin looked anxiously in the wing mirror at the *bakkie* until finally the farmer emerged from the store and drove away.

They arrived at the airport and Hamidullah took a small holdall from the back of the *bakkie*. In the toilets he changed into a jacket and tan pants, had a shave and emerged looking utterly unremarkable. He bought a one-way ticket to Cape Town and settled back to wait for the flight.

In Charlie's laboratory the team was waiting anxiously. Finally the speaker came alive.

'It's Telcom here,' said a voice, 'we managed to get a fix but only approximate. The target was moving - on the outskirts of Windhoek. In a one kilometre grid between Loop and Kaiser Streets.'

'Did you get that?' Katja asked the Namibian SB.

'Got it,' came the reply. 'We'll send some people to take a look.'

'Thank you, Namibia.'

'Try and get another fix if you can. It's like looking for a needle in a haystack,' said Namibia.

Katja raised an eyebrow at Charlie who shrugged. 'Give it a try,' he said.

'Standby Telcom, we're trying for another intercept. Standby Mpho.'

Petrus dialled the number again and everyone was surprised to hear it ring. It rang for 30 seconds then defaulted to the standard message.

'Did you get that?' said Tau.

'In one minute,' said the Telcom operator. 'OK, he's left Windhoek now and is moving south along the B1 towards Rehoboth.'

'Can you get a chopper in the air?' asked Gerry.

'Who is this?' said Mpho.

'Gerrit Viljoen and Tau Molepe, sir. Jonas Chitepo said that you would lend whatever support you can.'

'I appreciate that,' said Mpho, 'but I can't put a helicopter into the air just like that!'

Gerry rolled his eyes at Tau.

'I'm looking at the map right now,' said Tau. 'There aren't that many places to go on the B1. Can you get some cars from Rehoboth to intercept?'

'That's possible,' said Mpho. 'Give me five.'

He cut the connexion.

'Bladdy amateur hour!' yelled Gerry at no-one in particular.

'Keep calm,' said Tau. 'If he's on that road we'll nail him.'

Mpho came on the line. 'Hello? Okay, Rehoboth have sent two cars with armed officers onto the Windhoek Road. Have you got another fix?'

'Hang on,' said Katja, indicating that Petrus should dial again. The phone rang and eventually defaulted to the standard message.

'Telcom? Did you get that?' asked Gerry.

'Ja. We're just working it out… Approximately 47 kilometres south of Windhoek. Six K's further than our last call which makes his speed about 140KPH.'

'Good,' said Mpho. 'We'll keep in touch until there's a contact.'

The next call to the phone produced the same result revealing the vehicle proceeding steadily southwards with the Rehoboth cops closing all the time, but the following call produced a strange anomaly. The signal appeared to have left the main road and was proceeding West. Charlie had the area displayed on a large electronic map – the only possible destinations were some isolated farms.

Dan Nettles was having a bad day. His mailbox at the post office had been broken into and his copy of *The Fly Fisherman* has gone missing, not to mention a cheque from the bank and a furniture catalogue that his wife had been waiting for. Then his *bakkie* had started making a strange knocking noise and smelling very hot and he hoped that the big ends weren't going. To cap it all he'd ridden over a Cape Cobra that had flipped over the roof of the cab to land in the back with his main stockman, Elifas, who had started screaming and tried to jump out at over 100 KPH. Dan had pulled over and picked the dead snake out of the back with a stick and threw it into the sand at the side of the road and said that Elifas could ride up front with him but Elifas preferred to stay in the back in the breeze.

Dan could almost taste the cold lager from his fridge as he turned onto the track leading to his farm, Sonderwater. He lit another Gunston and drew in the blue smoke, trying to avoid the smell of burning coming from the engine, when Elifas started banging on the roof. Dan's eye flicked irritably to the rear-view mirror and was startled to see two Police Hiluxes barrelling along behind him, their lights flashing. Assuming there was some emergency up ahead, Dan pulled onto the shoulder of the dirt road and was surprised when the police cars boxed him in and four cops in flack jackets leaped out holding stubby Heckler & Koch sub-machine guns.

'Out! Hands in the air!' yelled one cop with a red raw face and teenage pimples. Dan sighed – his day had just got worse. He climbed out of the cab and saw Elifas already on the ground, his hands clasped behind his head.

'What's going on here?' demanded Dan.

Just then they heard a cell phone ringing. Dan looked around mystified. Elifas pointed into the back of the *bakkie* where one of the cops gingerly rummaged between the mealie meal sacks and found the instrument.

'Hello?' he said.

'This is Jurgen De Wet and I want to buy your tractor,' said Petrus. In the background the cop heard someone say 'Bladdy idiot!'

'What? This is officer Zendie of the Namibian Special Branch. Who am I talking to?'

Tau sighed and took the phone.

'This is Tau Molepe of the South African National Intelligence Agency. Who is with you?'

By the time everything had been explained and Dan and Elifas released, Hamidullah was flying at 35,000 feet and preparing to buckle up prior to landing in Cape Town.

Chapter 20

Tau and Gerry were in a bad mood when they finally left Charlie's laboratory. Their target had slipped away and could be anywhere. They had received the flight manifests from Windhoek International Airport, and learned that within the space of six hours over 1300 passengers had departed to Cape Town, Johannesburg, Lusaka, Nairobi, Frankfurt, London and Lisbon. There were also numerous internal flights to be examined, plus the roster of car hire firms, trains and coaches. The land borders were all on high alert, but for whom?

They drove out towards Stellenbosch and turned off to the flight school where Leon was waiting on the strip with his hand outstretched even before they could even cut the engine.

'Leon Wessels,' he said. 'I heard you guys wanted to speak with me but the chappie on the phone wouldn't say anything more. Do you want to come to the office?'

'Is that where you've got your records?' said Tau.

'Ja. Mind you, I can't say I'm the tidiest bugger that ever lived. Jeez, you can ask my wife. She's always saying 'Leon, if you didn't have your head screwed on you'd lose it.' Funny, hey?'

'Hilarious. I'm Gerry Viljoen and my partner is Tau Molepe,' said Gerry. 'Can we see all your flight trainee records for the past year.'

'Just trying to break the ice,' said Leon anxiously, sweat popping out on his brow. 'This way.' Leon led them into his office where four school desks were laid out neatly facing a blackboard with various navigational problems written in yellow chalk. 'Do you guys want a cool drink?'

'Coke would be good,' said Gerry.

'No,' said Tau. 'Just the records.'

Leon took a can of Coke from the small fridge in one corner of the office and tossed it to Gerry, then crossed to a wooden filing cabinet.

'Anyone in particular?'

'Farouk Parveen,' said Gerry.

'I KNEW there was something funny about that bugger, you know. Very cool customer. Always paid cash, hey. Worked hard and studied well. Can't take that away from him. He qualified just last week,' said Leon.

'Have you got his application on file?'

'Ja,' said Leon. 'I sent the photocopy to Cape Town like I was supposed to... Now where's his file?' Leon rummaged through the files several times. 'I can't seem to find it...'

'Are you sure you're looking in the right place?' demanded Tau.

'Ja. Sure I'm sure. This top drawer is just for pilot training and we've only had four others in the past six months. Here they are, look – Bronkhorst, Evans, Volker and Grieves.' But no bladdy Parveen. I don't understand...'

'He took the files,' said Gerry.

'But he couldn't have!'

'Did you ever leave him here on his own. Even for a minute?'

'Of course not!' said Leon defensively.

'Not even to take a leak?'

'Well, I mean, I'm only human. Jeez.' He said.

'That's debatable,' muttered Gerry. 'Have you got any photos of him? CCTV or anything?'

'I've got a CCTV looking at the hangar but it's on a seven day loop,' said Leon. 'That means it will have wiped last week's stuff.'

'Damn!' said Tau. 'What about his vehicle. How did he get here? Car? Motorbike?'

Leon pursed his lips. 'Car most of the time but one time he came on a motorbike. Blue and white, I think, but I can't remember. It was nearly six months ago.'

'The car registration or make?'

'It was a blue Mazda 323. I know that because my brother-in-law has one. Not blue. Silver. My brother-in-law's, I mean. But the registration – beats me. I don't check every registration – I'm not a bladdy traffic cop.' Leon was starting to sweat. 'But I took a copy of his flight exam and that's got his photo on it. Can that help?' Leon smiled triumphantly and opened a small safe and took out a slim cardboard file.

Gerry took the documents from him and spread them out. There was indeed a photocopy of a small passport-sized photo, but it was of such poor definition as to render it totally useless.

'Lousy bladdy copy,' growled Gerry. 'You don't have the original?'

Leon shrugged.

'Why did he want to fly? What was his story?' asked Tau.

'Said he had an uncle in Gauteng who grew cotton and he wanted to get work as a crop-sprayer, but when he graduated I offered him a bit of crop-dusting work and he didn't seem interested.'

'Let me get this straight,' said Tau. 'He came here specifically to learn crop-dusting?'

'I guess so,' said Leon. 'There's a lots of other flying schools around and flying clubs where you could get a normal licence for a bit of social flying, impress the chicks, that sort of thing. But I'm the only one in the Cape offering this specialist stuff.'

'Crop-dusting? What does that entail?' asked Gerry.

'It means you've got to be able to fly at very low altitude – between 15 and 25 metres. Otherwise the spray just dissipates in the wind.'

'And with his licence can he now fly anything?'

'Not legally, no. His licence is limited to small aircraft, daylight only and instruments. Anything bigger and he would have to go for a commercial licence.'

'But with what he knows already, could he fly a bigger plane?' asked Gerry.

'Well,' said Leon cautiously, 'because he has the basics I suppose he could learn the rest from a programme.'

'What sort of programme?'

'A flight simulator. You can get them these days to run on a PC. Bladdy realistic too,' said Leon. 'I saw one the other day for a 757. Jeez, it was like being right there on the flight deck.'

Gerry and Tau looked at each other.

'D'you think this guy's gonna do a 9/11?' asked Leon anxiously.

'Thanks,' said Gerry. 'If you can recall anything else, no matter how small, call us.' Gerry handed him a card.

'One more thing,' said Tau. 'Double the security on your planes. Take the keys home at night, get a guard with a radio, extra locks on the hangars.'

'It'll cost a packet,' grumbled Leon.

'How about if this bastard takes one of your planes and commits a national catastrophe just because you couldn't be arsed to lock it up. How would that look?' asked Gerry.

'I'll attend to it, sir.' Said Leon.

Chapter 21

Sayeed's eyes were driving him insane. He wanted to tear them out. He had left the Jew's office an hour previously with his eyes watering but the change in his appearance was startling, and he determined that he would wear the coloured lenses until such time as they were comfortable. Fortunately, he didn't have far to go. In the same strip mall as the optician was a jeweller's shop.

Sayeed entered through the steel security gate and marched up to the counter. An elderly man was seated at the counter with a jeweller's eyepiece screwed into his eye as he delicately probed the planet wheels of a fine gold watch. Finally he looked up.

'Yes?'

'I need a valuation,' said Sayeed.

'Insurance valuations cost a hundred Rand,' said the man and resumed his work. Sayeed peeled off the money and laid it on top of the watch so that the man couldn't continue. He looked up again. Sayeed opened an envelope and put two white diamonds onto the counter. The man adjusted his eyepiece and turned on a bright work lamp.

'White, good quality, very few occlusions...' He weighed one stone. '1.2 carats. And this other one of similar quality, 0.8 of a carat. These look like they come from Sierra Leone. Blood diamonds.'

'All diamonds are blood diamonds. What are they worth?' asked Sayeed.

The man wrote a figure on some letter-headed paper.

'For insurance purposes,' he said handing it to Sayeed.

'And if I were to sell them?' asked Sayeed.

The old man looked shrewdly at him. 'Knock off 50%,' he said.

Sayeed nodded and put the stones back into the envelope and walked out.

Sayeed drove to Mitchell's Plain to A-Z pawnbrokers, where he sold the stones for 35% of their true worth to the owner, Flet Albertyn, and came out with a thick wad of cash. He put in a call to a 'friendly' estate agent, a nervous Jackie Amrahamse, whom he met an hour later outside a modest little bungalow in Hout Bay. Money changed hands and that he parked his car in the adjoining garage, unloaded his suitcase and stashed his weapons before heading out again.

He made his way to the office at the back of the 11th Street mosque, and slipped into the secret cellar where he found two messages waiting. The first was from Tariq Dar saying 'I will come to discuss Uncle's party with you. I know that your house is small so arrange for me to stay at the hotel where will we have the function. Blessings on you and your family,' followed by a long prayer. The way in which the prayer had been laid out gave Sayeed the information he needed – the flight details, the assumed name that Dar was travelling under and the date of his arrival – two days hence. Sayeed was thrilled and excited but suddenly anxious, as he had not had much time to assemble a team. Hamidullah was on his way but he still needed three more men. He knew that with Hamidullah's help he could pull the unit together, but for Tariq Dar's visit Sayeed alone would be the focus and the fulcrum. Sayeed sent a reply saying 'Looking forward to seeing you.'

Sayeed deleted the message and opened the second one. It was from Hamidullah and said simply that he would meet Sayeed at the mosque the following night, at eight o'clock. If he could not make it then Hamidullah would keep returning for three nights, after that he would disappear. Sayeed also deleted this message and shut down the computer.

Half an hour later Sayeed drove through the Athenian portico and up the tree-lined drive of the Mount Nelson Hotel. This splendid colonial structure with its azure pool, pink stucco and majestic pillared frontage stood in the lee of the Mountain and was celebrated as one of the finest hotels in Africa, if not the world. Sayeed looked around at the discreet opulence and smiled to himself as he imagined the columns tumbling down, chandeliers torn from the ceilings and the rooms collapsing in an avalanche of blood and rubble. A tomb as solid and long-lasting as the Twin Towers, but rather than greedy businessmen, the targets would be the leaders of the G8, headed by the President of the United States.

Sayeed walked up to the desk, smiling. The clerk on duty looked up and blinked a couple of times then smiled. His name tag said 'Mohammed' and he wore a black suit and tie over a crisp white shirt. He was one of three PAGAD people working at the hotel, including a sous chef and a cleaner. Mohammed had of course known about Sayeed by reputation and had seen him some years previously at a radical prayer meeting at the 11th Street mosque.

'How may I help?' he asked.

'I need to reserve a room for two nights, starting this Tuesday,' said Sayeed. 'Something discreet.'

'Of course, sir. In what name?'

'Djibril. Hakimlah Djibril. Should I put down a deposit?'

'No need.' said Mohammed.

'Excellent,' said Sayeed. 'Our guest will settle in cash. Will you be on duty on Tuesday?'

'I will make sure I am,' said Mohammed.

Sayeed left with a bounce in his step.

Chapter 22

Tau was driving while Gerry dialled.

'Charlie? Why would someone want to learn how to fly between 15 and 25 metres off the ground?'

'Easy-peasy,' said Charlie. 'So that he can travel below the radar shadow - at that height you are effectively invisible'.

'Thanks,' said Gerry. 'We've got something else – that camera footage of the N7– be on the lookout for a blue Mazda 323.'

'Is that all? I've got three new murders overnight, a taxi which may have had its brakes tampered with and enough ballistics work to keep us busy for a year. You promised extra help – all I'm seeing are the usual dummies.'

'We're on our way to Chitepo now to see what we can do,' said Gerry. 'And stop bitching so bladdy much! We're all stretched!'

Gerry hung up, muttering to himself. 'Thinks he's the only one who's busy.' He turned to Tau. 'It seems our boy can hedge-hop all the way to his target and nobody will know about it until they get blown to Kingdom come.'

'Do you think that was his plan for Koeberg? A low-level run and fly the plane into the reactor?'

'Makes sense. But if they've aborted the Koeberg plan then they might just want to do the same thing with the Mount Nelson.'

'A small plane like that flying into the building would probably do more harm to the plane than anything else.'

'Unless it was packed with explosives which would turn the thing into a flying bomb. Then the whole game changes.'

They drove to HQ and outlined their surmise to Chitepo. He listened in silence then said, 'The military people have got back to me with the following. The driveway and entrance to the hotel are very easy to secure. That long drive means that someone has to make a hell of a noise getting past the gate security before charging up the drive by which time everyone is out of the way. They are also looking at putting an anti-aircraft battery at the back of the hotel.'

'And if they fly in from the front?' asked Tau.

Chitepo sighed. 'They have a smaller ak-ak unit which is attached to a mobile launcher which can be parked round the front.'

'That's something,' said Gerry.

'Not much. Both the mobile unit and the bigger guns are guided by radar. If these guys are flying below the radar umbrella they're about as much use as tits on a bull'.

'What about the AWACS the Yanks were talking about? If they're up above then their radar cone will be projecting downwards. It wouldn't be possible to fly below the radar,' said Tau.

'I'll examine that possibility,' said Chitepo. 'I read the report on the phone intercepts. A bit of a balls-up from our neighbours.'

'If the Namibians had put a chopper into the air when we first made the intercept we could have had him!' said Gerry hotly. 'They couldn't find their arses with both hands and a compass!'

'Thank you for sharing. Anything else?'

'There are two other things,' said Gerry. 'One, Charlie Brits is overwhelmed by the workload. There is in our opinion a very clever and dangerous terrorist out there, who, apart from his war on the police, is planning a major attack. We have to have more resources.'

Tau and Gerry looked expectantly at their boss.

'The other thing?' asked Chitepo.

'The other thing is that we met with Chris Pieterse and worked out a plan to infiltrate him into the Pollsmoor gang,' said Tau. 'But to make it look credible we are going to have to stage-manage an event and then have him very publicly sentenced and sent down as Public Enemy Number One.'

'Write it all down,' growled Chitepo. 'I want time, venue and the numbers of personnel required. Only then can I give an answer. Regarding the help for Forensics, I will speak to Pretoria and see if they can release any people.'

'There's always the Americans,' said Gerry.

'Don't push it, Viljoen,' said the chief. 'I said I will attend to it and I will. If and when we need to call in the Yanks, I'll let you know.'

'You'll have the Pieterse plan on your desk in the morning, sir,' said Gerry getting to his feet.

Just then Miss Naidoo came in bearing some files. Tau grinned at her and also got to his feet. 'Miss Naidoo,' he said. 'Agent Molepe,' she replied. Tau and Gerry exited as Chitepo flicked through the documents while Miss Naidoo waited patiently.

'Conference,' said Gerry as they walked down the corridor.

The sea was calm as pooled mercury. Long strands of kelp floated half-submerged beneath the swell and a stream of white cloud poured over the summit of Table Mountain. Tau peeled back the wax paper on his toasted cheese and tomato while Gerry attacked his Heiferlump double deluxe. A seagull hopped towards them, ever hopeful of scraps.

'Now fuck off,' said Gerry affably as he tossed the bird a corner of the burger.

'Let's recap,' said Tau. 'So far we've lost our inside man, many officers, three firemen and one critical. And now we learn that our boy has just qualified as a low-level pilot. Where do we go from here?'

'We know this much – he's an Indian or Coloured, mid-to-late 20's, and with blue eyes. How many people fit that description? The blue eyes, I mean. It's pretty rare.'

'I keep coming back to PAGAD. This guy's connected at the highest levels. Someone inside the organization must be able to point a finger.'

'Then we need to implement the Pieterse plan.' Said Gerry.

Tau sucked his teeth and shrugged, meaning that he agreed but wasn't happy about it. Just then his phone rang.

'Molepe,' he said.

'Tau? Listen mate, just had a call from those rock-crawlers in Pretoria. They're sending down three of their finest to help out here. Thanks, man. We needed the extra juice,' said Charlie.

'Good,' said Tau. 'Now what progress?'

'O-kay,' said Charlie, 'because you're my favourite cops I'll fill you in. One of our people, Katja actually, scanned a picture of a Mazda 323 into the computer and set up a primitive image recognition system coupled to the motorway tapes. Bingo. We got a hit.'

Tau covered the mouthpiece of the phone and spoke to Gerry. 'They found the Mazda,' he said. He uncovered the mouthpiece again. 'Did you do a trace?'

'Yup,' said Charlie, enjoying himself. 'It's registered to a Farouk Parveen at an address in Green Point…Oh shit. That's the same address as the bike, isn't it?'

'Right,' said Tau wearily. 'Same old same old. Thanks anyway, Charlie.'

Tau hung up, looking depressed. Gerry raised an eyebrow. 'The Spar on Main Road?' Tau nodded.

'We're missing something,' said Tau. 'Guy has top quality ordnance, false identities, obviously getting money from somewhere and we don't have anything on him!'

'I hate to say it,' said Gerry, 'but we were first given the PAGAD link by Stanton Fitzwarren. The Yanks are listening in to all the foreign traffic. Maybe they've got some Signal Intelligence. If this guy is talking to his buddies abroad it must be by phone or email. There must be some sort of electronic footprint.'

'We can't approach Fitzwarren without the chief's go-ahead,' said Tau. 'If we can get some sign from our own SigInt then perhaps we could make a case.'

Gerry nodded. 'Let's go through everything again,' said Gerry.

'That's exactly what we're doing,' said Tau tartly.

'No. I mean a nice drive. Some country air. A bit of open space for some blue sky thinking.'

'You want to go and pick up your fucking car, don't you?' said Tau.

'That's a bladdy good idea!' cried Gerry. 'Thanks. I'll just give Stoffel a call to see if he can do it.'

'I'm driving halfway to East London to meet with some arsehole called *Stoffel*?!' Said Tau, murder in his eyes.

'Don't be prejudiced,' said Gerry. 'What this guy doesn't know about engines isn't worth knowing. He can strip down a four-barrel carb with one hand behind his back in the dark.'

'Well colour me purple and call me impressed,' growled Tau. 'Let's get this misery over with.'

Chapter 23

Cairo. Although it was barely 9AM, the heat was already stifling. The air conditioning had broken down and the modern, high-tech terminal building was at the mercy of the sun streaming through its glass dome. A couple of old fans had been brought in and they were churning the air, not so much cooling it as shifting the humidity from one area to the next. Even the 'WELCOME TO EGYPT' sign seemed to be sweating.

The flight from Teheran was packed and Abasi was taking his time scanning each passport through the new digital readers, provided at no cost by the ever-helpful Americans. He looked up with the practised stare of hostile indifference at the short, chubby man with the luxuriant moustache standing before him. The man held a light jacket over his arm but his blue nylon shirt was already stuck to his body and Abasi could see the tight little black curls on the man's chest as he stepped up to the desk with an apologetic half-smile.

'Salaam' said the man, his voice serrated with the harsh saw of a heavy smoker. Abasi glanced at his fingers and saw that there were none of the usual telltale yellow stains which indicated a lifelong love affair with nicotine, and thought idly of his brother-in-law who had died of throat cancer some years before. He'd never liked him much but the endless days of coughing up bloody phlegm had made his final demise seem like a welcome respite, not only for himself but also for Abasi, who lived downstairs.

'What is the purpose of your visit?' asked the Egyptian as he scanned the passport.

'Business,' said the other man, looking sad.

'And what business is that?'

'Water. I'm a water engineer.' The man shrugged apologetically.

'Who are you seeing?'

The man nodded understandingly and opened his briefcase and produced a shiny roll of fax paper that he pushed across the desk to Abasi.

'All of these people. This afternoon I am seeing Hakim Simir, the head of Nile Pumping. I think we can do some business with regard to his pumping system. You see, his pumps are currently rated at five thousand gallons an hour, but could easily be uprated. Then tomorrow I am meeting Mister Haq, of International Boreholes. We can offer a great range of…'

Abasi held up his hand indicating silence, the coffee rising in his throat to provide acidic punctuation to the general dyspepsia of the early morning shifts. But more important, he had a sense that the little dumpling standing before him was not quite the man he pretended to be. There was nothing specific, but after years in the job Abasi had developed a sixth sense, which seldom failed him.

'Wait. I will take a copy.'

Abasi went into a side office and closed the door. The two men looked up from their computers. Abasi silently cut off one corner of the fax scroll and held a lighter under it for a moment. After a few seconds the purple outline of a thumbprint came up clear as day. Abasi handed the print to the shorter of the two men.

'Run this at once,' he said and went out into the customs hall.

The short man was mopping his face but looked up with a smile.

'Everything satisfactory?' he asked.

Abasi ignored the question. 'How long are you here?'

'Two nights.'

'And where are you staying?

'The Marriott,' said the man, shrugging again.

Abasi grumbled to himself and found a clean page of the passport and stamped a large elaborate stamp on the document and waved the little man away. The man smiled gratefully and hurriedly packed away his papers and went through to the baggage hall.

A moment later the door to the side office opened and the shorter man bustled out and handed a computer printout to Abasi whose face slowly lit up.

An old man with a long beard and a snowy dishdash shuffled up to his counter. Abasi glared at him.

'I'm shut,' he said curtly and pointed to the next desk.

Abasi went into the small office at the end of the arrivals hall, knocked briefly and strode inside, shutting the door behind him. Colonel Halawi looked up irritably.

'I've had a hit, sir,' said Abasi. 'This man just arrived off a flight from Teheran, travelling under the name of Mehmet Talafani. Claims to be a water engineer.' Abasi passed the Colonel the computer printout.

Colonel Halawi barely blinked as he typed the name into his computer and sucked on his cigarette. A moment later he glanced up with a slight smile.

'You have done well to bring this to my attention, Abasi.'

Abasi waited, but the Colonel resumed his typing.

'Anything further, Colonel?' he asked. 'Should I detain him at customs?'

'Delay him for half an hour or so. I will let you know when we have our people in place. Thank you.'

Abasi ducked his head and exited. He walked back to his control desk, buoyed up by the knowledge that his alertness had paid off, and it could even result in a promotion. After all, it wasn't every day that one of America's most wanted walked through Cairo Airport, pretending to be an engineer.

As soon as Abasi had left the room, Colonel Halawi crossed to the squat grey safe that was bolted to the floor and dialled in the codes. The heavy door swung open and Halawi extracted a slim, black, leather-bound book. Colonel Halawi thumbed slowly through the list of names and contact numbers until his eye alighted on the one he was searching for – Cyrus Dandridge, station chief of the CIA in Egypt. Despite the regional upheavals wrought by the Arab Spring, the real-politik of the region had endured, with Western powers anxiously seeking to ensure their influence against the rising tide of Islamization sweeping across the Middle East. Colonel Halawi dialled swiftly, hoping to catch the American still in bed, but the phone was answered on the first ring.

'Dandridge,' came the Texan drawl.

'Good morning, Cyrus, I hope this isn't too early for you', said the Colonel.

'It's never too early, good buddy. What's happening?' Dandridge was sitting on the balcony of his apartment overlooking the Nile, having just returned from a fierce game of squash. He wiped his face with a towel and took a long pull of a lurid orange isotonic drink.

'Are we secure?'

'We are now', said Dandridge, activating an electronic box attached to his phone that fragmented data into meaningless chaff for anyone outside of the closed loop.

'One of my men just picked up Tariq Dar at the airport.'

Colonel Halawi could almost feel Dandridge lean in closer and clench the phone tighter.

'You say 'pick up' meaning you're holding the guy?'

'No. He's waiting in the luggage Hall. I'm looking at him right now on the CCTV. He's travelling as a water engineer under the name of Mehmet Talafani.'

'I've got one of our best people near by, Gemal Hussein. Have one of your guys tag Tariq and we can do this a joint op.'

'You don't want to arrest him and transport him to Tunis where you can kick the shit out of him until he tells you something useful?'

'It's sure tempting, but no. If this bastard's on the move it's for a reason and if we stick to him like glue we might just learn who he's coming to see. Once he's in our sights, we can pick him up at our leisure.'

Colonel Halawi kept his thoughts to himself, reflecting on the number of cockups that had affected all of the intelligence services in the Middle East. Even Shin Bet, the Israeli Secret Service, who were usually the slickest, had botched the occasional operation, but if Dandridge was sticking his neck out then it would be on his neck that the axe would fall.

'Get Gemal to come straight to me, but be quick, eh. This Tariq Dar isn't a fool and if senses that we're stalling he could make things difficult.'

'He'll be with you inside ten minutes,' said Dandridge. 'Best wishes to your good lady,' he said and the line went dead. Colonel Halawi smiled ruefully wondering what exactly Dandridge did about women. Or relaxation. Or a life. He was single, 42 years old, a fiercely competitive squash player, fluent in several languages including Farsi, and seemed to live solely for his job and his love of country. Colonel Halawi sighed to himself once more and picked up the phone.

'Find me Faisal. Now.' He said and hung up.

Within two minutes an unshaven young man wearing black Levi jeans and a cheap leather jacket was sitting before the Colonel. They were watching the CCTV images being relayed from the closed customs cubicle where Tariq Dar was laboriously having his luggage searched. Faisal tapped a Lucky from its pack and sparked it up.

'Are the Yankees leading us again?' he asked, blowing a plume of smoke into the air.

'Not leading. Being guided by us. We were the ones who intercepted him, after all. Have you worked with this Gemal character before?'

'Yah. He's smart. Looks and sounds like an Arab but trained with the CIA in Virginia.'

Just then there was a rap on the door that opened to reveal a tall young Arab wearing a smart blue suit with white shirt, buttoned at the neck, and tugging a suitcase on a handle. He looked like an earnest young teacher on his way to the Madrassa.

'You're in the wrong place,' barked the Colonel.

But Faisal was on his feet, smiling, hand outstretched.

'Good to see you again, Faisal' said the young man, turning to the Colonel with his hand outstretched. 'I am Gemal, Colonel. Pleased to be working with you.'

The Colonel grunted, feeling somewhat wrong-footed.

'How did you get here so quickly? Does Cyrus have you on permanent stand-by in the coffee-shop?'

'Actually, I'm at billeted at the airport hotel. It allows us quick access.'

'Why the luggage?' asked the Colonel.

'So that I look like I've just got off a flight rather than being the only person at the airport with nothing to do,' said Gemal affably.

The Colonel growled something incomprehensible and glared at Faisal, then pointed at the screen where a customs official was just finishing his business.

'That's him. Tariq Dar. Travelling as Mehmet Talafani.'

'What triggered the hit?' asked Gemal.

'Mehmet Talafani has his passport stolen in Oslo last week. One of our alert officials took a print and ran it through the Interpol scan. It threw up Tariq Dar. It seems like your computers did a good job, for once.'

'It's most fortunate we didn't have a power outage at the time or he might have strolled straight through,' said Gemal with a smile. 'Air conditioning's gone again, I see.'

Colonel Halawi glared at him, sensing some vague insult but nothing you could actually be offended by. He'd have to watch him carefully, this American chameleon.

'We can't keep him any longer,' said Colonel Halawi. 'Get going!'

'Let's tag him at the exit,' said Faisal. 'Can you have Ali wait out front, Colonel?'

'Do we have an address where he might be going, sir?' asked Gemal.

'The Marriott,' said the Colonel. 'But he could be going anywhere.'

'Of course. Good to meet you, sir,' said Gemal sticking out his hand again.

He and Faisal left quickly, leaving the Colonel feeling oddly disturbed. He glanced up at the CCTV monitor in time to see Tariq waddling quickly out of the customs booth, tugging his suitcase behind him like an obedient dog. The Colonel picked up his phone again.

'Ali, get in position. Faisal and one other emerging in a few minutes.'

Faisal and Gemal passed within feet of Tariq Dar waiting in the taxi queue. As they emerged from the airport into the maelstrom of hooting and seething traffic, a silver Nissan pulled up driven by a young man wearing wraparound sunglasses, making him look like an alien. Faisal and Gemal slipped into the back seat.

'There,' said Faisal. 'The dumpling. Getting into the taxi now.'

'Got him,' grunted Ali and swung into the traffic two cars behind the taxi.

'Keep back,' said Faisal. 'If we lose him he could be heading for the Marriott,' said Faisal.

'If we lose him,' murmured Gemal leaning forward, 'then your Colonel and my boss will take great delight in cutting off our balls and feeding them to us one by one. Then we'll come looking for you, Ali,' said Gemal affably.

Ali flashed a glance in the rear mirror and tightened his grip on the steering wheel.

'Don't worry, teacher. I won't lose him.'

In the taxi Tariq Dar sank back into his seat, taking in the views. Cairo had changed since his last visit as a young man back in the early 60's. He had come to Cairo to meet the underground leaders of the first Islamic revolution. The impressionable young man had listened spellbound as those visionaries sketched out their dream of a unified Caliphate, stretching from the dusty backstreets of Cairo to embrace the Arabian Peninsula and eventually encompass the whole world, Insha Allah. It was this vision that had so inspired the young Osama Bin Laden and ignited the flames that now spread to every corner of the globe. Tariq Dar had plotted with Bin Laden to get rid of the corrupt leaders of Saudi Arabia, but eventually his vision of holy war came to embrace oppressed Muslims everywhere – in Afghanistan, Chechnya, Palestine, the Horn of Africa, and throughout the West. Dar believed that soon the terror backlash would force all of the Western nations to band together to unite against the Muslim faith, and when that moment came the universal call to arms could no longer be ignored. The uprising would be universal, swift and painful, but it would lead to a cleansing and purification of a world freed of infidels, led by men of faith.

He sighed and gave himself up to the moment. Cairo was still noisy and chaotic, but now alight with neon signs and trappings of Western decadence everywhere. Glass and steel buildings reaching into the sky – billboards for Nike, Levis, Bank of America. The streets were clogged with Toyota vans, cars, expensive limousines and donkey carts. Souks and crumbling old buildings jostled side by side with modern shopping malls. Women walked the streets without veils or shame, and the men smoked and chatted in cafes without a care in the world. The taxi circled Tariyha Square, the seat of the revolution that ousted the Western puppet Mubarak, then took the second turnoff, towards the hotel.

Tariq Dar smiled to himself – the West might be corrupt and immoral, but they really understood four star hotels. The taxi slowed and turned into the entrance of the Marriott – a vast, yellow stone building majestically flanked by date palms, its reflection tremulous in the huge blue pool out front. The taxi glided up to the door and a uniformed doorman held the door for Tariq Dar as he paid and over-tipped the driver who shot away. The doorman gestured for a bellboy who materialised from nowhere to take Tariq Dar's one piece of luggage. Tariq Dar would not part with the slim laptop computer case that he held in his hands.

Moments later the silver Nissan swept into the driveway of the hotel and Gemal and Faisal got out and waved Ali away.

'Let's go to the bar,' said Faisal.

'Lobby might be better,' said Gemal scanning the area. 'Let's see if they'll serve us some breakfast.'

'On your expenses or mine?'

'Uncle Sam always pays,' said Gemal finding a squashy sofa that gave a commanding view of the desk, front doors and lobby.

Chapter 24

Contrary to his expectations, Tau had found the drive through the wine country to be refreshing, the acres of vines in neat rows flanked on one side by purple mountains and on the other by the sea. He and Gerry had systematically reviewed the case from all angles and Tau felt that there were some fresh avenues to explore.

However, his *sang froid* was disturbed by their eventual arrival in the small *dorp* of Kleinmond.

'He said you can't miss his place. It's on the main street,' said Gerry.

Tau looked in vain for a car shop or garage, but was alerted to a yellow and black striped shop called '*Stoffel's Stokkies.*' His heart sank – 'Please God, no', he murmured to himself.

'There!' Said Gerry, pointing at the wasp-striped building.

Tau took a slow deep breath as he stopped the car outside the store that billed its owner as 'The Biltong King of Kleinmond,' with two crowns titled jauntily over the 'O's. Tau and Gerry went inside. Despite his misgivings, Tau had to admit that the selection of biltong on display appeared appetizing. The same thing though couldn't be said for Stoffel Van Staden, who looked as though he might have killed the kudu that was now decorating his shelves with his bare hands. His neck was thicker than his head, which was itself as thick as a fence post. Arms like anacondas, muscular but strangely hairless, stuck out of a tight red T-shirt on which was written BLIKSEM. Baobab thighs projected from tight shorts beneath a striped butcher's apron, ending in feet like soup tureens that squashed a pair of flip-flops into the green cement floor. He looked quizzically at Tau and Gerry.

'Ja?' he said, looming over them.

'Is your meat all ethically killed?' said Tau.

Stoffel's eyes screwed up in bafflement. 'Come again?'

'Hi,' said Gerry brightly, hand outstretched. 'I'm Gerry Viljoen. I've come about the Piranha.'

Stoffel wagged a warning finger in Tau's face and said 'Too clever, mister,' then turned to Gerry and crushed his hand.

'Good to see you, man.' He gestured at the car outside and said 'it looks like you need a decent ride. What did you come in – your wife's car?' He started laughing at his joke. Tau felt for his pistol in his shoulder holster without even realising it, but Gerry noticed, and stepped between them.

'Actually,' said Tau, 'it is my wife's car. But because I've already got a huge dick, I don't need to compensate. I'll take some of the kudu while I'm here. Let me have 150 Rands worth.'

Stoffel opened his mouth to speak but then shut it again and carved off some biltong that he wrapped. Tau took it with a smile and handed him the money.

'I'll leave you boys to your toys. See you back in town, Gerry,' said Tau as he exited. He got into the car and drove away with a jaunty little wave.

'Is he your ..uh.. *partner*?' said Stoffel. 'Shit, rather you than me, pal,' he said.

'The car,' said Gerry, feeling the red mist starting to descend. 'Where is it?'

Stoffel took off his apron and balled it up and locked the shop then led Gerry out back to where the bright yellow Piranha stood, twin black drag stripes extending along the hood into the vinyl roof, and exiting at the rear four thick chromed exhaust pipes. Gerry was in love.

'She's a beauty! Can you pop the hood?'

Stoffel was beaming like a proud father. Gone was the bumbling oaf of the dried meat emporium – standing before Gerry was a poet in steel, a sculptor in chrome. Stoffel flipped a button on a key fob and the car yelped and flashed its headlights twice, winking at Gerry. Then Stoffel opened the driver's door. A Recaro seat with a three-point race harness awaited. Full instruments, with everything possible lightened and drilled, and the *piece de resistance*, a chromed skull with ruby eyes sitting atop the gear stick. Stoffel reached under the dash and pulled on a lever and the bonnet jumped. He went around to the front of the car and lifted the hood. The engine was immaculate and still wearing its Mustang logo.

Gerry's eyes were misty. 'Five Litres?' he croaked.

'Ja. And of course the Boss hi-spec. I had to put on extra wide rubber to take all the power,' he said, kicking a racecar-wide tyre.

'Can we fire her up?'

Stoffel handed Gerry the key. Gerry felt the seat close around him to hug him tight. He inserted the key and turned the ignition. The starter gave a high-pitched whine then suddenly the bass baritone of the tuned V-8 kicked in. Gerry gently trod the throttle and the revs leaped. He wondered idly if he could find someone to arrange the Wedding March to be played on a V-8, but the image of Aletta's face banished the daydream as quickly as it had come.

'Take it for a spin,' said Stoffel. Gerry nodded and shut the door. He eased the stick back and felt the car jump. He nosed it slowly out into the street and up the main road and within minutes was on the coastal highway. He nailed the accelerator and felt the shove of a giant hand as he was pushed back in his seat. 'Whoeeeee!' he cried. After a couple of miles he turned the car around and chugged back to the shop, the engine barely ticking over. Stoffel was waiting behind the counter.

'She goes some, hey?' he said.

'Like a bat out of hell,' said Gerry. 'Have you got the papers?'

'Have you got the money?' asked Stoffel.

'Bank certified cheque OK?'

'I prefer cash, but that'll do,' said Stoffel. He opened a drawer under the counter and rummaged around until he produced the vehicle's registration papers. He pushed them across to Gerry who opened his pocket book to extract the cheque.

'I don't know how you can bear to work with them,' said Stoffel.

Gerry looked up, an icy douche drenching his ardour. 'What's that?'

'Working with a *kaffir*. I couldn't. The day one of those bastards comes walking in here and tells me that he now owns my farm, I'll deal with him one way.' Stoffel slapped a heavy, 9mm nickel-plated Vektor General onto the counter. 'Fuck affirmative action. I've worked too long and too hard to hand it to them on a plate.'

Gerry had pains in his chest. He struggled for breath. Despite looking at it every way he could, he knew that it was over. The brief sweet romance that had promised so much had turned to smoke.

'I tell you what I'm going to do,' he said softly and crooked a finger so that Stoffel leaned over the counter in anticipation of a whispered confidence.

'Look at this,' said Gerry pointing to a spot on the white marble counter-top. Stoffel frowned and leaned forward.

'See?' Said Gerry insistently. When Stoffel bent down to examine the marble, Gerry grabbed his meaty ears and slammed the thick head down onto the marble slab of the butcher's counter with a satisfying smack. Twice. Blood sprayed everywhere from Stoffel's nose and he bellowed as he struggled upright. He reached for his Vektor but Gerry kicked it away and whipped out his Sig Sauer and aimed straight at Stoffel whose broken nose was gushing blood down his shirt. Gerry held aloft his ID.

'National Intelligence Agency. If you want to lodge a formal complaint, be my guest. But I reckon when the judge learns what a bigoted sack of shit you are, you won't get very far.'

'Just give me the fucken cheque,' said Stoffel through a bubbling froth of blood and snot.

'Sorry,' said Gerry. 'Changed my mind.'

Gerry tucked the cheque away and walked out of the shop, cursing. He was still cursing when he rang Tau and asked him to turn around and come and fetch him.

Fifteen minutes later Tau pulled up at the petrol station and Gerry got in, slamming the door. Tau observed a few moments of silence, then finally asked, 'Car no good?'

'Car was good. Beautiful. Excellent. A chrome-plated fucking dream!'

'So why didn't you buy it?' asked Tau.

'Leave it, OK?' snarled Gerry. 'No more questions - I didn't get it. That's enough.'

'You've got blood on your shirt,' said Tau helpfully. Gerry ignored him.

Tau nodded and they drove in silence for about 45 minutes, then Tau flipped the indicator stalk and took a turn-off towards Stellenbosch.

'Where are we going?' said Gerry.

Tau grinned to himself and said nothing.

'Are you bladdy deaf?' said Gerry.

'Tee-hee,' said Tau.

'What's *tee-hee*?' Gerry growled murderously.

'You know what old man Koornhof used to say on the farm when I was growing up?' said Tau.

'Oh Jesus no, not more bladdy stories about the farm,' said Gerry. 'Is this the one about "Never sleep with a wild pig?" Or "How to catch a baboon that's raiding your pumpkin patch?" Or maybe it's "How to find water with a green willow twig?"'

'Glad to see that you've been listening over the years,' said Tau. 'No, this is one you haven't heard before.'

'Okay,' said Gerry holding up his hands in submission. 'Why don't you tell me what old man Koornhof used to say.'

'Very well,' said Tau. 'He used to say, "Ask no questions, hear no lies".'

'Very fucking profound,' said Gerry grinding his teeth. 'If I'm ever writing a *Little Book of Stupid Farm Sayings* remind me to look you up.'

'Tee-hee,' said Tau and concentrated on the road that was winding upwards into the mountains.

'So you're not going to tell me,' said Gerry.

Tau put a finger to his lips. 'Ssshhhh!' He said.

Gerry nodded and picked up a can of Coke that he started shaking vigorously.

'What are you doing?' asked Tau sharply.

'Nothing. I'm just gonna pop this can all over you in about ten seconds,' said Gerry.

'Juvenile.' Said Tau. 'How does this sound. A '65 BMW 2000 CS coupe, Bauer turbo and tuning kit, bringing up an extra 20KW. The fastest in the country. Less than 30K on the clock.'

Gerry, a man seldom stuck for words, could only gawp. Finally he spoke. 'What you just said – that was car talk.'

'Duh,' said Tau. 'I knew you'd recognise it.'

'But what do you know about bladdy cars?' demanded Gerry.

'Nothing,' said Tau smugly. 'But my pal Basil, he knows about cars. Tee-hee.'

Tau turned off the road where a farm sign written on a plough disc said 'Overberg – Basil Verdin.' They bumped along a single track road for some distance then rounded a bend and saw thousands of acres of vines stretching away as far as they eye could see. Nestling in the lee of the kloof was a splendid Cape Dutch house shaded by oaks, and beside it some barns. A wiry man with salt and pepper hair who was walking across the yard stopped when he saw Tau's car. He frowned as he tried to recognise the driver then broke into a broad grin as Tau drew up beside him.

'Hi Basil,' said Tau. 'How are you?'

'Tau. Fighting fit, thanks. You?'

'Ja, still here. This is my partner, Gerry.'

Gerry got out of the car and shook hands with Basil.

'So you're the petrol head?' he said.

'I appreciate good engineering,' said Gerry cautiously.

'Excellent. So do I. Tau here wouldn't know a socket set from a sack of spuds. Come take a look at this.'

He led the way to one of the barns and threw open the door. Inside was a burnt orange BMW CS coupe, immaculate.

'I bought her for the wife but she's a bit of handful,' said Basil.

'You shouldn't have married her then,' said Tau.

Basil laughed. 'The Beemer. Too fast for these roads and not really a farm vehicle. Anna much prefers her Land Cruiser.'

'Ouch,' said Gerry.

'Ja,' said Basil sucking his teeth. 'I mentioned to Tau some time ago that it was a shame that nobody was using it and so when he called today and said you were an enthusiast, well naturally…' he shrugged.

'I always liked the CS coupe best,' said Gerry. 'It's gorgeous – and bladdy fast.'

'The turbo helps a bit as well,' said Basil. 'But I heard you were more in the market for a muscle car.'

'Sometimes hairy-arse bad boy is the way to go. Other times, European cool takes it. I've got a Cobra in the garage at home.'

'Nice,' said Basil. 'I used to have a 'Vette. The Stingray. Also a beauty, but you need long straight roads – this Beemer also goes round corners. You want to try her out?'

An hour later Gerry and Tau were heading back to Cape Town in convoy. Gerry marvelled at the smooth power and handling of the German car, and when he put down his foot and the car leaped ahead with a yowl and sped past Tau he gave his friend a thumb's up and sped away.

'Enjoy!' yelled Tau at the fast-disappearing orange dot. His expression became more sombre as he reflected on the enormity of the task ahead of them, and of the negligible part enjoyment would play.

Chapter 25

Gemal was nursing a tomato juice while Faisal ate a burger with a stack of pancakes on the side, American style. Instead of coffee, he was drinking alcohol-free beer, ruminating that it was rather like orgasm-free sex. They were preparing for a long wait and Gemal was scanning the menu for something to eat when, out of the corner of his eye, he saw a movement from the front of the hotel. He turned around just in time to see Tariq Dar's backside slide into a taxi and speed away.

'Go!' said Gemal, pointing. Faisal turned just in time to glimpse the fat Iranian's face as he disappeared down the long drive. Something about him was different – he had changed his clothes and was now wearing a light suit and white shirt. Faisal leaped to his feet, frantically calling Ali on his cell phone. Gemal dashed out front and was joined moments later by Faisal. There was no sign of Ali but a Mercedes taxi was idling in the rank. Faisal and Gemal jumped in.

'Follow him!' said Faisal, pointing at the fast-disappearing taxi ahead of them.

'You are joking, yes?' asked the driver.

'Is this funny enough for you?' asked Gemal handing him 100 dollars. 'There's another 100 if you can keep up with him without being seen.'

The driver sped into the traffic and threaded his way through the fast- moving maelstrom until he was three cars behind Tariq Dar. Faisal was on his phone.

'You see us yet, you stinking dung beetle?' He cried.

Just then Ali's car appeared beside them and Ali was screaming into his phone and veering across the road as he made violent gestures at Faisal. 'Not me, camel turd. HIM!' Faisal gestured at Tariq Dar's car. Ali nodded and dropped in behind Tariq Dar's car.

'Good motivational leadership there,' said Gemal quietly.

'Where's he going?' muttered Faisal.

'It looks like back to the airport.'

'We're fucked,' groaned Faisal. 'He must've met someone and we didn't even pick it up. I must call my boss.'

'Wait,' said Gemal. 'Let's see how this plays. If we've screwed up we can perhaps make things right again. If we're dead, we're dead.'

Faisal muttered some curses under his breath as Tariq Dar's taxi pulled in to the Foreign Departures lane at the airport. Ali was directly behind him, two cars back were Faisal and Gemal. Tariq Dar bustled into the airport building and was followed moments later by Gemal and Faisal, with Gemal still tugging his suitcase behind him.

'Where's he?' asked Faisal.

Gemal nodded. Tariq Dar was standing at the Olympic Airlines desk. There was something about him that was different — he had shaved off his luxuriant moustache and his bare lip was pale compared with the rest of his face. He quickly bought a ticket and sent through his luggage. He walked up to passport control and moments later disappeared from sight inside the security cordon. Gemal and Faisal rushed up to the desk.

'Where is he going?' demanded Faisal showing his Identity Card. The startled sales girl quickly checked her manifest.

'Cape Town via Athens,' she said. 'The flight leaves in an hour.'

Gemal and Faisal went through the secure area and entered the embarkation lounge where Tariq Dar was sitting at one end of a row of chairs, reading a copy of Time magazine and minding his own business. He would occasionally glance up at the TV monitor to see whether or not his flight was being called, but otherwise remained entirely unobtrusive except for occasionally touching his bare upper lip.

Gemal was speaking to Dandridge and the conversation was not a comfortable one.

'Let me get this straight,' said Dandridge. 'Our target went in the front entrance, checked in, and fifteen minutes later left via a side door and you boys didn't register?'

'We were surveilling the lobby, sir, which is how we picked up that he exited the premises,' said Gemal. 'We tailed him back to the airport where he bought a ticket to Cape Town via Athens. We are sitting in the departure lounge right now and he is in visual contact.'

'You don't know if he met with or spoke to anyone while at the hotel?'

'I couldn't say, sir. He certainly didn't encounter anyone while passing through the lobby.'

'Gee,' said Dandridge. 'Just like a real pro. He didn't stop and talk to some guy in an explosive belt holding an AK. These guys must be smarter than we think!'

Gemal was now starting to sweat. 'Yes sir.'

'Why on God's green Earth did this son-of-a-bitch go all the way to the Marriott only to leave again straight away?' bawled Dandridge.

Gemal had been wondering the same thing.

'He changed his clothes and had lost his moustache. Perhaps to throw off any followers,' he said.

'He damn nearly did. Why else?'

'Possibly to collect something?' Said Gemal, thinking aloud.

'Go back to the hotel, you and Halalwi's feller, and don't come back until you've worked out what he was doing there. Get Halalwi to get all of the CCTV tapes and watch him check in, ride the elevator and go to his room. If he even went to his room! He went there for a reason and I want to know what it was!'

'Sir, the plane departs in 40 minutes. Do you want me on it?' asked Gemal hopefully.

'No. Just make sure he gets on board. Then go to the hotel and don't come back until you have the answer. I'll alert Athens and perhaps they can put someone on board who doesn't trip over his Goddamn dick!'

Gemal held the phone away from his ear and winced. He outlined the conversation to Faisal who called Colonel Halawi and had him get the necessary authorizations to seize the Mariott's CCTV tapes. Shortly afterwards the flight was called and Tariq Dar was amongst the first passengers to waddle down through the gate and onto the plane.

Faisal and Gemal raced back to the Mariott where a flustered manager was assembling the CCTV footage for review.

Cyrus Dandrige put in an encrypted call to the Head of the Africa station, Stanton Fitzwarren. After some minutes an irritable Fitzwarren came on the line.

'Speak to me, Cy,' he said. 'This had better be important. I've just had to leave a lunch with the President of Kenya.'

'It couldn't be more important, sir. Tariq Dar is currently on a plane for Cape Town. I thought you might want to know.'

'Is this 100 per cent verified?'

'They stop in Athens in an hour then arrive in Cape Town at 10.35AM tomorrow.'

'Are any of our people on the flight?'

'No sir, I took a decision here to follow up his contacts. Our people are onto it as we speak. I figured once he was up in the air he couldn't go anywhere except down. Oh Jesus! I didn't mean…' said Cyrus, as the horror dawned on him of what he had just said.

'Is there a security threat in the air? Do we have to bring the aircraft down?'

'It's my understanding that he does not have any weapons with him, sir,' said Dandridge, now sweating more heavily. 'They even checked his shoes before he got on board. I think, sir, he's travelling to meet other jihadis.'

'If you thought there was any kind of airborne threat you should have prevented him from boarding,' said Dandridge.

'We can halt the flight in Athens and do a full security check, sir.'

'If the plane hasn't blown up by then. If he disembarks in Athens I want him arrested – are we clear?'

'Crystal, sir,' said Dandridge, grinding his teeth. 'And if he doesn't disembark but remains on board?'

'Then I'll handle it in Cape Town. Keep me posted, and send through all known details immediately.'

The line went dead. 'Shit,' said Dandridge, feeling his world starting to collapse about him. Dandridge was opening his computer when the phone rang.

'Cyrus,' said Colonel Halalwi. 'Beween them, our men have managed to fuck up a simple surveillance operation, forgive my French. I will have Faisal directing traffic by next week!'

'Gemal didn't cover himself in glory either,' said Dandridge.

'They did manage one thing,' said Halalwi. 'The CCTV footage shows Tariq Dar getting an envelope when he checks in. The house manager said it arrived yesterday by courier, no details. The cameras show Dar going into his room and coming out ten minutes later. No sign of the envelope.'

'So he did pick something up,' said Dandridge, wondering why Colonel Halalwi had the information before him.

'I just want it noted,' said Halalwi, 'that I suggested we pick him up as soon as Egyptian intelligence identified him.'

'Relax, old buddy,' said Dandridge. 'It's my titty in the wringer, not yours. But he's in the air now and we'll tag him every step of the way.'

'I hope so,' said the Colonel. 'We must have lunch when this is all over.'

'Love to,' said Dandridge, seething. He hung up and stared at the phone for a long minute, then dialled Gemal. The number rang and defaulted to message – Dandridge hung up without saying a word. Dandridge sent Fitzwarren a brief summation of what had transpired, adding under 'Personal Information', a note that Tariq Dar had shaved his moustache and was travelling under the name of Mehmet Talafani. Dandridge then contacted the Athens bureau and filled them in, with less than 20 minutes to put people in place to intercept Dar if he should disembark.

Dandridge sat back and breathed deeply. There was little else he could do other than wait for Athens to respond. The return call came sooner than anticipated. The head of the Athens bureau, whom Dandridge had known briefly at Langley, was Orville Gretsch.

'We got a problem,' said Gretsch. 'Here's the thing – there's no Mehmet Talafani on the flight.'

'That's impossible,' said Dandridge. 'Our man saw him embark onto the aircraft!'

'Have you checked the passenger lists?' Said Gretsch.

'No I have not,' said Dandridge feeling his ass exposed as if in a surgical gown. 'He entered Cairo under that alias which is how we picked him up in the first place.'

'Well, I suggest you get your people to pull their thumbs out of their asses and find out whose passport he's travelling on this time.'

'Will do,' said Dandridge, 'but you guys must be able to make a visual ident.' But the line was already dead.

Dandridge started dialling Gemal again when the doorbell rang. The TV monitor showed an anxious Gemal on the step. Dandridge buzzed him in.

'You're in all kinds of shit, boy,' he said.

'After the hotel, Faisal went back to Colonel Halalwi. I returned to the airport to check what ID Talafani was using.'

'Smart thinking,' said Dandridge sourly. 'You should've checked it out at the time.'

'The check-in girl had left her shift and apparently boarded a plane for Sharm-El-Sheik for a week's holiday, but by going through the crew list and aligning their check-in times against the time we saw Dar arrive, I've narrowed it down to four possibles.'

'Four?'

'Yes,' said Gemal quickly pressing on. 'Bendi, Djibril, Mansour and Al-Hussein.'

'And how do we know which of these four he is?'

'With visuals and prints we can work it out pretty quickly,' said Gemal.

Just then the phone rang.

'Cyrus? It's Fitzwarren. Listen, your hot tip on Talafani doesn't pan out. He's not in any passenger lists.'

'I've just had an update,' said Dandridge seizing Gemal's manifest. 'I will send through the names immediately.'

'Names? As in plural?'

'We have a short list of four possible aliases,' said Dandridge. 'We figure he went to the hotel to pick up a new ID and shave his moustache. The boys in Athens can match him on that data.'

'You'd better be right,' said Fitzwarren and hung up.

'You'd better be right,' said Dandridge to Gemal. 'Otherwise your next posting is counting penguins in the Falkland Islands.'

When the plane touched down at Athens International, 22 passengers boarded including a curly-haired olive-skinned man in his early 30s, Avigdor Grunewald. Seven passengers disembarked, amongst them Ali Al-Hussein. Although he was over six feet tall and painfully thin, the perplexed physiotherapist was interrogated for five hours before being allowed to continue his journey. By the time word reached Fitzwarren, he was on board a private executive jet heading for Cape Town.

Chapter 26

It was just past 6AM. Tau had woken a few minutes previously and was in the kitchen fiddling with the new coffee maker when the phone rang. He seized it, his heart hammering as the jangling instrument shattered the morning calm. He listened for a few moments then hung up and went through to the bedroom where he quickly pulled on his clothes. Joyce was half-awake.

'Who was that?'

'The boss – he needs us right away.'

Joyce rolled over and peered at the alarm clock and grunted. Tau quickly kissed her and slipped his arm through the shoulder holster.

'See you later,' he said.

'Call me if you're gonna be late,' she said.

Tau was already out the door.

When he arrived at HQ Gerry was pulling up in his new BMW. He also looked as if he had just been woken, but had the presence of mind to pick up a couple of coffees and croissants.

'You get a heads-up?' asked Gerry.

'No,' said Tau. 'But he sounded edgy.'

Gerry nodded and they rode up to the top floor silently.

'That's just so depressing,' said Gerry as Miss Naidoo buzzed them in.

'What is?' she asked.

'That you can be up so early and look so perky,' growled Gerry.

'I'm a morning person,' she chirped.

'Me too,' said Gerry. 'But this is the middle of the bladdy night!'

'It's serious,' she said. 'Go straight through.'

Gerry and Tau entered the inner sanctum. Chitepo was behind his desk looking pouchy and sleep-deprived, but Stanton Fitzwarren looked fresh as a Permapress Shirt.

'Sorry to get you boys up out of your beauty sleep, but seven kinds of hell are about to land on your doorstep and I figured you'd want to know. In three hours time Tariq Dar touches down in your fair city.'

Gerry looked blank. Tau frowned as he trawled through his memory.

'One of the original jihadi leaders. Engineer and bomb maker.'

'Very good,' said Fitzwarren. 'He is also responsible for suicide car bombs in Saudi Arabia, Jordan, Chechnya and Indonesia, not to mention funding and supplying warlords in Somalia and Ethiopia and is a long time pal of Hezbollah. He's also very active in Iraq through his proxies. This guy makes his pal Osama look like an amateur.'

'What does he want here?' asked Gerry.

'We don't know, but rest assured, he's not here to check out the safari parks. He went to great lengths to cover his identity, rerouting via Cairo and Athens and changing ID twice along the way, so he doesn't want anyone knowing he's here.'

'So how do we know?' asked Chitepo.

'One of our agents in Cairo picked him up,' said Fitzwarren. 'We've been tracking him ever since.'

'And who is on the ground here in Cape Town? We need to know this so that we don't have any disasters,' said Tau. Chitepo nodded. Fitzwarren breathed deeply.

'I understand your concerns, which is why I'm here. We don't have anyone on the plane...' Fitzwarren intercepted a glance between Gerry and Tau. 'I know. We dropped the ball. But we have positive information that he will be here shortly. And as I've discussed with Jonas, we will co-ordinate the surveillance on him from the moment he touches down.'

'Are you going to let him go back to Iran?' asked Gerry.

Fitzwarren studied his fingernails for a long moment. 'We've been after this son of a bitch for seven years and, if it was up to me, I'd make sure he never caused any further trouble. But as you know, the White House is already under pressure over Guantanamo and extreme rendition, so the ultimate order on what to do with Mister Dar will come from the Supreme Commander.'

'But, and I need to make this absolutely clear,' said Chitepo, 'if he commits any crimes within our borders he will pay the price. Similarly, any hostile actions by foreign governments on our soil will be viewed as unfriendly.'

'Understood,' said Fitzwarren, flipping the latches on his Halliburton briefcase. He extracted two thin files and handed them each to Tau and Gerry.

'He's lost the 'tache but everything else is the same.'

'What name is he travelling under?' sad Tau.

'Ahm… it could be Bendi, Djibril or Mansour…' Tau flicked another glance at Gerry.

'And who said military intelligence is an oxymoron,' said Chitepo and they all laughed.

'Truth is,' said Fitzwarren, 'our point guy in Cairo screwed up. Anyway, this is the list of names on the flight and we know that one of them is our boy.'

'And what exactly do you want us to do?' asked Gerry.

'If I was a betting man, I would say that this links in with your other investigations into the PAGAD people. I think he's here to help plan a big operation – something to coincide with the G8 summit. So, stick with the bee and you'll eventually find the honey pot.'

'We'll need backup,' said Gerry to Chitepo. 'At least two other teams.'

'You can have Mangope and Edwards' teams. Good enough?'

'Fine,' said Tau, 'but we need operational precedence on the ground. I don't need to be arguing with Fix Mangope about who does what where and when. Gerry and I have to be the seniors here.'

Chitepo nodded. 'Anything else?'

'Yes,' said Tau. 'We still need Mister Fitzwarren to identify his agents on the ground here, and to whom they will be reporting.'

'The second part is easy – they will report to me. They have no jurisdiction in your country aside from inside the US Embassy, and I hope to hell we won't have Tariq Dar inside there.'

'We need names,' said Chitepo. 'If we don't know who they are and there's some sort of fire fight, anyone seen with a gun will be assumed to be hostile.'

'OK, OK.' Fitzwarren sighed and opened the briefcase once more and took out two sheets of paper, each dominated by a full colour photo, front and profile of two crop-headed tough nuts. 'Anders and Servadjian. Two of our finest.'

'And these guys are supposed to fit in?' demanded Gerry. 'They look like they just stepped off the parade ground at Langley.'

'Those were their service IDs. They look more like civilians these days.'

'Glad to hear it,' said Tau. 'So the CIA is putting just two guys on the ground for a major terrorist? That seems a bit light, sir. With respect.'

Fitzwarren sighed again. 'There is another team in deep cover. I really can't divulge their identities.'

'CAN'T?' barked Chitepo, incredulous. 'Why not?'

'Because they're looking into aspects of your own government's activities regarding possible arms sales to rogue states. That's all I can give you.'

'Christ!' Cried Chitepo, struggling for breath. 'Are you telling me that we have a CIA team inside our country spying on our own government?'

'Correction,' said Fitzwarren. 'We were *invited* in by the Minister himself because he was concerned about a possible leak from within your own ranks. The deal was that once our initial findings were handed over to him he would pass the files to you for implementation. I'm saying this all off the record because we need to work together on this, and some form of transparency is best.'

'So Zak De Bruyn invited you in?' Said Chitepo.

'Exactly.'

Chitepo sighed and heaved his bulk from the chair and opened a wall safe. He took out a dossier and flipped through it.

'According to our sources,' said Chitepo, with a slight smirk, 'it appears that you have five agents in Cape Town, six in Johannesburg, three in Pretoria and one in Durban. What are *they* all doing during this current crisis?'

Fitzwarren flushed slightly and then grinned. 'I understand you're pissed, Jonas, but take it up with your minister, not me, OK? We're all batting on the same team here. I also hardly need add we are the world's only superpower, and our reach is long and our pockets are deep.'

'Until China comes on stream,' muttered Gerry.

'Point,' said Fitzwarren. 'Anyway, guys, as much as I'd like to sit here discussing global geopolitics for the next few hours, there's work to do. Jonas?'

'Agreed. Get to it. I'll notify the other teams and get them to the airport and await your instructions.'

Gerry and Tau left quickly. Fitzwarren was shutting his briefcase when Jonas came around the desk and closed his meaty hand around the American's bicep.

'Listen carefully, Stan,' he said, 'if I ever get word of covert ops in our country by a supposed friendly power, all hell will break loose. Are we clear?'

Fitzwarren unpeeled the fingers and smoothed his jacket. 'I hear you Jonas, but be advised that if we hear that any of your guys are selling forbidden material to rogue regimes, then your government will no longer be seen as friendly. Do your own housekeeping so we won't have to.'

And with that, he exited the room. Chitepo sat heavily. He was aware that a junior civil servant in the government's procurement and sales department had met with Peruvian guerrillas while on holiday in South America, but he was an idiot and a low level idiot at that. Chitepo would send him a scare before he got into serious trouble. But what nagged at him was the concern that someone within his own department might be untrustworthy. He would have to investigate. He was about to summon Miss Naidoo but when he glanced up she was already standing there, a smile on her face and a cup of coffee and biscuits laid out on a plate. It was a comfort to him that in an uncertain world there were at least some things that were dependable.

Chapter 27

A flight had just arrived from Frankfurt and a British Airways 747 was making its approach as Tau and Gerry entered the security offices adjacent to the arrivals hall at Cape Town International Airport. Standing with his hands in his pockets and looking as surly as ever, was Fix Mangope with his partner JoJo. The other team, consisting of Jez Edwards and Sipho Banzi, was sitting at a table enjoying a Coke. They all looked up as Tau and Gerry entered.

'The plane lands in just under 20 minutes,' said Tau dispensing with niceties. 'We will be the primary team in the airport and will make the ID. Fix, you and JoJo wait in the taxi rank. Jez, have you got your bike?'

Jez held up his crash helmet in silent acknowledgement.

'Good,' said Tau. 'Sipho, you're in the car park, free-floating and ready to react to whatever goes down. Understood?'

They all nodded and mumbled. Gerry outlined the basics in a few minutes and they pored over the summary of Tariq Dar's file and photo ID.

'Are we working alone on this?' asked Fix.

'No,' said Tau, holding up the photo of the American agents. 'These guys are CIA. Anders and Servadjian.'

'We're fucked,' groaned JoJo.

'Listen up,' said Gerry. 'The Yanks are our intel on this one and we could need their help, so it's time to start acting like pros.'

'Rah-rah,' said Jez. 'How come it's you two who get to call the shots?'

Tau walked up to Jez until they were nose to nose.

'It's because we're smarter,' said Tau.

'And better looking,' said Gerry.

'If you've got a problem take it up with the boss. But right now we're in charge,' said Tau.

Just then the airport PA kicked in. 'Flight OL 213 from Athens will be touching down in five minutes.'

'That's us,' said Tau. 'Let's get in place. And guys, this fucker is a bad one. If he succeeds in his mission Cape Town will become a ghost town.'

The levity died away and everyone filed off.

Tariq Dar was one of the first off the plane. He stretched and yawned while scanning the arrivals hall, then took his place in the queue for the immigration desks. Tau and Gerry were standing three metres from him, looking through one-way glass.

'That's our boy,' said Gerry referring to the mug shot. Tau nodded.

Tariq Dar stepped up to the vacant desk and handed over his passport. The official typed the name into the computer that immediately appeared on a screen inside the room where Gerry and Tau were standing. Tau hit PRINT and the printer buzzed and he tore off a sheet of paper.

'This is his alias,' said Tau handing it to Gerry.

'Hakimlah Djibril. No hits on the Interpol database.' Gerry punched a button and the small microphone buried in the immigration officer's desk came alive. The sound quality was not good, but sufficient for the job.

'My daughter is getting married in September, Insha Allah,' said Tariq Dar in his husky voice. 'I want to give her and her husband a trip they will always treasure. That is why I am here,' he said with his mournful smile.

'Do you have any friends, relations?'

'Sadly, no. But my travel agent has assured me I will be well looked after in your wonderful country.'

'Where are you staying?'

There was a loud rustle of paper as Dar squinted at a note.

'Here. The Mount Nelson.'
'Very good sir. Enjoy your holiday. Welcome to South Africa.'
Tariq Dar went through to the baggage reclaim.
Tau and Gerry flipped open their phones.
'Got him.'
They were already on their way to baggage claim when the next person stepped up to the desk.

'Good morning Mister Grunewald,' said the official. 'What is the purpose of your visit?'

'I'm here to see my mother. She lives in Rondebosch.'

The area where Gerry and Tau went was off limits to the public. The small baggage train drove into an area under the hall where two conveyor belts stood, ready to transport the suitcases to the upper level. As they arrived the baggage was being unloaded from a wagon just prior to being put onto the belts. A dog handler was walking along the luggage, his Beagle febrile with excitement, tail wagging in anticipation. Tau had the luggage identifier and he and Gerry went quickly through the suitcases until they found Tariq Dar's suitcase.

They took it to one side and ran the suitcase through the X-ray machine. Once they were confident that it contained no explosives, they used the security guard's skeleton key to open the cheap lock. They quickly scanned the contents - clothes, shoes, personal items and a copy of the Koran. No contraband and no information about possible contacts. They quickly repacked the suitcase and put it onto the luggage carousel and went upstairs to the reclaim hall.

The first thing they noticed was a surfer dude with long stringy hair standing at an adjacent carousel to the one from the Athens flight, which had started disgorging its cargo. The surfer was holding a boogie board and was waiting for the remains of the previous Frankfurt flight luggage to clear. He glanced up and caught Tau's eye – Savadjian, the American. Tau nodded slightly towards the fat Iranian, standing patiently with his jacket folded over his arm as he watched the suitcases emerge from the belly of the building.

Gerry nodded briefly at Tau and exited the hall. He ran to his car and brought it around to the front of the hotel where he sat with engine off, his face hidden behind a copy of the Cape Argus. Jez was parked nearby on his Fireblade, also watching the exit.

Five minutes later Tariq Dar's suitcase was on a trolley and he was pushing it towards the exit. Tau picked up a dummy suitcase and followed him at a distance. Moments after Tau emerged he noticed a tall rangy man standing at a newsstand, reading a paper. He glanced up and Tau recognised Anders just as Savadjian emerged with his surfboard. They also took a leisurely stroll across the airport to the taxi rank where Tariq Dar was waiting in line. Just then a Mount Nelson courtesy bus pulled up and Tariq Dar jumped in and was away before anyone realised fully what was happening.

Nobody noticed Avi Grunewald get into a waiting Toyota and drive off, two cars behind the Mount Nelson bus.

Anders and Savadjian started cursing and ran towards the car park but collided with Fix Mangope pushing a luggage trolley at high speed. All three collapsed in a sweating cursing heap, with Fix apologising profusely while trying to dust the Americans down. Gerry's car swept up and Tau hopped inside and they were off, followed at a distance by Jez on his bike and Sipho who had drawn up and was hooting for Fix and JoJo who rushed out and were away while the Americans were still disentangling themselves.

Gerry was grinning. 'Did you see that?'

'I did,' said Tau. 'Bloody arsehole, that Fix Mangope. Always got to show what a big *bok* he is.'

Tau hit speed dial. A minute later Fix answered.

'Yes boss,' he said.

'What are you playing at?'

'Me? Nothing.'

'Don't fuck around, Fix. I mean it. It looks like he's heading for the Mount Nelson. We'll stick with him all the way. You and Sipho and JoJo go ahead and position yourselves.'

Just then Jez drew up alongside their car. Gerry signalled for him to go ahead and catch up with the Mount Nelson minibus that was about half a kilometre ahead. Jez nodded and dropped a gear and sped away. Gerry's eyes scanned the rear-view mirror and he frowned.

'Blue Ford Focus coming up fast behind.'

Tau half turned and saw Anders clutching the wheel fiercely and Savadjian beside him, talking on his phone.

Tau dialled a number. 'Boss, we're onto our target. But our Yankee friends are looking pissed off and might blow it. Can you get their cell phone numbers from Fitzwarren?'

Moments later Tau received a message and dialled a number. The Focus was now two cars behind. Savadjian answered.

'Who's this?'

'Tau Molepe. I'm in the orange Beemer ahead of you. We have the subject in visual contact. Suggest you keep back so you don't spook him. We assume his destination is the Mount Nelson.'

'Roger. Was that clown back at the airport one of yours?'

'Fraid so,' said Tau. 'Just pissing on his patch. I'll speak to him directly.'

'Appreciated.'

Tau shut off his phone and looked at Gerry. 'This is it, my friend. I can feel it.' Gerry nodded.

Chapter 28

When Tariq Dar checked into the Mount Nelson, Jez was standing at the desk beside him speaking to the concierge about arranging a trip to Spier for some opera-loving friends coming from England. Moments later Tau and Gerry entered and found a space in the lobby where they scanned the menu attentively. Fix had the foresight to remain outside where he and JoJo were ostensibly checking out the tennis facilities, when Anders appeared at the desk asking about a room for the night. Tariq Dar flinched slightly on hearing the American accent but the polite young man attending to him smiled sympathetically and handed him his room key.

'We've given you a suite on the top floor. You have wonderful views in all directions. Your luggage will be waiting in your room. Enjoy your stay, Mister Djibril,' said Mohammed.

The fat Iranian turned away with a smile and crossed to the lift. The doors opened and swallowed him up. Just before the door shut he punched the top floor lift button. As the doors closed he hit the button for the first floor and seconds later stepped out. Waiting for him was another of the PAGAD members working in the hotel, pushing a laundry cart. He led Tariq Dar into a small service well containing mops and floor polishers where the Iranian pulled a white overall over his head. The stitching on the back said 'Klenz Laundry'. A moment later Tariq Dar emerged pushing the laundry cart. He went down a service elevator to the back of the building where a Klenz van was waiting for him. He was driven quickly away by an earnest young man who said nothing until they were well clear of the hotel. Then he stuck out his hand with a smile.

'It is good to see you again, brother. Welcome to my country.'

Tariq Dar smiled broadly. 'It's Allah's will that we make this great work together, Sayeed. What have you done to your eyes?'

Sayeed grinned. 'There is much to discuss. But first we must get rid of this truck.'

Tariq Dar wrestled with the tunic and managed to get it off. They were stuck in traffic near Greenmarket Square. Sayeed handed a set of car keys to Tariq Dar.

'That blue Mazda,' he said, pointing. 'Get in and wait. I'll just ditch this vehicle.'

Tariq Dar got out of the Klenz van and walked towards the Mazda while Sayeed swung the truck into a side street and pulled in at a metered parking bay. He gave the car a quick wipe over with his handkerchief then left the windows open and the keys in the ignition and walked swiftly away. As he glanced over his shoulder Sayeed saw a street hustler checking cars for valuables. The thief's eyes lit up on seeing the van with the keys in the ignition. Laughing crazily, he jumped inside and took off at speed, pausing only to offer a ride to one of the low rent hookers on the next corner, before disappearing from sight.

Sayeed slid behind the wheel of his car and they drove quickly out of town towards the Kalk Bay safe house. Sayeed circled the house carefully but the street was deserted and the house looked exactly as it had when he had last visited it, to meet with that snake Achmad.

One inside Sayeed drew the curtains and offered Tariq Dar a drink and some food.

'Our time here is limited,' said Sayeed. 'We should address the work.'

Tariq Dar smiled indulgently. He recognized the impatience and fervour of the young jihadi before him, but what distinguished Sayeed from the normal canon fodder was that his fanaticism was tempered by intelligence, and a cool methodical efficiency.

'Your preparations for the nuclear plant were well advanced?' asked Tariq Dar.

'We had everything in place. We were undertaking the final reconnaissance but the enemy infiltrated our group.'

'How many in your operation?'

'Four. One martyred, one fled aboard, the third was the traitor whom we executed, and me.'

'But you say the planning was advanced?'

'Absolutely. I was just about to ask you for some assistance with the explosives, but…' he shrugged expressively.

'You have your pilot's licence and a light plane?'

'Yes. And we have half a ton of fertilizer packed into steel canisters ready and waiting. But not the high explosive.'

'The boat?'

Sayeed nodded. 'We have access to the main boat yard here in Cape Town. We can get a fast boat whenever we need it.'

'We are blessed,' said Tariq Dar. 'The planning and logistics for the previous operation can all be utilized, which saves much time. Do you have a sheet of paper?'

Sayeed drew a crude map showing both the Mount Nelson Hotel and the Simonstown naval base where the USS Alabama would be berthed during the Presidential visit.

'The final press conference will be at 6 PM,' said Tariq Dar. 'At that time everyone will congregate in the press centre of the hotel, just near the front. That is when we strike. The aircraft will fly below the radar all the way from the landing field equipped with 15 kilos of Semtex, enough to bring down the entire hotel.' He paused and popped a date into his mouth.

'At the same moment the attack will be launched on the Alabama. The ship will be moored approximately two kilometres offshore with an exclusion zone all around it. One of our people on shore will attack with a hand-held anti-aircraft weapon. When it strikes the ship all attention will be focussed on a land-borne assault.' Tariq Dar glanced up – Sayeed was nodding slowly as he committed each step to memory. Dar continued.

'That is when the speedboat charges in from the sea, carrying the half ton of explosive. The sun will be setting at that time and the ship's crew will have difficulty seeing the approaching speedboat. Besides, it should all happen so quickly that they won't be aware of it until the boat rams the hull. Questions?'

Sayeed went through the plan in his head. He couldn't see any flaws in the execution. The only problem was the materiel.

'We don't have an anti-aircraft missile,' he said. 'Or the Semtex. We have about a kilo of plastique but that's not enough.'

'Don't worry,' said Tariq Dar with a smile. 'I arranged for a fishing boat to leave Somalia two days ago with two of the Igla weapons for you. The landing co-ordinates will be SMS'd by the captain closer to the time, but we are looking to drop the weapons on a beach in Northern Natal, near the Mozambique border. I expect the captain to be in place in three days. You will pick up the weapons and bring them back to Cape Town to wait until they are needed.'

Sayeed nodded, impressed at the planning and organization which had already been achieved.

'As for the Semtex, this is the real thing. Original Czech manufacture with no smell and no metal markers. Fifteen kilos will be brought by hand across the Mozambique border. You will meet the contact on the old Nelspruit road at a place called Beyers Kloof in two nights time. Then you will drive to Kwa Zulu Natal to await the other weapons.'

Sayeed nodded thoughtfully.

'Tell me, with respect, how were you able to arrange this so swiftly?'

Tariq Dar blinked a couple of times, unused to be questioned by a much junior man, then barked a laugh and pointed a finger at Sayeed.

'I should hate to lose you, my friend. We need people like you to plan and run operations, not be sacrificed.'

'How?' said Sayeed, his gaze unflinching.

'When you signalled to me that you were advanced with your plans I went to Somalia to arrange these things. They have been standing by ever since. I am happy now that my preparations will not have been in vain.'

Sayeed nodded, satisfied. 'These anti-aircraft rockets – how big are they? Can I get them in my car?'

'No. I would say you need a pickup with a tarpaulin cover.'

'And who else knows of this arrangement?' asked Sayeed.

'Just you and me - the boat's captain will have your cell phone number as will the Semtex contact, but beyond that, nobody. How many men do you currently have?'

'I can get four men with whom I can entrust my life. They are all good strong jihadis. Would you like to meet them?'

'This will not be necessary. You have the plan and the means to make it work. I have done the easy part – the hard part is now up to you. Are you willing to sacrifice your life for the betterment of the Muslim faith?'

'I am not concerned to be leaving this life because I will be entering Paradise,' said Sayeed.

Tariq Dar nodded and inwardly breathed a sigh of relief. He knew, Inshah Allah, that his plan would work.

'Then you must drop me somewhere safe and I will take a taxi back to the hotel. We cannot meet or speak again.'

Sayeed stood and hugged the rotund little man tight, muttering a fervent prayer of thanks that he had been enabled by Allah-the-all-powerful to launch an attack on the infidel that would deal him a blow from which he could not recover.

He dropped Tariq Dar outside a curio shop on the Waterfront and was amused to see the little man's face light up as he gazed at the various masks and trinkets. Sayeed put the car into gear and drove away without looking back.

Chapter 29

Tau and Gerry were getting bored. They had been drinking coffee in the lobby for nearly an hour. Anders had set up at a table nearby and Jez was wandering around the grounds. Fix and JoJo were now examining the pool facilities. Suddenly they were alerted to a police car arriving at the front door and two burly cops emerging. Tau stood beside them at the desk as they asked for the manager. The concierge showed them through to a private office.

After about five minutes the cops emerged and left in their car. Tau nodded to Gerry and together they knocked on the manager's door and entered.

Charles Hennesy, the manager, looked up in mild irritation. 'May I help?' he said.

Tau and Gerry flipped their IDs at him.

'Yes,' said Gerry. 'Why were the police here?'

'Just a routine matter of no concern. I'm sure it's nothing to bother the National Intelligence Agency,' he said stiffly.

'Perhaps it matters that you are harbouring one of the world's top terrorists in your hotel,' said Tau mildly.

The expressions that flitted across the pink jowly face of the manager were both alarming and something quite wonderful to behold.

'I really had no idea…' he spluttered.

'That's bladdy obvious,' said Gerry now starting to enjoy himself. 'Why were the cops here?'

'One of our laundry vans was stolen this morning.'

'What time?' said Tau sharply.

'Just after ten. It took the police nearly an hour to get here.'
'Where was it parked?'
'At the back by the service hatch. Look, this has never happened before…'
'You need to go and check on a guest. Right now,' said Tau.
'This is most irregular…'
'Are you aiding and abetting?' snarled Gerry. 'Is this a conspiracy?'
Hennessy was now perspiring. 'Which guest?'
'The name is Hakimlah Djibril,' said Tau.
'I'll just call the desk…'
'Don't,' said Gerry. 'Look it up on your internal systems. If he slipped out in the laundry van then he has friends here within the hotel.'
'Impossible!' said Hennesy.
'Just do what he says,' said Tau.
Hennesy scanned the computer records and found the room.
'And what am I to say to Mister Djibril?'
'You are to go in with a bowl of fruit and tell him that the room service forgot to put it out.'
'Very well,' said Hennessy, sighing theatrically.
'We'll come too,' said Tau. 'Just to help if needed.'
'I don't know that will be necessary,' said Hennessy.
'And if he starts shooting?' Asked Tau. 'Fine, go on your own. I don't need to be putting my arse on the line for you.'
'I'm sorry. This is all just so… Irregular! Please, do whatever you have to,' said Hennessy, wiping his face with a snowy hankie.
'One more thing,' said Gerry. 'You have just been told classified information. If a single word this reaches any other ears, you will be locked up for so long your grandchildren won't even recognise your dust. Are we clear?'
Hennesy blinked at Gerry as if mute.
'Are we clear?' asked Tau.
'Quite clear,' said Hennessy.
'One more thing,' said Tau, 'he couldn't have done this without help from inside. We will need to vet your staff, without

their knowledge. Any hint or tip-off and we will hold you personally responsible.'

'You may be assured,' said Hennesy, 'that after many years of running a top hotel the one thing I can guarantee is utter discretion.'

'Bully for you,' said Gerry. 'Let's go.'

The manager picked up a fruit basket from the kitchen and rode to the top floor. Gerry waited at one end of the corridor, Tau at the other. Hennesy walked stiffly to Tariq Dar's door and knocked. Nothing. He knocked again. No response.

'Open it,' said Tau.

'This is highly irregular,' said Hennesy.

'For God's sake open the damn door before I kick it down!' Said Gerry.

Hennesy fumbled with a key and a moment later threw open the door. Gerry and Tau rushed inside, weapons drawn. Aside from Tariq Dar's suitcase standing in the middle of the room, it was empty. The bathroom too was empty. The sheet had been turned back and a Swiss chocolate was resting delicately on the pillow.

'He hasn't been in,' said Gerry.

'How can you be sure?' asked Tau.

Gerry snatched up the chocolate and popped it in his mouth.

'The fat fuck wouldn't have passed up a good chocolate.'

Tau turned to Hennesy.

'Do you have CCTV we can run through?' said Tau.

The manager nodded, deathly pale.

'He didn't even come to this room,' said Gerry. 'He somehow got away in your laundry van.'

'But I had no idea…' blustered Hennesy.

'Where can we review the tapes?' demanded Tau.

'In the security office,' said Hennesy.

Twenty minutes later Fix and JoJo were sitting in the cramped security room, going through the tapes.

'We're going to be back in position,' said Tau. 'As soon as you've got something, get us.'

Fix nodded grimly.

Tau and Gerry resumed their places in the lobby. Anders wandered over.

'Is this seat taken?' he asked. Gerry waved him into a seat.

'So?' Hissed Anders. 'What the fuck is going on? You huddle down with the manager then pull your guys off surveillance.'

Tau filled him in briefly and said that he should in fact help Fix and JoJo in the security office. Anders went off to join them, leaving Savadjian lounging by the pool.

'He got away right under our noses,' said Gerry. 'The boss isn't going to be impressed.'

'That's an understatement,' said Tau, 'but it tells us a lot. He's got accomplices, he's here for a reason and we need to…'

Just then a taxi drew up and a sweating Tariq Dar emerged carrying a large African mask. He waddled up to the hotel desk with a big smile.

Mohammed smiled back at him. 'You've been to our markets already?' he asked.

'Yes. This is a fine present for my wife. But I think I may have paid too much for it.'

'Pay a third of what they ask,' said Mohammed.

'Thank you for that advice,' said Tariq Dar. 'Can I get something to eat by the pool?'

'Of course. The steward will bring you a menu.'

This time when he ascended the lift Tariq Dar was accompanied by a muscular black man who nodded pleasantly at him.

'This your first visit to South Africa?' asked Tau.

'Yes. I am most impressed,' said Tariq Dar.

The lift doors opened on the top floor.

'Enjoy the rest of your stay,' said Tau walking past him to the end of the corridor. Tariq Dar nodded and entered his suite.

When he emerged ten minutes later wrapped in a fluffy white robe over his swimsuit, five pairs of eyes watched as he descended to the pool level and waddled out onto a sun-lounger and pored over the menu.

'I think we need to trigger Chris Pieterse,' said Gerry.

'Now?' asked Tau, frowning.

'Ja. Look, this bastard has just met someone – it could even be our blue-eyed boy. We need a break. I think if we can get Chris inside the Pollsmoor Madrassa then we might get something back in exchange.'

'I'm not so sure…' said Tau.

'And what if fat boy just gets back on a plane and disappears?'

'How soon could we get it all ready?'

'Chris is standing by. He just needs the go-ahead.'

'He's got all the equipment?'

'Yup. Charlie made it up - it looks pretty convincing. Let's just hope the security guards don't shoot him.'

Tau flipped open his phone and dialled. 'Chris? Tau Molepe here. Are you ready to go? Good, I'll notify the guards. Good luck.'

Tau closed the phone, looking worried. 'That's less than two hours.'

Gerry meanwhile was working his own phone call to Charl Gerber, who ran security for the whole Waterfront complex. He brought Gerber up to speed and added, '…There will be a press photographer standing by, maybe even a news crew so you can be big *bok* on the six o'clock news. Call me as soon as it's over. And Charl, if there's a fuckup, I promise you, you won't find work guarding a kindergarten after this. Have a nice day.'

Tau put in a call to a friendly freelance photographer and also to the news desk at the SABC.

'We're ready,' he said.

Gerry was on another call. 'Charlie? We're at the Mount Nelson. Ja, ja. Now shut up and listen! We need a room bugged. Now. Phone and general atmos. Can you send someone good - that smart girl, Katja. Thanks.'

Just then Fix emerged from the corridor leading to the security office and nodded at Tau. He and Gerry strolled across the lobby and slipped into the security room.

Charles Hennesy was already there, stony-faced.

'Got it,' said Fix. 'Run it.'

JoJo hit the PLAY button and the black and white image showed a hotel cleaner standing by the lift doors while leaning against a laundry cart. The doors opened and Tariq Dar emerged and was hustled briefly out of sight then re-appeared a moment later in the cleaner's tunic, pushing the cart. He entered the service elevator and disappeared from sight.

'So that's how he did it,' said Tau. 'The cleaner, who is he?'

'His name is Parminder. He's been with us for some years.'

'Get him. Now.' Said Gerry.

Hennesy picked up a phone a dialled. 'I need to see Parminder in my office right away…Very well, send all his personal details to my office immediately and if he returns I am to be notified at once.'

He turned to Tau and Gerry. 'He went off sick this morning. He hasn't been seen since 9.30.'

'He's not the only one here,' said Tau. 'Someone alerted him. I want all the front of house staff files as well.'

'That could take some time,' said Hennesy.

'Now,' said Gerry. 'Fix, JoJo, get onto it.'

Fix held his eye for a moment then nodded. 'Where will you be?'

'Out at the pool,' said Gerry.

'You guys get all the tough jobs,' said JoJo.

Tau and Gerry found a table under a striped parasol and pored over various tourist maps as if preparing for a grand tour. Tariq Dar lay on a recliner some metres away, drinking a lurid cocktail and watching the bathers in the pool which was largely deserted. Avigdor Grunewald and an attractive blonde in a skimpy bikini were chasing each other noisily. Savadjian was carving through the water in a resolute fashion, and a young newly wed couple spent most of the time cuddling in the water and whispering to each other. Tariq Dar became more animated when the waiter brought him a steak and chips and he started steadily working his way through the food.

On cue, Gerry picked up the menu and ordered a peri-peri steak roll and cherry soda while Tau went for calamari rings and sparkling water.

'I don't know why Fix and JoJo seemed a bit resentful,' said Gerry, thoroughly enjoying himself. 'Mind you, for the cost of a sandwich in this place you could put down a deposit on a bungalow.'

'The rich are a race apart,' said Tau.

'While we're waxing philosophical,' said Gerry, 'It occurs that if we encouraged that fat fuck into the water where he had a terrible accident and drowned, none in this world would be sadder.'

'I know,' said Tau. 'It is tempting.' He glanced up just as Katja walked across the grass towards them, a smile on her face.

'Hi,' said Gerry. 'Didn't Charlie tell you that you had to wear your bikini?'

She rolled her eyes. 'Oh please,' she groaned. 'Too early for this *kak*. Let's get going.' Gerry slurped the last of his drink and glanced at his watch. It was 1:25PM.

Chapter 30

Chris Pieterse had the explosive belt wrapped around his waist. He had done his research thoroughly; made a "farewell video" prior to embarking on his mission and had shaved all of his body hair, as any true jihadi about to enter Paradise would. He was wearing a loose shirt over the belt to avoid any telltale bulges and had started to sweat as he sat in the car park watching the minutes crawl by. Finally he got out of his car and approached the southwest doors to the Waterfront, a collection of shops and restaurants built around the renovated shipyard that had become a focal point for tourists and locals alike.

He walked slowly and with some deliberation. A burly security guard was at the door where he was checking a white woman's handbag. He glanced up as he saw Chris approaching and shooed the woman away. As Chris entered the door the guard motioned him to one side and held up a black wand metal detector.

'Would you please raise your hands,' said the guard.

'Allah Akubar!' cried Chris as he frantically thumbed a red button that projected from a tube which was connected by wires into his sleeve. The guard shouted and wrestled Chris to the ground, and after a frantic scuffle the guard pulled his gun and sat astride Chris, the gun in his face. Chris' shirt had ridden up to expose the canvas body-belt packed with fake sticks of dynamite. A crowd had gathered and the guard bawled at them to get away. The guard punched the panic button and an alarm started howling as people fled, streaming out of the building into the car parks as the other security men came running. A camera flashed and from nowhere a small mobile news crew appeared just as the head of security, Charl Gerber, led the furiously struggling Chris away. Back in his office Charl phoned Tau and let him know that the operation was a success and that Chris was alive and well and on his way to jail, the whole thing captured on film.

After an hour everyone was allowed back into the complex, but by then the story had already appeared on the news about how a daring suicide bomber had been captured by a vigilant security guard at the Waterfront. The chief of police was interviewed and said that although the investigation was ongoing, they had reason to believe that the man arrested was a Muslim fundamentalist who was bent on mass murder. By the time of the evening news the police had found Chris's taped confession where he spoke straight to camera, a green battle headscarf tied around his head, behind him a black Islamic flag. He mouthed a few clichés about the decadent west and the Zionists who oppressed his brothers across the globe, and that his martyrdom would light a fire among the Muslim brothers in the Cape and they too would rise up and soon a black flag would fly over Cape Town.

Chris was whisked at high speed with a blaring police escort to Pollsmoor Prison where he was put in an isolation cell to await his appearance in court to face formal charges. As he was driven into the prison compound a cry went up from all the Muslim prisoners, and as his door was bolted shut Chris felt himself to be truly alone.

When he awoke the next morning, stiff and bruised, he found a note in his cell.

Chapter 31

Tariq Dar spent most of the afternoon lounging by the pool. After lunch he read slowly through Newsweek then lowered himself into the water and did a few leisurely lengths, breaking water to puff and gurgle like a manatee. He emerged panting from the pool and sprawled face down on the sun bed where he dozed until the late afternoon. Various other guests came and went during this time, but the only other couple who remained were the curly-haired man and his girlfriend, who swam and played in the pool, then threw a frisbee for some time before collapsing under an umbrella and taking tea and scones.

Tariq Dar was followed on CCTV as he made his way from the pool back to his room. Katja was working the audio bugging devices and they all listened in rapt silence while Tariq Dar passed an explosive ten minutes in the toilet, and then sang loudly and off key in Farsi while he showered. He neither made nor received phone calls. Katja went off duty at eight leaving Savadjian and Jez listening to the bugs. Tau and Gerry had been pulled into Chitepo's office for a debrief and were listening as he railed against their incompetence at losing their quarry for a crucial few hours during the day.

Finally Tau had had enough and stood quietly.

'If you want me to resign from this case then I will,' he said. Gerry nodded. 'Me too.'

'Sit down and shut up, the both of you!' roared Chitepo. 'This man Dar is due to fly out of here tomorrow morning. He is not to be let out of your sight for even five seconds during that time.'

Tau nodded. 'Have you heard anything back about the stolen van?'

'Didn't Charlie Brits tell you? The traffic cops sighted it and chased it across town until it finally crashed. The driver was a small time drug dealer called Smous who says he found it with the keys in Green Market Square. It's being dusted for prints at the moment but forensics aren't hopeful.'

'This was set up in advance,' said Gerry. 'We're going through the hotel staff lists and are still looking for Parminder who seems to have disappeared in a cloud of smoke.'

'I also heard from Fitzwarren that your boys had blocked his people at the airport. I hope that he's wrong.'

'He's right,' said Tau, 'but we straightened it out. We're co-operating fully with the Americans.'

'Glad to hear it,' said Chitepo. 'If you're going to mess them about, be more subtle.'

'Where is Chris Pieterse now?' asked Gerry.

'The operation went smoothly,' said Chitepo. 'And I think will yield results. He is currently in Pollsmoor Madrassa in isolation, but the Muslim brothers are aware of his 'crime' and have welcomed him like a conquering hero. I've no doubt they'll make contact soon.'

'I saw the coverage on the TV in the hotel. It looked very good.'

'Let's hope so,' said Chitepo. 'Because so far all I see in this investigation is a big fat zero. He ran rings around the Yanks in Cairo and now he seems to be doing the same thing with us.'

'We're onto it,' said Tau, standing to leave.

'Keep me informed.'

'One question, sir,' said Gerry. 'Are you going to let this arsewipe get onto a plane and fly away?'

'I need proof that he's done something illegal in our country,' said Chitepo. 'So far he's gone shopping and eaten lunch and sat by the pool. Dressing up as a laundry man may be in dubious taste but it's not illegal. So the long answer to your question is – get me proof of conspiracy or even putting bent pennies in a parking meter and this bastard will rot in jail for the rest of his life.'

Tau and Gerry made their way back to the hotel. The news was that Tariq Dar had not left his room but had ordered a lobster dinner and a bottle of Krug and was watching The Bold and the Beautiful on TV. Fix and JoJo had reviewed the staff files and pulled out a dozen names that they were currently running through the national crime computer, but so far nothing. Anders was sitting with Fix and JoJo and seemed resigned to an all-night surveillance. Savadjian was in the bar drinking cola tonic and fraternising with the natives while keeping an eye on everyone who came and went.

Finally at 9.42 Tariq Dar picked up his phone and dialled. Tau leaned forward to hear everything recorded on the small digital tape machine. He listened as Tariq Dar called an escort agency, and requested the company of a blonde lady to come to his suite, a blonde lady with big breasts.

It was going to be a long night.

Chapter 32

It was early evening, just getting dark when Sayeed parked near the Mosque on 11th Street. He took an unusual route this time, walking around an extra block before cutting through a small park and entering the grounds of the mosque from the rear.

He stood in the shadows for half and hour and on the stroke of 8PM a figure loomed up out of the darkness.

Sayeed and Hamidullah embraced and then walked back swiftly to Sayeed's car. On the way back to his new flat Sayeed explained everything that had happened since his comrade had fled to Namibia, and that the operation was to be even bigger and more spectacular than before.

They ate a simple meal while watching the news, and cheered when the story of Chris Pieterse's audacious attack on the Waterfront was featured.

'Have you heard of him?' asked Hamidullah.

Sayeed frowned. 'No. I don't know whether or not he was one of our younger recruits or if he was working alone, but Allah be praised, more and more of our young jihadis are taking up the cause.'

That night they slept the sleep of the self-righteous, and awoke early, filled with excitement. Sayeed drove Hamidullah to the downtown Hertz depot where he rented a 4x4 Hilux with a flatbed and tarp in a false name for a week and paid cash. He followed Sayeed back to his flat and parked a couple of blocks away and then walked to join his friend. Sayeed parked his car in the garage and locked the doors, threw a few clothes into a sports bag and then walked back to the Hilux with Hamidullah.

'Where to?' asked Hamidullah.

'We're going to Durban, then cut up through Swaziland and towards Nelspruit.'

'That's a good few thousand Kilometres,' he said. 'Why are we going there?'

Sayeed smiled. 'We can take turns driving. I want us to be at the Swazi border by tomorrow morning.'

'OK,' said Hamidullah, accepting that he would be told more as and when necessary.

They drove steadily Eastwards. Through the wine lands of Paarl and Worcester until finally they broke free of the towns and were driving along the coast, the roaring Indian Ocean on one side, the verdant woodlands on the other. They stopped in the Tsitsikama Forest to eat some sandwiches and to change over. Sayeed was feeling a well of emotions. He had never driven along the Garden Route and found it breathtakingly beautiful. He also felt a poignant sadness that he would never enjoy it again, and so he was saying farewell to the sights that he had just embraced.

Hamidullah was altogether more prosaic and chattered incessantly as they drove, but after a while even he was silenced by the grandeur of the landscape. When Sayeed took over the driving Hamidullah put his head back and within minutes was snoring. Sayeed was grateful for the peace and concentrated on the task ahead. Weapons. Warfare. Smoke and blood – the way of Jihad, the way into Paradise.

Chapter 33

The grunting and cries of delight coming from the bug in Tariq Dar's room were more embarrassing than erotic for the small caucus of hard-boiled CIA and National Intelligence Agency officers who were seated in the security office of the Mount Nelson.

They tried to divert their attention by continuing the trawl through the personnel files, and were visited every few hours by a sweaty and anxious Charles Hennesy who seemed to never sleep and was vacillating between being outraged, angry and scared witless that his hotel and by implication, his job and reputation, would be compromised.

Finally there was a dying gurgle and the heaving bedsprings stopped their rhythmic pounding.

'Horny little fucker, isn't he?' said Gerry. 'Perhaps he's had a heart attack.'

'Dream on,' said Fix.

'Shh! Listen,' said Tau.

'Jesus! He's haggling over her rate! Cheap bastard!' said Anders.

For some minutes they listened while Tariq Dar argued with the prostitute. Finally she took some money and left, cursing him with a colourful stream of epithets in a mixture of English and Afrikaans.

'What'd she say?' asked Anders.

'I don't want to make you blush,' said Gerry.

Then they heard Tariq Dar's noisy ablutions, and finally he subsided into a medley of snores and farts that both amused and repelled the listeners.

'Going to be nothing much for the next few hours,' said Tau. 'I suggest we break into shifts. The manager has offered us a room to rest in.'

'Double or single beds?' asked JoJo.

'Singles,' said Tau. 'Why don't you take a break. Anders?'

'Me? Hell no. Sleep is for pussies where I come from.'

Gerry laughed. 'Well, I'm a pussy. Tau, do you want to grab some kip or should I?'

'You go,' said Tau. 'I'll come and get you in a couple of hours.'

'I'm gonna go find Savadjian,' said Anders. 'You've got our cell numbers in case anything happens before 0600.'

'Sure,' said Tau.

'And don't let me catch you sleeping,' said Gerry. 'Not even a yawn.'

Anders grinned and stretched. A couple of minutes later JoJo and Gerry left. Tau and Fix sat in silence.

'You holding up OK?' asked Tau.

'Sure,' said Fix. 'Besides, do I have an option?'

'Not really. This is what we signed up for.'

'Sitting in a posh hotel listening to some fatty screw a hooker?'

'This man's hands are covered in blood. And if he succeeds here…'

Tau shrugged.

'I looked at his registration. He's due to leave in the morning,' said Fix.

'Yup,' said Tau. 'Just hop on a plane then fly safely home. Meanwhile we're left sitting on a time bomb.'

'Do you know his target?'

'I've got an idea,' said Tau. 'But right now we need to close this net or it'll be too late.'

'And you can't tell me,' said Fix thrusting out his jaw aggressively.

'All I can say is that Iran has its dirty little fingers on some of our people, and its plans for Cape Town will make 9/11 look like a picnic. And this son of a bitch is here to help with the planning, or bankrolling the thing or indoctrinating young people to go and kill themselves to help achieve a world Jihad.'

'I tell you what,' said Fix, 'I'll go and kill the fucker myself.'

Tau laughed. 'Let's go through these files once more. He has accomplices here in this hotel. If we can squeeze them who knows what else will pop up?'

He divided the load of files between himself and Fix and they started sifting through the information. Fix looked up.

'Does this have something to do with Achmad?' he asked. Tau was momentarily surprised because he didn't know that Fix knew Achmad personally.

'Yes,' he said. 'We find the guys that killed Achmad and we'll find the guys who are planning to bring down our country.'

Tau and Fix switched shifts with Gerry and JoJo at 4 am. The grey pre-dawn light was leeching the darkness from the land and birds had started singing in the gardens. The night kitchen was able to rustle up a couple of bacon rolls and some good strong coffee, and just as Gerry started combing through the short list of files they heard a couple of phlegmy coughs from the bug in Tariq Dar's room as his alarm sounded and he spluttered awake.

Gerry put through a call to Tau and Fix's room, and by the time Tariq Dar had showered and dressed Tau was just sitting down to breakfast in the dining room. Seated across the room was Savadjian, also looking freshly scrubbed. Between them were a dozen wealthy tourists planning their days out in Cape Town, a couple of serious-looking Chinese businessmen dressed identically, a blue rinse old lady with her carer and Avigdor Grunewald and his girlfriend, holding hands and looking lovingly into each other's eyes.

Finally Tariq Dar came into the room and sat down two tables away from Tau. Tau glanced up momentarily and nodded in a friendly fashion then resumed reading his newspaper until his breakfast arrived.

When breakfast ended Tau walked out of the dining room, pausing briefly to touch Tariq Dar on the shoulder.

'Have a nice day,' he said and exited. Tariq Dar nodded off-handedly and attacked his steak and eggs. He had started the day with prayers and ablutions, asking forgiveness for his transgressions of the previous night, then reverted to analytical mode. He felt confident that the fiery young jihadi would carry through his plan. There was a chance that he would be intercepted or fail through some logistical error, but the road to freedom was drenched in the blood of martyrs, and if Sayeed Dhatri became another, then that was what Allah-the-all-seeing had deemed.

Tariq Dar finished his breakfast and went back to his room, elated at the prospect of getting out safely while leaving behind a primed human bomb, waiting to detonate. He left Ten Rands on the bedside table for the maid, then made his way down to checkout. He scanned the lobby and saw nothing untoward and relaxed, confident in his own ability to bring matters to a successful conclusion.

Gerry and Tau were in place in the car park. Jez was poised on his motorcycle and JoJo and Fix were standing by. The Americans were waiting in a side street, ready to pick up the convoy whichever way it went.

Tariq Dar exited the hotel just as the courtesy bus whooshed up and he jumped inside. The bus was heading for the airport where Tariq Dar was booked on a 12.30 flight to Athens. The airport was the last place where they could detain him before he left South African soil, and Tau had asked Chitepo and Fitzwarren to be on call so that a final decision could be taken.

The convoy was stretched out over a couple of kilometres, with Tau and Gerry in the lead car, some five vehicles behind the bus. A beaten up old green Datsun hatchback flashed past them in the fast lane, and Tau glimpsed the back of a blonde head carving through the traffic. Beside her sat another figure, his head obscured by the head-rest, but nonetheless Tau felt a tingle of recognition. He was momentarily distracted but Gerry brought him back to reality.

'I said, what do you think the boss will do?'

'I reckon we've enough to hold him on conspiracy while we try and find something that will stick.'

At that moment Tariq Dar was looking through his itinerary, shuffling the papers in his lap. He was going to deplane in Athens and take a boat to southern Italy where he was to meet a cell of North African jihadis in Naples, then back to Iran. He became aware of eyes upon him and glanced through the side window of the courtesy bus. The green Datsun was driving beside him, not five feet away, and in the passenger seat was the curly-headed young man from the hotel, looking at Dar with fierce concentration. All at once Tariq Dar knew what was happening and he leaned forward to shout to the driver. The silenced muzzle of the .38 Ruger appeared in the window of the Datsun as Tariq Dar started to duck down.

'What's that crazy bastard doing?' said Gerry, pointing as the Datsun.

Tau saw two quick puffs of smoke from the passenger window, then the bus suddenly veered across two lanes of motorway and smashed into the safety barrier, then spun out into the traffic where an oncoming car rammed it and two more slammed into it.

'GO!' yelled Tau as Gerry floored the throttle.

Tau just glimpsed the Datsun swerve across the traffic and onto the Khayalitsha off-ramp, the sprawling black township near the airport. As the BMW raced up to the mangled courtesy bus Tau was on the phone to Fix.

'Green Datsun hatch took the Khayalitsha turn-off. He was the shooter!'

Fix managed to turn off just in time and in seconds had put out an APB on the vehicle. Jez pulled up, and moments behind him the Americans who leaped from their car and were running to the courtesy bus. The driver of the bus staggered out, bleeding from cuts all over his face and holding his arm at an angle that showed it to be broken. Tariq Dar sat in the back seat, his head resting on his chest, seemingly asleep, except for the froth of grey matter and blood and bone chip sprayed across the seat beside him. There was a small bullet hole punched in the door of the bus and a starred hole in the side window. One bullet had entered Tariq Dar's temple, another had gone through the fleshy upper arm and entered his chest just above the heart. The exit hole on the other side of his head was an ugly wound that you could fit a ping-pong ball into, the result of a Hi Shok load at close quarters. There was only an entry wound to his body, the bullet tumbling around his ribcage and pulverizing his vital organs, before finally coming to a stop against his spine.

'Oh shit,' said Gerry.

Ten minutes later a grey Corolla drew up at the airport and Avigdor Grunewald and the blonde got out. The driver of the Corolla pulled away with a wave and melted into the traffic. They rushed through checkout and were just able to get the Frankfurt flight as the doors were closing. Twenty minutes later the plane had taken off over the ocean and turned inland again, preparing for the long flight up the length of Africa.

Fix and JoJo were standing in a Khayalitsha side street staring at the smouldering burned-out wreck of the Datsun. They drove back to the airport highway and became gridlocked by the traffic snarl that had bled back from the wrecked hotel bus.

Tau and Gerry were standing with Savadjian and Anders in the security room of the airport. Nobody spoke. A moment later the door opened and Jonas Chitepo strode in, followed by Stanton Fitzwarren.

'Right,' said Chitepo, incandescent with rage, 'who wants to kick off?'

'Somebody, operating without our sanction, decided to get rid of Tariq Dar,' said Tau. He turned his face slowly towards the Americans.

Anders looked briefly puzzled then his colour rose to his throat.

'Are you saying this had something to do with *us*? Motherfucker!'

'Who else knew about him?' asked Tau.

'Now hold it right there,' said Fitzwarren. 'As I understand it a beat-up car tried to ram the hotel bus, then the shooter popped off a couple of shots. Could be hijacking like happens ten times a day out here.'

'It was a hit,' said Tau grimly. 'It may have been made to look like a hijack, but it was a hit.'

'Could it have been one of yours, Jonas? Perhaps some rogue in your department?'

Chitepo leaned forward, resting his hands on the desk, speaking slowly. 'Nobody in my department is responsible for this. I think if there is any organization that behaves without thought for the consequences it is the CIA.'

A vein was throbbing on Fitzwarren's temple. 'This has the makings of a diplomatic incident, so why don't we all calm down. Let's wait for ballistics on the bullets and whatever else we can piece together on this investigation before we go accusing each other.'

'I'm happy to do that,' said Chitepo, 'but I don't like the inference that my department may have people operating outside the rules.'

'Well, it sure as hell wasn't any of my people! There they are! Sitting right in front of you!'

'And those that are on special assignment? What about them?'

'Now hold on...'

'It was Shin Bet,' said Tau, interrupting.

They all turned to look at him.

'Come again?' said Fitzwarren.

'That blonde at the hotel – I knew she looked familiar. I met her a couple of years ago at a barbecue at the Israeli ambassador's house. She said she was a junior trade attaché. She was as much a trade attaché as I am Mahatma Ghandi.'

'And her curly-haired "boyfriend." Jesus,' said Gerry. 'He was in the arrivals hall with Tariq Dar.'

'They must've tracked him all the way from the Middle East,' said Fitzwarren.

Chitepo hit speed dial.

'I want you to connect me with the Israeli Ambassador. Now! I'll wait.' The silence stretched out for a couple of minutes, finally contact was made.

'Jonas, how are you?' said Meir Gershon, a balding man in his early 50's. He was sitting in the office of the Israeli Consulate, the driver of the grey Corolla standing nearby, staring out of the window, smoking a cigarette.

'Put this on scramble,' said Chitepo.

'It already is,' said Meir. 'You are sounding troubled.'

'I understand that Shin Bet has just conducted an assassination on Tariq Dar. In my town. Under my nose. And without reference to us at all. This is wholly unacceptable and we will be pursuing this at the ministerial level.'

'Back up, my friend,' said Meir. 'These are very serious allegations. Have you any proof?'

'We want you to hand over…' he turned away from the phone, snapping his fingers at Tau.

'Leila Stern,' said Tau.

'Leila Stern,' said Chitepo. 'She was seen at the incident and is a key material witness. Now when can we speak to her?'

There was lengthy silence. Finally Meir spoke. 'You cannot speak with Leila.'

'Oh? And why not?'

'She is no longer here.'

'Where is she?'

'She has left the country.'

'OK Meir, this is starting to get cute. And her curly-haired boyfriend?'

'Also gone.'

'OK,' said Chitepo, trying to control his anger. 'I'm standing here with Stanton Fitzwarren and he's also pretty pissed with you guys. We were about to lift Tariq Dar to find out what sort of murderous mayhem he intends for our country, but your people have short-circuited that.'

'I am not saying that we had anything to do with it,' said Meir, 'but Tariq Dar was responsible for giving Hezbollah over a thousand Katyusha rockets which rained down on Haifa. He has paid and instructed over a dozen suicide bombers in my country in the past five years. He was instrumental in putting Iran on the road to being a nuclear power, and every day his people surface in Iraq, Afghanistan, Somalia, Indonesia and Chechnya. Basically, if he got wiped out in a hijacking it's not going to upset too many people.'

'Who said how he died?' asked Chitepo.

There was another pause. 'If your minister wants to meet me at any time my door is always open.' He hung up.

'Sonofabitch,' said Fitzwarren. He turned to Chitepo. 'So how do you want to play this?'

Chitepo thought for a moment, then said 'Press statement saying that an Egyptian citizen while on holiday in South Africa died in a failed carjacking.'

'But when you feed his name to the Egyptians it'll become clear the guy is someone else. Then the press will start digging.'

'Can't we turn this to our advantage?' said Tau. 'Why don't we send some digital pictures of the dead man to Al Jazira with a note saying Tariq Dar was killed in action.'

'Where?' said Fitzwarren. 'I don't think you guys want to admit it was in sunny Cape Town.'

'What would look best for the coalition? Baghdad? Afghanistan?,' said Chitepo. 'Eventually one of their people will come out with the fact that he was in SA, but by then nobody will give a shit.'

'And our friends the Israelis?' said Fitzwarren.

'My guess is that they'll get their wrists slapped and possibly and official warning, but that's not my concern at this stage. What IS my concern is who the hell did he see when he disappeared for those few hours and left us holding our dicks?'

He turned at glared at the agents in the room. Nobody could meet his eye.

'Maybe we should call the Israelis again?' he suggested sarcastically, 'perhaps they know.'

'That may not be such a crazy notion,' said Fitzwarren. 'I'll make some enquiries at my end.'

'And while you're at it,' said Chitepo, 'why don't you enquire where the Shin Bet agent got onto the plane. It will either be in Egypt or Athens. And at that stage the only people who knew about this were the CIA, so maybe you should look into that and let me know. You two,' he said turning to Tau and Gerry, 'I want you in my office tomorrow morning with a progress report, and it had better contain some progress or we might as well just give the keys to our country over to these bastards.'

He stalked out. Fitzwarren gestured for his men to follow him and they exited, after shooting a glance at Tau and Gerry. Gerry exhaled slowly.

'Conference?'

Chapter 34

The Hungry Heifer was hopping. Gerry attempted to overcome his sense of failure with a Humungus Heifer featuring two patties and cheese and bacon plus a slathering of their famous 'Secret Sauce', while Tau confronted his own inadequacies over a toasted chicken mayo and coffee. A stiff breeze was blowing off the brown sea, with clots of yellow foam sticking to the wave caps like Jersey cream. Far out a luxury yacht cruised slowly by.

They reviewed the case again and came up with no easy answers. Chris Pieterse hadn't been inside the Pollsmoor *madrassa* long enough to have made any headway, and all of the other clues in the search for the mysterious blue-eyed Asian had come to nought. There were a number of possible options amongst the staff at the Mount Nelson and common sense dictated that someone had been alerted to the fact that Tariq Dar was coming to town, and that arrangements had to be put in place to get him out of the hotel to avoid any possible watchers.

'Right,' said Gerry. 'Let's go and give that smug Englishman Hennesy a boot up the arse.'

'I don't think he knows anything. Let's just go and find these guys.'

Tau took his notebook from his pocket and looked at the first name on the list.

'I like this guy,' said Tau. 'Mohammed Butt. He's a bit of a smooth young operator, he was on desk duty when Dar checked in – he was very pally with our fat friend.'

'Where does he live?'

'Mowbray. Let's go.'

The break, when it came, was unexpected. Charlie rang up from forensics while Gerry was driving towards Mohammed Butt's house.

'Listen up, china,' he said. 'You know that phone number we were dialling when we were trying to nail your cop-killer?'

'Ja,' said Gerry, his heart hammering.

'Well, you're not gonna believe this but we got a hit about an hour ago. We alerted the uniform boys and they nabbed someone. He's in the Loop Street holding tank.'

'Thanks Charlie,' said Gerry. 'I owe you.' He turned to Tau, his face alight with enthusiasm. 'Now we see who fucks with the big boys!'

Gerry slammed the blue light on the car roof and hit the siren.

When they arrived at the old police station in Loop Street, Tau and Gerry were sent straight to the holding cells where a dishevelled young 'Coloured' boy was sitting on a cement bench, his hands thrust deep into the pockets of a huge overcoat. His trousers were threadbare and his shoes had cardboard covering the holes in the soles. He wore a pink T-shirt that said 'Malibu' in faded letters across the front. Tau and Gerry's excitement drained away as they entered the cell.

'Gots a smoke?' asked the boy hopefully.

'No,' said Gerry. 'You shouldn't be smoking anyway.'

'Who's you? The President?' demanded the youngster.

'Let's get this over with,' said Tau wearily. 'Where did you get your phone?'

'My bra' gave it to me, s'true's God!' said the boy, linking his pinkies and kissing them as proof of his eternal verity.

'That phone belongs to a killer,' said Gerry. 'Now where did you get it?'

'I tells you it's mine! Not some *skollie*, neh!'

Just then a uniformed cop entered and handed Tau a slip of paper.

'This says that the phone was stolen from the cubby-hole of a red Ford Focus belonging to Mrs Joanna Green of Fishoek last year.'

'I didn't steal it!' wailed the boy.

'Listen carefully,' said Gerry, eyeballing the boy from a distance of six inches. 'I don't give a rat's arse if you stole the phone or sold your granny to buy it. I'm not interested. But the number of the phone is different from the number it used to have when Mrs Green owned it. So my question to you is, now concentrate here, son,' he said, inches from the terrified youth's face, 'where-did-you-get-the-fucking-SIM-card?'

The boy blinked at Gerry a couple of times then turned to Tau.

'I didn't steal the phone, neh?'

'Just answer,' said Tau. 'Tell us about the SIM card. If you give us the right answer you walk out of here free. If you don't co-operate then...' He sucked his teeth and rolled his eyes dramatically.

'I found it!' blurted the boy.

'More shit,' said Gerry.

'S'true's God! I found it there in that little park by 11th Street.'

'What were you doing there?' asked Tau.

The young boy looked sullen.

'Guard!' yelled Gerry. A moment later a huge guard appeared at the door with a cartoonishly-large set of keys.

'Lock him up!' roared Gerry.

'I'm telling you s'true'sBob!' wailed the youngster. Gerry winked at the Guard who looked menacing but walked away.

'Last chance,' said Gerry. 'No more *kak*, hey!'

'We goes there to bust pipes,' said the boy sullenly, expecting a blow. When none came he perked up and started gabbling, eager to be off. 'So yesterday I was having a nice smoke when suddenly I sees this little Simmetjie lying there in the grass. Like it was winking at me. Now this old phone was no good because the Sim was cancelled but I put in the new one and tried it. Next thing I know six *bliksem* cops jump on me and bring me here! So now can I goes?'

'Not so fast,' said Tau. 'You're saying you just found this in the park?'

'Exactly right, my prince,' said the boy. 'You gots it just so.'

'I don't like it,' growled Gerry.

'It's God's word, my king!' wailed the young man. 'That's where I found it, there behind the mosque.'

Suddenly everything went still. Gerry and Tau swapped a glance.

'Carefully, now,' said Tau. 'Nice and slow - tell us once more where you found the SIM card.'

'There in the grass behind the 11th Street Mosque. Jehovah strike me down if I'm not telling the truth, neh.'

Gerry and Tau exchanged a glance.

'One last time – you found the SIM card outside the 11th Street Mosque?' asked Tau.

'Hunnerd Per Cent! Ten out ten! If I lie, I die,' said the youngster, kissing his entiwned fingers again.

'You got that right,' growled Gerry. 'Now go, before we change our minds.'

The search warrant took a little longer than normal to get because Tau and Gerry had to walk the tightrope of political correctness and urge Judge Sondergaard that the reasons for entering the mosque had national security at their heart, and that all respect would be shown to persons and property of the mosque. The Judge was still reluctant but a swift call to Jonas Chitepo helped make up his mind, and Tau and Gerry drew up outside the mosque an hour later. Prayers had just finished and the white-robed Imam was standing at the door chatting to the faithful as they streamed out. He appeared to be in his mid 40s, his long black beard showing the first touches of silver. He glanced up and frowned as he saw the orange BMW pulling up to the curb.

Tau and Gerry walked around the back of the mosque and saw the clutch of outbuildings and the dusty square that led onto the park. A group of feral street kids were huddled under a ratty palm tree, a plume of smoke rising from them as they smoked their bottleneck pipes.

The two NIA agents emerged at the front of the mosque just as the last straggler was leaving. The Imam spied them at once, and after saying a warm goodbye to the last of his flock, advanced with hands held meekly in front of him, a picture of humility and decorum, his sharp eyes missing nothing. He addressed Tau, pointedly ignoring Gerry.

'What can I do for you, brother?'

Gerry stepped into his face and held up the search warrant.

'We need to search your premises. Brother,' he said.

'But this is a house of God!' said the Imam. 'It is a sacred place.'

'We have reason to believe that some people may have abused your trust,' said Tau, 'and abused the sanctuary offered by the mosque.'

The Imam was about to reply but realised that he had no choice, and so snapped shut his mouth and turned on heel and walked quickly inside.

'Take off your shoes,' he said over his shoulder.

The examination of the mosque was very quick, and it became apparent that the offices at the back were more likely to be of interest.

The Imam led them around to the offices where he gestured at the door, fastened with a steel chain and heavy padlock.

'Where's the key?' Asked Gerry.

'Unfortunately it is with Fatima,' said the Imam, a hint of a smile on his lips. 'Today is Fatima's day off.'

'Where is she?' asked Tau.

The Imam shrugged. 'It's a big world.'

'Ja, and I wouldn't want to paint it,' said Gerry, as he reached under his arm and produced his pistol. 'Stand back,' he said.

'What are you going to do?' squawked the Imam.

'Shoot off the bladdy lock' said Gerry. 'Now mind – if the ricochet hits you I don't think our insurance covers that.'

The Imam spluttered briefly then delved into his robes and produced a key.

'A miracle! God is Great!' cried Gerry putting his gun away.

The Imam opened the door and Tau and Gerry entered.

'What is this used for?' said Tau looking around at the sparse, open plan offices.

'Administration. This is where we conduct the affairs of the mosque. The donations, the repairs to the buildings, our charity works.'

'How many people work here?'

'There is Fatima. She does the books and general office administration. Then there is Ramesh, who does the building and grounds maintenance, and on a part-time basis Ali, a young man who is training for the priesthood and helps out wherever he is needed.'

'And through there?' asked Gerry, pointing at the door at the back of the room.

'We use that room for storage and occasional get-togethers of our young people.'

Gerry tried the door. It was locked.

'Fatima got this key too?' he asked.

The Imam scowled at him and unlocked the door. The room was crammed with sports equipment and stacking chairs. Tau peered in over Gerry's shoulder.

'Doesn't look like it's been used for years,' he said.

'What's in that old filing cabinet?' asked Gerry.

'Nothing,' said the Imam quickly.

'Looks like a lot of nothing to me,' said Gerry.

'It's just old records – there is nothing of importance. All of our current files are out here,' said the Imam. 'Here, take a look, water rates, electricity bills…'

The Imam had opened a grey filing cabinet and was producing folders all neatly marked. Gerry ignored him and walked towards the old filing cabinet and pulled open the top drawer. It was almost empty, save for some curling yellow bills. The second drawer too was empty.

He frowned and started walking back to where Tau and the Imam were standing in the outer office going through the files. Suddenly he stopped. He walked back a step. Then forward again. Tau looked up, sensing something.

'Is there anything underneath here?' asked Gerry.

The Imam was now sweating.

'Of course not! Now please let me get back to my business. You've taken enough of my time.'

Gerry tapped the floor a few more times then looked around. He noticed that a fine patina of dust had settled on everything in the room but there was a smear mark where the ragged carpet was shoved under the filing cabinet. Gerry locked arms around the filing cabinet and lifted it easily into the air.

'Wait!' said the Imam. Gerry looked quizzically at him. Tau moved to block any possible thoughts of escape while Gerry flipped back the carpet revealing the trapdoor.

'What's down here?' demanded Gerry, suddenly recalling the booby-trap which decimated the firemen at Sayeed's old house.

'I don't know,' said the Imam. 'I have never seen that before.'

'Tell you what,' said Gerry affably. 'Why don't you open it.'

The Imam looked fearfully from Tau to Gerry. Tau nodded. The Imam grabbed the brass ring and wrenched it open, expecting something dramatic. All that happened was the room filled with the smell of damp earth and a cool silence. Gerry peered down into the darkness until his eyes had accustomed themselves to the gloom, then he climbed down the ladder. After a moment he found the light switch and the fluorescent tubes flickered into life.

Gerry whistled. 'Tau! Get hold of Charlie, pronto. We've found the motherlode. And while you're up there, you'd better get hold of our friend's collar before he decides to make a run for it.'

Chapter 35

It would take Charlie and his team nearly three days to complete their investigations of the cellar, but within hours of the find, the story became headline news. The Imam had been arrested and sent to Pollsmoor to await charges, but the good news for Tau and Gerry was that Charlie had managed to lift a set of prints which had registered a hit on the national crime computer – Sayeed Dhatri, aged 16, briefly detained on a PAGAD demonstration. Distinguishing features, blue eyes and 'Asiatic' appearance.

Finally, they had a name.

Chapter 36

Sayeed and Hamidullah had made good progress and were aiming to cross the Swazi border by dusk and stop at the first available resting place for the night. They had just circled Durban and were heading for the northern coastal motorway when Sayeed tuned the radio to the six o' clock news and was stunned by two stories. The first told of an Egyptian tourist who had been fatally shot in a carjacking on his way to the airport in Cape Town. Before the name was read out Sayeed knew that it was going to be his old comrade Hakimlah Djibril, *nom de guerre* of Tariq Dar.

The second news story was even more disturbing, as it listed some of the weapons found in a cache hidden in a cellar beneath the 11th Street mosque in Cape Town. Hamidullah was driving at the time and veered off to the side of the road and stopped the car.

'They murdered him!' cried Sayeed. 'The filthy sons of whores assassinated our comrade.'

Hamidullah looked at Sayeed in some mystification.

'Who? Who was murdered?'

'Our Iranian friend,' said Sayeed. 'He came to meet with me and work out our plan. Now they've killed him.'

'But…they said it was a carjacking.'

'Idiot! Of course that's what they would say, but he was shot down like a dog!'

'That means they must have been watching him,' said Hamidullah.

Sayeed thought for a moment, realising that his comrade wasn't all that stupid after all.

'I don't think they saw me,' said Sayeed, 'otherwise I would be martyred or in jail by now....'

'But how did they find out about the mosque?'

'I don't know,' said Sayeed, his eyes narrowing. 'Perhaps they were listening to your phone.'

'Don't try and blame me,' said Hamidullah. 'If it was as you say they could have picked us both up the other night. Is there anything in the cellar that ties you in?'

Sayeed thought. 'No. It's all clean - even the computer is wiped clean.'

'So what do we do?' said Hamidullah.

Sayeed pored over the map.

'I don't want to go across any borders if we don't have to. We will drive up through the Drakensberg and around Swaziland and join the Nelspruit Road just here...' He stabbed the map. 'It's not too far from where we are supposed to meet our contact anyway.'

Hamidullah was looking doubtful.

'It will add an extra three or four hundred kilometres,' he said.

'It's Allah's will that we make this trip and through his guidance we will succeed,' said Sayeed. 'Now, take the next turning and go back to the main Durban road, then we take the N3 towards Maritzburg.'

Hamidullah was cheerful once again – he had a direction and a purpose, and, Insh'Allah, they would be victorious.

Chapter 37

Shosho had been walking for nearly four hours and was certain that he was near the border. The sun was sinking towards the hilltops and the sweat trickled slowly down his face. He must have made the crossing at least 20 times and knew the way well, but he always felt the tension rise when he was transiting from Mozambique to South Africa. The Arab who had brought him from Maputo had said nothing in the five-hour journey, but Shosho didn't care. As he had nothing to say to the man and didn't like Arabs anyway, but the man had paid two thousand American Dollars and would pay another two thousand when Shosho returned to Maputo.

They had pulled in at a lay-by about seven kilometres from the road border. Shosho had got out of the car and hefted his rucksack onto his back and had walked straight into the dense bush at the side of the road. The Arab turned his car around and drove back towards Maputo, and within moments all that Shosho could hear was the screech of cicadas as he climbed steadily in the rising heat and humidity.

Inside the rucksack were three long grey rolls of Semtex plastic explosive, each weighing five kilos, and wrapped around with greasy paper covered in Czech writing. There were a couple of detonators in a side pouch and two spare clips for his .45 Star pistol that he wore in a webbing holster on his belt. Also attached to his belt were a water bottle and compass, and a diver's knife with a wicked serrated back and a razor-sharp blade. There was also half a loaf of bread in the bag, two sticks of biltong and some bubble gum.

Shosho wore camouflage combat trousers, cotton shirt and the lightweight hiking boots that he'd taken from a Boer farmer on his last raid. He swung a machete back and forth, both to clear away the clinging vines and undergrowth and also to deal with any snakes that might be lurking in the bush. Shosho had faced down seven drunk rebels armed with AK's, but he had frozen when a long black snake had slithered across the path just in front of him. This area was thick with snakes, and he was able to rationalise that they would get out of the way if they heard you approaching, but the deadly mambas were aggressive and could outrun a man, and he dreaded being trapped in thick bush with one.

After a couple of hours the bush started to thin and Shosho saw that he had climbed several hundred metres and was now on the spine of hills that ran through Northern Swaziland, the Eastern end of Limpopo Province and across the Mozambique border. Running along the top of the hills was the very faint remnants of a trail over a hundred years old, first mapped out by Paul Kruger as his wagon train route to the coast. Dotted along the route were a few tumbledown houses that had been used as way stations by the Boer President, and occasionally you could still find a broken wagon wheel at the side of the track, grass pushing through the split wooden hub.

Shosho sat on a rock, after first checking for snakes and scorpions, and had a deep pull on his water bottle. The day was starting to cool and he sat in silence, listening to the sounds of the bush. He knew that he had about five more kilometres to go, following the old wagon trail, then he had to cut down a gorge, cross the Crocodile River and make his way to the Kloof, about four kilometres along the road. He chewed some biltong then stood up and started walking – he had to keep moving or his muscles would cramp with the cool breeze. He dug in his pocket and found a black capsule that he swallowed – an old fashioned Benzedrine tablet to give his legs added energy for the long walk ahead.

Suddenly he heard a deep bark. He dived into the bush and pulled out his pistol and stared at the long elephant grass ahead of him. Then he heard another bark, this time off to one side, and then another, behind him. He realised that he was in the middle of a troop of baboons, moving slowly through the bush, turning over rocks to look for scorpions or small lizards. He remained still and a few moments later the dominant male of the troop stalked out of the grass on all fours and stared in Shosho's direction. Shosho slowly brought up his pistol and aimed straight at the big male.

But the baboon grew bored and sat down and yawned – his massive canines were longer than a lion's and Shosho had heard that an angry baboon could inflict as much damage as any of the big cats. But big male's interest was on the rest of the troop as they emerged singly from the grass and moved slowly away, up-ending stones as they went, uttering the occasional bark. Shosho exhaled slowly and put his pistol back into its holster.

A hundred metres ahead was the border fence. The tall wooden poles ran for hundreds of kilometres, strung with twin strands of razor wire three metres high with looping swathes of wire on top, and the inevitable electric strands running through the middle. Sosho glanced around and having determined that he was alone sprinted to a gnarled old marula tree that abutted against the fence. He glanced up at the silver humming wires beside him and smiled to himself. At the base of the tree was a large boulder that he rolled aside, revealing a shallow depression cut into the earth, passing directly under the wire. Sosho took a deep breath and pushed himself into the trench, and a minute was on the South African side of the border.

Two hours later, the sun had set and Shosho was starting to make his way down from the ridge. In the distance, he could see the lights of the Marais place, a rambling old farmhouse that was set high on the hillside. He could even see someone moving about in the kitchen, but he knew to give farms a wide berth, and as if on cue he heard a dog start barking in the distance.

He slipped a couple of times as he followed a stream as it tumbled down a waterfall and once sprang back in fright as a small buck leaped out of the stream bed. But finally he reached the flatter lands that were studded with avocado and mango orchards. In the distance he could hear the intermittent hum of traffic on the road and follow the headlights of the cars as they traced their path along the valley floor.

He almost walked straight into an electric fence that gave a warning click every five seconds. He was momentarily angry because the fence was new, but after the last raid the farmers were becoming scared of the bandits who marauded along the frontier, and had started to fight back. Shosho followed the fence for about a hundred metres until he found a tree overhanging the wire. He scaled the tree and dropped down on the other side, his lip curling in contempt at the ease with which the security had been breached.

Ten minutes later he was standing beside the gushing waters of the Crocodile River. The name was no romantic conceit – a small child had been taken by a croc barely 10 kilometres away and there were pools downstream with hippos which were if anything even more dangerous than the crocodiles. He took out his pistol as he stepped gingerly into the water. Once, when he had been fighting in the bush war, he had encountered a croc and had emptied his magazine into the creature before finally stopping it with a headshot through the eye. He finally threw caution to the wind and charged across and was up and into the reeds on the opposite bank, gasping to catch his breath.

He lay on the grass on the other side, breathing heavily and laughing to himself. After a few minutes he had sat up and swallowed another capsule and felt the energy flow into his legs. He jogged through an avocado plantation, climbed over a fence and saw the road ahead of him. He had come further than he realised and was barely a kilometre from Beyer's Kloof.

He took out his cell phone and sent a brief message. Moments later he received his reply and felt a surge of confidence. He now had the number plate of the vehicle he was to make his delivery to, waiting for him at the rendezvous. He looked up at the red sandstone cliffs towering above him and thought that it would be most secure to walk along the cliff tops then drop down into the Kloof. But after trying to scramble up the steep rocks in the darkness, Shosho decided that he would follow the road, ready at a moment's notice to slip into the black shadows of the bush.

Ten minutes later he was standing behind a thick stand of mimosa trees opposite the Kloof. Parked at one end of the dirt lay-by was a red Hilux with the number plate matching the text he had received. Seated inside he could see two men, sitting and waiting. He had taken off his rucksack and left it some distance away in case of a trap, but as he hunkered down and watched he became more confident that it wasn't a set-up. Just as he turned to go and retrieve his pack, another pickup truck pulled up into the lay-by, towing a ski boat on a trailer, with heavy-duty sea rods sticking over the roof of the cab. The fishermen were obviously planning to motor through to Mozambique for some marlin fishing, but had decided to break their journey at the Kloof.

Within minutes they had produced a cold box and had cracked out some beers, and started a fire in the collapsible Swanee Braai that they had taken out of the back of the truck. *Boerewors* was put onto the grill and Shosho felt his stomach growling as he smelled the cooking meat. He also felt a growing irritation because he knew that the men would be some time and might even stay for the night. He was now starting to get cold and could feel the stabbing pain in his legs as they started to cramp. He could also see the two men in the Hilux starting to become agitated. Finally he decided on a bold strategy. He retrieved his rucksack and walked along the road towards the Kloof. When he reached the Hilux he knocked on the window. An Indian man opened the window, glaring through hooded eyes.

'Good evening, baas, can you give me a ride?' Said Shosho loudly.

'I'm not going anywhere,' said Sayeed.

'I will get in the back. You will drive half a kilometre down the road and let me off. Then we will do the exchange,' hissed Shosho.

Sayeed's eyes momentarily widened, then he nodded and gestured in the back with his thumb.

'Get in.'

'Thank you, my *baas*,' said Shosho, ducking his head. He slung the rucksack into the back and hopped up after it. Moments later Hamidullah started the engine and they drove away from the Kloof, leaving the fishermen to their beers and *braaivleis*.

At a dark bend in the road Shosho banged on the roof of the cab and Hamidullah pulled over. Shosho hopped out of the back and came round to Sayeed's window.

'Salaam Alaikum,' said Sayeed.

'Whatever,' said Shosho. He took the rolls of Semtex from his bag and added the detonators and put them into a plastic sack and passed them to Sayeed.

'Thank you,' said Sayeed.

'My money,' said Shosho.

'What money?' said Sayeed, genuinely surprised.

'You think I risk my neck for nothing?' said Shosho. 'They said you would give me a thousand Rands.'

Hamidullah looked at Sayeed, suspecting a shakedown. But Sayeed raised his hand to calm Hamidullah.

'We weren't told. I have only got 400 Rand with me.'

He took out his wallet and held it up to Shosho for inspection. Shosho took the money from the wallet and threw it back into the car with a dismissive suck on his teeth. Within seconds he had sunk back into the darkness. Hamidullah started the van and did a tight U-Turn and drove quickly away. Both Sayeed and Shosho swore that if they ever saw the other man again, they would kill him.

Despite his apparent anger, Shosho was pleased with his luck. He had managed to secure an additional 400 Rands, plus the 2000 dollars waiting for him in Maputo. He sat down on a stone and opened his pack and took out some bread and *biltong* and water and made himself a simple meal. He thought briefly of going back to the fishermen and shooting them and taking their food, but in the end it simply wasn't worth the hassle.

He was exhausted, but knew that he should start back towards the border at once. He swallowed another speed capsule and started walking back through the avocado orchard towards the stream that would take him back up onto the old wagon trail. This time when he reached the electric fence he threw his rucksack over the top strand of wire and managed to clamber over without giving himself a shock, but his mood was ugly and he was becoming paranoid, starting at the sudden night noises and seeing shapes in the darkness.

He struggled up the waterfall and paused at the top to drink some of the fast-flowing water. A slip of a moon was hanging low in the sky. In the distance he saw the last light in the Marais farmhouse go out. And all at once he made up his mind.

Chapter 38

Although Tau and Gerry had been joined at the hip since their days at the academy, they seldom went on double dates. Joyce and Aletta had always been slightly wary of each other, which made for uncomfortable contact. Aletta, because she thought that Joyce, being an academic, was also an intellectual and somehow looked down on her and Gerry for being more materialistic. For her part, Joyce felt somehow oafish and out of the swim with Aletta, who always seemed to know the latest fashions and how to put them together with an ease and naturalness that Joyce could never match. But lately the situation had started to change, and there was a slowly emerging warmth between the two women, so when their mates suggested a night out at a new sushi place at the Waterfront, they leaped at the chance.

'Jeez,' said Gerry with total predictability, 'for these prices you think they could have cooked it.'

'Stop it,' said Aletta, turning to Joyce. 'The other day he brought home some tuna and we made a raw tuna salad with wasabi and rice. He likes to pretend that he's just off the farm.'

'Just don't tell them about my knitting,' said Gerry, laughing.

'Well, if you weren't brought up with it, eating raw fish isn't the first thing that comes to mind,' said Tau.

'We never ate raw anything,' said Joyce. 'My ma used to cook the meat until it was cinders and the veggies until they were like old *lappies*.'

'Saké?' asked Gerry looking around. They all nodded and moments later were presented with a carafe of steaming rice wine. Tau poured them each a thimbleful and they raised their cups in a toast.

'What are we celebrating?' asked Aletta.

'Celebrating having such wonderful partners,' said Tau.

'You old smoothie,' said Gerry. 'But I agree. Also, we've finally had a break in our case. Cheers!'

'So what was the big break?' asked Aletta.

'You know we can't say,' said Gerry.

'Gee, it's like being involved with the secret service,' said Aletta. 'Oh, wait! It IS the secret service!'

She and Joyce giggled.

'That man who was shot in a hijack on the way to the airport? It seems a bit strange…' said Joyce.

'Oh? Strange how?' asked Tau.

'Well, according the news, they shot the guy through the door. They didn't even try and stop the vehicle, and when they'd shot him they ran away. Pointless!'

'Who can figure out the criminal mind, eh,' said Gerry.

'Well,' said Aletta, 'Isn't that what you boys are supposed to do?'

'I swear,' said Gerry to Tau, 'if these two were to conduct interrogations the crims would just put up their hands and confess straight away!'

'Even if they weren't guilty,' said Tau.

'Hmmm,' said Joyce. 'I could tell you about some cases where the cops really screwed up. In fact…'

'So tell me,' said Gerry to Joyce, hoping to avoid the looming train smash, 'did your sister-in-law open her fancy boutique?'

Joyce glanced at Tau. 'She's going to Paris to do some buying,' said Joyce, wrinkling her nose. 'It'll open in about two months' time.'

'Paris! Wow,' said Aletta. 'I'd love to go to Paris. When will you take me, Ger?' she said, fluttering her eyelashes in a parody of cuteness.

'Maybe sooner than you think,' said Gerry, 'now, what should we eat?'

Aletta looked startled and was about to say something but realised that this was not the time, and looked at her menu instead. She glanced up and caught Gerry's eye – he winked at her. She smiled to herself and sat back to enjoy the evening.

The meal was excellent and they took a leisurely walk around the yacht basin, stopping to look in the various shops and chatting affably. The two women fell behind and Gerry and Tau walked ahead. Gerry seemed anxious and when they were out of sight of the women he reached into his pocket and produced a ring box that he showed to Tau. He opened the lid and held the ring up for inspection.

'At last!' said Tau. 'I'm touched, Gerry. I really am…'

'Not you, *poephol*,' growled Gerry. 'For Letty. What do you think?'

Tau reacted in an uncharacteristic manner – he embraced Gerry and patted him hard on the back. Gerry paused then patted his old friend on the back too.

'Well done, brother,' Tau said, just as a figure darted out of the shadows and grabbed the ring from Gerry's hand that was clasped behind Tau's back. Gerry sprang back as if electrocuted.

'What the fuck! Catch him! HEY!' Gerry started racing after the young black kid who ran like the wind. Tau joined in the chase and they charged past the two startled women. The young kid was heading for the exit of the complex when Gerry put on a burst of speed and at the last moment launched into a flying rugby tackle that would have done him proud at Loftus Versveld. He locked arms around the youngster's ankles and they crashed to the ground. Gerry was astride him in a second and wrestled his ring out of the boy's clenched fist.

'Got it!' he cried, holding up the ring triumphantly. The boy heaved his chest with strength beyond him and Gerry momentarily toppled forwards, allowing the kid to wriggle free and start sprinting for the exit. Tau was about to take off after him again when Gerry stood up, still holding his ring aloft.

'Let him go,' he said, panting. Tau stopped running and walked back to Gerry who had now been joined by the anxious women.

'What was that all about?' asked Joyce.

'He..uh…' stumbled Gerry, aware that they were all now staring at the ring in his hand.

'My God! That's a beautiful ring,' said Aletta. 'Did he steal it?'

'Ja,' said Gerry. 'Kind of…'

Tau was grinning and took Joyce's elbow and tried steering her away. She was about to protest when Tau whispered in her ear and she suddenly also grinned and said 'Come, let's go and see those shops over there.'

She and Tau walked quickly away.

'What's going on?' demanded Aletta, fearing that she was being set up for some kind of practical joke.

Tau glanced back over his shoulder to see Gerry slip the ring onto Aletta's finger, and even from a hundred metres they heard her delighted shriek as Gerry picked her up and twirled her around. A couple of minutes later Aletta and Gerry joined them looking in the window of a curio shop. Aletta's cheeks were glowing and Gerry was looking sheepish.

'Congratulations!' said Joyce, kissing them both.

'Congratulations,' said Tau. 'I'm damned if I'm gonna kiss you, Gerry.'

They all laughed.

'Did you all know?' asked Aletta.

'Know? Gerry's as tight as clam. He says nothing. I was as surprised as you.'

'Okay okay,' said Gerry. 'The night is still young. Can we treat you guys to a glass of champagne?'

'We'd be delighted,' said Joyce, slipping her arm through Aletta's.

That night Gerry and Aletta made slow and tender love, with Aletta showing him some new and exciting techniques that she'd discovered in a book from her feminist bookshop, entitled *So He Thinks you're Not Good Enough?*. Hell, she was nothing if not flexible.

'Will you still do this after we're married?' gasped Gerry.

'Forget it,' she said sweetly, and started all over again.

Gerry had never been happier.

At 2AM he was woken from a deep sleep by the jangling phone. Tau's voice on the other side said simply 'Chris Peiterse was murdered in Pollsmoor Prison late last night.'

Chapter 39

Hannes Marais had just checked every window in the property and settled into bed beside Sannie, when he heard his Alsatian, Prinz, emit a low growl.

'What's it, boy?' he asked. Prinz growled again and stood up, his hackles raised, his tail hanging low.

'Could be that troop of baboons again,' said Sannie who had spent the morning repairing damage to the small vegetable patch outside the kitchen.

'I'd better go check,' groaned Hannes, swinging out of bed.

'Take your gun!'

Hannes sighed. He opened the drawer beside his bed and took out his revolver, an old Smith &Wesson .38 that had last been fired ten years ago and Hannes wondered if it would actually work if required. He also picked up his powerful lantern torch and stamped through to the kitchen. Prinz was scurrying ahead of him, his nails skittering on the lino.

'Be careful!' called Sannie, throwing a dressing gown around herself.

Hannes opened the back door. He could make out someone standing at the gate, about 20 metres away. He shone the torch and saw the black man put a hand to his face to shield his eyes.

'Who is it?'

'It's Moses! I work for Baas Davenport. There's trouble at the farm. He wants you to come quick!' Shosho had noticed a name marker saying 'Vale Farm JG Davenport' as he walked to the Kloof.

Hannes half-turned to Sannie as he kept his eyes on Shosho.

'Get John on the Agric-Alert,' he said quickly, and then stepped into the yard, holding Prinz by the collar.

'What trouble?' he asked.

'Some men with guns came. Shooting, Baas. You must come now!'

Hannes frowned, sensing something amiss. He knew John Davenport's foreman well, and there was something about the way the man was standing with his hand dangling half hidden behind his back that put Hannes on guard.

'How many men?' asked Hannes, stepping up to the gate.

'Six. He said I must run to Baas Marais and get help,' said Shosho, panting dramatically.

Hannes pulled a bunch of keys from his pocket and started to unlock the gate. Shosho stood back respectfully until the lock fell away then strode forward and pushed his pistol into Hannes' face and shot twice, in quick succession. Hannes flew back into the dirt, his eyes open wide in startled disbelief. Shosho was aware of a high-pitched scream coming from the house and looked up to see Sannie's mouth open in a howl of despair as she struggled to shut the kitchen door. Shosho rushed across the yard as Prinz flew at him - he shot the dog in mid-air and it fell in a heap as he reached the door and kicked it open.

Sannie was up against the fridge, her face wrinkled in ugly terror. Shosho seized her by the hair and started to undo his trousers, but the Benzedrine pills had left his penis totally without feeling. Enraged, he smashed her in the face with the butt of the gun. As she fell he shot her once in the stomach and once in the chest. She was making some pitiful moaning noises as he stepped over her and quickly found the safe. He tried a number of keys from Hannes' ring until he found the one that fitted. He hauled open the heavy door and inside found a small jewellery box containing some rings and diamond earrings, a neatly-wrapped bundle of cash, and some yellowing boxes of ammunition for the old revolver. Shosho quickly took the cash and the jewels and stepped over Sannie on his way out.

She moved slightly and Shosho suddenly saw a small silver gun in her hand. Before he could respond the gun emitted a sharp snap and he felt a punch in his shoulder. He looked down angrily at where the .22 had entered his body, and then fired four more shots into Sannie at close range. She flopped back onto the ground, and this time did not move. Just then he heard a crackly squawk from an inside room. He approached cautiously and threw open the door only to find the Agric-Alert radio on a side stand.

'Come in, Hannes. Calling Hannes Marais, this is John Davenport. I heard shots. Is everything OK? Come in Hannes…'
Then another voice crackled onto the open party line.

'John. It's Fanie Ferreira. Is there trouble?'

'Ja Fanie. I can't raise Hannes and I heard shots.'

'I'll get the cops, you round up the others.' 'Roger, will do.'

Shosho wrenched the radio out of the wall and threw it down. His shoulder was starting to throb and the pain was intense. He felt around and could locate the bullet in the fleshy muscle of his shoulder, but couldn't get it out. He knew a medic in Maputo who would remove it, but first he had to get back. He went into the bathroom and threw open the medicine cabinet and swallowed a handful of aspirins and took a length of bandage. He left the house walking swiftly towards the ridge and shook out another Benzedrine capsule from the bottle. He was furious at having been impotent, and even more furious at having been shot by a woman.

Still, he would make the rendezvous by midday and be back in Maputo by nightfall the following day. Then he could rest.

Chapter 40

'What happened?' asked Tau. They were sitting before Chitepo once again.

'He was standing in the food line. There was a crush of people against him, when everyone stood back he just fell over. Sharpened bicycle spoke into his spine.'

'His cover was excellent!' said Gerry furiously. 'Every bladdy news bulletin was running stories about the major terrorist event that was thwarted at the last minute.'

'When they took him into Pollsmoor there was cheering,' said Chitepo. 'So what went wrong?'

Tau spoke softly. 'On our side, only Gerry, me and Chris knew the detail.'

'Plus the security head at the Waterfront,' said Gerry. 'Charl Gerber, but I've known Charl for a hundred years and he's reliable.'

'Perhaps they rumbled him inside,' said Chitepo.

Nobody spoke for a few moments.

'Perhaps we've got a leak,' said Tau.

Chitepo paused for a moment, the said, 'Here's what's going to happen - I am going to bring in someone from Internal Affairs, from Jo'burg, to go through this department with a fine tooth comb. I will find out whether or not there is a mole within our organization. Only you two know about this and that's how it will remain. Understood?'

Gerry glanced at Tau and both men nodded.

'Back to the present - you have a lead with Sayeed Dhatri and some of the staff at the Mount Nelson. Go and shake that tree until he falls out. I want that bastard and I want him now!' Said Chitepo.

'We've got the Mount Nelson suspects to speak to, and we have to starting tracing all of Dhatri's movements for the past 18 months, at least. We need more resources,' said Gerry.

'Then take them,' said Chitepo. 'The teams you used at the airport. Is that enough?'

'Yes sir,' said Tau, standing.

'There is one other thing you might like to know,' said Chitepo. 'I just got off the phone to Fitzwarren. The Israeli hit man was called Avigdor Grunewald and his associate within the Cape Town Embassy was Leila Stern. The Israelis learned about Tariq Dar from a leak within the Athens station of the CIA and the lead man there is already on his way home. But the pertinent point is that the Israelis, within two hours of learning this information, had put together a plan and put everything in place for a successful operation. And they got their people out again before we even knew what day it was! That's the kind of operational efficiency I want from your team. Understood?'

Chapter 41

Shosho didn't realise that he had fallen asleep. His eyes were gummy and the pain was burning a fiery path from his shoulder all the way down his side. He tried to sit up and work out where he was, then the events of the previous night came flooding back. He had walked for a couple of hours from the Marais farm house before finally collapsing in the lee of a small rocky kopje. Shosho checked that he still had the money and the diamonds in his rucksack, and took a drink of water and swallowed some more aspirins. He was pleased that he had had sufficient foresight to bring the pills with him and hoped that within a few minutes the pain would start to abate.

He took stock of where he was and realised that he had only covered a couple of kilometres from the farm and that he had strayed some distance from the old wagon trail. The sun was just starting to rise and he would have to make good progress to meet his pickup on the Mozambique side of the border. He also knew that the police would soon be on his trail, and so stood cautiously, eyes and ears straining for any sounds of pursuit. He carefully pulled on his rucksack and started walking back up the slope.

At the Marais house John Davenport and Fanie Ferreira and the other members of the local farmers' militia had gathered in a sombre group. The bodies of Hannes and Sannie had been covered but lay where they fell, awaiting the arrival of the police from Nelspruit.

'Waste of fucking time,' said Fanie savagely. 'They don't even have a murder squad these days. And between you and me, they don't give a fuck if white farmers get taken out anyway.'

'That's right,' said Kobus Van Zyl. 'When Dan Roberts and his family were wiped out they didn't make one arrest. Not one! And a reward of ten thousand Rands too!'

'It was an inside job,' said Barend Pretorius. 'The houseboy even pointed out who he thought did it.'

'I think it's someone or some gang who works the border area,' said John Davenport. 'Twice they brought in trackers and lost the trail near the Mozambique border.'

'Have you met the local police chief?' asked Fanie.

'Ja,' said John. 'Seems OK, but overworked.'

Hmf!' snorted Barend. 'So are we going to sit on our arses doing nothing until the cops get here?'

Barend made a show of chambering a round in his M-1 assault rifle. He gestured at a sleepy-looking dog in the back of his *bakkie*. 'My dog can track a flea at a thousand metres. I say we go after the bugger while his spoor is still fresh. Let the cops catch up when they can.'

'I agree,' said Fanie.

'I'm in,' said John.

They all looked at the only man not to have spoken so far. He carried a nylon webbing gun case, inside which was a sniper rifle and bipod and scope. Willie Joubert had been short-listed for the South African Olympic rifle team, and was the best shot in the entire Mpumalanga region. Willie simply nodded.

'Someone going to stay to deal with the police?' asked John.

'I'll wait,' said Kobus. 'Make sure none of these jokers steal anything from the house.' He gestured at the farm employees who sat in a morose group in the dusty yard, waiting for something to happen.

Barend brought his dog from the *bakkie* and led him to a rag that they found on the bathroom floor. The dog's tail went up and he started snuffling his way out of the yard, heading for the high ground with the team of men following eagerly behind.

Shosho had been going for about 20 minutes and had just stopped to take another drink of water, when in the distance he heard a dog barking. He squinted through the dawn light and on the far-off hillside he saw four white men, all with weapons, being led by a dog, moving swiftly through the grass. Shosho pushed ahead with all speed – the border could not be more than a couple of kilometres away. He kept low, keeping a screen of bushes between him and his pursuers.

Fanie and the others had stopped to get their breath. Fanie was scanning the bush with his field glasses and suddenly cried out 'There!' He pointed at the far slope and passed the binoculars to John who scanned the bush to no avail. Finally his vision settled on something behind a rock – he couldn't make it out but it didn't look like the surrounding veld.

It was, in fact, the top of Shosho's rucksack as he hunkered down behind a large boulder. The sun was making him feel faint and the pain in his shoulder meant that he could not carry his rucksack on both shoulders but had to wear it across his body. The sweat trickled into his eyes, but he felt keenly the imperative to keep moving. There was an open area ahead of him and he realised that if he broke cover he would be a sitting duck.

He noticed that the pursuers were about to enter a copse of dense woods and he would use their limited visibility to make good his escape. He peeped through a narrow fissure between the rocks and saw that the four men had stopped and were scanning the terrain with binoculars. He would have to wait.

As he squatted down he smelt a rodent smell, a musty, earthy odour that came from a rat run. He heard something slowly moving through the dried grass and leaves, very close by. His heart started hammering and he unstrapped his pistol and snapped in a fresh clip. He wiped the sweat from his eyes and licked his lips, ready for action.

Across the valley the men were arguing.

'It's nothing,' said Barend. 'A bit of twig or leaf. Why don't you check it through your scope, Willie. It's better than this piece of shit from OK Bazaars,' he said, dismissively passing the field glasses back to Fanie.

Willie sat down and unzipped his rifle case. He took out the weapon with the strange polymer stock, and opened its bipod legs then peered through the scope at the spot indicated.

'It could be something,' said Willie.

'Let me crack off a few rounds and see if we can flush him out,' said Fanie, raising his M-1.

'Waste of time from this distance,' said John. 'Just make him run faster.'

'If I let my dog off the lead he'll go straight to him. You watch,' said Barend.

'He'll go off chasing some bushbuck,' said Fanie. 'That dog's even more stupid than his owner.'

Shosho suddenly remembered something he had learned as a youngster that snakes often waited along rodent runs to catch their prey. In that instant he knew that he had to get away from that place, even if it meant being seen by the white men. He reached for his rucksack when he heard a long slow hiss. He froze. Rearing up directly in front of him was a *rinkhals*, a young ring-necked spitting Cobra. The snake had raised itself nearly a foot off the ground and its hood was extended. Shosho knew that it targeted movement, which is how it found it's victims' eyes. His left hand was still low and he slowly started moving it back and forth. The cobra followed his hand movement and suddenly discharged a spray of venom that hit against his hand. Shosho gave a cry but remained where he was. He would try and draw the snake towards him then shoot the fucking thing in the head. He slowly cocked the pistol in his right hand while starting to move his left hand again. Two more jets of venom struck his hand.

'Come. Just a bit closer,' said Shosho. A fat bead of sweat dribbled into his eyes, and at that moment he blinked.

'Tst!' Twin jets of venom shot straight into his eyes. The pain was scorching, blinding, like hot acid on his eyeballs. Shosho leaped to his feet, groping helplessly for his water bottle as the snake shot more poison into his face.

'Jesus!' cried Fanie. 'What the fuck's he doing!' They looked in amazement as the muscular black man suddenly reared up from behind the cover of the rocks and did a strange jerky dance, beating at his face and stumbling around.

'Snake,' said John.

Willie held up a pinch of sand and watched it blow away. He adjusted the scope for windage and took a deep breath. He peered through the eyepiece, made another slight adjustment, and then he squeezed the trigger.

'Twa!' The gunshot echoed across the valley. It seemed to take forever but suddenly Shosho's head exploded in a red spray, and he cart-wheeled backwards over the rock and lay on the ground, unmoving.

Fanie and the others looked in disbelief.

'You got him!' Cried Barend. 'Fucking gold-medal shot there! Jesus, must be nearly a bladdy kilometre.'

'I hope your dog didn't fuck up,' said Willie as he grimly packed up his rifle. But the others were already charging ahead, racing through the long grass towards the dead African.

Just then Fanie's cell phone rang.

'The cops are here,' said Kobus, peering from the Marais kitchen window as a 4X4 crawled up the dirt track towards the house, a whip aerial on the back and a blue light on its roof.

'Typical. Arriving when the party's over,' grunted Fanie.

'Where are you?'

'We're on the old wagon trail. Just near the border. We got the bugger.'

'Alive?'

'Dead dead dead. Willie popped his cork at a thousand metres. Unbelievable fucken shot! Listen, you must tell the cops it was self-defence. He started shooting at us first. You got that?'

'Check,' said Kobus and hung up just as a fat policeman in a tight uniform got out of the 4X4 and came towards the house. The van's driver, Thomas, a lanky man in a putty grey uniform, got out and followed his boss at a respectful distance. Kobus went out to meet him.

'What have we here?' said Chief Inspector Mangope.

'Suicide,' said Kobus. 'Hannes Marais shot himself in the face a few times, then Sannie got so upset she robbed the safe then shot herself a whole lot more.'

Mangope looked hard at Kobus and wagged a warning finger at him.

'You are a funny man, Mister Van Zyl. Have you got your Sig Sauer licensed yet? I just might have to confiscate it.'

Kobus realised that the Chief Inspector was staring at his pistol, stuck cowboy-style into his waistband.

'Another thing,' said the Chief Inspector. 'If the gun goes off you'll blow your balls off.'

'Thanks for the tip. They got him,' said Kobus, trying not to gloat.

'Uh-huh,' said Chief Inspector Mangope, turning to his lieutenant. 'You hear that Thomas. While we were dealing with a rape these people did their own policing and caught the alleged criminal. Impressive, yes?'

Thomas nodded. 'Impressive, Chief Inspector.'

'Where is the prisoner? I need to speak to him,' said Chief Inspector Mangope.

Kobus' eyes slid to the ground.

'He tried to shoot down our people. There was a gunfight and he's dead.'

'Dead? I see. And where are they?'

Kobus gestured vaguely into the hills.

'Why don't you show us,' said the Chief Inspector 'Thomas, better bring the stretcher and body bag.'

John, Fanie, Barend and Willie stood around staring down at Shosho. The high velocity round had blown half his head away. Fanie's dog had settled beside the body and was whining.

'See?' said John pointing at the toxin drying in silvery flakes on Shosho's black skin. 'Cobra. Might still be here.'

They all looked anxiously around.

'Is he the killer?' asked Barend, feeling slightly queasy as he looked at the greyish pink pulp spilling out of Shosho's head.

'Of course!' snapped Fanie. 'Check his rucksack.'

Barend gingerly opened the rucksack and showed the others the contents, then let it fall back. 'It's him, all right. That's Sannie's necklace.'

Suddenly Fanie unleashed a volley of kicks into the dead man's side.

'Piece of shit,' he said, breathing heavily.

Fanie picked up Shosho's pistol and forced it into the dead man's hand and fired a couple of shots into the air.

'What the hell's that for?' asked Barend.

'Cops are on their way. The story is we were tracking this arsehole and he opened fire. We returned fire and killed him in self-defence. We have to stick to the story or next week we'll be standing in the dock in Nelspruit charged with murder. Are we all agreed?

He held out his fist. Barend clasped his hand over the fist, and then John put his over theirs, then Fanie.

'Agreed.'

Chapter 42

Sayeed and Hamidullah had spent the night in the Lowveld Motel, with the Semtex in a cooler bag under a row of Cokes. They had breakfast on the terrace of the Motel, overlooking the Crocodile River.

'I can't wait to get out of here,' said Hamidullah.

'We have to go to Northern Natal,' said Sayeed, 'and wait until the shipment arrives. Could be as early as tomorrow or the next day.'

'Where will we stay until then? I get the creeps here,' said Hamidullah. He had been propositioned by a drunk woman the previous night and had seen her sitting alone in the dining room, which is why he steered Sayeed out onto the terrace.

Sayeed took out his map and they studied it carefully. He identified an area around Cape Vidal that was designated a nature reserve and indicated the small town of St Lucia bordering on Lake St Lucia.

'There,' he said. 'We'll go to Vidal until we get the call.'

They quickly loaded up their pickup and filled up at the petrol station and loaded some more Cokes and bottled water for the journey ahead.

'I'll take the first shift,' said Sayeed, settling behind the wheel. They were just in time for the 8 o'clock news on the radio. Sayeed was relieved that there was nothing further on the hijacking of Tariq Dar, his mentor and comrade, residing in Paradise at the side of the Prophet.

They swung out onto the open road and started the journey south.

Chapter 43

Pollsmoor Prison. A depressing complex of orange-brick cubes with grey steel window bars and festoons of razor wire making up the perimeter fence. It had been home to Nelson Mandela and was now housing some of the roughest and most violent criminals in the world.

A cleaner at the prison had found a note in Chris Pieterse's cell that he had passed to his senior officer who had in turn passed it to Tau in the warden's office. The warden, a career officer with a scar across his nose was slow and deliberate, and did not like facing criticism, especially from outsiders.

'Once again,' said Gerry, who had grown tired of the endless litany of denial. The warden took his time lighting a Lucky and blowing a jet of blue smoke at Gerry.

'I advise you to not do that again on health grounds,' said Gerry.

'My health's fine,' said the warden. 'It's yours you should worry about.'

Gerry snatched the cigarette from the warden's lips and mashed it out on the table in front of him, making a small circular burn in the oak top. 'You need to be more worried than me,' said Gerry, holding his eye. The warden sighed.

'Like I said, he was sent into lockdown in his own cell on the first night. Next day he exercised in the yard and my people saw him make contact with some of the lifers here. The PAGAD hard boys…'

'We'll need a list of names,' said Tau.

The warden waved dismissively. 'Ja. Anyway they went back to their cells and then nothing until they all turned out for supper in the mess hall. While he was standing in line he got *moered*.'

'Uh-huh,' said Gerry. 'Does anyone know how a sharpened bike spoke got into the prison?'

The warden spread his hands wide, and leaned forward with studied patience. 'They're criminals. They do that sort of thing, you know.'

Gerry leaned forward with equal emphasis. 'We're police. We're supposed to stop that sort of thing, you know.'

The warden shrugged.

'You send undercover into my prison there's always a risk someone will hear about it. Maybe if you'd let me know I could have kept an eye out for him. As far as I'm concerned, I had a big terrorist in lockup and some prisoners got to him. One less burden on the tax payer – end of story.'

'He was one of ours,' said Tau.

'Not ours. Yours.' Said the warden, pointing his finger. 'Like I said, if you'd told me I could have helped. And one more thing I'll tell you for free – if there's an enquiry into this I'm not eating the shitty end of the lollipop.'

Tau got to his feet.

'We're leaving now. But you can be sure there will be an enquiry, warden, and nobody will escape scrutiny. However, your own situation can be helped by mounting an investigation into who killed Chris Pieterse and how they got their information.'

'As the Pope said to the Bishop, "Kiss my Ring."' Said the warden, lighting another cigarette.

Tau and Gerry left without another word.

In the car Tau passed the paper to Gerry. 'Take a look,' he said.

Written on the paper in Chris' small neat hand were three names – Rashid Khan, Mustafa Ali and Six Moreno.

'Fuck!' said Tau. 'That poor bastard! We've got his blood on our hands.'

'Nobody forced the guy to go,' said Gerry. 'We warned him.'

'Come on! We pitched it to him. He was like a kid, so keen to show what a big *bok* he was!'

'The guy wanted to prove himself. So fucken what?' yelled Gerry. 'We all did! You. Me. We did a million dangerous operations!'

'Ja, but we're still here and he's lying on a slab.'

'I know,' said Gerry angrily. 'I know and I can't do a damn thing about it, other than trying to do my job and find out what the hell is going on here! Someone is leaking information and it's coming from right at the top!'

'Chitepo? Bullshit! I'd swear on my mother's grave that it's not him,' said Tau vehemently.

'I'm not saying it's necessarily him, but it's someone with access to the inner sanctum. That's all.'

'Ja, well maybe this Internal Affairs guy from Jo'burg will find the mole. Meanwhile, we need to put in some hours tracking down these other people.' He tapped the list that the warden had given him.

'I wish Chris had left something more,' said Gerry.

'It's enough to start,' said Tau.

'I've been thinking,' said Gerry. 'Should we put out an APB on Sayeed Dhatri? I mean, if he's splashed on every newspaper and TV in the country the guy won't be able to break wind without someone noticing.'

'My feeling is that it's a last resort. If we flag up that we're onto him then he could just disappear. I'd rather try and track him down and nail his whole cell rather than just cut the head off the snake and watch another one grow.'

They drove back to town in silence. A room had been set aside in the basement of HQ and the team from the airport was there. The mood was downbeat and nobody greeted Gerry and Tau when they entered. A whiteboard had been put up at one end of the room and Gerry marched up to it and picked up a pen. He wrote on the board 'Rashid Khan – Mustafa Ali – Six Moreno.'

'Right,' he said. 'These names were found in Chris Pieterse's cell. His brief was to locate any senior PAGAD men who had not been arrested or were not on our main radar. I don't know if these are the men, but we have to check them out anyway. Any of these names ring any bells?'

For a moment nobody spoke then Sipho spoke.

'I came across Mustafa Ali a couple of years ago. It was rumoured that he was bringing in large quantities of Mandrax from Amsterdam. We couldn't ever catch the guy and after that he pretty much dropped out of sight. Rumours were that PAGAD had a little talk with him and told him to fall into line.'

'If Chris was right then he's moved up the feeding chain. Anyone who has international smuggling links would be of great use to the organization. Any of these others?'

There was no response.

'Okay,' said Gerry, 'there's some procedural stuff we need to put in place. Here's the thing – this investigation is to be conducted under maximum secrecy. That means that nobody outside this room knows anything.'

'If you need a photocopy, do it yourself. Don't ask a secretary to make a call for you or set a meeting. Nothing. This is a strictly need-to-know operation,' said Tau.

'What the hell's going on, Tau?' asked Jez. 'Everything we do is supposed to be strictly secret anyway.'

'Ja, but we all involve others in our work. This time we do everything ourselves.'

'Is there a leak?' asked JoJo.

'Put it this way,' said Tau. 'Chris went into Pollsmoor in deep cover. Twenty-four hours later he's dead. Someone, somewhere, said something they shouldn't have. We will operate a strict pyramid with Gerry and me at the top. All notes and records are to be stored in this room. We will brief every morning at eight sharp.'

'That's our first angle,' said Gerry handing out files 'Next, we need to do background on these guys – all low-level PAGAD and all employees at the Mount Nelson.'

'Anything else?' asked Jez.

'Ja,' said Tau. 'The cherry on the cake.' He stuck up a picture of the young Sayeed Dhatri. 'Him. Sayeed Dhatri. Head of the Cape Town cell that we believe was planning the Koeberg attack and is now planning an attack at the AIDS conference.'

Gerry passed out more files.

'He's gone AWOL. We'll break into teams. Fix and JoJo you take the Chris Pieterse contacts. Sipho and Jez, you do the Mount Nelson employees. Tau and me will chase Dhatri. These leads will all overlap to some extent, so it's important that we liaise often and keep up to date. Get to it.'

'And make sure your weapons are clean and ready to go and your phones are charged. We don't want to be butt-fucked because you forgot to put ten Rands on your phone credit. These guys are planning something major and we know that they're lethal.'

Sipho put up his hand. 'Question – there are seven names on our list. If we speak to them one by one isn't there a chance that the others will get wind and bugger off? What if a team of uniforms picked them all up at say 4AM tomorrow morning then we can interrogate them without fear of tipping off the others.'

'Good idea,' said Gerry. 'Again, the uniform guys don't know anything other than they are making arrests. Anything else?'

'Do you think they've got a chance of pulling it off?' asked Fix.

'The AIDS conference attack? You bet,' said Tau. 'They came within a hair of acing the nuclear plant at Koeberg. The summit is a much easier target.'

'Except we're onto them,' growled Fix.

Nobody seemed convinced as they filed out of the office.

Chapter 44

At Nelspruit Police Headquarters Chief Inspector Mangope was sweating as he stared at the rumpled rucksack on his desk. Shosho's body lay in the meat locker in the basement, awaiting a post mortem certificate. He carried no ID and his fingerprints hadn't thrown up a hit on the national computer. The Chief Inspector knew that Shosho would remain a John Doe, unrecognised and unmourned.

The Desk Sergeant entered and dropped a file on his boss's desk.

'It's so hot you could fry an egg in the carpark,' said the Sergeant.

Mangpe grunted, wondering if his Sergeant meant frying the egg on the tarmac itself which would result in getting bits of gravel in the yolk, or if he meant using a pan, which would take some considerable time to heat up. He realised that he was involved in this pointless speculation because he was frustrated, and reluctantly turned his attention to the file marked MARAIS.

The Chief Inspector had brought in the posse of white farmers who swaggered and preened and exuded an air of confidant braggadocio until the Chief Inspector had put them into separate cells and taken statements one by one and then compared them. He knew that the men had concocted the story about coming under attack from the fleeing man, but no court would be able to disprove it, and quite frankly, the Chief Inspector's strained resources didn't warrant launching a pointless prosecution that would only inflame the already strained relations between the local farmers and the state.

He had cut the men loose and they had gone straight to the nearest hotel bar where they spent many rowdy hours drinking and regaling each other with stories of their bravery and prowess. In point of fact, the Chief Inspector actually understood that after a number of unsolved murders of white farmers in the valley, the killing of Shosho was seen as a victory for the farmers.

Though not overtly political, the Chief Inpsector recognized that the war against South Africa's farmers was a hidden conflict. Since the campaign had started more farmers had been killed than in the whole of the Zimbabwean war, but nobody mentioned it. The conflict had its roots in the issue of land distribution. Many of the landless peasant farmers in the rural areas had felt that after independence the government would seize the vast white farms and parcel them out to subsistence farmers, but this had not happened and the simmering anger was increasingly spilling over into violence. It fell to men like the Chief Inspector to pick up the pieces, and while not exactly covering up the crimes he was not broadcasting their rise either.

He understood that the reasons the government had not undertaken wholesale land seizures were twofold – first, they realised that the white farmers fed the country and were a major earner of Foreign Exchange through their agricultural exports. Second, and more important, South Africa's image as a magnet for foreign investment would be badly hit if there were to be a mass takeover of white-owned farms. This would be seen as nationalization by the back door, and the government was keen to project an image of a progressive, developing economy.

Mangope also knew that the government was working steadily behind the scenes to buy out farms and hand them over to black farmers with the requisite skills and expertise so that the country could continue to grow and prosper, and the issue of land inequality could be methodically redressed. The warning about handling the land issue wrongly could be seen from Zimbabwe, which had gone from being a net exporter of food to being a basket case reliant on charity from the rest of the world. In Zimbabwe the land had been seized from the whites in an arbitrary fashion to try and buy a few more votes for an ailing dictator whose grip on power was being eroded, and sacrificing the white farmers was a small price to pay for his continuing tenure.

The Chief Inspector knew that as pressure for land reform grew, more violence would inevitably follow. Many of the landless were taking inspiration from their neighbours in Zimbabwe who had simply driven the white farmers off the land and then squatted the farms. The clandestine war of intimidation and was now spilling over more and more into outright murder, so that when a farmstead was attacked, it was hard for the police to establish whether the motive was political or purely criminal. Mangope's loyalty was to the law, but he felt there was a certain justice about blacks seizing land that may have been taken illegally from them, even if it was 200 years ago.

It sat heavily with the Chief Inspector but he knew his duty, and marked the death of Shosho as 'self-defence.' However, something else was nagging at him, a tiny fragment of a clue that excited his interest. He laid out all of the rucksack's contents on his desk and went through them again, trying to find the small anomaly that had piqued his interest. There was a knobbly chunk of stale bread, a gnawed stick of biltong, a canteen of water, almost empty, a small brown bottle containing black capsules which the Chief Inspector assumed to be speed, a leather sack tied with a thong which contained Sannie Marais' rings and jewellery, a neat stack of Rand notes still bound with a paper bank strap, a compass, a cell phone, and the pistol, ammunition and diver's knife. There was also a box of matches with a Mozambique logo, which indicated where the dead man had come from. There was one other thing that the Chief Inspector noticed – on his feet the dead man wore hi-end Reebok hiking boots. He recalled that 15 months previously the farmer who lived in the crook of the valley had been murdered, and when the police had found the body he was barefoot.

The Chief Inspector sighed, regretful that he hadn't caught Shosho alive, but at the same time relieved because there was one less armed criminal roving along the border. Then he saw it – a small scrap of greasy grey paper that contained some foreign writing on one corner.

He lifted the greasy fragment of paper carefully with the tip of his pen and put it on the clean blotter in front of him.

'Thomas!' he roared. The startled lieutenant skidded into the room almost immediately. 'Yes sir?'

'Do we have a magnifying glass here?'

Thomas frowned and then his face lit up. He turned to go.

'Wait! I also want you to go and get Betty. Right away.'

'From her work?' asked Thomas anxiously.

'Exactly. From her work. Get her boss to ring me if there's a problem. It's national police business.'

The words had a magical effect. Thomas stood up straight and snapped off a salute and rushed out of the office. He returned a moment later and put a large Sherlock Holmes-type magnifying glass onto the desk.

'Where did you find this?'

'Captain Du Preez collects stamps,' said Thomas proudly, and dashed out of the office.

The Chief Inspector looked carefully at the letters on the greasy paper. They appeared to be Russian. The Chief Inspector was no expert but he had spent some years in Zambia with the ANC, and much of their materiel came from the USSR and the Chief Inspector had in fact expended many hours laboriously trying to translate a landmine manual from Russian into English with the help of a dictionary that lacked most of the critical words. Something was nagging at him – he knew that he had seen such paper previously and thought back to the dusty camp near the Zimbabwe border. He was suddenly inspired and turned to the Internet and called up the Cyrillic alphabet. He managed to translate the fragment …'ublic of Czechos.'

What could a thief in the middle of the African bush be carrying that came from the Czech Republic? All at once it came to him. He recalled the day that young Godwill Ndlovhu had arrived in camp in a state of high excitement with a wooden crate labelled as 'tractor parts.' Underneath a pile of scrap metal were ten small sausages of Semtex, bearing the same greasy wrapping. He also recalled how a few days later Ndlovhu had blown off his hand while trying to detonate a small lump of the plastique. The Chief Inspector carefully put the scrap into a plastic bag for sending to Pretoria for further analysis, but he knew that it would confirm what he already suspected.

As he was pondering the significance of his discovery there was a polite tap on the door and there stood Thomas with his girlfriend Betty. She was as wide as he was lanky and the pair had the aspect of a comedy team, but Betty was bright and determined to get ahead in life, and the Chief Inspector was in no doubt that she would be able to instil some backbone into his somewhat lacklustre lieutenant.

'Thank you for coming,' said the Chief Inspector. 'Should I give Mr Jaspers a ring?'

'No sir,' said Betty. 'It's my lunch hour anyway.'

'Good. I need your help, Betty. On a security matter. Most sensitive.'

Her eyes grew wide.

'Please, put these on,' said the Chief Inspector handing her a box of latex gloves. She looked around at Thomas who nodded gravely and she snapped on a pair of the gloves. The Chief Inspector pushed the cell phone across the desk to her.

'I understand that you can tell who called this phone and also get a log of calls made.'

She brightened. 'Oh yes, sir. It's not hard. There's an interface at work which lets me download that information from any phone,' she said brightly.

'This is a vital piece of evidence and I don't want it removed from the station. Is it possible to bring this ..uh..*interface* to the office here and plug it into my computer?'

She sucked her teeth dramatically. 'Look, there's no problem as far as I'm concerned, but you really should talk to Jaspers first.'

The Chief Inspector nodded and picked up the phone. Betty dialled the number. A moment later the phone was answered.

'Ringtones, good-day. Barry Jaspers speaking. How can I help?'

The Chief Inspector told him quickly what was needed and five minutes later the safari-suited Jaspers stood in the office holding a lead with a strange coupling at its end.

'Can I bill the police for this?' he asked.

'No,' said the Chief Inspector. 'You are doing your civic duty and helping to solve a murder. The nation will thank you.'

'Hey, no need to need to be arsey. I've got a business to run.'

'Well you should go and run it. Betty will help me and I'll send her back as soon as she's finished.'

Jaspers turned and walked out. Betty picked up the cell phone and inserted the plug into the base then put the other end of the cable into the USB port at the back of the Chief Inspector's computer. Thomas was watching in slack-jawed amazement.

'Thomas, go and finish the paperwork on the case while Betty does her job.'

Thomas looked injured but left. Betty was fixed on downloading a string of data from the phone and didn't notice his exit. She hit the print button and the printer whirred out one sheet of paper.

'Not much,' muttered the Chief Inspector looking at the paper.

'I'd say it's either a new SIM card or he only uses the phone for special purposes,' said Betty. 'This line here are calls made, and this shows calls incoming.'

'What's this?' asked the Chief Inspector pointing to a mixture of numbers and letters.

'That's an SMS message he received last night. There are no others.'

'But this doesn't look like a phone number. It looks more like a number plate,' he said.

Betty shrugged, unplugging the umbilicus from phone and computer and coiling it neatly up. 'If there's nothing more then I should get back.'

'Thank you,' said the Chief Inspector. 'If Jaspers gives you a hard time just let me know.'

'He's OK,' she said and exited the office. Moments later Thomas put his face around the door.

'Everything all right, sir?' he asked.

'Excellent,' said the Chief Inspector. 'She's a fine young woman. Treat her right,' he said. Thomas puffed up with pride and carefully shut the door behind him.

The Chief Inspector stared at the paper. The SMS was worrying him. He accessed the Vehicle Registry and tried punching in the numbers. The computer thought about it for a few seconds then flashed up an answer – a Red Toyota Hilux registered to Hertz Car Rental in Long Street, Cape Town. He wondered why a cross-border thief carrying Semtex would be interested in the number plate of a Cape Town car when he was several thousand kilometres from Cape Town.

The phone had thrown up a number from which the SMS had been transmitted. The Chief Inspector dialled the number but received no signal and no message facility so he rung off.

He sat back and tapped his teeth with a pen – something wasn't right. This was not a simple case of banditry. He remembered that Oliver Chang from training school had been seconded to the detective branch in Cape Town. He would give him a ring, but first he should await confirmation from Pretoria that the paper scrap had indeed been used to bind a cylinder of Semtex.

Chapter 45

Tau and Gerry had emailed the mug shot of Sayeed to the flight school near Stellenbosch and Leon Wessels had immediately replied that the photo was indeed that of the man who had recently completed his instruction under the name of Farouk Parveen. Their next stop was the flagship store of Dhatri Brothers.

Tau and Gerry walked through the acres of sofas and dining suites until they found an office at the back, presided over by an elderly Asian man with black rings around his eyes and a bad comb-over. He glanced up at as they knocked on his door.

'We're looking for Sayeed Dhatri,' said Tau, flashing his badge. The old man put on a pair of bifocals and studied the badge carefully then seemed to deflate slowly.

'I am Sayeed's father. What has he done?'

'We need to speak to him on a range of matters,' said Gerry. 'When was the last time you saw him?'

'Must have been a month ago. Since then, nothing.'

'Do you know where he's living?'

'He had a flat in Deep River, but he said that he was going to see some people in Jo'burg. I didn't want him to go.'

'Who was he going to see?' asked Tau.

The old man shrugged. 'He didn't say. He just said goodbye and left. Didn't even bother to see his mother.'

'Please think carefully,' said Gerry. 'Did he ever mention any friends, girlfriends, anyone in Johannesburg?'

'No. I just had the feeling he was getting in with a bad lot.'

'Why do you say that?' asked Tau.

'He was always very…intense. I know he wanted to do things for his community, but I always said: get a good career, a qualification, then you can help people. But he would never listen…'

'Do you know if he was ever involved with PAGAD?' asked Gerry.

The old man's face hardened in an instant. 'Those rubbish! They think you can make things better by shootings and stabbings! I warned him about those people. I warned him!'

Just then, an angular young man with an unruly mop of black hair entered the room.

'Any problems, Poppa?'

The old man waved vaguely at Tau and Gerry.

'Police. Looking for your brother.'

'Sayeed is dead to us.' said the young man firmly. 'Now, please, can you go? You're upsetting my father.'

'You don't know where he might be?' asked Tau.

'No. I heard his place in Deep River burned down. Too bad he wasn't in it.'

'Final question: do you have a recent photo of your son?' asked Gerry.

The old man sighed again, pulled open a drawer and produced a glossy 8x10 in a cardboard frame. It showed a family gathering around a groaning table. To one side stood Sayeed, looking sullen and aloof.

'Thank you,' said Tau. 'When was this taken?'

'Last year. My 70th Birthday.'

'We need to take this away to have copies made and then I will return it to you,' said Tau. The old man was no longer listening, staring into space.

Half an hour later Tau and Gerry were driving along De Waal Drive.

'Not much love lost there,' said Gerry.

'That stuff about PAGAD – he must have been involved from early on. The old man didn't seem to like them one little bit.'

Just then, Tau's cell phone rang.

'Tau? It's Jez. We were reviewing some old security tapes here at the Mount Nelson and who do we see making a reservation at the desk? Our blue-eyed boy.'

'Sayeed?'

'In person. And he's chatting with that youngster, Mohammed.'

'Excellent,' said Tau. 'Keep on it. Let's cook Mohammed until he gives something up.'

'Let's revue,' said Gerry, glancing at his watch.

'We've got to go to the range,' said Tau.

'Dammit, I forgot,' said Gerry. 'Can we do it now then catch a bite?'

Tau shrugged. Gerry cut across three lanes and took an off-ramp.

The shooting range was in the basement of an anonymous government building that housed a local tax office and the main vehicle registry. There was an outdoor range as well but neither Tau nor Gerry felt the need to waste an hour just for the joy of seeing the cordite puffs disappear into the open air.

There were six lanes, with paper targets hung from mechanical pegs that brought them to the shooter on the touch of a switch. The instructor was an old Pole called Vladek. He had a constant nasal drip that he treated with a spray, and so earned the nickname of Vlad the Inhaler. Uniform cops were using two of the lanes. Vladek came over and gave Tau and Gerry some ear muffs.

'I haven't seen you for long time,' sniffed Vladek.

'Ja,' said Gerry. 'Been kinda busy.'

'Too busy to remember how to shoot straight, eh?'

'I do OK,' said Gerry stiffly.

'We see,' said the instructor, fitting two new targets into their holders and sending them to the end of the lane.

'Come on,' grumbled Gerry, 'that must be over 25 metres.'

'You want gunman to always be six feet away? Now shoot. Ten rounds then we check. You too, Mister Tau.'

Gerry and Tau took up position in adjacent lanes.

Gerry managed four shots in the inner ring, Tau five. Gerry was irritated.

'Now look,' said Tau in as condescending a manner as he could muster, 'you've got to just squeeze it gently.'

'Fuck you and the horse you rode in on,' muttered Gerry. 'Another ten rounds, and I have 20 Rands says I beat you.'

'Watch,' said Vladek. He produced a handgun and aimed carefully then shot ten rounds in rapid succession. He brought back the target and revealed that he had achieved ten out ten.

'Now you boys stop playing and start getting serious. If you need headshot then it no good to say Wait! I still got six shots! I not give you certificate until you get all ten in inner circle.'

After an hour Tau and Gerry had improved their skills to the required level and had cleaned and oiled their weapons and finally were able to leave the building.

By this time Gerry was in a filthy mood because he was missing his daily dose of saturated fats, sugar and carbohydrates. He put the blue light on the roof and hit the siren and raced through town and pulled up with a screech outside the Hungry Heifer. Tau shook his head in silent disapproval at using the emergency equipment, but Gerry was beyond caring.

'Double Heiferlump with jumbo fries on the side and a coke float,' he barked at Missie in the serving hatch.

'Coming right up, boss,' she said with her gap-toothed smile.

'I'll have a toasted cheese and ham with an iced coffee, Missie,' said Tau, turning to Gerry. 'You're still pissed 'cause I beat you at the range, aren't you?'

'You didn't beat me,' said Gerry, his eyes small and flinty. 'You beat me by one shot on the first round then we were level pegging then I got the full ten first! If that's being beaten then I'm a Dutchman's uncle!'

Tau looked at him for a moment then burst out laughing.

'You ARE a bloody Dutchman's Uncle – look at your nephew, Neelsie. I believe his full sobriquet is Corneels Johannes Willem Jocobus De Jager. He couldn't be much more Dutch if you put him in clogs and gave him a clay pipe.'

Gerry shook his head and also started laughing. They both laughed hard until the tension had ebbed, then they settled down and faced the more pressing issues.

'OK,' said Tau. 'Sayeed may be in Jo'burg.'

'Or he may be in bladdy Timbuktu for all we know.'

'What's in Jo'burg?'

'Money. Stupid tourists. Mine dumps.'

'Not many Muslims.'

'Are you doing a spot of racial profiling?'

'Look, the vast majority of terror incidents worldwide in the past five years have all involved militant Islamists, and mainly Asian ones at that. I'm not getting many hits on white old ladies. All I'm suggesting is that if he's gone to Jo'burg it must be for a very specific reason, and if he's working within a tight-knit cell structure the chances are that his brothers will also be young Asian Muslim men.'

'But it isn't very likely, because Jo'burg doesn't have a big Asian Muslim population.'

'Where does?'

'Cape Town. And of course Durban…'

The words hung in the air for a few moments while Gerry attacked his burger. Neither he nor Tau wanted to look too hard at the Durban option because Durban had the single greatest Indian population outside the sub-continent, and to start an investigation with a police force from another city and no local informants of their own would be slow and tortuous. But the possibility could not be overlooked.

'Next question – would he necessarily tell his parents where he was going anyway?'

'Not if he's planning a major terror attack. Of course he bladdy wouldn't.'

'Ergo, he could still be here, or possibly in Durban.'

'But he needs to move around. His Mazda must be somewhere.'

'Perhaps he got rid of it, or changed the plates. Or bought another bike.'

'Then there are flights, trains. This guy must be leaving footprints behind him.'

'Maybe we should check in with Charlie. He's had a lot of material to go through since we discovered the cache in the mosque. You're right – he can't mount an operation of this size without support. And although forensics are about as much use as tits on a bull when you're on the ground, this is the kind of stuff they're good at,' said Gerry, hurling his paper napkin into the wire waste bin.

Chapter 46

Sayeed and Hamidullah reached Cape Vidal by early evening. The camp was located in a small wildlife reserve carved out of the semi-tropical bush which served as a holiday base for fishermen and tourists. Cape Vidal was 200 kilometres north of Durban, bordering both Lake St Lucia and the Indian Ocean. Lake St Lucia is a freshwater lake that lets into the sea and hosts a unique species of crocodile that can exist in both saltwater and freshwater. The Lake has been designated an area of outstanding natural beauty and has been declared a World Heritage Site, and in the short drive from the gates to the log cabin compound, Sayeed and Hamidullah had marvelled at the number and variety of game, including a white lipped rhino and her calf, a herd of buffalo and numerous Springbok and other antelope.

They took a log cabin at the far end of the compound. Hamidullah was delighted by a small troop of yellow macaque monkeys that chattered onto the veranda and promptly stole all of the fruit out of his cool bag, and then one of them had run off with sunglasses. Sayeed had become irritated and told Hamidullah to come inside and shut the curtains.

'When are you going to fill me in?' demanded Hamidullah, who was becoming tired and hungry. He prepared a Spartan meal from the few canned goods that they had, and grumpily set it before Sayeed.

Sayeed spent the next hour describing the plans for the simultaneous attacks on the G8 leaders at the Mount Nelson and on the USS Alabama that would be berthed at Simonstown. Sayeed would lead the assault on the Mount Nelson by flying his crop-dusting plane loaded with Semtex into the convention, bringing down the entire hotel. Hamidullah would drive the speedboat bearing the half ton of ammonium explosive straight into the side of the Alabama, while on shore one of their men would be drawing the ship's fire by launching a couple of Igla anti-aircraft missiles at the aircraft carrier.

Hamidullah was fired up with enthusiasm and admiration for the taciturn Sayeed. He knew that his star would be amongst the brightest when he took his place in Paradise.

'But we are two,' he said. 'Who else will join us?'

'I will need one other man, you will need at least two, making our cell a five people unit. Things are getting hot and the NIA are all over us, so we can either use known faces or we can activate one of our sleeper cells. You are my second in command – what would you do?'

Hamidullah thought for a moment. 'The experienced people mean that there is less chance of cock-up on the actual operation, but the new faces are not known to police so there is less risk of being intercepted before we get under way. I would suggest one experienced man to work with you and me, and one newcomer.'

Sayeed was pleased with this analysis and felt that he had somewhat under-estimated his fellow warrior. 'I want to bring in Rashid Khan as my Number Two,' said Sayeed. 'Who do you want?'

'There's a bloke I know from the early days. He still does a bit of cleanup work but he's been quiet for some time so should have no heat around him. His name is Yussuf Anwar.'

'I know Anwar,' said Sayeed. 'He's a good man and a strong heart, but has he got the courage for a martyrdom operation?'

'His wife died last year. I know that he's eager to meet her again in the life hereafter.'

'And the sleeper?'

'You are the one who knows the sleeper cells,' said Hamidullah. 'You should tell me.'

Sayeed thought for a moment, and then sucked his teeth. 'Young man. Been active in the movement for some time but holds down a job and keeps a very low profile. His name is Hakim-Quddus.'

Hamidullah choked on the Coke he was drinking. When he got his breath back he spluttered 'That white boy? The convert?'

'His previous name was Martin Chisholm, but when he took the faith he took the new name.'

'But how can we trust him?' demanded Hamidullah.

'He has embraced the one true faith. He is loyal, dedicated and wants to become a jihadi. Besides, the security forces will be looking for brown faces only. Being white, he can probably go places where we can't.'

'I still think you should test him,' said Hamidullah.

'Oh, I intend to,' said Sayeed. 'And if he doesn't rise to the standard which our faith demands, then…' He gave Hamidullah a sinister grin.

Hamidullah grunted. 'Look,' he said, 'let's go back to the little town. It's only about 15 kilometres. I can't eat this shit.' He angrily held up a tin of corned beef. 'There's a steakhouse on the outskirts.'

ayeed leaped up, his pistol in his hand. Hamidullah opened the curtain and fell back laughing when he saw it was just monkeys.

Sayeed exhaled slowly and put his gun away. 'Let's go,' he said, 'all this nature is driving me crazy.'

They drove out of the compound as the sun was starting to sink, the suck and roar of the Indian Ocean audible behind the line of scraggy palmetto palms.

Chapter 47

Charlie was buoyant and humming softly 'The sun has got his hat on, hip hip hip hooray!'. He was wearing a Hawaiian shirt and baggy surfer shorts that hung at half-mast, exposing an unattractive hairy arse crack whenever he bent over.

'Are you becoming a surf bunny?' growled Gerry.

'Ah. Agents Viljoen and Molepe. My favourite defectives.'

'Have you been in the contraband cupboard?' asked Tau. 'Sampling the stock?'

'Just trying to spread a little cheer. Isn't that so, Katja?'

She looked up from behind her desk and gave the cops a slow wave.

'We're hap-hap-happy here in forensics,' she said.

'Good,' said Tau. 'We like a bit of *joeie de vivre*. But even more than happy-clappy, we enjoy results. What have you got for us, Charlie?'

'If you don't take time to smell the flowers...' said Charlie, about to embrace his theme of universal one-ness and the cosmic imperative, but stopped suddenly as Gerry stepped forward cracking his knuckles ominously.

'We are making headway,' he said quickly. 'Not spectacular, but solid. Katja now has the full inventory of the room under the mosque and everything transcribed from the computer's hard drive. And – guess what? That sniper rifle in the cellar – a Russian SV-98 - it fired the bullet that took down Moosa Ibrahim and the plainclothes cop and that civilian in the Beemer on Boyes Drive. '

'So if nothing else we've got the guy on first-degree murder.'

'Well, if you can prove he pulled the trigger, yes.'

'Anything new?'

Katja smiled and held out a plastic folder for Tau. 'Lots,' she said.

'The thing is,' said Tau, 'we know the guy's identity. We know what he looks like. Oh, by the way, Charlie, can you copy this and do a blow-up,' he said, producing the Dhatri family photograph and pointing at Sayeed.

'What we don't know,' said Gerry, 'is where he is. He used a false name for his flight school training and his vehicle registration. He must have shown documents that were convincing.'

'There were 16 passport blanks at the mosque,' said Katja. 'He could have used one of those.'

'But unless the guy's a forger he would still need someone to stick in the picture and laminate it and provide all the stamps. And I don't think he's a forger. He used to be a furniture salesman.'

'But now he's a killer,' said Charlie. 'People change.'

'I think Gerry's on to something,' said Tau. 'This guy needs support – he must be getting money from somewhere and documents. With fake ID and a ready source of finance he can stay out of sight for a long time.'

'What forgers do you know about?' asked Gerry.

'The bad ones,' said Charlie. 'If they were any good they wouldn't be in here.'

'We need to speak to CID,' said Tau.

'Were you able to look into bank accounts in the name of Farouk Parveen?' asked Gerry.

'Zilch,' said Charlie. 'Not even a Post Office savings book. And, no surprise, there's no National Insurance number either. And no passport. So he obviously has a full set of phoney docs.'

'What about in Dhatri's own name?'

Charlie sucked on his teeth and opened a file. 'Ja, here we are. He's got 458 Rands in the Standard Bank. No withdrawals for the past four months.'

'We need to put a trace on his cash point card and on the account. Any action and we have to be notified immediately.'

'Have you got the paperwork? I can't go around just freezing accounts without the necessary authorization.'

'You have the authorization. From me.' said Tau, looking him hard in the eye.

'If I could say something,' said Katja They all looked expectantly at her. 'If he's not maintaining any banking arrangements then he must be relying on cash.'

'It takes a hell of a lot of cash to put an operation like this together,' said Gerry. 'I don't think he earned it selling sofas.'

Katja opened the safe and held up a sparkling stone.

'Blood diamonds,' she said. 'In the past month we must have had a dozen at least come in from various raids. Last year we saw exactly two.'

'So you're saying our boy could be cashing in diamonds whenever he needs some hard cash?'

Katja smiled and shrugged. 'You're the detectives.'

The CID headquarters were in an old colonial building downtown. When Tau and Gerry entered the detectives' room the place was empty except for a lone figure sitting at his desk, typing a report on his computer with a laborious two digit hunt-and-peck technique.

'Just love those dancing fingers,' said Gerry. 'If I ever want a secretary I know where to find one.'

Oliver Chang looked up with a glare, then his face broke into a grin.

'Well, we are honoured. Hotshot One and Hotshot Two, visiting our humble detective division. Obviously you want some real work done.'

Tau and Gerry shook Oliver's hand.

'You guys busy?' asked Tau.

'Us? Nah. The criminals have all gone on holiday this month, so we're just standing around scratching our arses.'

'No change there then,' said Gerry.

Tau quickly outlined the need to put all jewellers on notice about people wanting to cash in raw blood diamonds.

'Not to mention fences, pawnbrokers and drug dealers. Anyone handling diamonds will be our number one priority,' said Gerry.

'Been a couple of busts lately where the stones have appeared,' said Oliver. 'We just thought it was some guys coming from up North with whatever they could carry. You think there's something more to it?'

'Can't give details,' said Tau, 'but there is a major security angle here. The guy at the centre of this is certainly the worst we've come across. It's not the money we care about, it's what he's using the money for.'

'This wouldn't have anything to do with that so-called Egyptian who was gunned down by the airport?' asked Oliver.

'Ja, and you can factor in Achmad and Chris as well. That's just the ones we know about. I can't say any more right now.'

Oliver held up his hands. 'OK,' he said, 'I'll speak with Boytjie Steyn. He used to head up the IDB squad for years. He knows more about diamonds than De Beers.'

'Great,' said Gerry. 'There is something else. This guy is deep underground because he has access to first-rate forged documents. ID, Passport, Identity Documents – the works. Who in Cape Town is capable of putting together an operation like that?'

Oliver looked hard at them for a few moments, and then sighed. 'Look, we've been watching this guy for 14 months now and we're almost ready to bust him. He has graduated from doing driving licences to full ID sets and now he's starting to turn out American Dollars. Quite crude, but he's getting better all the time.'

'I understand,' said Tau. 'I'll get Chitepo to speak to your boss.'

'The boys on the ground aren't going to like it.'

'Since when did *like* have anything to do with anything,' said Gerry. 'Who else have you got in the frame if this bust turns bad ?'

'Two others,' said Oliver. 'One is a small-timer who works in his garden shed. The other is more geared up, but still a novice. I'd say if you're looking for the good stuff, then our target is the one.'

'Thanks,' said Tau, shaking hands once more.

'One thing,' said Oliver. 'When's Chris Pieterse's funeral?'

'Tomorrow,' said Gerry.

'He was a good kid,' said Oliver.

Gerry nodded and held out his hand. Oliver shook it.

'You'd better find who did it,' he said, and returned to his report.

Chapter 48

Hamidullah and Sayeed were finishing off their meal at the St Lucia Tuck Shop. There was only one other customer and the atmosphere was slow.

'What's this *à-la-mode* shit?' grumbled Hamidullah. 'If all they mean is *with ice cream*, why don't they just say it?'

Sayeed looked at him and didn't bother to reply. His apple pie hadn't been properly heated and was cold in the centre. He would have been happy to get an early night without traipsing back into town, but Hamidullah needed some food and so Sayeed obliged.

The cell phone in Sayeed's pocket gave a short blip. Sayeed fished it out and read the text message. He smiled at Hamidullah.

'Drop off 6AM tomorrow. There's a Diaz Cross about 30 K's north of here. That's where he'll be.'

Hamidullah nodded. 'That means we have to be up by 5AM,' he said.

'Yes. So we should finish up here and get back.'

The camp was dark apart from one cabin when they returned to it. Sayeed locked the cabin door securely and checked out the accommodation. The beds were fine but the bedding was slightly damp from the salt air, but both men were exhausted. At least the hot water worked properly and after having showered they went to their bedrooms and prepared for what sleep they could get.

The monkeys spent the night clambering noisily across the roof. A bird with a piercing scream would cry out every time Sayeed was drifting off to sleep, and the constant roar of the surf had him burying his head under the pillow. Eventually, at 4.30AM, he walked into Hamidullah's room and roughly shook him awake. Sayeed's irritation was further increased by the fact that Hamidullah had slept deeply and awoke feeling refreshed. They made some black instant coffee and Hamidullah produced a couple of Lion Bars for breakfast., They were driving out of the camp by 5 AM as the first fingers of a lead-grey dawn were starting to penetrate the darkness.

They got lost a couple of times because the beach where the landing was due to take place was not marked on their map, but then Hamidullah finally found a small cross on the map and argued that the place indicated was the Diaz Cross. They turned off the single strip road onto a track and Hamidullah engaged four-wheel drive. After ten minutes they emerged onto a small cove of white sand. At one end an ancient stone cross stood at a steep angle, having been battered by wind and spray for over 600 years. In fact it was not a genuine Diaz Cross, as erected by the Portuguese explorer Bartolomeo Diaz as he sought a route to the Indies, because Diaz had only managed to explore the East Coast as far as Mossel Bay, when he turned back. The journey had been taken further by Vasco Da Gama in 1497 who had sailed up the East Coast as far as Zanzibar then made it across Indian Ocean to landfall in India. It was Da Gama who had erected the marker, proclaiming the Kingdom of Prester John for Portugal and for Christianity.

At one end of the beach was a Nissan Pathfinder, and standing in the surf holding a sea rod was a thickset fisherman. He turned when he saw the Hilux emerge from the dunes and waved briefly then resumed his fishing.

'Oh shit,' said Hamidullah. 'Now what?'

Just then Sayeed pointed to the horizon where a small fishing boat was visible, making its way slowly towards the shore.

Sayeed indicated that Hamidullah should stop. They were about a hundred metres from the fisherman, their vehicle pointing out to the ocean. Just then a light flashed on the deck of the fishing boat. Three times. Sayeed flicked his headlights three times in reply. The fisherman turned around and looked at the Hilux again. Sayeed cocked his pistol and put it into his pocket.

'Do you want me to come?' Hamidullah asked, anxious.

'No,' said Sayeed. 'Cover me. Wait until I call.'

Sayeed walked along the cold sand towards the fisherman. The man was wearing bathing trunks and stood in the water, with a sweatshirt around his upper body. As he got closer Sayeed could distinguish his features. He was overweight and red faced with a mop of unruly brown hair. His strong blunt hands fiercely gripped his reel and short stubby rod. A steel peg was driven into the wet sand and a keep net was tethered to the peg, half immersed in the water, heaving with large silver fish.

The fisherman squinted at Sayeed.

'Morning,' he said. 'Yellowtail are biting,' he gestured at his keep net. Sayeed nodded, his hand in his pocket.

'You here for the fishing?' asked the fisherman.

'Yes,' said Sayeed and took out his pistol and shot the man in the head. The fisherman dropped into the water and bobbed in the surf, face down. His rod started to drift out on the waves. Sayeed gestured for Hamidullah and he came at a run.

'Jesus,' said Hamidullah, staring at the body.

'Look in his truck for a spade. We need to bury him.'

Hamidullah nodded and pulled the man out of the surf. He crossed to his Nissan and threw back a tarpaulin. The fisherman had everything for an extended camping expedition and Hamidullah quickly found a short-handled foxhole shovel. He dug a hole at the top of the beach near the tree line and he and Sayeed quickly pulled the fisherman into the hole and covered him over. Hamidullah found some heavy stones nearby and piled them onto the grave to prevent animals digging up the body.

When they turned to look out to sea again they saw a small powerboat heading towards them. One man was standing in the prow holding a rifle while the other held the tiller. The man in the prow was wearing a loosely knotted turban and waved at Sayeed.

Ten minutes later Hamidullah had waded into the surf and was helping to pull the small boat ashore.

'Salaam Alaikum' said the man in the prow.

'Alaikum Salaam,' Sayeed said.

'Quickly now,' said the man, in heavily accented English. He passed Hamidullah a long thin crate and another one to Sayeed. They stashed the crates on the beach then pushed the boat back into the water. The man at the tiller spun the little craft around and headed back to the fishing boat at high speed. The entire operation had taken less than an hour.

Sayeed grinned at Hamidullah. 'Let's get this into our truck and get back to Cape Town.'

They put the two crates into the flat bed and then took a variety of camping equipment from the fisherman's truck and covered the wooden crates so that nothing was visible. Hamidullah started the engine and turned slowly around.

By 8 AM they were back on the main road, heading towards Durban and then the Garden Route Back to Cape Town. The first part of their mission had been accomplished they were buoyed by success.

Chapter 49

Aletta had woken early to strange noises. Gerry was in the kitchen, attempting to iron a shirt while eating a bacon sandwich, doing neither especially well. She put her arms around him and hugged him. There was nothing to say – it was the morning of Chris Pieterse's funeral and Gerry had fallen into a deep depression the night before. It took half a bottle of whisky for him to start talking and then the words had poured out. He had fallen asleep nestling against her shoulder and had woken with a stiff neck, a filthy hangover and vengeance in his heart.

Tau was also silent and withdrawn, and Joyce had sent him to meet Gerry earlier than the arranged time because she felt that he needed to be with his partner. When Tau arrived he found Gerry waiting. He climbed into the car without a word and they drove to the cemetery in silence.

The funeral was as awful as anticipated. Chitepo had trouble finding words of consolation through the usual clichés and platitudes, and Chris' elderly parents stood to one side, their faces grey with grief and shock. Chitepo had visited them on the night of Chris' arrest to explain that it was an undercover operation and that his reputation would be restored once he had learned all he could, but instead he had had to visit their small house 24 hours later with the news which no parent can bear to hear.

Gerry hadn't heard most of the service. He spent his time brooding on the nature of the enemy that had brought such grief and pain, and savouring the terrible revenge that he would exact upon them. 'Revenge' was frowned upon these days, it needed to be the administration of justice. Swift, decisive justice that allowed no room for legal niceties – in this situation his father's words of an 'eye for an eye' seemed to make perfect sense. Tau too was removed from the service, his rage tempered by a bottomless guilt. He felt responsible for Chris' death, not because he had lured him into an operation that he knew to be dangerous, but because he hadn't intervened to stop the young man becoming a victim of his own hubris.

Although Gerry was arguing that Chris was a responsible adult and a police officer who knew the risks, he too felt a lingering guilt that he had somehow put Chris into a position that had ultimately cost him his life. But for both Tau and Gerry introspection was of limited value when there was still a job of work to be done, and they excused themselves from the ceremony as soon as was decent.

As they headed for Tau's car Oliver Chang came up to them.

'You got a sec?' asked Oliver.

'What's up?' said Tau. 'Lots of uniforms are giving us the evil eye.'

'The boys are feeling bad that one of our own is being put in the ground. So soon after Achmad, too.'

'Not half as bad as we feel,' said Tau. 'It was our operation. Everything was watertight, but somehow word got out....'

'Ja,' said Gerry. 'He made his choices like the rest of us. If we wanted a safe job we could have found work in the post office!'

'Whoa! I'm not here to bust your balls,' said Oliver. 'I just had a call last night which might mean something for your investigation.'

Gerry exhaled slowly. 'Sorry for jumping down your throat,' he said. 'A guy I knew from Pretoria is now Chief Inspector in Nelspruit,' said Oliver.

'Poor bastard,' muttered Gerry.

'Anyway,' said Oliver, 'rolling straight along, it's a long story but the upshot is he found a guy who he believes carried Semtex across the border from Mozambique.'

'Interesting,' said Tau, 'but this is relevant how?'

'Here's the kicker – the guy had a number on his cell phone that belongs to a car registered in Cape Town. So my mate called me to see if we knew of any action going on down here with high explosive. Now in CID we're just the normal robbery, murder and arson, but I thought I'd share with my obnoxious buddies from NIA.'

'Can we speak to him, the guy with the Semtex?'

'Not unless you know a good medium.'

'I don't suppose you've got the Cape Town number plate?' said Tau.

Oliver handed him a slip of paper. 'Hertz. Downtown. And the number of the cell phone which sent it. Have a nice day,' he said and disappeared.

Because of the funeral, the daily debrief had been set back to 11AM. Tau and Gerry arrived on time and found everyone there.

'Listen up,' said Gerry. 'We've just been to bury Chris Pieterse and it was pretty grim. However, we've had what could be a lead. But let's recap first. Who wants to kick off? Fix?'

Fix flipped through a notebook for a few seconds. 'We started with the first one on the list, Rashid Khan. We went round to his house and met his mother who said he was at work at the Hi Fi Warehouse. We went to his work and they said he hadn't turned up for six months, so we went back to his house and the place was locked up. We've left one plainclothes guy hanging around seeing if Rashid comes back. He's got a record – he used to be a car thief when he was younger but, after 18 months inside, he came out a reformed character. A devout Muslim. Guess where he used to pray?'

'The 11th Street Mosque,' said Tau.

'Correct. Then we tried to get hold of Six Moreno. We couldn't locate him – Six is obviously some kind of nickname. We located an Elifas Moreno who is 63 years old and works for the Parks Department. There was also a Chamba Moreno who is 34 and works for Ned Bank. He's also leader of a gospel choir. But no *Six*.'

'You need to look at the 11th Street Mosque again,' said Gerry.

Fix shrugged. 'Final one on our list is Mustafa Ali. As we know, after being a Mandrax importer he's totally dropped out of sight. Dead end.'

'Jez? Sipho?'

Jez opened his notebook. 'Some movement here. The uniform boys did their thing this morning and we managed to grab six of the seven.'

'Good work' said Tau.

'I can see the posters now –*Free The Mount Nelson Six*,' said Sipho.

They all chuckled. 'Anyways, we've been speaking to young Mohammed Butt – the desk clerk kid - and after toughing it out for an hour, he suddenly wilted when I said we were going to tell his mother he was a major terrorist and wouldn't be out before he was 97 years old.'

'I hope you had a lawyer present,' said Tau.

'No. But we got it on tape. That's the thing – our jihadi turned down our offer of a brief: he wanted to become a martyr until we told him he would end up being buggered rotten in jail and would enter Paradise on all fours.'

'What did he give?'

'He said he was approached by a certain man – we ID Sayeed for him and when we showed him the tape he started to spill his guts. He said he knew Sayeed from the 11th Street mosque and knew he was a big man in PAGAD and so when Sayeed had booked a room, Mohammed said he would do whatever he could to help. We asked him if he knew who his guest was and he said no. I believe him.'

'Good,' said Gerry. 'Sipho, anything to add?'

'We asked about who set up the switch around the cleaning van and he said Sayeed had given him a note to pass to the cleaner.'

'So Sayeed knew all the PAGAD men at the hotel. I think we should tell that snotty Englishman that his hotel is a nest of vipers.'

'Have we got the cleaner?' asked Gerry.

'He's in the tank. He's our next call as soon as we leave here.'

'Good. We've got a lead, a bit of a long shot but worth a look. Some bush cop caught a guy carrying Semtex across the Mozambique border, and he thinks it's bound for Cape Town. The guy had a contact – a CT number plate. We're going to check on it right now.'

'If it pans out then it means they're shipping in the hard stuff,' said Sipho.

'It also might just put our boy somewhere in Mpumalanga Province. Which means we have a chance of picking him up on the road home.'

'Let's get to it, people,' said Tau.

As everyone started dispersing the sole phone in the room started ringing. Gerry snatched it up. 'Ja?'

'It's Chitepo. I've spoken to the head of the CID and they're raiding the suspected forger's place tonight. You want in?'

'Absolutely,' said Gerry. Chitepo gave him the address.

'There is one other thing,' said the boss. 'I am having a joint security ops briefing tomorrow morning. I want you and Molepe there.'

'Very good, sir,' said Gerry. 'Which heads will be there?'

'The whole lot. USA, UK, France, Germany, USSR, Japan, Italy and Canada. And they'll all be looking to you – to us – to bring them up to speed on current security arrangements.'

Chapter 50

Sayeed and Hamidullah had been making good progress, sticking to the speed limits and driving carefully so as not to attract attention. It had taken nearly four hours to reach the environs of Durban when they connected with the maze of motorways that finally put them on the road back to the Transkei and the Eastern Cape.

Sayeed was driving when he turned on the radio to catch the midday news. He heard the newsreader say that the American forces in Iraq had scored a significant blow against Al Queda with the killing of their Iranian leader, Tariq Dar. The report went on to detail a heavy firefight on the outskirts of Mosul, with two Americans wounded and half a dozen jihadis killed, amongst them the notorious Tariq Dar.

Sayeed hit the brakes so suddenly that a Ford behind him almost rear-ended them, and the driver had gone past waving his fist.

'What is it?' said Hamidullah.

'Those filthy sons of whores! Those lying bastards!' screamed Sayeed.

'But what?' said Hamidullah, mystified as to why his leader was becoming apoplectic. Sayeed realised that Hamidullah didn't know the identity of the mysterious visitor, nor the untimely manner of his passing. He calmed down slightly.

'The enemy is clever,' he said by way of explanation. 'Never forget that!' He resumed driving in a more normal manner. But his brain was racing – the Americans knew that Dar was assassinated in a minibus near Khayalitsha, so why were they claiming to have killed him in action halfway around the world? Sayeed realised that the game had entered a new phase, a level of psychological tactics that he had not previously encountered, certainly not when working as a cut-rate vigilante taking down crack dealers in the township. He knew that the National Intelligence Agency was sending him a message of sorts, but he couldn't divine the sense of it. He also realised that he had no choice but to proceed.

'Look,' he said to Hamidullah, 'the cops are aware of this operation and after the discovery at the mosque I'm sure they must be aware of me. The issue now is how do we get the stuff back to Cape Town without being busted on the way? We could detour via Gauteng but that would add another day to the journey, or should we put our heads down and go for it – the sooner we're back in the Cape the sooner we can disappear.'

Hamidullah felt honoured to be consulted on a matter of strategy, although Sayeed just by verbalising the problem had already arrived at his solution. 'I was the one who hired the Hilux,' said Hamidullah, 'so there's no direct link with you there. And I also used false papers, so we should be safe to carry on the shortest route back home.'

'I agree,' said Sayeed. 'But I don't trust that black bastard who gave us the explosive. He knows the number plate.'

'We could steal some new plates,' said Hamidullah.

'That might help but if the cops are on the lookout for a red Hilux they'll pull us over anyway. There is one other option…'

'What's that?'

'There is a sleeper cell in Durban. Perhaps they could exchange the vehicle for us.'

'You don't think we're just being a bit paranoid?'

'Tariq Dar was gunned down in Cape Town two days ago! By the fucking NIA. Now they put out this ridiculous story that the Americans killed him in Iraq! You tell me if I'm being paranoid!'

Hamidullah's mouth dropped open. 'That was Tariq Dar? In Cape Town?'

'Yes. He is our sponsor and the main planner. And now we must carry his work forward.'

Hamidullah thought for a few seconds, and then indicated a turnoff to North Durban. 'Let's go and see our comrades,' he said.

Sayeed put on the indicator and the Hilux left the motorway, heading for Durban's Northern Suburbs.

'One more thing,' said Sayeed holding up his cell phone. 'From now on, no more phones.'

Chapter 51

Tau and Gerry were going to the downtown Hertz depot when Gerry looked at the scrap of paper on which Oliver had written the information. He suddenly slammed his hand on the dashboard, causing Tau to swerve violently.

'What the hell!?' barked Tau.

'This number – does it ring any bells?' said Gerry.

'Most phone numbers ring bells,' said Tau tartly.

'This is the number that we tried calling from Charlie's place.'

'The Namibian connexion?'

'No. The other end. The Cape Town end. And I bet my arse against a used Q-Tip that this is one of the stolen SIMs. Could even be our blue-eyed boy!'

Tau cut across a couple of lanes of traffic and turned off towards the forensics laboratory.

They rushed inside to find Charlie waxing a boogie board.

'How's it hanging, dudes?' asked Charlie.

Gerry pulled the board out of his grasp and stowed it under the desk and rested his feet on it.

'Hey! Give that back!'

Tau took Charlie's upper arm in a steel grip and steered him to a desk and sat him down hard.

'Now listen here, Charlie Brits,' said Tau, his voice dropping an octave. 'While I enjoy seeing you reinvent yourself as a middle-aged lunatic trying to recapture a youth he never had, this is neither the time nor place.'

'Hostile,' said Charlie. 'You're frankly hostile.'

'No. A kick in the nuts is hostile,' said Gerry, drawing back his leg.

'Sheesh, you guys need to chill. I gather you're invading my headspace for a reason?'

Gerry put the paper down on the desk and stabbed the phone number with his finger.

'Whose number is this?' he demanded.

'That's Cape Town unconfirmed ID, the same sequence as the mosque SIM cards.'

'Have you had a trace on this?'

'No,' said Charlie. 'We can't keep traces on all lines at all times.'

'Try now,' said Tau.

Charlie sighed and stood up. He fiddled with a jack plug on a circuit board and put on a headset. He dialled some numbers from a keypad and moments later they heard a click.

'Telcom? Ja, Charlie Brits. We need to see an activity log on this number…'

He gave out the number and drummed his fingers while he waited. He cupped his hand over the mouthpiece and addressed Gerry. 'Maybe you should threaten to kick this guy's arse too?' Just then the Telcom operator came back on line and spoke for a few seconds. 'Thanks,' said Charlie. 'You able to find where it was sent from?' He waited a few more seconds the said 'Thanks mate. I owe you one,' and hung up.

'They recorded message text two nights ago from somewhere in Eastern Mpumalanga. Since then – nothing.'

'Thanks,' said Tau. 'Please keep a monitor on this number, Charlie. I think it's our boy.'

Charlie nodded. 'Katie! Keep this log updated and let Tau and Gerry know if there's any action.'

She gave a thumbs-up and continued with her work.

'Conference?' said Gerry.

A South Easter was blowing and fine sand was leeching the colour out of the daylight. Everything seemed bright and harsh, as if lit through yellow Cellophane. The sea was undulating in oily swells, the wind catching a light spume and blowing it onto the shore.

'I'll have a tuna salad,' said Gerry.

Tau swung his head around as if stung. 'What? What happened to your high fat, high carb diet?'

Gerry patted his belly. 'Letty thinks I'm starting to pork out. I need to get down to my svelte fighting weight again.'

Tau shrugged. 'Pastrami bagel, please Missie, and sparkling water.'

They sat on the bench eating in silence, until a gull hopped up, looking for scraps. Gerry absentmindedly threw it a piece of lettuce. The gull, initially excited, picked up the leaf in its beak then dropped it and walked off, offended.

'I agree, pal,' said Gerry. 'Fit only for rabbits and lesbians.'

Tau gave him a sideways glance and shook his head.

'What?' said Gerry. 'Should I rather have said 'homosexuals of either gender.' You're right, I shouldn't have excluded the *moffies*.'

'That's much better' said Tau. 'I'll get the Gay Police Association to invite you as their guest speaker.'

'The phone call links our boy in with the Semtex and the Eastern Mpumalanga,' said Gerry. 'I think we should put out a traffic alert on all vehicles coming from Durban.'

'Let's get to the car rental place and see what they have. It's good to know who's on this trip.'

At Hertz they encountered a pretty young woman sporting a name badge that identified her as BRIGID. Tau smiled at her.

'Brigid with a *d*, that's unusual,' said Tau.

She shrugged and smiled, revealing a brace on her top teeth.

'My folk*sh* like to be different,' she said by way of explanation.

Tau nodded and handed her the slip of paper bearing the Hilux's number plate. 'Who booked this vehicle?'

She glanced anxiously at her boss seated at a corner desk.

'Mishter Shnyman?' She said. Mr Snyman glanced up with an irritated grimace.

'We don't reveal that information,' he said and resumed work.

'Hey, you. Snyman,' said Gerry. 'Please see what you can do to help.'

Snyman looked even more irritated. 'I already told you,' he said.

Gerry walked slowly to Snyman's desk, leaned over and prodded him in the chest. Hard. 'Now I'm telling you. This is my ID – call the Head of the National Intelligence Agency, Jonas Chitepo, and explain to him that you're being arrested for impeding a major security investigation. Oh, and tell your wife, if you've got one, which I doubt because you're such a hopeless sack of shit, that you won't be home for Christmas.'

Snyman's face took on a mottled hue like fine Roquefort. Breathing stertorously, he got up and examined Gerry's ID, then Tau's, as if he knew what he was looking at. Suddenly he smiled, not a pretty sight.

'Apologies, gentlemen, we may have got off on the wrong foot. Now, what did you want to know?'

Tau slid the registration across to him and the man quickly riffled through some cards and produced a docket.

'Here we are,' he said proudly as if he'd just made a major scientific breakthrough. 'Red Hilux, less than two thousand kilometers on the clock. Full spec. She's a beauty of a truck. Alloys, chrome pipes, bull bars.'

'Quite frankly,' said Tau, 'I couldn't care if it was an ox wagon with a broken wheel. I want to know who hired it.'

'Yes sir,' said Snyman, starting to sweat profusely. He fanned through some more paper. 'This is the fellow,' he said. 'Six Moreno. Bladdy funny name if you ask me,' he said with a smirk. Tau's eyes hardened.

'My father was called Six' said Tau. 'It means *slayer of the ignorant*.'

Tau snatched the document from Snyman's hand and stared at it for a moment. There was an address and various personal details.

'Photocopy this,' he said.

Gerry glanced around and saw the glass eye of a CCTV camera beamed on the front desk.

'Did you get him on CCTV?' asked Gerry.

'We must have,' said Snyman, mopping his brow with a dirty hankie. 'Bridgie, go see if you can locate the tape for these gentlemen,' he said.

She smiled and led them through to a cluttered back office where a row of tapes was neatly laid out on a shelf. She took one off the rack and popped it into a machine. She fast-forwarded through a blur of grey images, date stamped and time coded at the bottom of the screen. Finally she hit PLAY and the image stabilised. They saw a tall, well-built man wearing a baseball cap that covered most of his face, enter the office and walk up to the counter. He spoke to Brigid for a few moments then nodded and handed her some documents and a pile of cash.

'Stop there,' said Gerry. 'He paid cash?'

'Yes*h*,' said Brigid, 'for a week'*sh* rental.'

'Don't you take a credit card as backup?'

'He exs*h*plained that he'd just los*ht* his card and was*h* doing everything with cash and left an extra two thousand Rand*sh* a*sh* deposit.'

'That's pretty unusual,' said Gerry. 'I'm surprised Snyman accepted it.'

'We need to make our quota*sh*,' she said.

'OK,' said Tau. 'Run the rest.'

There wasn't much more to see. Hamidullah kept his face averted from the CCTV camera. While Brigid filled out the documentation he fiddled with a large globe that identified Hertz dealers worldwide. Finally she put everything in an envelope and handed them to him with a smile. He nodded and exited.

'That'*sh* it,' she said apologetically.

'Can you describe him?' asked Gerry.

She looked briefly perplexed, as they had just viewed him on tape, but seeing Gerry's intense stare she tried to recall him.

'Tall. About 1.85. And s*h*trong.'

'Colour?' said Tau.

'He was ..uh… coffee-coloured. Like an Indian,' she said.

'Not black?'

'No. I'm *shertain*. He could have been a coloured, but I think he was Indian.'

'Thanks,' said Gerry. 'We need to keep this tape. The lab will try and enhance these images.'

'Of *coursh*,' she smiled and passed the tape to Gerry then led them out into the main office. Snyman looked up anxiously.

'Everything alright, gentlemen?' he asked. 'Were we able to help?'

'A great help,' said Gerry. 'I'll mention it to Chitepo personally. He'll probably brief the President tomorrow and I wouldn't be surprised if it was on CNN by the evening and you get asked to address the United Nations the day after. Now you have a very good day.'

He exited, Tau following after him. Their final image was of Snyman flopping down at his desk and mopping his sweating brow.

'You did well,' said Tau. 'I think you're getting even more obnoxious than before.'

'Six my bladdy arse. Your Pa's name is Mandla. Don't you start pulling my bladdy chain now,' growled Gerry. 'We're finally starting to see some progress here.'

'Should we get this to Charlie now or can it wait until after the raid?'

Gerry glanced at his watch and saw that they had half an hour to get to Paarden Island and the rush hour traffic was starting to build up.

'Let's go and find our forger,' he said, sticking the blue light on the roof and hitting the siren.

Chapter 52

Sayeed pulled up next to Calcutta Café, a greasy little convenience store with a single petrol pump outside and a picture of a phone on the window. He told Hamidullah to have the car filled while he went inside to make a call.

The interior of the cafe was gloomy and smelled of stale cooking oil and curry. There was a Coke cooler near the door and a counter with a board advertising the various culinary disasters on offer. An Indian man with one eye blinked at Sayeed.

'What's a *bunny chow?*' asked Sayeed.

The shop keeper said nothing but lopped the top off half a loaf of white bread, scooped out the soft dough with his fingers and squashed it into a conical crown, filled the cavity with brown curried gravy and various unspeakable lumps and popped the crown on top and handed it to Sayeed.

'Bunny chow,' he said. 'Six Rands.'

Sayeed paid the money and took the offending loaf with some distaste. Just then Hamidullah entered the store and Sayeed handed it to him. His eyes lit up and he took the food outside and started eating hungrily. Sayeed shook his head.

'I need to phone,' he said. The one-eyed shop keeper pointed at a payphone in the corner. Sayeed had committed half a dozen key numbers to memory and dialled the relevant one. After a few moments a husky voice answered 'Ja?'

'Is that my cousin Deepak?' asked Sayeed.

There was a long beat, then the husky voice said 'This is Deepak. How is our uncle Sulli?'

'Sulli says Benares is hot,' said Sayeed.

'Where are you now?'

'Some place called the Calcutta Café in Verulam.'

'Stay there. I'll be with you in five minutes.'

The line went dead. Sayeed looked outside. Hamidullah was leaning against the Hilux, eating contentedly.

'How much for the petrol?' asked Sayeed. The one eyed man squinted at the pump, decided he couldn't read the dials and went briefly outside. He returned a moment later.

'Four seventy Rands plus another ten for the Cokes.'

'What Cokes?' demanded Sayeed.

One-eye gestured with a grubby thumb at Hamidullah.' Your friend wanted two litres,' he said. Sayeed said nothing but counted out the money and received his change in silence. Just then he saw a silver Datsun pull up outside and a shifty-looking character with long black hair get out of the car and look around. Sayeed went outside.

'Deepak?' he said.

'Howzit,' said Deepak looking less than delighted. He lowered his voice. 'We better get the fuck out of here. That old bastard is an informer,' he gestured at one-eye who stared through the window.

'Right,' said Sayeed. 'We'll follow you.'

They drove for about ten minutes until they entered a small wooded area, very hilly, covered with thick semi-tropical trees and dense undergrowth. The houses here were more ramshackle and on separate stands, the faces peering anxiously from windows were more suspicious. Finally Deepak pulled up outside one of the larger houses and came urgently to the Hilux as it coasted to a stop.

'Come inside quickly, neh.'

'There's stuff on the truck that needs watching,' said Sayeed.

'My son will watch it. Come.'

He led the way quickly inside. It took Sayeed a couple of moments for his eyes to register in the darkness but a young Indian woman in a saree sat silently in the living room. Sayeed nodded briefly. She ignored him and turned to Deepak.

'Who are these now? More rubbish, neh?'

'You shut your bloody face, woman!' said Deepak drawing back a fist threateningly. She shrunk away, expecting a blow.

'Go get us some food. These are important visitors.'

She shuffled off to the kitchen.

'Is it safe here?' asked Sayeed. Deepak shrugged.

'Police are raiding here all the time. Looking for *dagga*. What do you need?'

'I need the bloody toilet,' said Hamidullah. 'That food I just ate…'

Deepak pointed to a door along a dark corridor and Hamidullah fairly flew inside.

'Thank you for helping. If it was not urgent I would not have called,' said Sayeed. 'This truck — we have to get it and its cargo back to Cape Town. But the cops have the number plates and the van's description. What can you do?'

Deepak thought for a long moment then sucked his teeth.

'Suleman has a garage and paint shop. He can do a respray.'

'Excellent,' said Sayeed. 'How long?'

Deepak shrugged again. 'He's not one of us. He'll need paying.'

Sayeed nodded wearily. 'If he can do it overnight I'll give him a grand.' He said. 'And new plates.'

'Let me call,' said Deepak. He took his cell phone outside and muttered a few words then returned.

'He'll do it.'

'Is he reliable?'

'Ja. If he says anything to anyone he'll die. Good enough?'

Sayeed nodded. 'But what about your ..uh… merchandise?'

'That comes inside here. Can we stay overnight?'

'Of course,' said Deepak just as his sullen wife entered the room with a tray of sweetmeats. She silently thrust them down onto the low table and left the room.

'Let's bring the goods inside and then get the truck to the garage,' said Sayeed. 'We can eat later.'

Just then Hamidullah emerged from the toilet doing up his trousers and looking pale.

'Let's go,' said Deepak.

'One more thing,' said Sayeed, 'your wife – she won't mention this to anyone?'

'She better bloody not,' said Deepak.

Just then the door flew open and a young kid of about 12 years in jeans and a T-shirt rushed in.

'The *manne* are coming!' he cried.

'Where?' said Deepak.

'Just there by Sollie's place. They gripped him and his old lady. Found a whole sack of *poisons*!'

'We need to go now,' said Deepak urgently. 'You will have to stay the night with your truck in the garage. Leave at first light. I'm sure informers will tell the cops we've been here.'

They moved swiftly and minutes later were following the silver Datsun on narrow back roads, climbing steadily out of the small township until they hit a major road. Five minutes later they turned off again and Deepak pulled up outside the Lucky Ace Garage. A man in greasy overalls came out to meet them and had a hushed conversation with Deepak then opened the doors to the garage and ushered the Hilux inside. Moments later the doors shut.

'I got to go,' said Deepak. 'Insha Allah you will have good fortune.'

'Insha Allah,' said Sayeed. 'Stay away from your home until tomorrow. If the police cannot find you then you cannot say anything. Understood?'

Deepak looked away, then turned back and looked Sayeed in the face. 'I am ready,' he said. He embraced Sayeed and Hamidullah then let himself out through a side door.

Suleman looked the truck over. 'What colour do you want?' he said.

Chapter 53

Gerry cut the siren and took the blue light off the roof as they approached the industrial site where Raj Printers was located. Parked at one side of the road in sight of the premises was a Toyota Crown with a single occupant - Captain Coetzee of the CID. Gerry pulled in behind him and they slid into the Captain's car.

'Hi Captain,' said Tau.

'Can't say I'm pleased to see you,' said Coetzee. 'We wanted a few more weeks surveillance but Chitepo gave some sob story about national security. If we get a result on this it's my boys who get the credit, understood?'

'I don't give a rat's arse about credit, Captain. We just have to get some information and then we'll leave you to walk alone down Glory Road.'

'I don't much like your tone,' said Coetzee.

'You don't have to,' said Gerry. 'Look!'

He pointed. A couple of workers were starting to emerge from the factory unit.

'GO! GO! GO!' Yelled Coetzee into his walkie-talkie. Suddenly about 20 cops appeared from nowhere, sprinting hard towards the cinder block building, guns drawn, yelling for everyone to get down on the ground. Coetzee leaped out of the car and raced towards the place, followed by Tau and Gerry.

After about 20 metres the Captain's run had slowed to a stagger and he was gasping for breath as Gerry and Tau sailed past, legs pumping.

'Need to do some cardio!' yelled Gerry as he flew by.

By the time they reached the inner office Raj was lying on the ground, his hands bound with nylon cable ties. Oliver Chang was supervising the systematic clearing of drawers and shelves while another detective itemised the contents of the safe. Even from the doorway Tau could see half a dozen passports and various forms of ID.

'Hi,' said Oliver. 'You guys made me very unpopular when NIA instructed us to go in early.'

'Don't worry about it,' said Gerry, 'you were never that popular to start with.'

'Seriously,' said Tau, 'that tip-off you gave us yielded gold. Thanks.'

'We need to speak to this beut,' said Gerry indicating Raj.

'The deal was that we would take him downtown and you guys could have access,' said Oliver. 'This is still our bust.'

Gerry bridled, but Tau calmed him with a wave.

'Good,' said Tau. 'Let's get him there straight away.'

'They're still searching the premises.'

'That's CID stuff,' said Gerry. 'Our business relates to a set of specific false documents.'

Raj glared angrily at Gerry.

'Let's go,' said Oliver, hoisting Raj to his feet. 'See you downtown in 15 minutes.'

Gerry and Tau nodded and followed them out into the lowering dusk.

In fact it took half an hour for Raj to be booked in and then he refused to be interviewed without his lawyer present. Tau and Gerry waited in the canteen until finally the brief appeared. Henry Frolichman was Cape Town's leading defence lawyer, famed for his numerous victories and exorbitant fees that fuelled a lavish lifestyle. He was in his 60s and walked with a cane, the result of a car crash when he rolled his new Porsche on Hospital Bend. Tau and Gerry made their way down to the interview room where Henry was already in place with his client, whispering to each other while Oliver set up the tape recorder and video. Finally they were all ready.

'Before we start,' said Henry, 'I would like to be assured that my client was detained under proper procedures and that the warrant was correctly served.'

Oliver was starting to oblige when Tau put out a restraining hand.

'Let's cut to the chase, Henry,' he said. 'We aren't interested in criminal charges against your client – what we want from him is information.'

'What can you offer?' asked Henry, 'assuming, of course, that my client may be in a position to assist the police.'

'Regarding this specific case of document forgery, no charges will be brought. However, the CID will, I am sure, wish to lay other charges against your client.'

'And whatever help he gives you will not in any way be deemed admissible in any other counts which may be brought?'

Oliver sighed. 'We agree.'

'Excellent,' said Henry. 'Do you agree, Raj?'

Raj whispered to his lawyer who smiled broadly and patted his client's knee.

'My client will not admit on tape that he is involved in any way with forged documents,' said Henry.

'Look at it from this perspective,' said Gerry. 'We are in pursuit of a major terrorist whom we believe has been given substantial material assistance by your client. When, not if, *when*, we run him to ground we will be able to find the identity he has been using. If we are able to trace a link back to your client, we will prosecute him to the full extent of the law. Not under normal civil law, but under the terrorism laws as they apply.'

'Our offer is good for five minutes,' said Tau. He and Gerry and Oliver walked out.

They stood behind the one-way mirror watching Raj locked in earnest discussion with Henry.

'That sounded impressive,' said Tau, 'where did you get all that legalese?'

'LA Law,' said Gerry.

Henry waved at the glass.

'Showtime,' said Oliver, leading them back into the room.

'Gentlemen, in the light of wishing to assist our security services in dealing with this threat to our nation, my client will co-operate within the strict lines of enquiry delineated,' said Henry. 'But I should caution that any comments made cannot be used to incriminate my client. Is that clear?'

'Clear,' said Oliver.

'Right,' said Gerry. 'What ID did you give Sayeed Dhatri?'

'Whoa!' yelped Henry holding up his hand. 'That question contains so many infractions of the guidelines we've discussed that my client cannot possibly say anything.'

'Okay,' said Tau, breathing deeply. 'Does your client know what identity papers Sayeed Dhatri may be using?'

Raj whispered something to Henry who nodded sagely.

'My client cannot possibly know what identity Mister Dhatri is currently using,' said Henry. 'To make such assumptions would be presumptuous at the least.'

'This gets cuter by the minute,' said Gerry. 'Tell me Henry, when your lovely wife – Lydia, I believe, is out shopping for a new Carrera and the place is blown sky-high by some Islamic fundamentalist who doesn't favour sharing the planet with you, I hope you will remember this little chat.' He turned to Oliver. 'Throw the book at him so hard that he kisses his arse goodbye. And you' – he pointed a finger in Henry's face – 'should be struck off for failing to help your client when he had the chance. Now I'm going to find Jonas Chitepo and the Minister himself and tell him that your skanky client is helping international terrorists and should be dealt with accordingly. The Americans will want to speak to him as well, I'm sure. We will of course seize all of his assets and property and freeze all bank accounts.'

'Intimidation!' bawled Henry, standing and banging the desk.

'No,' said Gerry. 'Reality check. This isn't the movies and you aren't Clarence-fucken-Darrow.'

Gerry turned and stamped out. Tau shrugged and walked after him. They had gone barely five feet when Oliver opened the door and called after them.

'Canary time,' he said.

Tau was the first to re-enter the room followed by a reluctant Gerry.

'Speak,' said Gerry.

'This is all most…' said Henry but this time Raj held up his hand.

'I believe he is using the identity of Ishak Fendi.'

Tau put a pad on the table before Raj. 'Spell it,' he said. Raj wrote the name in block capitals. He and Gerry turned to leave.

'Hold it,' said Henry. 'My client has fully co-operated. I want your assurance that no further action will be taken on this case.'

Tau looked at Gerry, who made a great show of slowly looking at his watch.

'The time limit was five minutes. That was eight minutes ago.'

'Your filibuster cost your client three minutes,' said Tau sucking his teeth. 'Three minutes and it's another ten years. Bad move, shyster.'

'This is outrageous!' Thundered Henry. 'There is still rule of law in this country. I will fight you all the way to the Supreme Court!'

'Jeez, that's scary,' said Gerry. 'Tell you what Henry, since we keep our word, we'll honour the deal if your client is telling the truth. If he's bullshitting us then all bets are off. Are we clear?'

'As crystal,' said Henry.

'Excellent start,' said Oliver. 'Now, about the plates for American Dollar bills which we found in your safe…

Chapter 54

Sayeed and Hamidullah spent a restless night in the small back office of the garage, unable to sleep because of endless thumping of the compressor and hiss of the spray gun. Finally at five AM Suleman had come to get them.

The truck was a gleaming forest green, and sporting new number plates.

'What plates are those?' asked Sayeed.

'They're from a green Hilux registered in Maritzburg,' said Suleman.

'Great job,' said Hamidullah, patting the side of the car. His hand came away with a green smear on it. Suleman glared.

'It needs to bake under the lights for at least another hour,' he said. 'My cash?'

Sayeed nodded and reached inside his pocket. Suleman stepped forward as Sayeed whipped out his pistol and pushed the gun hard into Suleman's chest and fired. Blood splattered on the wall behind him and Suleman fell to the floor, his shirt filling with blood. He gurgled once then coughed and was still. Hamidullah pulled a dust sheet over the body and dragged him into the corner.

Sayeed felt alive and vibrant. The dawn was breaking and soon the roads would become busy. Inside the car the smell of paint was overpowering and they drove with their windows open, but within an hour had cleared the outskirts of Durban and were heading back to Cape Town.

In two days' time the foreign heads of state would arrive, and two days after that, on Friday the 28th, the attack would take place.

Chapter 55

The last thing that Tau and Gerry had done before going home for the night was to circulate a 'stop and detain' notice on a red Hilux bearing the registration CA 767 25 and carrying two Asians, Six Moreno and Ishak Fendi. Both men were armed and extremely dangerous, last seen in Mpumalanga Province. The alert had gone out nationwide and they felt certain that the truck and its inhabitants would be found, sooner or later.

Gerry staggered into his house after ten and was delighted to find that Aletta was still awake and that supper had been kept for him.

'You look shattered, sweetheart,' she said, pouring him a brandy.

'Thanks,' said Gerry. 'We're finally starting to make some progress. We've nailed down the IDs and the vehicle – someone, somewhere will pick them up. How was your day?'

'Interesting,' she said.

'Interesting as in good, or interesting as in bad?'

'Could be good. Louis Eksteen called. About the job in George.'

Gerry's jaw clamped tight. How often were Eksteen and Aletta speaking? How long had he had her phone number? He fought against his natural instincts and managed a half-nod. 'Ja. Go on.'

'Initially he wanted a full-time person there, but I told him that couldn't work for me. But he's found a young graduate and reckons that it could be a three day a week supervisory role.'

'But that would still mean you staying over?' said Gerry.

'I guess so. I said I'd talk it over with you and get back to him.'

Gerry's mind flew back to article he'd read in *Cosmo* in Chitepo's reception area called 'Why Men Don't Listen.' He put on his most attentive and considerate face. 'So?' he said, taking a long pull on his beer bottle. 'What do you think?'

'It's a great opportunity. I'd still have a partnership but it would be a bit smaller.'

'Three days a week? That would mean giving up your present job. Could you afford it?'

'I already spoke to Morne and he said I could do two extra shifts on Sundays.'

'Sounds like you've got it all worked out already,' said Gerry. 'Don't know why you bothered to ask me.'

'Is it always going to be like this? Is it the fact that it's Louis or is it that you want me to always be some second assistant?' Cried Aletta. She stalked out of the lounge and slammed the bedroom door.

Gerry sucked his beer for a few moments, feeling shame wash over him and at the same time a surge of pride in his fiancée, but his predominant desire was to meet Louis Eksteen and kick his sorry arse all the way to hell and back. He had once seen a photo of Louis with his arm around Aletta when they were students. In truth, he looked like a fairly timid sort with a pudding basin haircut and wing-nut ears and a stupid T shirt with 'Free Boksburg' written on the front, but in Gerry's mind he had become dazzlingly handsome, rich as Croesus, and a superlative lover, capable of transporting Aletta to regions that Gerry could not even dream of.

Gerry cracked another beer, sunk in dark thoughts. Knowing that he could no longer delay the inevitable, he squared his shoulders, sucked in his gut, and prepared to dine on a heavy portion of humble pie.

Tau had returned to an empty house, to find a terse note saying 'Where are you? We had a cocktail party at the university at 6PM.' Tau had shaken his head wearily, showered and climbed into bed. Moments later he was asleep.

By dawn, Gerry had done his best at reconciling with Aletta, but she was still angry with him and their breakfast passed in silence. Finally, as she was about to leave, Gerry had pulled her into his arms and said 'Look, I'm sorry, sweetheart. But the idea of us spending three nights a week apart doesn't sound like a marriage to me. You wanted my thoughts, here they are.'

'It was work,' she said. 'And I'm not going to take the offer. But it's a matter of trust, Gerry. Think about it.' With that she kissed him and went to work.

Gerry shaved carefully, put on his suit and tie and waited for Tau.

Tua had woken at about three-thirty to discover that Joyce hadn't returned. He slept fitfully until dawn, and she still hadn't come back. Tau's thoughts went to obvious concerns about traffic accidents and hospitals, but then became darker as he started to worry that her absence could be intentional. He tried her cell phone, which was turned off. He left a message, trying to sound more concerned than angry, then prepared for work. He was just backing his car out of the drive when Joyce returned.

'Hi,' said Tau. 'I was worried about you.'

'I was fine,' she said stiffly.

'Ja? Well you could have let me know. I thought you'd got mashed up.'

'As you see, I'm OK,' she said.

'Where did you spend the night?' asked Tau, concerned that the answer might not be what he was seeking. She paused, and then sighed.

'The party went on late. I was a bit drunk and so I stayed over at Rachel's place.' Rachel was a bright young thing who had recently joined Joyce's department and kept a flat close to campus.

Tau took her hands. 'Are we OK?' he said.

'No,' said Joyce quietly. 'I think we might need some help.'

Tau nodded. 'I can't promise when I'll be back. The case is developing very quickly. But I'll keep you posted. Oh, I'm sorry I missed the cocktail party.'

'No you're not,' she said.

'You're right. But I didn't miss it on purpose. Had I been here, I would have come, not because I love stupid damn cocktail parties, but because I love you.'

Joyce smiled sadly. 'You'd better get going. You look very smart, by the way.'

Tau backed out of the drive, not knowing what lay ahead. Ten minutes later Gerry plopped into the car with a sigh.

'Women,' he said by way of explanation.

'Another species,' said Tau.

Gerry nodded sagely and sighed once more. Something was bothering him.

'Tell me,' he said, 'are black women as difficult as white women?'

Tau sucked his teeth for a long moment before answering. 'Which question do you want me to answer first, the black part or the women part? Actually, I think they're all the same. Tricky.'

Gerry raised an eyebrow. 'You reckon? When I was growing up in Graaf there was this old Boer, Van Biljon, who every Friday night would screw his black maid. Everyone knew about it.'

Tau glared at Gerry. 'And? What's your point? Some racist shitbag who exploited the help. Nice.'

'Actually,' said Gerry, 'when the colour bar ended in '94 he divorced his wife and married the woman. They're one of the happiest couples I know.'

Tau growled something incomprehensible and stared stonily ahead.

When they arrived at Chitepo's office, Miss Naidoo told Tau and Gerry to proceed to the conference room at once. They went down a floor and opened the door to the vast chamber dominated by a U-shaped table bearing eight little national flags and nameplates. At the head of the table sat Jonas Chitepo, flanked on one side by Stanton Fitzwarren, who gave a small wave, and on the other a florid man with brown hair, the British delegate, Tobias Clore. The other G8 security officers were unknown to Tau and Gerry who stood somewhat awkwardly at the door until Chitepo gestured for them to enter and take up a position opposite him. A thick file was laid out on the table before each of them.

'Gentlemen,' said Chitepo. 'To bring you up to speed. We have spent the past hour discussing security arrangements in general, but request that you brief our colleagues on any specific threats that may arise. You kick off, Officer Viljoen.'

Gerry stumbled to his feet, his mouth suddenly dry.

'We have identified a terrorist cell which we believe will mount an attack on this summit. Probably on the final day when everyone gathers in front for the press conference.'

He sat down. The other delegates looked thunderstruck. The German, Joachim Schmidt, spoke.

'Who is behind this cell? Have you got them targeted? What is the nature of the attack? Should we cancel the proceedings?'

Tau stood up. 'The cell is funded by Teheran…' The Japanese delegate, Joshi, said 'PAGAD, yes?'

'To be clear, PAGAD is fairly benign and low key. These guys were a splinter faction who broke away and became radicalized. The operation was devised by Tariq Dar.'

There was a buzz around the table.

The Canadian delegate, Russell Hulme, said 'Didn't Dar get killed in Iraq recently?'

'He was actually assassinated by Shin Bet here in Cape Town,' said Chitepo. 'We issued the story about Iraq in conjunction with our American colleagues to send a message to Al Queda.'

There was some more buzz around the table, then Fitzwaren said 'Please continue your briefing, Tau.'

'We have identified the ringleader and his number two,' said Tau, 'we have also learned that the leader recently completed a pilot's course.'

Groans ran around the table.

'So he's going to try another 9/11,' asked Clore.

'Not quite. We believe that he will use a low-level plane like a crop duster to hop below the radar, and then fly the plane loaded with Semtex into the building.'

'And what are you doing to prevent this attack?' demanded the Italian delegate, Roberto Regazzi.

Gerry's face darkened. He didn't bother to stand.

'We are doing all we can'– he peered at the nameplate –'Robbie. We have put out an APB on the vehicle that the cell leader and his number two are driving, we have discovered the alias he's using, we've identified the likely source of the aircraft and the source of his explosives.'

'If you know who the leader is why haven't you detained him yet?' asked the Russian, Oblomov, who had so far said nothing.

'Because we wanted to take out the whole cell,' said Tau.

'This sounds too loose for me. I think I will have to recommend that my minister stays away,' said Lascelles, the French delegate.

'No change there then,' muttered Gerry.

'What?!' yelped Lascelles, furious. 'You run a shambolic, amateur operation whereby you cannot guarantee the safety of our heads of state and you expect us to collude?'

'I thought you guys were pretty good at collusion,' said the Canadian softly.

Lascalles leaped to his feet. *'Merde!'* he cried, pointing at the Canadian.

Chitepo thumped the table with his huge paw.

'Sit down Jean. This is not time for hissy fits. The French record is hardly one to brag about. To cut and run plays straight into the terrorists' hands. Sometimes 'no surrender' can be more effective than 'here's my backside, boys.' But more to the point, we closed down an operation to bomb the Koeberg nuclear plant a few weeks ago, and buried one of our best undercover agents. We lost another deep cover agent just last week while infiltrating this network. My people have now gained enough intelligence to thwart the operation, and we believe that the conference will pass off without major incident.'

Lascelles examined his nails for a moment, then said quietly, 'Fine words, Jonas, but if you recall, it was the French who were the go-betweens during the ending of apartheid because the ANC could not trust either the British or the Americans.'

'We're not here to score points,' said Chitepo, 'but to try and ensure that the conference passes peacefully and that our political masters can do what they are mandated to do – namely try and improve the lot of the AIDS sufferers worldwide.'

He pointed at the folders in front Tau and Gerry.

'Those files contain all of the security arrangements that have been put in place. Review them and come back if you feel that anything needs to be modified. And I believe Stanton has a few words.'

'Thanks Jonas,' he said, getting to his feet. 'The USS Alabama will be arriving tomorrow and be berthed at Simonstown with a two kilometre exclusion zone around it. The aircraft carrier will be the President's base while he is in Cape Town. He will daily attend the conference by helicopter…'

Gerry's hand went up. 'Excuse me, sir, but how secure is a chopper? They bring those birds down all the time.'

'There are two identical aircraft, nobody, not even me, will know which one the President is on until it lands and he emerges. But more importantly, each aircraft is fitted with the latest anti-aircraft missile technology, and will be supported from an AWAC circling above and two F-14's and Apache support from the carrier.'

'When does the President actually arrive?' asked Chitepo.

'I do not know,' said Fitzwarren with a smile, 'and even if I did, I am not empowered to tell you. Suffice it say Air Force One will touch down at a military airfield and the President will be flown straight to the carrier in ample time to attend the conference. Any further questions?'

The Frenchman raised his hand. 'Is there room for my President on the Alabama too?'

There was some laughter. 'If there's nothing more,' said Tau, 'then we'll get back to doing what we do best. Gentlemen.'

Gerry looked at the Frenchman, and coughed 'Arsehole!'

Tau and Gerry exited and rode the lift down to the basement where the team was waiting for their morning briefing.

'Nice,' said Tau. 'I thought you handled him with great tact and maturity.'

'Bladdy French dick,' said Gerry as they entered the windowless secure room that they were using for their operational HQ.

The briefing was quick and everyone was jubilant that Six Moreno had been identified and that they knew of Sayeed's new identity. Two more of the Mount Nelson PAGAD people had been interviewed but it was plain that they were small fry who knew nothing of significance. Gerry had said that Ishak Fendi should be fed into the computers, looking for a bank account, house address, anything to tie him down. The agents dashed off to their appointed jobs with a new sense of urgency. Tau tried calling Joyce but was patched through to Rachel's office. He was about to ask her what had happened the previous night, but thought better of it and just left a message saying that he'd called.

Chapter 56

The road was shimmering in the heat. A tin-coloured mirage floated off the tarmac and disappeared into the haze, to be replaced by another one in an endless cycle. There wasn't a cloud in the sky and the truck's aircon was pumping. They were travelling through the Transkei and were about 10 kilometres outside Umtata and were making good progress. Sayeed had just taken over the driving from Hamidullah when they rounded a bend and saw ahead of them a police roadblock. Hamidullah eased a bullet into the breech of his pistol as he slid it under the seat.

'Here we go,' said Sayeed. 'Get your ID ready.'

Hamidullah put his head back and pulled a baseball cap over his eyes, apparently napping, as Sayeed pulled the car to a gentle halt beside a young policeman who was holding a clipboard. His older companion sat in a yellow police van, drinking coffee.

'Morning,' said Sayeed affably. 'What's the problem?'

'Vehicle check,' said the cop. 'Can I see your Driver's Licence?'

Sayeed made a show of going through his pockets and had just located his new licence when he saw the names ISHAK FENDI and SIX MORENO together with their truck's original number plate on the cop's clipboard. Sayeed managed to locate his old licence and hand it to the cop. It said 'Sayeed Dhatri' and showed a younger Sayeed looking stonily at camera. The Cop checked the licence against his clipboard then waved them through.

'Thanks,' said Sayeed, and drove slowly away, checking in his rear-view mirror that the cops hadn't suddenly started chasing after them. He drove for a couple of kilometres in silence then Hamidullah exploded with a huge guffaw.

'That was close. Oh God, that was close!'

'They have our new IDs. Both of us. I don't know that we can keep going on this road.'

'Maybe it's time to ditch the car,' said Hamidullah.

'And how do we get another one?'

'Hijack. Steal. Buy.'

'Shit!' said Sayeed. 'How the fuck did they get the new ID?'

'I don't know, but there will be more roadblocks and you can bet that one of them will be smart enough to look in the back.'

'We're going to the Kei River Mouth,' said Sayeed.

'Why?'

'Because we're fishermen,' said Sayeed gesturing at the rods and tackle in the back.

The Durban police had been looking around the Lucky Ace Garage since 7.45 when Amir, Suleman's stolid, middle-aged receptionist had called in hysterics because she had found the garage open and on looking around had discovered her boss lying under a tarpaulin, drenched in blood and stone dead. By the time the cops arrived Suleman's mechanic, Shak, had also turned up and was gloomily watching as the police secured the site and waited for forensics to come and take body away. The cops noted that Shak didn't seem too upset by his boss' demise and learned that Suleman worked him hard and paid very little, and that Shak had been planning to go and find other work soon anyway. The interviewing officer, Detective Dube, made a note that he would need to discuss things later with Shak but was distracted by one of the junior detectives who came in holding a pair of number plates.

'Look what I found,' he said. 'In the bin outside.'

Detective Dube held a plate up for Shak. 'Ever seen this?' he said. Shak shrugged listlessly.

'Suleman was always messing around with stuff like that. I don't know what he got up to. I just did the spannering, yeh? Oil change, sparkplugs, new filters, that sort of thing.'

Detective Dube was about to press his point when he looked again at the number plate. It was somehow familiar but he couldn't place it.

'Hey!' he yelled at the young cop. 'Run that plate for me!' He turned back to Shak. 'Was Suleman running a side-line in false number plates?' Shak shrugged again as the detective burst in.

'Boss,' he said. 'We've got something. Cape Town has issued a national alert for this vehicle with a severe health warning about the driver.'

'Too late for him,' said Detective Dube gesturing at Suleman's body as the ambulance arrived. 'Is there a contact number in Cape Town?' He took out his cell phone and was about to dial when he looked again the scene before him.

'Tell me,' he said to Shak, 'when was the last time you or the boss spray-painted anything?'

'Last week,' said Shak. 'A rust bucket needed a paint job. An old Valiant. Piece of shit, but now it's a cool piece of shit.'

'And what colour was that?'

Shak pointed at a tin on a shelf with a red drip down the side. 'Carmine.'

'Uh-huh,' said the detective. He rested his hand on the cooling fins of the compressor – it was still warm. He opened the spray gun canister revealing a small amount of green paint still in the bottom.

'You haven't used green recently?'

'Nah,' said Shak lighting a Lucky. 'I'm positive.'

Detective Dube dialled the number referenced on the 'stop and detain' notice. It rang a couple of times and was then answered by a terse 'Ja?'

'Who is this?' demanded Detective Dube.

'You phoned me, you *poes*! Who are you?'

'I'm Detective Dube of the Durban Murder and Robbery Squad.'

'Sorry,' said Gerry. 'I'm Gerry Viljoen, NIA. What's your news, Detective?'

'Are you always so bladdy rude?' demanded Dube.

'Not always, but mostly. I said I was sorry, what more do want?'

'You know what,' said Dube, 'why don't you go fuck yourself.'

He hung up. Moments later his phone rang. Dube looked at the caller ID and refused to answer. The phone rang again with another number displayed. This time he picked up.

'Is that Detective Dube?' said a voice. 'I'm Tau Molepe of NIA. Please excuse my partner, but his haemorrhoids are killing him and he feels bad because he has a tiny penis, so try and overlook his inadequacies and tell me your news.'

Detective Dube smiled to himself. 'OK. We got a call at 7.38 this morning to a garage and body shop in North Durban. The owner was found shot dead. Outside we found the hot plates that you had circulated. The sprayer was still warm and had green paint residue inside. So if you want my best bet, you should recirculate your 'stop and detain' but note that the Hilux would now be a dark green.'

'Thank you,' said Tau. 'I know it's a long shot but you wouldn't happen to know what his new number plates were?'

'I'll see if any green Hiluxes have been stolen recently,' said Dube. 'Have a good day now.' And he hung up.

Tau and Gerry were sitting outside the Hungry Heifer. Tau noted that Gerry was tucking into his Jumbo fries and peri-peri Heiferdoodle – half a spring chicken soused in chilli - his salad days no more than a distant aberration. Tau was listlessly eating a toasted cheese and tomato.

The surf was high and the heavy crashing of the waves created a evanescent rainbow that hovered briefly over the breakers before disappearing only to reappear when the next wave burst.

'Charlie might be onto something with his surf bunny lifestyle,' muttered Gerry staring at the waves. 'Wouldn't it be nice – load up your Kombi, put your board in the back and head up the coast to Jeffries Bay. Sun. Surf. And if you can get a woman mad enough to spend her time doing that, perhaps a bit of the other as well. Not a bad life.'

'Do you and Letta still go running together?' asked Tau. Shortly after they met Aletta and Gerry would run each Sunday morning, for kilometres. With time this had started to ebb, but occasionally they still managed to find the time. Gerry raised an eyebrow in query.

'Why?'

'Just thinking,' said Tau. 'Shared interests, that sort of thing.'

'Uh-huh. You and Joyce got problems?'

Tau's mouth fell open. He was stunned by Gerry's insight and somewhat awkward about how to voice his concerns.

'Ja. I think we're drifting apart. Our worlds are so different.'

'Do you love each other?'

'Yes. But I don't know if that's enough any more,' said Tau.

'Used to be enough in the old days. Hell, a lot of the time they didn't even have that but made the marriage work.'

'Uhm,' grunted Tau. 'Anyway, let's get back to work.'

'If you need help, then find it. Don't just fuck up because you're too uptight to admit it. Joyce is worth fighting for – go ahead and fight.'

'Enough already!' roared Tau. 'Ten minutes ago you were ripping apart a chicken with your bare hands, now you're mister sensitive. Since when did you become all touchy-feely?'

'I was reading Letta's Fair Lady in the lavvie,' said Gerry with a shrug.

'This Detective Dube, whom you managed to piss off in only two sentences, has thrown up a big problem - if our boy is in Durban then we don't stand a chance.'

'But he can't stay in Durban' argued Gerry. 'What's he going to attack – the International Curry Convention?'

Tau shook his head. 'You are a deeply reactionary person,' he said.

'Oh, mister hoity-fucken-toity, what target is there in Natal that's worth blowing up? Especially when the world leaders are meeting in Cape Town? Huh? Answer me that?'

'OK,' said Tau. 'So we must assume he's coming back. And we must assume he's driving because he'd hardly fly with Semtex given the current state of airport security.'

'We should put out a flash that his truck might now be green. Basically the cops should stop anyone, anywhere, in a green Hilux and make their life hell until we find him.'

'And if he gets the stuff back here safely?'

'Then we're screwed.'

Tau held up the security-briefing file. 'We need to go through this. See what our international colleagues are cooking up.' Just then Tau's phone blipped and he frowned at the SMS message. 'Charlie – he says he's got something for us.'

Seven hundred kilometres away, Sayeed was still driving when they pulled into the small resort of Kei River Mouth, built on a slow wide estuary opening into the Indian Ocean. There were a couple of clusters of whitewashed *rondavels* with thatched roofs and Sayeed headed for the furthest camp, which had only two cars parked outside.

He had driven fast from the roadblock and they had made good time, and felt much more secure having turned off the main road onto the narrow trunk road that served the little community of Kei River. Sayeed walked into the cool bungalow at the entrance of the compound and pinged a brass bell on the counter. A moment later a sunburned man emerged from the back room wearing khakis.

'Good day,' he said. 'How can I help?'

'We need a couple of rondavels for two nights,' said Sayeed.

'Certainly,' said the man taking two keys off a board behind him. Each key was secured to a large wooden disc with a number burned in pokerwork on one side.

'How are you paying?' he asked.

'Will cash do?' said Sayeed. The man nodded and Sayeed counted out the notes. 'My friends will be coming through later,' he said.

'Doing a spot of fishing?'

'Yes. One last thing,' said Sayeed. 'Is there a phone in the room?'

'In this one, number 4,' said the man. 'We can provide bait and boat trips up the estuary if that's what you want. There's a restaurant just around the headland. Nothing fancy but good basic cooking. Enjoy your stay.'

'Thank you,' said Sayeed, 'we'll be fine.'

He got back into the Hilux and drove to bungalow number 4 and parked round the side behind a large bougainvillea bush, ensuring the vehicle was not visible from the road.

He and Hamidullah quickly brought the crates carrying the anti-aircraft missiles into the rondavel and the rucksack of Semtex, plus the rods and various bits of tackle. Finally Sayeed picked up the phone and dialled a number. After a few moments it was answered.

'Can I speak to Martin Chisholm please,' said Sayeed. In the background he heard someone yelling 'Maa-artin!' Finally the phone was picked up.

'Hello?' said Martin.

'Hakim-Quddus, we require your assistance.'

There was a beat, then the voice came back strong and confidant. 'What must I do?'

'Listen carefully. You must get a car - a *bakkie* - and drive to Kei River Mouth. At the Sea Breeze rondavels you will go to rondavel 4. If you leave now you can be here by early evening. Do you understand?'

'Yes,' said Martin, his heart hammering.

'You must discuss this with nobody. Understood?'

'I understand.' He hung up.

Sayeed then made a coded call to Rashid Khan and gave him a similar message. Then it was Hamidullah's turn to use the phone and he rang his old comrade in arms, Yussuf Anwar. Within six hours all of the conspirators would be gathered in one place and the final logistics for the attack would be readied.

'I don't like using the phones,' said Sayeed. 'But by the time they've worked out who were are and who we are speaking to we will be safe in Cape Town, preparing for Holy Jihad.

Hamidullah laid out his prayer map and they knelt down together, confidant that soon their names would be added to the roster of glorious martyrs for Islam.

Chapter 57

Tau and Gerry were on their way to the forensics lab when they received an urgent call from Chitepo's office. Twenty minutes later they entered the outer sanctum.

'Afternoon, Miss Naidoo,' said Tau.

'Gentlemen,' she said. 'The boss is waiting.'

Tau and Gerry pushed their way into the office where Chitepo was locked in conversation with a stocky man in a grey suit who looked like the manager of a small provincial bank. He took off his reading glasses and stood up as they entered, hand outstretched.

'Pat Kavanagh,' he said. 'Internal Affairs.'

Both Tau and Gerry gingerly shook hands.

'Sit down,' said Chitepo, 'Pat's been going through the upper echelons of the department with a fine-tooth comb. What have you found?'

'Thus far, a whole lot of nothing. We found a couple of low level leaks which probably require a reprimand, but as far as I can ascertain so far there is nobody with the degree of security clearance who could make the alleged security breeches.'

'Not alleged. Actual,' said Tau.

'As you like. I have interviewed all senior staff with two notable exceptions – you two.'

'Just hold on a bladdy minute!' said Gerry jumping up and pointing at Kavanagh.

'Sit down and listen,' rumbled Chitepo. 'You need to be screened same as everyone else. But rather than go through hours of slow and painstaking interviews and surreptitious background checks, Mister Kavanagh has agreed that you two can take a polygraph test. Shouldn't last more than a half an hour.'

'And if we don't agree,' said Tau softly.

'Then you will be on immediate suspension and we will take our time to trawl through every aspect of your lives to see whether or not you are the source of the leak. Also, it will be noted on your record that you proved unco-operative.'

Tau nodded. 'You've been through everyone?' he asked Kavanagh.

'There are only six people in this department with sufficient clearance to have access to this information. I have cleared all of them, with the exception of you two.'

Just then Miss Naidoo entered with a tray of coffee and biscuits. She smiled at Kavanagh and put the tray down in front of him.

'Thank you,' said Chitepo. She ducked her head and exited. Four pairs of eyes followed her from the room. When she had shut the door Gerry spoke softly.

'We'll be happy to take your tests, Kavanagh. As soon as possible. I've just got one question, sir,' he said turning to Chitepo, 'who does all your photocopying and places your phone calls?'

As one, they all looked again at the door. Chitepo sighed, 'Seven people have access to all this information. Not six,' he said to Kavanagh. 'Nobody is exempt from this investigation.'

'How could we be so bladdy stupid?' muttered Gerry.

'I should remind you that I still need to conduct an investigation,' said Kavanagh stiffly.

'Should have done it right in the first place then,' said Gerry smugly.

Kavangh's face turned beet red and he shuffled with the papers in his hands.

'I want to suggest two immediate courses of action,' said Tau. 'One, we let it be known that Kavanagh's work turned up nothing. We can then keep an eye on her – sorry, on the mole – and bust the entire contact chain. Two, we should set up a smokescreen of disinformation ASAP, then we can take her down.'

'Him or her,' said Kavanagh, weakly. 'We can't act on supposition.'

'Point,' said Gerry. 'Let's roll. Where's your lie-detector?'

Kavanagh had set aside an empty office and tested first Gerry then Tau, and they flew through the polygraph analysis. They were silent as they rode down in the lift, but once in Gerry's car Tau shook his head.

'Bladdy lie detectors,' he said.

'Stupid,' said Gerry. 'You can fool them, if you've got the right training.'

'Joyce was saying that there are some pathological liars who are so accomplished that none of their vital signs register any changes whether they lie or tell the truth.'

Gerry looked at Tau. 'It's her, isn't it? Miss Naidoo. Our fucken PAGAD mole right in the heart of the National Intelligence Agency.'

Tau nodded. 'Let's wait to see what friend Kavanagh turns up, but I know the outcome. We all missed it.'

'It's not what we were expecting. Besides, isn't everyone supposed to be vetted before they join the service, even if it's to make the tea?'

'It's good that we've found out who it is,' said Tau, 'so that we can stop any further leaks. If Sayeed and Six Moreno have somehow made it to Cape Town then they're preparing for the attack.'

'I just thought – those security briefing documents – do you think she had access?'

'Ja,' said Tau, 'she laid them out before the meeting started.'

'Okay,' said Gerry, 'we're going to have to brief everyone to explain why everything must be restructured.'

'They'll love that,' said Tau, 'especially when we tell them that it's because there was a mole in the boss' office.'

'Old Kavanagh didn't look too pleased when we pointed out who the mole might be,' said Gerry with a chuckle.

'I thought he was going to pop a blood vessel,' said Tau, joining in.

'That lie-detecting works up an appetite,' said Gerry veering off towards the Hungry Heifer.

'Weren't we on our way to the forensics lab?' asked Tau.

'Ja, but that was traumatic. Just a quick *snork* and then we can go.'

There was a raw edge to the wind, a distant harbinger of autumn. The waves were dark and troubled, and filaments of seaweed rolled in the water like coiled ropes. Gerry was scowling at his Noo Yawk Dog which had lost some its onions when Tau pointed to the horizon where a vast grey aircraft carrier was making its way sedately towards Simonstown.

'Jesus,' said Gerry. 'Look at the size of the bladdy thing.'

'The USS Alabama,' said Tau. 'A symbol of the world's last superpower.'

'I think we should go public now with Sayeed's ID. Splash the bastard's picture all over the TV, newspapers – everything. Ask the Yanks if they'll put up a reward. We've got to nail him.'

'Eat your sausage – we've got work to do.'

When they walked into the forensics lab the atmosphere was different, subdued. Katja was sitting at Charlie's desk.

'Hi,' said Gerry. 'Where's Hang Ten?'

'Haven't you heard?' said Katja, trembling. 'Charlie had a heart attack.'

'What?! I mean, is he OK?'

'He's in Groote Schuur. It wasn't too bad and they think he'll be all right but it gave us a bad scare here, I can tell you.'

'When did this happen?' asked Tau.

'Last night. I was just locking up when I heard a groan and he kinda fell onto his desk and crumpled on the floor. I thought he was dead.'

'My God,' said Gerry. 'So what did you do?'

'I put him into the emergency position and made sure his breathing was OK and then ran to get Doctor Schneider from upstairs. She gave him a shot of adrenalin and waited for the ambulance.'

'How old was he?' said Gerry.

'Forty two,' she said. 'And there's no need to talk about him in the past tense. People have heart attacks and carry on for years!'

Tau looked carefully at her and saw how genuinely distraught she was. He put an arm around her.

'We'll go and see him just as soon as we can, but if you see him first give him our best, eh?'

She nodded miserably.

'He asked us to come in,' said Gerry softly. 'Do you know what it was about?'

'Ja,' she said. 'CID raided a pawn-broker in Mitchell's Plain looking for pirate DVDs, and in the guy's safe they found four blood diamonds. You said we should give you a call if any more came in.'

'That's great,' said Tau. 'Thanks. If you could just write down the details…'

She wrote everything down and handed Tau the slip of paper.

Gerry took her hand and pressed it warmly, 'Look, tell the old bastard to stop shamming – we need him back here.'

Katja smiled but her eyes were brimming with tears.

'One more thing,' said Tau, 'were you able to do an enhancement of that family photo of Sayeed Dhatri?'

Katja nodded and opened a drawer and pulled out a sharp print of Sayeed looking in three quarters view. Good enough to put out on the wires.

'Thanks,' said Gerry.

Gerry and Tau drove towards Mitchell's Plain.

'So what do you think?' said Tau.

'About Charlie? Scary, man. It must be all that crap he eats.'

'And Katja?'

'What about Katja?' asked Gerry, puzzled.

'If I didn't know better, I'd say she was in love with him,' said Tau.

'Charlie? Are you saying she's in love with Charlie Brits?' asked Gerry, incredulous.

'Why not?'

'Well, where should I start? The bladdy obvious or the more obscure.'

'Fifty bucks says I'm right,' said Tau.

'Never mind Beauty and the Beast. Have you spoken to Joyce today?' demanded Gerry.

'What?' said Tau, irritated that he had been foolish enough to open a window on his private affairs.

'Joyce. That smart lovely woman you're married to. Have you called, shown her how much you care?'

'You think it's that simple?' said Tau angrily.

'No mate, I think it's bladdy hard, but you know, you got to start somewhere.'

Tau glared at him and fell into a moody silence all the way to Mitchell's Plain. It didn't take them long to locate the pawnbroker's shop and they marched inside. An Asian woman was behind a counter with bars to the ceiling, like an old-fashioned bank, her head covered with a veil.

'Are you the owner?' barked Tau.

'No,' she said.

'We need to speak to the owner,' said Gerry flashing his ID.

'He's not here,' she said.

Tau took a slow breath. 'OK, now this is how it goes. We want to speak to him now. Wherever he is, whatever he's doing, you must get hold of him and bring him here. Right now. OK?'

The poor woman shrunk back in fear. She went into a back office and shut the door. She appeared a moment later.

'He's on his way,' she said.

'Good,' said Tau, lightening up. 'What's his name?'

'Flet Albertyn,' she said.

'And you are?'

'I'm his wife. Jamilla.' she said.

Just then a bell over the door tinkled and a burly man with a fringe beard entered. He stood with feet far apart, his arms folded over his ample belly.

'Who the hell are you?' he said.

Gerry and Tau showed him their ID.

'I just spent two days in lock-up. What more do you want?' Demanded Flet Albertyn.

'First,' said Tau, 'lose the attitude. We aren't some local cops interested in a few stolen DVDs…'

'Nothing here is stolen,' he interrupted. 'I have receipts for everything.'

'So does the guy who bought London Bridge. Now keep your mouth shut for a minute and hear what we have to say then maybe you'll sleep at home tonight,' said Tau.

Gerry gave his partner a sidelong glance. Normally Tau was the model of probity while Gerry acted like an arse, but today it seemed that Tau was bent on carving out a niche for himself as something of a hard case. Gerry sat back and was happy to watch it all unfold.

Albertyn said nothing but took a step back. Tau moved into the space. 'When CID raided your premises the found blood diamonds in the safe…'

Albertyn started to speak but Tau put a finger against his lip, gently, but with terrible menace.

'Shush. *Asseblief.* I want to know – who sold you those diamonds?'

'I got a receipt!' wailed Albertyn. 'I don't know blood this or blood that – I sees some gemstones and I buys them. Finish and *klaar.*'

'Ssshhh!' said Tau, moving closer to him. Tau took the picture of Sayeed out of his pocket.

'Have you ever seen this man?' he hissed. Albertyn wondered for a millisecond what his options were, then seeing the terrible resolve in Tau's face he made up his mind.

'Yes sir, he's the one. He told me I wasn't to say but that's him. Yes.'

'Good,' said Tau. 'Has he ever been in before?'

Albertyn's eyes darted to his wife. He licked his lips. Tau widened his eyes just a fraction. The effect was instantaneous.

'Yes sir. I sometimes made donations to the .. organization… Before that my shop got broke into every week. After I paid him it all stopped like.'

'PAGAD?,' said Gerry.

'Yes sir,' said Albertyn. 'They didn't leave business cards or nothing, but we all knew it was them.'

'Does he stay around here?' asked Tau.

'I don't know, sir. True's God is my witness!'

'Here's what you are going to do. If this man comes in again, you are to call me immediately.' Tau gave him a card. 'If you don't do this, or if you fuck up in any way, no matter how small, I will come after you and you will truly feel my wrath.'

Tau turned around and stalked out. Flet Albertyn had gone pale and his hand was shaking as he held the card. His wife was looking at them with saucer eyes, biting her knuckle. Gerry shrugged and smiled.

'You don't want to feel his wrath, hey?' he said, and went out and joined Tau in the car.

Chapter 58

It was just after evening prayers when the first headlights wobbled down the track towards the bungalow. Sayeed pulled out his pistol and stuck it in his waistband under his shirt and went outside to meet the approaching vehicle. It was a Toyota *bakkie*, driven by a young Caucasian man with short hair and a wispy blonde beard. He stopped next to Sayeed and got out, his hand outstretched.

'Salaam Alaikum' said Martin Chisholm, aka Hakim-Quddus.

'Aleikum Salaam,' replied Sayeed. 'Come inside.'

Within half an hour both Rashid Khan and Yussuf Anwar had also arrived. There was some unease about the white Muslim in their midst, but Sayeed started to calmly and methodically lay out the plans for the next three days, culminating in the combined attacks on the USS Alabama and the assembled G8 presidency. They were spellbound.

'You should also know,' said Sayeed, 'that the famous warrior Tariq Dar died a *shaheed* here in South Africa, not in Iraq as the infidels claim. I met with Tariq and this plan is his own, approved at the highest levels by brother Ayman Al-Zawahiri himself.'

There was a low murmur of appreciation, then one after another they got to their feet, crying 'Allahu Akbar!' Finally they calmed down.

Hamidullah said 'Come Yussuf. Let's go and get us some food.'

'Very good, said Sayeed. 'We will eat then set off by ten o' clock tonight. From now on, brothers, we will not be separated until the attack. Please, your cell phones.'

Everyone put their cell phones into a plastic bag which Sayeed took. Shortly thereafter Hamidullah and Yussuf returned from the restaurant bearing foil cartons of take-away lamb curry and rice. They ate while chatting in low voices, their excitement simmering beneath the surface. Sayeed took time to study Martin Chisholm – the young man was keen and enthusiastic, but inexperienced. He would have to be watched.

Finally the meal was over and the remains thrown into plastic rubbish sacks and placed in an outside bin. The antiaircraft weapons were loaded onto the back of Martin's *bakkie* and covered with fishing equipment. The sack of Semtex was also stowed out of sight and the fishing rods tied over the cabin's roof and a tarpaulin secured over the lot. Finally the vehicles set out in convoy – Martin driving the Hilux in front, then Rashid and Sayeed in the *bakkie*, then Hamidullah in Rashid's battered old Land Cruiser, and finally Yussuf in his Corolla.

They drove slowly to the main road then spread out along a two kilometre stretch. They were making good progress, heading towards East London, when they hit their second police roadblock. As Sayeed arrived he saw that the Hilux had been stopped and Martin was standing outside the vehicle, gesturing for the cop to look inside with his torch. The other vehicles were waved through and stopped at a rest spot about five kilometres down the road. After half an hour the Hilux came barrelling down the road and pulled in to the rest spot. Martin's face was glowing with excitement.

'Jeez. There were looking for you guys! They had names, registrations everything. They knew the truck was now green and wanted to keep me but I obviously wasn't you and they couldn't find anything so had to let me go!'

'You did well,' said Sayeed. 'Now let's press on.'

The convoy set off again, this time with the Corolla leading. At the outskirts of East London they pulled into the parking lot of an all-night convenience store. Martin left the keys in the Hilux and got into the Corolla and they drove slowly through town and then hit the open road. Within eleven minutes the Hilux had been stolen and disappeared forever into the sprawling township on the outskirts of East London. They turned back onto the highway and carried on through the night.

They were leaving Mossel Bay just as the sun was rising, a scarlet fireball blasting its way into a pale green sky, the final light of the last star dying in its glare. Five hours hard driving brought them into Cape Town. Nothing could now stand in their way.

It was Tuesday the 25th of March. The countdown had started.

Chapter 59

Tau and Gerry had worked late the previous night, their final act being to brief all of the G8 intelligence heads about the security leak and advising them to make changes. The heads had gone back to their own embassies where they had worked through the night changing various aspects of their arrangements. Chitepo had taken the heat for the rearrangement and the mood was fractious, with the French once again threatening to pull out their President. They were all due to reconvene the next morning at ten to review the situation.

Tau and Gerry had started their day with a breakfast with Charles Hennesy in the Okapi Room at the Mount Nelson. On their arrival they saw that oil drums filled with concrete had been put across the driveway in a zigzag formation, forcing cars to crawl through the gap before they could even approach the hotel. Flanking the drums were two light armoured cars, capable of blowing up any vehicle which did not comply with their strict vetting procedures. An anti-aircraft gun had been put at one side of the hotel, covering the seaward approaches. It was draped in a camouflage net which only added to its obviousness in the rose garden. Around the back of the hotel a flatbed truck was parked, with a light anti-aircraft gun mounted on the back, covering any approaches from the mountain. Two men on ladders were stringing a banner across the portico saying 'SOUTH AFRICA WELCOMES AIDS AWARENESS.'

'Feels like the Normandy landing,' said Hennesy as he poured coffee.

'What about internal security?' asked Tau.

'All guests have been cleared out and each floor is swept twice a day for bombs,' said Hennesy.

'Staff?' said Gerry.

'Well obviously those dodgy PAGAD characters have all been weeded out, thanks to you fellows,' said Hennesy. 'I've had a small team here from God-knows-where reviewing all of our staff credentials, and so far I am delighted to inform you that everyone has come up smelling of roses.'

'How are the guests distributed?'

'Basically two nationalities per floor, meaning each President will have his own luxury suite with another six rooms for his entourage. On the first floor we have the Italians and the French, second floor, Canadians and British, third floor Japanese and Germans, and on the top floor the Americans and the Russians.'

'I thought the American President was going to be billeted on the USS Alabama,' said Gerry.

'*Entre nous*,' said Hennesy leaning forwards, 'but he must obviously have his suite here, if he needs to freshen up between conference speeches or whatever.'

'And when do they arrive?' asked Tau.

'The Italians are already here. Enjoying the pool,' said Hennesy with a chuckle. 'The rest will be in during the day for the inaugural dinner tonight and the official conference launch tomorrow.'

'When is the final press conference?'

'It's scheduled for 6PM on Friday, in the Eland Room, which we usually use on such occasions.'

'Keep that schedule intact,' said Tau, 'but we may have to move it at the last minute.'

'Why?' asked Hennesy nervously.

'Because Al Queda wants to blow us all to hell,' said Gerry, 'and if we have to prevent that by shuttling a few people around then that's what we will do.'

'How safe is your perimeter fencing?' asked Tau.

'It's three metre razor wire with an electrified top strand. And now I see there are armed soldiers patrolling all the time,' said Hennesy. 'I'd say, pretty damn safe!'

'Is there roof access?' asked Gerry.

'Uhm, well, there is a trap letting out onto the east roof. Strictly for maintenance.'

'Show me,' said Gerry.

'Right now?'

Gerry nodded and within moments he and Tau were following Hennesy to a service lift which rode to the top floor. Hennesy then unlocked a door at the end of the corridor and led them up a steep flight of stairs and heaved open a hatch, exposing the sky. They all clambered out onto the roof and looked around. The apex of the pointed portico was in front of them, facing towards the ocean. Behind them loomed the mountain, vast and imposing. Gerry saw that there were walkways laid out between the tile and he walked quickly around the entire perimeter of the roof before finding his ideal location. He jogged back to Tau and Hennesy.

'This is where we'll be,' he said to Hennesy. 'Nobody to gain access to this place without our say-so. Not you, not the Yanks, not the bladdy president himself, OK?'

'If you think that's really necessary,' said Hennesy stiffly.

Gerry gave him a dirty look.

'Come on,' Gerry said to Tau. 'We've got to debrief.'

On their way to HQ they received a call from Chitepo. When they arrived in his office they found Miss Naidoo in buoyant mood.

'Morning gents,' she chirped. 'Boss is waiting for you.'

They entered and found Kavanagh seated with Chitepo. A radio was playing noisily in the corner.

'I didn't know you were into Kwaito, sir,' said Gerry, gesturing at the radio.

'A simple precaution,' said Kavanagh. 'Although this office is regularly swept, the phone itself can easily be used as a transmitter.'

Tau nodded, turning to Chitepo, who looked stormy.

'Pat has uncovered the leak within this organization. It gives me no pleasure to confirm your original suspicion. Immediately after the conference we will arrest and charge

Miss Naidoo with breaching National Security and providing information to persons and organizations hostile to the state.' He gestured to Kavanagh to continue.

'It seems that Soraya Naidoo, although bearing an Indian name, is in fact of Pakistani origin – her family is from the Peshawar region which borders on Afghanistan. Peshawar is a lawless town, and a major transit point for Mujahedeen going to Afghanistan, or for Taliban and Al Queda fighters coming the other way. She lost a brother fighting for the Taliban four years ago, and had her head turned when she attended his funeral. She was put in touch with a major PAGAD figure when she got back here, and he convinced her that she could greatly help her fellow Muslims in their Jihad. Since then she has been feeding them information on a fairly consistent basis, using a dead letter drop in the Botanical Gardens.'

'We've set up a camera to observe who picks up the material, and we will keep following the trail until we break up this cell,' said Chitepo. 'They're waiting for us in the boardroom. Thank you,' he said, shaking Kavanagh's hand.

The meeting with the G8 security heads was difficult. Given the parameters of the venue there was not a lot which could be changed, especially at such short notice. Chitepo managed to cool things down slightly by saying that the mole had been identified and fed a stream of misinformation to take any plotters away from the venue.

'Do we have any guarantee that everyone will be safe?' demanded the German, Lehmann.

'Bladdy stupid!' Muttered Gerry under his breath. 'What we can guarantee is that we have all jointly done our best. The odds are always against us.'

'And this hotel, the Mount Nelson – how secure is that?' asked the Canadian.

'We've just come from there,' said Gerry, 'it's like an army camp.'

'Very good table too,' murmured the Brit. 'The wife and I were there in the summer.'

'The place was also filled with all of your people,' said Gerry, looking pointedly around the table. 'What's their reconnaissance?'

'I don't think this is appropriate,' murmured the Frenchman.

'*Au contraire*, Lascelles,' growled Chitepo. 'We aren't doing a solo dance here for you guys. We're supposed to be working jointly. Spill.'

Each chief gave a brief summation of what their field agents had achieved in helping to secure the conference venue. It reiterated what Gerry and Tau already knew, but they enjoyed briefly the spectacle of foreign heads having to account publicly for their services. Gerry was goading Lehmann and they were starting to argue about whether or not the German state security apparatus was still riddled with old Stasi spies, when Tau stood up and banged his glass on the table until he had everyone's attention. He held up the forensic lab photos of Sayeed Dhatri. 'This man is the leader of the terror cell. His picture was circulated this morning on the TV news and is front page in every newspaper. And thanks to our generous American colleagues,' – he nodded towards Fitzwarren, who bowed his head at the compliment,' – we are able offer a Million Rand reward for information leading to his death or capture.'

By the time Gerry and Tau exited the office they were drenched in sweat. As they headed down to the secure parking area, Gerry tugged off his tie and slung his jacket over his shoulder.

'Full of crap,' he growled. 'Telling us how to do our job.'

Just then Tau's phone started to ring but died as the signal faded. When they emerged onto the street the phone blipped that he had a message.

'That's weird,' said Tau. 'Oliver Chang says he had an urgent call from an optician in Sea Point who wants to see us right away regarding the picture Ident on the telly.'

'Let's go,' said Gerry sticking the blue light on the roof and punching the siren.

Chapter 60

Sayeed and Rashid slipped into the new house on the perimeter of the sprawling 'informal settlement' that had sprung up on the edge of Hout Bay. They swiftly unloaded the *bakkie* and left it parked in a nearby side-street. The others were told to leave their cars a kilometre away and to walk. Hamidullah was the next person to appear, and then Martin in a highly excited state – he produced that morning's Cape Argus with the picture of Sayeed on the front, listing his real name and his alias, and the huge banner headline offering a Million Rand reward. Moments later Yussuf arrived and they hurriedly drew the curtains and put on a pot of coffee.

'Do the neighbours know you?' asked Hamidullah anxiously.

'No. I moved in one night and have only been here once,' said Sayeed. 'But obviously now security is paramount. There are still a number of outside preparations to be made, but nobody goes anywhere alone. You will always travel in twos, and carry guns. If it looks like you're going to be taken, kill as many of them as you can, but save the last bullet for yourselves. The death of a *shaheed* is a glorious one, and one which we will not flinch from! Now, put your weapons on the table.'

Hamidullah laid out his Glock on the table and slapped down a spare clip, and then took a nickel-plated .38 out of his back pocket and put it down. Rashid contributed a .45 Star with a spare clip, Yussuf a .357 long barrelled Python, and Martin smiled shyly and said 'I don't have a gun.' The others looked incredulous then started laughing, but Sayeed handed him an old revolver. 'Webley,' said Sayeed. 'Used by the British military for years. A very fine weapon,' he winked at the others behind Martin's back. Martin took the gun and weighed it in his hands, his dreams of glory blazing bright. Sayeed put his own gun on the table and went into a back room and brought out a black nylon carry-all from which he withdrew another four handguns and ammunition.

'First,' he said, 'we must clean every weapon here, check that they are all primed and oiled. Then we will break into teams – Hamidullah and Yussuf will be in charge of the sea and land attacks, while Rashid, Hakim and myself will take care of the aerial assault.'

'Where will we all sleep? What about food?' asked Hamidullah.

'Good point. You and Yussuf go to Pick 'N' Pay and stock up. There's also that little camping shop there – grab some sleeping bags for all of us. And listen, no credit cards, no debit cards. Cash for everything.' Sayeed peeled off some money. The fat roll of cash he'd obtained from Flet Albertyn had dwindled and he was concerned about going out to pawn more diamonds – especially to a lowlife like Albertyn who would sell his mother for 50 Rand, never mind a cool million. He would think about that later – in the meantime they had a vast amount to do, and so little time.

'How do we get in touch if there's an emergency?' asked Yussuf.

Sayeed dug into the bag of cell phones and produced Martin's.

'What's your number?' he asked. Martin reeled off the nine digits.

'Emergencies only. This phone will stay on all the time that anyone is out. But before you go shopping, there is some business to take care of.'

Sayeed led Hamidullah and Yussuf into his bedroom and shut the door. The others could not hear what was said but a couple of minutes later they emerged, looking solemn. Hamidullah picked up his Glock and checked it, and Yussuf did likewise with his weapon, and moments later they slipped out of the door.

They walked quickly to their car and drove over the hill to Llandudno, the upmarket suburb built on hills overlooking a picturesque beach, where the estate agent who had rented Sayeed the flat lived. Although Jackie Abrahamse was a 'friendly,' Sayeed knew that the reward of million Rands would not give him even a second's pause for thought. It was barely seven AM as Hamidullah and Yussuf parked in a lay-by overlooking the man's house.

It was a beautiful, pearlescent day, the sea a patchwork of turquoise and blue, changing as the wind and currents subtly shifted the water. A cool breeze blew in off the ocean, the positive ions invigorating the air. Hamidullah was just tuning in the radio for the news when they saw the Abrahamse's door crack open and the man emerge in running shorts and a loose vest. He was in his early 40's, slightly built, with a receding hairline and a neatly-trimmed beard. He glanced around then started jogging up the hill straight towards them.

A car went past and the driver slowed to check out who was sitting in the parked vehicle at this time of day – Hamidullah smiled and waved at him and the man accelerated away. By this time Abrahamse was barely 30 metres away. Yussuf chambered a round in his Python and Hamidullah started the engine. As the man approached, Yussuf opened his door and stood on the pavement, the gun dangling loosely at his side. Jackie Abrahamse had to break his stride, and looked up with an irritated frown as Yussuf squeezed off two quick shots into his chest and one in his head as he fell, then hopped back into the car and they raced away, whooping like teenagers with the thrill of the kill. The dead man lay half in the street, face down, blood pooling around his body.

Twenty minutes later Hamidullah and Yussuf were walking round a busy supermarket pushing a trolley laden with food. They were both still high from the execution, but their excitement cooled when they reached the news stand and saw that Sayeed's face was plastered over every newspaper with the banner headline reward. As they approached the checkout, Hamidullah pointed out some action at the far end of the car park where a police van had stopped beside their car and two cops were scrutinising it closely and making notes.

'We leave. Right now,' said Hamidullah, abandoning their trolley. He and Yussuf walked quickly out of the supermarket and into the adjacent shopping mall. They carried on walking and emerged at the far end of the complex where a bank of pay phones stood beside a deserted taxi rank. Two of the phones were broken but the third worked. Hamidullah dialled the number and waited, then fed in some coins, cursing at the delay. Yussuf too was starting to panic and kept anxious watch, fearing at any time the sound of sirens. Finally the other phone was answered.

'Listen,' said Hamidullah. 'Business is taken care of but we've been made. We need someone to come and collect us. We'll be waiting under the flyover bridge in ten minutes, neh.'

They walked through a stand of dusty bluegums and emerged onto a tarred road. Their destination was a busy overpass about half a kilometre away and they walked swiftly towards it, heads down, alert for trouble.

Back at the flat Sayeed was cursing. He instructed Martin to go on his own and fetch the hapless two, and pressed the revolver into his hand as he was about to leave.

'Six shots,' hissed Sayeed. 'Five for the enemy, one for you. Allahu Akbar,' he said.

'Allahu Akbar,' said Martin slipping the gun into his pocket and emerging from the flat, his baseball cap pulled low over his eyes.

Martin drove within the speed limit and approached the bridge but could see no sign of the other two. He doubled back and stopped under the bridge, his hazard lights flashing. Suddenly he saw Hamidullah and Yussuf emerge from a wide storm drain and run to the car. They drove back to Hout Bay in tense silence.

Sayeed was waiting for them and as soon as they opened the door he slammed his pistol into the side of Hamidullah's head. Hamidullah groaned and slumped onto the floor, his eyes glazed.

'That was *your* operation,' hissed Sayeed. 'So simple a child could have done it. What went wrong?'

'It wasn't our fault,' said Yussuf and Sayeed wheeled around, his pistol cocked, aiming at Yussuf's head. Yussuf put up his hands slowly.

'Steady, my bra,' said Yussuf staring hard at Sayeed.

'Be a man! Take responsibility! Now say what happened.'

Hamidullah shook his head to clear the fuzziness. 'We were just parking up to check out his house when this guy drives past and stares at us, like 'what are you doing here kind of vibe.' A minute later we see our guy come out of his house and he's jogging up the hill straight towards us. Bang! Bang! Bang! Three taps and he's dead and we're out of there. Drive away nice and slow, then go the shops. While we're in the supermarket we see the cops checking out our car. Maybe it was nothing but we don't want to take chances.'

'He made you. The guy who rode past in his car fucking saw you and gave the cops a description when he learned about the shooting. Stupid!' Sayeed was breathing heavily and was toying with the magazine on his pistol. Rashid stepped forward.

'Look, it's done now. We're back here. Nobody followed you, did they?'

They all looked at Martin who suddenly blushed.

'No. I don't think so. I'm certain of it. No.'

'Good,' said Rashid. 'We took out the estate agent, who was the last link to this place. We can get more food later, it's not important. While you've been away we have been working out what needs to be done next.'

Sayeed had recovered his composure and put his pistol down on the table.

'Hamidullah, you must go and secure the boat. Yussuf will go with you. If you fail then we abort the mission.'

Hamidullah nodded. His head was still ringing but this time he would achieve what he had to. There would be no mistakes.

Chapter 61

Tau and Gerry were sitting in Milton Goldman's optician shop in Sea Point. The man appeared anxious, but eager to help.

'I made him a set of brown contacts a week ago,' said Milton. 'Paid cash too.'

'So we should amend the description that's gone out?' asked Gerry. 'Can't you tell that he's wearing lenses?'

'Not the way I fit them,' said Milton.

'How did he find you?' asked Tau.

Milton twitched. 'Come again?' he said.

'Why did he come here?' asked Gerry. 'Did someone refer him?'

'No! No, I don't think so. I mean, he could have just been going past.'

'You seem a bit nervous, Mister Goldman,' said Tau. 'Is there something we should know?'

'No. Nothing's wrong. I mean, if you catch this guy will I be eligible for the Million Rands?'

'That depends,' said Tau. 'You're certain it was him?'

'RACHEL!' yelled Milton. She anxiously put her head around the door. 'Remember that guy who came for the brown contacts two weeks ago? I told you to put the CCTV tape away. Did you do that, doll?'

She came in a moment later proudly bearing a tape. She smiled at Tau and handed it to him. Milton took it from Tau and opened a cupboard behind him and popped it into the player. He fast-forwarded the images then stopped when Sayeed came on screen.

'That's him, isn't it?' said Milton. 'Just like in the newspaper. But you mustn't say where you heard about the contacts, hey. That guy had killer eyes. I mean it. He freaked me out. That's why I told Rachie to keep the tape, isn't that so, doll?'

She nodded.

'Well, thank you Mister Goldman,' said Tau, standing.

Just then Gerry's cell phone rang.

'Speak to me,' he said. 'Where was this? OK, we're in Sea Point now so we can be there in a few minutes.' He snapped shut his phone and gestured with his thumb they should exit.

'Thanks again,' said Tau. 'That was a great help.'

'A pleasure,' said Milton. 'And if you guys ever need any glasses, even just a pair of shades, I'll do you the best deal, OK?'

Milton watched them get into the burnt orange BMW and race away. He shook his head and turned to Rachel.

'A million bucks, babe. We could have some fun, hey?,' he said, patting her bum.

'Yes,' said Rachel squirming away. 'If you ever leave your wife.'

Milton sighed and slumped back down at his optical bench.

'What time is Mrs Pinchus coming in for her eye test?'

Gerry was driving fast along the twisting coast road.

'Oliver said that a guy out jogging was gunned down this morning in Llandudno. No robbery, no clear motive.'

'And this is of interest why?'

'Some busybody Neighbourhood Watch guy saw the shooters waiting in their car and he took a photo on his phone. The cops tracked the car down to a supermarket parking lot.'

'Apart from getting a good citizenship badge how does this help anything?'

'Because,' said Gerry, enjoying his pedagogical role, 'he showed his photos to Oliver Chang and Oliver thought the guy looked very much like that ID shot we circulated of Six Moreno at the Hertz depot.'

'Jesus,' said Tau. 'If Moreno's back then it means that he and Sayeed must have got through. We've got to tell Chitepo.'

'Wait, it gets better. Oliver was able to make a positive ID on Moreno's mate in the car with him. He's a *skolly* who was a PAGAD G-Man called Yussuf Anwar.'

'Now we're talking,' said Tau. 'Doesn't this heap of shit go any faster?'

Gerry grinned and hit the siren.

Chapter 62

Hamidullah and Yussuf parked Rashid's old Land Cruiser at the side of the Hout Bay house for less than a minute while they loaded the Iglas into the back under a bright picnic blanket and drove off without attracting any attention. They parked in the open lot at the Waterfront, then sauntered round to the yacht basin and marina, looking for all the world like tourists, mingling casually with the crowds that were already starting to gather.

Hamidullah turned into a bank of public phones and made a call, then he and Yussuf sat down in the shade and waited. Ten minutes later a tall man with strong arms and the rolling gait of someone who has spent many years at sea sauntered up to them and sat down a few feet away from Hamidullah and took out a newspaper which he started reading, ignoring the two men seated nearby. Jamal Mansour was in charge of refitting and maintaining the multi-million Rand yachts and ski boats that were berthed in the marina.

'Salaam Alaikum,' said Hamidullah.

'Aleikum Salaam,' replied Jamal without looking up. 'I see from the papers that our friend is very popular, neh.'

They all chuckled.

'It's a busy time,' said Hamidullah. 'We're ready to go.'

'Now?' said Jamal, startled.

'Friday morning six AM we need the boat.'

Jamal sucked his teeth and shrugged. Then he brightened.

'Got a ski boat. Very nice and fast. She's got a 375 horse inboard gas turbine engine.'

'And we can get it?' said Hamidullah.

'The owner is a German who's just gone back to Munich for a month. I've got to service the boat and get her ready for his return.'

'Excellent. How much weight can she carry?'

Jamal frowned. 'Not sure. If her tanks are full, I'd say about a ton.'

'But won't full tanks will slow her down?' said Yussuf.

'Slightly,' said Jamal. 'But she's got so much excess power that it shouldn't make a difference.'

'I want her half full,' said Hamidullah. 'We aren't going far. Is she easy to drive?'

'Like a car. Get in and turn the key.'

'Which one is she?' asked Hamidullah.

Jamal gestured with his chin at a row of boats tethered to the quay.

'That white one with the blue flash along the side. *Schadenfreude.*'

'I'll be here at 6AM Friday. I'll load up and take the boat out of the harbour.'

'Drive slowly,' said Jamal. 'If anyone stops you then you've just had the engine rebored and you're taking her out for sea trials, OK?'

'No problem,' said Hamidullah. 'Where will the keys be?'

'In the ignition. And I'll leave a set of overalls with our logo in the hold. Wear that and nobody will challenge you. When he learns that his boat has been stolen this guy will go apeshit. Still, that's why God invented insurance.'

'God requires no insurance,' said Hamidullah. He took something out of his pocket and handed it surreptitiously to Jamal. Jamal looked down and saw a white stone gleaming in his hand.

'To help take away your pain,' said Hamidullah. Jamal smiled and slipped the stones into his pocket.

'I'd better get back,' he said. 'If there's any trouble you took the boat on your own, neh?'

'Sure,' said Hamidullah. 'Allahu Akbar.'

'Allahu Akbar,' said Jamal folding his newspaper and walking away without looking back. Hamidullah and Yussuf remained for a few moments then walked slowly off in the opposite direction.

It took nearly an hour for them to reach the stretch of deserted bush behind Melkbosstrand. Both men had received weapons training in the early days with Zapata, and had fond memories of the place. They parked the car off road behind a stand of *fynbos,* and started walking.

'Whatever happened to Zapata?' asked Yussuf. 'He was one crazy son-of-a-bitch.'

'I heard he went to Indonesia,' said Hamidullah.

'What for?'

'Jihad. I think his family had some connection. The way I heard it he was linked up with *Jemaa Islamia.*'

'Those brothers behind the Bali bombs?'

'Ja. Finally he found his war.'

'If he'd stuck around here he would have found a war on his very own doorstep,' said Hamidullah, pausing to get his breath. 'Through there.'

He pointed at a small cave mouth, covered by a couple of boulders and a screen of bush. They managed to roll the boulders aside and inside were four steel propane tanks with the regulators removed. Each was filled with a mixture of ammonium nitrate and aluminium powder. All they needed was a primer and the final chemical ingredient and the crude fertilizer bombs were ready to detonate. They carried the gas bottles to the Land Cruiser and then returned to the cave. Hamidullah stuck his hand deep inside the rock fissure.

'I hate this. Could get bitten by a bladdy snake or scorpion,' he said.

He gingerly felt around until his hand fastened on something cool. He carefully drew out a package wrapped in oilskin. He held it up triumphantly.

'Detonators. All we need is a battery and BOOM!'

Yussuf laughed. 'Those fuckers will get the shock of their lives, neh.'

'It was a boat just like this that nearly sank the USS Cole off Aden. Punched a hole right on the waterline. If we can do the same to the Alabama, especially when the Great Satan is on board…'

They laughed at the prospect.

Hamidullah carefully backed the Land Cruiser out of the long grass and rejoined the road. They took a slow drive back towards Kalk Bay where the safe house had remained undisturbed for the past month. They took a road that enabled them to look down on the house. Nothing untoward. Standing just offshore was the vast grey bulk of the USS Alabama.

'Look at that!' said Hamidullah, whistling. Yussuf's jaw dropped in disbelief.

'Wow!' was all he said. 'Wow!'

'We're gonna nail that bitch,' said Hamidullah. 'From land and sea. They won't know if they're coming or going.'

Hamidullah was just about to release the handbrake when he saw a car slow down on the lower road, with the driver staring hard at the empty house, then accelerate swiftly away.

'Cops,' said Hamidullah. 'Let's wait a bit and see if he comes back.'

After ten minutes the police car had not returned and Hamidullah rushed down the hill and quickly entered the garage and shut the doors behind them. Yussuf climbed onto a crate and peered out at the street through a small hole in the top of the garage door.

'Anything?' asked Hamidullah.

'No. I reckon they cruise by every so often and just take a look, but it doesn't seem like a permanent surveillance.'

'I bloody hope so,' snorted Hamidullah, 'otherwise…'

'BOOM!' said Yussuf.

They laughed and unloaded the gas tanks and set them down in the back of the garage and covered them with a sheet. Next were the Iglas. Hamidullah unlocked the interleading door and they entered the house carrying a ladder. It smelt musty and a layer of dust was everywhere. In the hallway Hamidullah pointed to a trapdoor in the ceiling, operated by a pull cord which released a swing-down ladder. They did two trips to the garage and carried the anti-aircraft weapons up into the loft.

The loft was spacious with a glazed skylight each side. Hamidullah looked through the seaward window and found that he was looking straight at the USS Alabama. He took a range-finding device like a small telescope from his pocket and twirled the ring on the collar then read off the distance.

'Two point seven Kilometres. Perfect. The Igla has a range of up to six Ks. Have you ever fired one before?'

'No,' said Yussuf. 'But I saw how on that video I got from Afghanistan. It's easy as a rifle – you just rest it on your shoulder, prime the thing, and fire.' They laid one of the wooden weapon crates out on the dining room floor and jemmied up the lid with a screwdriver. Inside were the missile launch tube and the missile itself, nearly two metres long with its antenna projecting out the front. There was also, fortunately, a simple manual which explained the workings in Russian, Spanish, French, Italian and broken English. It was in fact a supremely easy weapon to use, more or less a simple point and shoot, as Yussuf had indicated. The warhead was smart enough to track down the heat signal from its target, and the model in the crate had the latest anti-jamming software inside it. It was also described as being an 'all aspect' weapon which meant that it could home in on any portion of the target, and not simply the hot exhaust gas. Satisfied that they had mastered the theory, they broke for prayers and then prepared to leave.

'Well,' said Hamidullah. 'This is where you will be on Friday afternoon.

At six sharp you open fire.'

'Brother,' said Yussuf gripping Hamidullah fiercely. 'In this we cannot fail. Allah wills it. We shall deal the enemy a mortal blow.'

'Inshah Allah,' said Hamidullah.

'Inshah Allah,' said Hamidullah, feeling a tingle of excitement run down his spine.

Chapter 63

'Oh God, it's the heavy brigade,' muttered Oliver Chang as Tau and Gerry walked up. They had just arrived at the high road overlooking Llandudno where a dark stain on the tarmac was the most visible sign that a man had recently died there. Tau and Gerry stepped over the yellow police tape and joined Oliver

'Thanks for letting us know,' said Tau. 'Where's Spark?'

'Didn't you hear? Spark's gone to Joeys. Murder and Robbery, stupid arse. My new pard is a farm girl, Hester Hofmeyer. She's back at base right now…'

'Doing the bladdy paperwork,' Gerry made a sympathetic tutting noise. 'This where it happened?'

'Yes,' said Oliver. 'Abrahamse apparently came up here every day for his run, rain or shine.'

'And these two guys just blew him away?' asked Gerry.

'Seems like it. His wife's still too upset to give a proper interview, but she says nothing seemed out of the ordinary. Jackie was his normal self, and they were looking to go to the Cape Town ballet tonight.'

'But he took a bullet instead,' said Gerry, sucking his teeth. 'Lousy fucken choice.'

'Nothing stolen?' asked Tau, glaring at Gerry.

'No. He had nothing on him anyway. Just a little iPod thingy taped to his arm which was still on when they found him.'

'So robbery wasn't the motive. You think it could have been random?

'With Yussuf Anwar and Six Moreno? Puh-lease,' said Oliver.

'OK,' said Gerry. 'So they came here to slot him. But why?'

'Affiliations. Gambling. Drugs. Debts. Something must have gotten them pissed off,' said Tau.

'The guy's got no record. Nothing. Not even a parking ticket. He's your perfect family man - doesn't drink, doesn't smoke. In other words, a model citizen,' said Oliver.

'How about sex?' asked Gerry.

'Look, I like you,' said Oliver, 'but not that much.' Tau snorted back a laugh. Gerry ploughed on, determined not to let his duty be deflected by a slur on his masculinity.

'Religion? Was he a churchgoer?'

'He's a Muslim,' said Oliver. 'As a matter of fact his wife said that he was very active in his community.'

'Can I guess which community he belonged to?' asked Tau.

'Five Rand says you can't,' said Oliver.

'The 11th Street Mosque,' said Gerry. Oliver nodded.

'I'm well-impressed. You finally did some detecting, Gerry.'

'Where's the fiver?' asked Gerry.

'Sorry, my bet was with Tau,' said Oliver. 'You invalidated the terms of the wager.'

'Jesus, you should be a bladdy loss adjuster,' grumbled Gerry.

'Back to business,' said Tau. 'OK, so we have a link with the PAGAD crew. But why should they kill this guy? What was his line of work?'

'Estate agent,' said Oliver.

'You think that in itself is reason enough?'

'It works for me,' said Gerry.

'If it's related to his work then it's either something he did, or something he didn't do,' said Oliver.

'Right,' said Tau. 'Estate agents sell and lease properties. Now either he failed to give our boys a bolt-hole and they whacked him, or else he *did* give them a safe house, and they feared that the reward might cause him to blab. It's unlikely they'd risk their necks for something he didn't do.'

'Were you guys able to ask his missus if Jackie saw a paper or watched the TV news this morning? Did he know about the reward?' Asked Gerry.

'That was the first thing I asked,' said Oliver. 'She said that he normally listens to the radio news when he has breakfast after his run, and the paper hadn't been delivered yet.'

'Where's his office?' asked Gerry.

'Elite Properties in Hout Bay,' said Oliver. 'You can't miss it – it's in the main street.'

'Thanks,' said Gerry and started walking back to his car.

'Hey! Where are you going?' asked Oliver.

'To his office, duh,' said Gerry.

'Wait a minute! So far this is just a normal homicide - it's my call, fellas.'

'Six Moreno and Yussuf Anwar make it a terrorist hit. Sorry,' said Tau, 'this is now National Intelligence Agency's headache. But you should be there – this is still your case.'

'Jeez, you throw me scraps and expect me to be happy,' grumbled Oliver.

'Look,' said Gerry, 'if this pans out you'll look good, believe me. It was your lead that helped make the case.'

'Get out of here,' muttered Oliver.

'You're wasted in the CID,' said Gerry. 'You should come and play with the big boys.'

Oliver grabbed his crotch and hefted his package in eloquent dismissal.

Gerry and Tau got back into the car and raced away, over the hill towards Hout Bay.

'He's a good guy, Oliver.'

'Yup,' said Tau. 'Can't blame him for being pissed.'

'No. There it is,' said Gerry pointing to a blue building in a strip mall along the main street with a cop car parked outside. Gerry pulled in behind the vehicle and they entered the building. A young guy with shoulder length hair sat at one desk, playing with his computer in a distracted manner, while an attractive brunette woman sat sniffling into scrap of tissue, her eyes red with crying. The young guy looked up as Tau and Gerry entered. 'We're closed,' he said.

'Not to us,' said Gerry flipping his ID. 'Just the two of you working here?'

The woman let out a wail, causing Gerry to flinch.

'Is there anyone else?' asked Tau.

'No. Well, there was Barney, but he left last year to go travelling.'

'And you are..?' said Gerry.

'Mike McGuiness,' said the young man miserably. 'That's Charlize De Kok,' he said indicating the distraught young woman.

'OK,' said Tau. 'I know this is difficult time for you but you've got to concentrate. We believe that Jackie was killed because of something to do with a recent property transaction. We need to get hold of all the property deals in the past two months.'

'Rentals or purchases?' snuffled Charlize.

'Both,' said Gerry.

'You run off the rentals, I'll do the sales,' said Mike, taking charge. Charlize blew her nose again and turned on her computer, happy to be distracted. Within minutes they handed Tau a list of 133 rentals and 47 sales.

'Does everyone who concludes an agreement come into the office to sign off?' asked Gerry.

'Ja, pretty much - I mean, we've got all the docs on computer here and we can adjust anything as we need it, so I would say yes,' said Mike.

'Is there ever a situation where Jackie might take the documents out of the office, to sign somewhere else?'

'Don't think so,' said Mike.

'There was that one time,' said Charlize in a high-pitched voice. 'When Jackie sold that last penthouse at Bantry Bay and the guy insisted that we bring all the documents to him. He was the big shot type – you know 'If I'm spending two million bucks then yadda yadda yadda.'

'Oh ja,' said Mike. 'Some double-barrelled Brit who acted like it was beneath his dignity to come into our office.'

'Look at this picture – was he ever in here in the past month?' said Tau, showing the Sayeed photo. Charlize's eyes grew large.

'That's the bloke on the TV!' she said.

'Did he ever come in?'

'Him? No. I'm pretty sure.'

'He might have had brown eyes, not blue,' said Gerry.

'No,' said Mike. 'I think we would have remembered.'

'OK,' said Tau, 'here's what we need. You must go through every contract in your lists and make a note of who came into the office to sign, and who didn't.'

'It could take a while,' said Mike doubtfully.

'You've got an hour,' said Gerry.

'Final question,' said Tau, 'is it possible that Jackie could have let or sold a place without it appearing on the database?'

They took some moments.

'I suppose,' said Mike. 'I mean, he was the boss, he could do what he liked.'

'But I don't think he would!' blurted Charlize. 'He was a good man!'

'I know he once let a friend stay at one of our empty properties for a week while he was in Cape Town for some conference. That never went through the books,' said Mike.

Charlize stared at him. 'Which property?' she asked.

'One of those town houses near Clifton called Sea View, or Fairmont. One of those new ones overlooking the bay.'

'Oh,' said Charlize. 'I didn't know.'

'Are they still vacant?' asked Gerry.

'No. They all went pretty fast,' said Mike.

'Double check and get back to us as soon as you've reviewed the other material we asked for.' Gerry handed them each a card.

They got back into their car and sat for a few moments before Gerry started the engine and they drove down the winding street to the harbour. The sea was sparkling blue with white horses riding the crests and a stiff breeze blowing inland. Gerry got out and stretched his legs. Tau joined him.

'He could be right here,' said Gerry. 'The bastard could be sitting somewhere over there watching us right now,' he gestured at the maze of new houses crawling up the hillside.

Tau's phone rang. He listened in silence then put it away.

'That was our CID hotline. So far 5,772 calls on Sayeed with some from as far afield as the Kalahari, the Zimbabwe border and Northern Lesotho.'

'We should tell them to restrict everything to within 20Ks of Cape Town. He's here,' said Gerry angrily. 'I can smell him!'

'That's fish and chips,' said Tau, sniffing the air. 'Let's grab a quick bite while those kids at the estate agent do their business.'

Gerry led the way into a modest restaurant with a couple of tables and chairs outside, shaded by grapevines. He squinted against the glare.

'It's not the Hungry Heifer,' he said.

They ate plain *kabeljou* and chips. The fish had been landed straight from the incoming fishing boats and was lightly grilled over charcoal. The chips were thick cut from waxy potatoes and had first been par-boiled so that the outer layer was crisp while the interior was soft. There was even a sprig of parsley on the fish that Gerry held up and said 'Salad,' before tossing it aside. And the Cokes were bottled, not from cans or pumps.

'Not too shabby,' said Gerry, wiping his mouth on a paper napkin.

'To recap,' said Tau. 'We must assume that Sayeed and Moreno are here, with their Semtex. They also have a bolt hole that they believe to be safe. Sayeed has his pilot's licence and we must assume that he plans to use it…'

'I know that Chitepo authorised troops to help guard Leon Wessels' flying school, but I think we should go and check it out for ourselves.'

'Agreed,' said Tau. 'But what about all the other flying schools around the Cape – he could steal a plane from any of them.'

'He could also hijack a commercial flight, then we'd be really fucked,' muttered Gerry.

'I don't think he will – he couldn't get the Semtex on board, and with his picture on every billboard I think he'll go low-key.'

Gerry pulled out his notebook and riffled the pages. 'Here we are. When we were first looking into the flying school angle I checked it out – there are seven flight schools within a hundred Ks of Cape Town. We should get all of them secured with some troops, if not as many as Wessels' place.'

'I'll notify Chitepo,' said Tau. 'There is one thing we're not addressing, though: if this is a typical Al-Queda assault, then there will be several simultaneous attacks.'

'Ja, that's been bugging me too,' said Gerry, 'but we don't have any proof that there's another cell, unless of course Moreno is leading one cell, and Sayeed another.'

'Too many *ifs* and *buts*,' said Tau. 'Besides, while there might be other targets, the biggie must remain the G8 leaders.'

'Let's go see Leon Wessels now,' said Gerry. 'We can do it in half an hour, I reckon. The car needs a good run.'

At times Gerry nudged 230 KPH on the drive to Stellenbosch. They turned off the road and bumped along the dirt track towards the landing strip and cluster of small buildings that comprised the flight school. Suddenly two soldiers in combat fatigues carrying R1 rifles stepped into the road ahead of them, forcing them to stop.

'Well, that's something,' said Tau.

'Where are you going?' demanded the first soldier.

'NIA' said Gerry showing his pass.

'You?' said the second soldier gesturing at Tau with his gun.

'Also NIA,' said Tau, slightly irritated but also relieved that the men had been briefed to make no assumptions.

'Who are you here to see?' demanded the first soldier.

'Leon Wessels,' said Gerry.

'Wait,' said the soldier sternly, then turned away and spoke into his walkie-talkie. Finally he stepped back and lowered his rifle.

'Proceed,' he said.

Gerry waved and drove on down the bumpy track. When they arrived at the perimeter fence they found other two soldiers on duty guarding the gate that had been reinforced with iron bars. An armoured car was parked near the hangar, and several squaddies were sitting around smoking. As Gerry's Beemer was waved through, a couple of soldiers on the armoured car followed with their light machinegun, ready to open fire at a moment's notice. As Gerry's car stopped at the office, Leon Wessels strode out holding a Belgian FN rifle in his hands, wearing green combat trousers and an olive vest that was straining to contain his gut. He looked about as much an invincible fighting machine as the Michelin Man. Hanging from his belt was a mesh holster packing an Eagle pistol.

'Jesus,' muttered Gerry in alarm, 'if that doesn't scare the shit out of Sayeed then nothing will.'

'Hi gentlemen,' cried Leon. 'Look at this bladdy show - like Fort Knox, hey! Security's so tight you couldn't get a fucken fly in here!' he said proudly.

'It's not a fly we're worried about,' said Tau. 'But you've done a good job here, Leon. How many squaddies are on site?'

'Twenty of the buggers working 12 hour shifts. I tell you, nothing gets past Leon Wessels.'

'And your planes?'

'Come look,' said Leon, dancing away across the apron. They followed him to the double doors of the hangar, shackled shut with a heavy chain and padlock.

'Case-hardened steel. Even bladdy bolt cutters won't get through that chain, and that lock cost me over a grand!' Said Leon. 'Nothing, but nothing, can get through it!'

'Great,' said Tau. 'Who has the keys?'

'Here,' said Leon taking a key from his pocket. 'Safe as houses.'

Leon unlocked the doors and pulled them back. The yellow Piper was standing inside. Leon got into the cockpit and turned on the ignition and hopped out and threw the prop. The engine caught and he clambered into the cockpit, yelling at Gerry.

'Pull the chocks away!'

Gerry pulled the wooden blocks from under the plane's wheels and Leon revved the engine and the plane started rolling slowly forwards until it was out of the hangar and stood on the runway. He cut the engine and clambered out.

'Why are you taking it out?' said Tau.

'Got a lesson in an hour,' said Leon.

'Someone new?' asked Tau.

'Ja,' said Gerry. 'I feel good about this one. He's a smart-sounding young man who's well-spoken and respectful. The chappie's name is Martin Chisholm.'

'OK,' said Tau. 'Remember to send his original photo in this time – not a copy.'

Leon Wessels saluted. 'Got it, chief.'

Gerry nodded and got back into his car.

'After the 28th it's demob,' he said to Leon.

'It'll be a shame,' said Leon. 'I quite like all this,' he said, raising his pistol into the air and firing off a couple of shots. The soldiers immediately leaped to their feet, weapons ready, and the air crackled with walkie-talkie squawk.

Gerry waved at them and he and Tau drove steadily towards the exit. In the rear-view mirror they saw the squaddies' commander giving Leon an earful.

'What a *poes*,' said Gerry.

'A league of his own,' said Tau.

Gerry's phone warbled.

'Hello? Officer Viljoen?' Said Charlize nervously. 'There's nothing to report here. Every lease or sale was completed in the office, so sorry, we can't help.'

'It's in there somewhere,' said Gerry. 'You have to think outside the box here, Charlize. Your boss was murdered for a reason – help us work out who did it and why.'

He hung up and turned to Tau.

'Nothing.'

'Bugger,' said Tau.

Chapter 64

Hamidullah and Yussuf slipped out of the Kalk Bay house without encountering any more police attention and made their way back over the Nek to Hout Bay. They parked a couple of streets from Sayeed's bungalow and walked swiftly back to the house.

'Everything OK?' asked Sayeed anxiously. 'We were getting worried.'

'Sweet as a nut,' said Hamidullah, who had laid out the plans for the ski boat and brought the others up to speed with their own preparations. Sayeed led them through to the bedroom. A green banner had been strung across one wall, declaring 'La Ilaha Ila Allah', there is no God but Allah, faced by a camcorder standing on a tripod. Sayeed handed the men each a black battle scarf that they carefully knotted onto their heads.

'We are preparing our martyrdom videos,' said Sayeed. 'Take a few minutes to compose yourselves and work out what you want to say. These messages will be played around the world and be an inspiration to our brothers in the Jhiad, wherever they encounter their enemy. By our words and our deeds we will be known as the South African *shaheeds* who took on the Great Satan and won.'

'Insha'Allah!' they cried, and then solemnly went before the camera one by one, each declaring their passionate desire to take on and defeat the enemies of the one true faith. Martin put on his scarf too and made his declaration and afterwards was embraced by the others and called by his Muslim name. Sayeed took the tape out of the camera and put it into a prepaid box marked for the Head of News at the BBC in Cape Town. Then, Sayeed announced that Martin and Rashid had work to do and after checking their weapons they slipped out of the house.

Sayeed sent Hamidullah to the garage where he found a red empty steel fire extinguisher, and Hamidullah sat down with a hacksaw and started sawing at the discharge valve to create an opening large enough to accommodate the plastique explosive.

Martin and Rashid made their way towards the flying school but Martin stopped and let Rashid out at a café attached to a petrol station and arranged to pick him up in an hour or so, after his lesson with Leon. Rashid had ordered a long slow meal and was on his second coffee when Martin arrived and waved at him through the window.

'That place is tight! Jeez, soldiers on the approach roads, at the gate and then this fucken tank next to the hangar itself. There's no way you could get in there without an army!' Said Martin.

'Just drive,' said Rashid calmly.

'Uh…where are we going?' asked Martin.

'Sayeed and I discussed this possibility exactly, which is why we have a secondary plan. This man who runs the flight school – is he armed?'

'Ja. Tooled up like a cowboy. Personally I think he'd shoot his thumb off, but he's packing an FN rifle and a huge bloody pistol.'

Rashid nodded absently. 'Take the next turning,' he said.

Martin complied and they drove along a rutted rural road between vineyards and oaks trees on one side, and purple mountains on the other. Finally Rashid said, 'Pull over there - under that tree.'

Martin stopped under a spreading oak, listening to the tick of the engine as it cooled. Rashid checked that there was nobody else about then said, 'Come.'

Martin was mystified as Rashid led them up a steep hill at a swift pace. They paused for breath only when near the top, by which time Martin was gasping.

'What are we doing?' he demanded.

Rashid led him through a small copse of trees in silence, and suddenly they had a view down the other side of the hill. Vine lands stretched away on all sides, punctuated by the occasional farmstead and small clusters of labourers' houses. About 150 metres from where they were hidden was the back of a modest whitewashed bungalow with a thatched roof, standing alone in a couple of acres of land. The back yard was planted with squash and runner beans and some mealies, and a woman in her thirties was hanging washing from a line at the back of the house, a toddler on a trike riding around nearby.

'I still don't understand…' said Martin.

'That's Leon Wessels' wife and child. Now do you understand?' said Rashid.

They drove back to town in silence and debriefed Sayeed and the others as to what they had learned. Hamidullah had cut away the neck of the fire extinguisher bottle and it was tightly packed with the three sausages of Semtex, linked by wires attached to detonators that had been pushed into the explosive. A simple bell push was connected to one end of the wires, a nine volt battery to the other. All that was needed to activate the device was to push the terminal block onto the top of the battery.

Dusk was starting to fall, and it was time for prayers.

Chapter 65

Tau and Gerry had returned to Elite Properties only to find the building locked and the two young people gone.

'That's a piss-poor show,' muttered Gerry. 'Couldn't they wait a while to see if we had anything further? There has to be some link with Abrahamse's death.'

'Maybe it's something else altogether,' said Tau. 'We should go and speak to the wife.'

'Oliver already did,' said Gerry. 'I don't know about you, but I'm starting to shit bricks. The conference kicks off with the launch dinner in three hours time and we're in the middle of butt-fuck nowhere without a compass.'

'Jesus,' said Tau. 'The opening gala! I must remember to pick up my dinner jacket from the cleaners.'

'Dinner jacket?' asked Gerry, suddenly going pale.

'The opening dinner, remember? We are all guests, although of course we'll spend most of the time running around with the security people.'

'Fuck!' muttered Gerry He had even forgotten to let Aletta know that she was invited until the night before, and they had had another row, and now Gerry recalled that he didn't possess a dinner jacket. He put the blue light on the roof and hit the siren.

'What's going on?' asked Tau.

'Stuttaford's,' said Gerry.

'What?'

'Fucken Stuttaford's fucken clothing store to get a fucken jacket for some fucken dinner, that's what!' Yelled Gerry.

'Gerry, we're chasing Public Enemy Number One. Forget the fucking jacket!' Tau yelled back at him.

'At the moment we're chasing our tails. Rule Number One – go and do something irrelevant and then something significant will happen.'

'More superstitious white man mojo?'

'Do YOU want to explain to Aletta why I'm the only *poes* at the dinner in my jeans and *takkies*?'

Twenty minutes later Gerry was paying at the Men's counter in Stuttaford's when his phone rang. He passed it to Tau while the cashier carefully wrapped the dinner jacket. Tau listened in silence, grunted once and terminated the call.

'What was that?' asked Gerry as they got into the car.

'Pat Kavangh. Says they've put up a sting for Miss Naidoo and wanted to alert us to *act normal*,' said Tau with a curl of his lip.

'See?' said Gerry. 'I told you something would happen! Viljoen's First Law of Entropy – things fall apart, then they get worse.'

Tau muttered darkly as they rushed off to their next meeting.

At the Long Street Police Station a special operations room had been set up to deal solely with the calls relating to the reward. There were six harried operators wearing headsets and making notes as fast as their fingers could fly. Overseeing everything was Étienne De Jager.

'Look at the bladdy work you've created,' he said.

'Anything likely so far?' asked Tau.

'We've got a dozen cop cars out at this precise moment. To date of the nearly 6,000 calls at least 500 sound promising.'

Gerry whistled. 'Amazing the effect a bit of cash has on peoples' memories, hey?'

De Jager nodded vaguely, overwhelmed by the mountain of information incoming.

Tau gave him a card. 'If there's even a whiff of anything positive call us any time, day or night – we need to nail this bastard.'

Their next stop was HQ where all of the G8 security people had gathered for a final briefing. Tau and Gerry rode the lift in silence. As they emerged on the conference room floor, Gerry drew in a deep breath.

'I want to kill her,' he said.

'Who?'

'Naidoo. I don't know that I can be all smiley for the treacherous bitch. Maybe she'll make a run for it and I can shoot her.'

Tau looked sideways at Gerry. 'Shooting her would probably tip her off,' he said.

They strode down the corridor to the conference room and arrived at the same time as Stanton Fitzwarren.

'I hope you boys have got big *cojones* because I've got some news that'll curdle your milk. Let's go inside,' he said.

They briefly greeted the other chiefs and took their seats. Fitzwarren remained standing.

'Without further ado, gentlemen, let me bring you up to date on some disturbing developments. One of our high-speed patrol vessels working off the East Coast of Africa pulled over a Somali fishing boat that was hundreds of miles off course. The Somalis opened up with a couple of Russian anti-aircraft missiles, which I've got to tell you, scared the Bejesus out of us. When we eventually overpowered them we found that the boat was loaded with military-spec radio equipment. Turns out that these guys were gun-runners working for one of the Islamist warlords. The captain told us, after some persuasion, that they had dropped off two of the Iglas at a rendezvous on the Northern Natal Coast two days ago, the place marked by a Diaz Cross.' He stopped for a sip of water.

'We alerted the Durban CID who found an abandoned vehicle with the owner lying under a pile of rocks. The bullets in him matched the bullets found in your garage owner in Durban the next day. So in summary it appears that our friend Sayeed Dhatri now has some sophisticated anti-aircraft weapons as well as the Semtex. The party just got larger.'

He sat down to silence. Then the German delegate spoke.

'They could bring down an aircraft as it's coming in to land,' he said.

'Doesn't the US President use choppers to ferry him from the carrier to the land?' asked the Japanese delegate.

Everyone started speaking at once. Jonas Chitepo rose to his feet.

'Quiet!' he thundered. 'We will immediately order a review of security around our airports. The military aircraft have sophisticated jamming equipment that can neutralize a hand held anti-aircraft weapon, so there is no need for alarm.'

'I am not happy,' said the Frenchman.

'What's happy got to do with anything?' asked Fitzwarren. 'Tau? Gerry? Your assessment of this new information.'

'We suspected that there may be another cell,' said Tau, 'and we have identified the probable leader. We believe him to be with Sayeed Dhatri and we are certain they are now in a safe house until such time as they launch their attack.'

'We believe that we have an inside track as to the location of the safe house,' said Gerry, trying to sound confidant, 'and we hope to neutralise any attack before it starts.'

'Ja, believing and hoping is one thing,' said the German. 'But what do you actually *know*?'

'I'll tell you when we've made the arrests,' said Gerry. 'Now if you don't mind we have some urgent work to attend to. Our agents are waiting for our debrief.'

Gerry and Tau rode the lift the briefing room. Jez, Sipho, Fix and JoJo were all there.

'Bad news,' said Tau. 'It looks likely that Six Moreno and or Yussuf Anwar will lead a second cell. We need to regroup and modify our strategy.'

'Updates?' snapped Gerry. 'What have we got? Anyone have any joy with Rashid Khan?'

'No,' said Sipho. 'We went back to his mother's house and she said he had not returned from work a few days ago. I believed her – she was pretty sick with worry.'

'OK,' said Tau, 'it's all assumptions at this stage but it's a fair bet after Chris Pieterse's tip-off that Khan is a big fish and that he's also involved. We need mug shots if we're going to plaster the whole bunch of them over the media. What else?'

'I think I might have something,' said JoJo. 'That bad camera shot of the guys who whacked Jackie Abrahamse…'

'Moreno and Anwar,' said Gerry.

'Ja. The guy you're calling Six Moreno looks very much like a bad boy we were keeping tabs on some time ago who suddenly disappeared.'

'PAGAD?' asked Tau.

'G-Man. He was supposed to have more than a dozen executions to his name. His real name is Hamidullah Hamid.'

'That would explain why we couldn't find any links to Six Moreno,' said Gerry. 'Good work, guys.'

'We need to find out anyone who's suddenly gone missing. I think they've put their operation together now and are waiting for the 'go' signal.'

'I think we should put a couple of our people onto the lead from Jackie Abrahamse. Go and find those two young kids who worked for him and go through each transaction until you find something - Abrahamse was killed for a reason, and we think it's related to their safe house.'

'This information about the anti-aircraft weapons is bad news,' said Sipho. 'It looks like a multiple attack is likely.'

'But what's the target? Commercial airliners? The President's flight?' Asked Jez.

'Chitepo's throwing up a cordon around the airports – securing the access roads and making sure nobody can get through without security clearance,' said Tau.

'What about the actual hotel?' asked Sipho.

'The warhead on those hand-helds are too small to make a real difference to a large structure like the Mount Nelson,' said Gerry. 'No, I think it has to be a secondary target.'

'Thier priority now is to find the safe house,' said Tau. 'Gerry and I checked on the flight school where Sayeed trained and it's pretty secure, but can the rest of you go and check the other facilities personally. This guy learned low-level flying for a reason, and my bet is that's how he's going to choose to deliver his payload. I think the Iglas are to mount some kind of diversionary attack, away from the main event.'

'And if we don't catch them in time?' asked Jez.

'Then we relocate the final press conference faster than you can blink, so that even if the attack gets through, they'll be bombing an empty shell. I want you and Sipho to draw up a swift evacuation and relocation plan.'

'Can't they just cancel the damn press conference and send everyone home?' asked JoJo.

'Not an option,' said Tau. 'Loss of face. Caving in to terrorism. But a swift removal – sirens and choppers – will let the world see how brave our political lords and masters are. Now let's go, gentlemen, I don't intend for the attack to succeed, nor for us to be running for cover with our pants round our ankles.'

They all left swiftly except for Gerry and Tau.

'Good speech,' said Gerry. 'So what now?'

'Now we pray,' said Tau.

'Great if you're an atheist,' muttered Gerry.

Chapter 66

Scotty Chisholm was 64 years old. She had Martin late in life, in her 40s, after years of being unable to conceive. Her husband Clive had worked for most of his life as an engineer at the Post Office and was looking forward to a comfortable retirement when he'd been felled by a heart attack while swimming at Muizenberg. At the time Martin was 14, and was already something of a handful. Scotty had done the best she could as a single mother to raise him, but at 17 he'd left school with only two Matric subjects and had drifted from job to job. Eventually, he had found a vocation – the army. He'd tried to enlist three times but was rejected each time because he was asthmatic, and found solace in drink for the next two years.

Finally, after spending a weekend in jail, after being thrown out of a bar for fighting, he'd started to turn his life around. By his early 20s he was more settled and was renting a flat while working at a large electrical goods emporium called Aeon. He had also started dating a rather shy girl, Cheryl, and it looked like they might eventually settle down together. Scotty was a strong believer in a woman's reforming influence and she was confident that if Martin and Cheryl could make a life together he would start to find his direction.

Then something had happened between them, and Martin had broken off the relationship, leaving Cheryl distraught. After a few weeks she stopped calling him and started to accept that they wouldn't be getting married. Martin had become sullen and moody. One night, when he was watching TV at Scotty's house, the news featured a scene of a young Palestinian child shot by Israeli troops in Ramalla.

'Why did they do that!?' Martin shouted, deeply upset.

'The Arabs and the Jews are always fighting,' said Scotty, with a resigned shrug.

'But that kid wasn't fighting!' said Martin, tears springing unexpectedly to his eyes.

'It's terrible,' said Scotty. 'Do you want a coffee? I've got some tart as well.'

In the following months, Martin had started reading about the Israeli/Palestinian conflict. He trawled through websites and slowly came to believe that the conflict had arisen because the Palestinians were Muslims, and the Jews were allowed to steal their land and kill them at will because nobody in the West cared. His web-surfing led him to other conflicts where Muslims were being deprived of land, their oil seized and their men and young boys mercilessly shot down by the agents of the Great Satan, the Western god of money and greed. In turn this led him to a tentative exploration of Islam, and he had been entranced by its poetry and its certainty, and his conversion to the faith became inevitable.

When he had first told Scotty, she had laughed, thinking that he was joking, but she wept when she realised that he was serious, and she saw less and less of him as the months went by. The final schism came when he demanded that she call him Hakim-Quddus and refused to answer to his birth name, so when Cheryl suddenly phoned her out of the blue asking if she knew where Martin was, Scotty started to become fearful.

'I haven't seen him for a few weeks,' Scotty said. 'Has he been in touch with you?'

'That's just the thing,' said Cheryl. 'He broke up before Christmas and I haven't heard a peep from him, but two days ago I got a message on my mobile phone just saying *goodbye*. I was just calling to check if he was OK.'

Scotty felt the blood drain out of her face.

'Like I said, I haven't heard from him but when I do I'll let you know,' said Scotty, and hung up. She dialled Martin's cell phone but it defaulted to message.

'Martin? It's Mom. I'm just checking you're all right. I heard from Cheryl and she's also concerned. Give me a bell just to let me know that everything's fine. 'Bye.'

She hung up and stared at the phone for a long moment before calling directory enquiries and getting connected to Aeon. After various dead ends she finally reached the personnel department where a snotty young woman told her that Martin hadn't turned up in the past few days. That was the point at which Scotty started to get seriously worried and at 10PM she finally called the police and reported her son missing.

Chapter 67

The setting was spectacular. The double ballroom, with its yellow-wood floors and marble columns, was laid with two long tables seating 120 guests. Portraits of past colonial governors were hanging on the walls, with special prominence given to Cecil John Rhodes and Lord Charles Somerset, but the pride of place was taken by portrait of Nelson Mandela. The centrepieces featured strelitzias with their bird-like shapes and vibrant colours, setting off the pale gold table linen and white plates with their simple gold rims.

Tau and Gerry and their respective partners were seated far from the dignitaries, as expected, but Jonas Chitepo had made a point of coming over and complimenting the women and praising their husbands, who stood like store dummies in their dinner jackets. Both Joyce and Aletta were thrilled to be there and had endured agonies of choosing the right clothes for the occasion.

They had taken their places with their husbands and found that they were sharing a table with the Chief of Police, his frumpy wife, and a dapper young Chinese man who simply announced himself as Deng. The Minister of Security, Zak De Bruyn, had briefly stopped at their table and muttered something to Tau and Gerry who nodded as he moved away.

Joyce and Aletta watched the unfolding spectacle with delight as the various national presidents filed into the hall to muted applause to take their places at the head table. Finally, the South African President entered the hall, his elegant wife on his arm, and the applause rose. His Vice President,

Silas Maponya, twinkling behind his spectacles and beaming at everyone, followed him.

After the usual welcoming speeches, Silas Maponya got his feet and made the inaugural address stressing the need for an international co-operation in research to defeat the HIV virus and of the progressive measures being taken by Africa to combat the devastating disease.

'In conclusion,' he said, 'it behoves the rich multinational drug companies of the world to make their drugs available at cost price so that the real victims of HIV can benefit.'

This was greeted with a warm applause, although some of the representatives of those same drug companies looked less than enthusiastic.

'Finally,' he said, 'I look forward to welcoming the President of the United States who will be joining us tomorrow. Now let's enjoy the evening, and we'll show you how truly welcoming we South Africans can be.'

'Very slick,' said Joyce softly to Tau.

'If you knew what I know about our good friend Maponya you'd know why they call him the *Vice* President.'

Joyce smiled and, for a moment, Tau felt some of the old warmth returning. Aletta was gossiping to Gerry about what the French President's wife was wearing, and judging by the glazed expression on his face, Gerry was nearing the limit of his endurance.

The food was excellent and the women enjoying themselves thoroughly when Tau had signalled to Gerry that they needed to speak. They excused themselves and left the main hall. Guarding the doors was a phalanx of security men from the G8 countries, all wearing black suits and coiled earpieces disappearing into the bulging jackets.

'Thank God!' breathed Gerry. 'I felt like attacking those fat cats myself.'

Tau smiled thinly. 'Let's take a walk about and check on things,' he said.

Gerry unlocked the roof hatch and they emerged onto the parapet, seeing the lights of Cape Town spread out below. It all looked quiet and peaceful.

'Somewhere up there is an AWAC, looking down on us,' said Tau.

'We should go the Alabama tomorrow and take a look at their electronic tricks,' said Gerry.

'If the plane does get through we'll be reliant on the AWAC to be our eyes and ears.'

'To guide in the F14s to shoot the bastard out of the sky.'

'Hmm,' muttered Tau.

'What's 'Hmmm,?' demanded Gerry.

'I spoke to a colonel in the airforce and he confirmed that the F14s are so fast that they would overshoot a slow little prop plane like a crop-duster. And their weapons are all electronically guided, and the signal coming from a tiddler isn't really enough for the weapons to lock onto. They're designed to combat high-speed jets, not puddle-jumpers.'

'Thanks for telling me now,' said Gerry hotly.

'Didn't want to ruin your dinner,' said Tau.

'Haven't they got some VTOL planes on the carrier? Sea Harriers or something that's slower than the Tomcats?'

'Yes, and Apache attack helicopters, but to have them all airborne and circling for hours isn't on, and they take 15 minutes to scramble by which time the hotel could be rubble.'

'So it's down to the muppets on the ak-ak guns in the yard?' asked Gerry.

'No,' said Tau. 'It's down to us. Only if we drop the ball do those guys get a look in.'

'Now I feel a WHOLE lot better,' said Gerry. 'I always thought in the back of my mind that the Yanks and their hi-tech glitz would bail us out.'

'Fraid not,' said Tau. 'But the AWAC could give us a heads-up if a plane is incoming.'

Gerry rubbed his eyes then looked out at the city lights.

'Are you and Joyce staying here tonight?' He asked.

The hotel had prepared a couple of rooms for Gerry and Tau, not so much from largesse but from necessity to be close to the operations room in the basement.

'Yes,' said Tau. 'Joyce has never stayed here before and was excited by the prospect. Come to that, I've never stayed here either, but quite frankly if I'm going to spend the night prowling around it won't make any odds anyway. You?'

'Ja, 'Letta was also very excited. Do you think they could attack tonight?'

'I had to tell Joyce there was a possibility,' said Tau. 'She said, 'We all have to die sometime and I'd rather it was in five star luxury than in a pile-up on the N1.'

'And you?'

'If Joyce was to be killed in an attack I don't think I'd want to go on. Especially if it was through my failure to protect her,' said Tau.

'You always were a cheery bastard,' said Gerry. 'Let's go down to the ops room and make sure that those dicks know what they're doing. But I just want to stop off in the ballroom to first.'

They returned to the ballroom as the band was striking up. Tau led Joyce onto the dance floor and Aletta made it plain that she too expected to be dancing but Gerry was distracted until the Chinese guy asked Letta for a dance at which point Gerry seized her by the wrist and led her onto the dance floor, provoking a smile from Aletta.

'So, mister big *bok* security, are we all safe in your hands?'

'You're not,' growled Gerry nibbling her ear.

'Ger,' she said, 'I just want you to know how proud I am of you.'

Gerry was stumped for a response and kept her pressed close for the entire dance, then he held her away from him and said, 'Tau and I will be working tonight. I'll come to bed when I can, but you've got the number of our room, yes?'

'I'll be waiting,' she murmured.

'And I don't want you dancing with that bladdy Chinaman as soon as my back's turned,' he said darkly.

The temporary operations room had been set up in the basement of the hotel and six operatives sat at computer screens sifting through data as it poured out of the ether. The atmosphere was of restrained hysteria, presided over by a South African SigInt major called Zwelake and an American CIA geek by the name of Sturgis. Tau and Gerry were not part of the hour-by-hour planning of the conventional security measures, but were free to concentrate on their single operational goal, which fed off and informed all of the other operations going on underground.

'So?' said Zwelake, 'have you caught them yet? Can we all go home?'

'Ja,' said Gerry. 'This whole thing is just an exercise.'

'I wish,' said Sturgis. 'The SigIntel we've been picking up is massive. It seems that everyone from Pakistan to Tashkent is waiting for something to happen down here.'

'No pressure, then,' said Tau.

'Have you got the E-fits ready?' asked Gerry.

Zwelake pulled out some photos and electronic renderings of Hamidullah, Yussuf and Rashid Khan. 'They're with all the news agencies right now. We'll aim to catch the late night bulletins and be all over the papers tomorrow.'

'Good, we want to make it so hot that these guys can't breathe. Anything else?'

'Yes, there was a call from a CID cop called Oliver Chang. He wants one of you to ring him.'

Gerry pulled out his cell phone. 'No signal down here,' he muttered.

'Thanks,' said Tau, 'we'll keep popping in throughout the night. If anything breaks you know where to get us.'

'Yes,' said Zwelake, 'in bed on the bloody fourth floor.'

'Ja,' said Gerry, 'but you know we'll be thinking of you.'

'I could do with some air,' said Tau.

They emerged onto the front lawns of the hotel and Gerry dialled a number that was answered almost immediately.

'Oliver? I got your message. Where are you?'

'I'm at the Hungry Heifer eating a greasy steak roll. You?'

'Well, we've just finished a five course meal with the world's presidents and now are strolling in the grounds of a sumptuous hotel.'

'Well, I think I'll leave you alone then. 'Bye.'

Gerry stared at his phone in disbelief. 'He hung up. I don't believe it. The little shit hung up on me.'

Gerry redialled. 'Oliver? Listen! Don't hang up again, you *poes!*'

'That'll do it,' said Tau taking the phone from him. 'Oliver? It's Tau. Sorry, but Gerry just had a double helping of smug for supper. Now what's up?'

'One of your guys, Sipho, asked us to notify any messing persons. There have been three in the past 48 hours.'

'Any look likely?'

'What's the profile of 'likely?'

'Young 20–30, male, probably Asiatic or Indian or 'Coloured.'

'No,' said Oliver. 'One's a white woman in her 50's who ran away from an abusive husband, then there's a black guy, 62, who's a notorious womanizer and disappears at least once a month, and finally a young white guy, 24, walked out of work because he'd had a bust-up with his girlfriend.'

'Thanks,' said Tau. 'Please keep us posted if anything else comes up. Can you send the details through to the ops room anyway - mark it for me care of Zwelake. Thanks, mate.'

'I'm gonna go and see Letta for a few minutes if that's OK,' said Gerry.

'Good idea,' said Tau. 'Meet at the bunker at 1PM.'

'You got it,' said Gerry, walking towards the hotel.

Chapter 68

Fix and JoJo had spent most of the day at Elite Properties, working through the various property lists with Mike and Charlize and by the time they finished their first trawl, night had fallen. Fix brought in four portions of Nando's chicken and chips, which they ate in silence, then resumed their task with renewed vigour, verifying that each and every signature matched a person who could be contacted or whom they could positively identify as not being Sayeed.

'What properties do you still have available?' asked JoJo.

Charlize took out a couple of files, bulging with glossy photos. She handed one file to Fix and one to JoJo.

'That's everything. Rentals in the blue file, purchases in the red – the lot,' she said.

'Is it possible that one of these could have been taken off the market without your knowing?' asked Fix.

'Possible,' said Mike. 'Like I said to that other guy – Jackie was the boss and could do what he liked, but normally he was very tight about keeping his books in order.'

Fix started going through the 'for sale' files while JoJo tackled the rentals. With no criteria to go on, they were flying blind, but Tau and Gerry were convinced that the answer lay somewhere in their property lists, and so they ploughed doggedly on.

'We're going round in bloody circles,' said Fix.

'If you were looking for a place – a short term let,' said JoJo to Mike, 'where would you go?'

'That all depends,' said Mike. 'I mean, if I wanted a bachelor love nest I'd go for a penthouse in one of the new blocks overlooking Clifton or Bantry.'

'No, I reckon it would be something quieter, not likely to attract attention,' said Jez.

'A big detached house would attract attention. The neighbours at those sorts of places are always nosey and would want to know who was moving in.'

'So a flat then?' asked JoJo.

'Yeah, a flat's pretty easy to be anonymous,' said Mike.

'I don't think a flat,' said JoJo. 'Reason being they might be carrying a lot of heavy gear that they'd want to keep away from prying eyes. In flats you're always bumping into people in the lifts or the car park.'

'Then you'd be looking at a bungalow,' said Charlize. 'Something modest on its own little plot with a fence and maybe a garage.'

'That's right,' said Mike. 'But we don't have too many of those on our books. We tend to specialise in upmarket properties - the bigger houses, luxury apartments, sea views, that sort of thing.'

'Do you have anything like Charlize described?'

'Yes, about half a dozen.'

'Now you're talking,' said Jez. 'Show us.'

Chapter 69

It was two minutes to one when Tau met Gerry walking across the lobby to the lift.

'You get some sleep?' asked Gerry.

'Unh,' said Tau, looking evasive.

'You dog!' said Gerry. 'You've been up in the room making the two-backed beast!'

'I don't know what it is about a good hotel, but it seems to have a liberating effect on a woman's libido,' said Tau.

'That and the thought of imminent death,' said Gerry.

'You too?'

'Hot,' said Gerry. 'Ts!' He pulled his hand away as if from a flame.

'At least if I die, I die happy,' said Tau.

'Not if I've got anything to do with it. You two Lotharios come with me,' boomed Chitepo who had appeared silently behind them. They rode down to the basement and headed for the ops room but Chitepo kept on walking. He stopped outside a nondescript door.

'When I left my office this evening I placed a set of plans on my desk purportedly showing the hotel security. I asked Miss Naidoo to file them for me as I was running late. Yesterday I had my office fitted with a miniature CCTV camera hidden in the aircon duct and I caught on film my personal assistant photocopying the documents and putting them in her handbag. She was arrested in the car park. She's in here now – I thought you might have some questions for her before she is shipped off to maximum security.'

'Are you not coming in, sir?' asked Gerry.

'No. I think if I'm in the same room as that poisonous bitch I'd rip her head off,' said Chitepo. 'Report back to me if she talks.'

Tau and Gerry exchanged a glance then entered the room. It was a storeroom of sorts without windows and contained some carpet end-rolls and a couple of broken chairs. Soraya Naidoo was seated in one of the chairs, her eyes black with smudged mascara, her hair awry. She looked up dully as they entered.

'I don't know where to start,' said Tau, 'other than to coin a cliché - you're in a whole heap of trouble.'

'I haven't done anything,' she muttered.

'How about the fact that your leaks resulted in Achmad's and Chris Pieterse's deaths,' said Gerry.

She picked at a piece of lint on her sleeve and said nothing.

'Your mail-drop in the Botanical Gardens – who are you feeding with information?'

She looked briefly startled then resumed her picking.

'Cute,' said Gerry. 'The baffled idiot works well. Especially as we've got you on film copying documents and putting classified data into your dead letter drop.'

'Not to mention your trip to Pakistan to bury your brother. You said he'd been killed in a traffic accident, but it turns out old Nazeem was wiped out in a fire fight with the Brits near Kabul,' said Tau.

She shook her head and looked away.

'Here's the deal,' said Gerry. 'Outside we have Stanton Fitzwarren who is dying to arrest you and have you flown to Uzbekistan or Saudi Arabia or any of those countries where the Yanks practise extraordinary rendition. You know why they choose those places? Because they can torture you and nobody will ever know until your father gets a call to fetch his daughter's body. I think we'll use the traffic accident story with him too. Nice touch.'

She finally looked up. 'I'm not scared of dying,' she said to Gerry.

'No,' said Tau, 'I think you might be scared of living. In a world where not everything is black and white, where reality doesn't conform to your dogmatic certainties.'

She turned away from him with a look of disgust.

'Here's the kicker, our little jihadi,' said Gerry. 'While you aren't scared of dying I'm sure that your family may not be so eager to follow suit.'

'You cannot threaten my family!' she spat.

'Heaven forefend,' said Gerry holding up his hands in horror. 'But what I can say is that when word gets out that you are a traitor to your country, responsible for many deaths and perhaps even that of the G8 leaders, then there are probably some unruly elements in the *volk* who just might fancy a spot of vigilantism, and we certainly cannot be held responsible for what they get up to.'

'And how many deaths are those fine presidents responsible for? Muslim deaths? Who cares? Nobody. NOBODY!' She screamed at him and flew at Gerry, her fists hammering against his chest.

Gerry grabbed her hands and shoved her roughly away.

'Where are they? Cut a deal and maybe you'll get out while you're still young enough to have a life. Sayeed. Hamidullah. Rashid. Yussuf. Where are they?'

She started to say something then shut her mouth tightly, only to say, 'I want a lawyer.'

'Enjoy Saudi Arabia,' said Tau as he and Gerry exited.

The rest of the night was spent prowling around the hotel and checking on the various security elements, until finally at 4.30 Tau and Gerry decided to return to their rooms and catch a couple of hours sleep.

Chapter 70

The Hout Bay cell awoke before six: they all prayed then had a simple breakfast. Sayeed turned on the portable TV set that Hamidullah had rigged up the previous night and they all sat down together to watch the morning news.

The top story was the arrival in Cape Town of the G8 leaders and there was extensive footage of various national heads of state waving to cameras as they stepped out of planes and were whisked away. The jihadis responded like a bunch of school kids, whistling and booing as each new leader emerged.

The action then cut to the exterior of the Mount Nelson, proudly flying the G8 flags outside with its AIDS banner undulating in the breeze.

'That,' said Sayeed, 'is our target and our mission.'

He was just about to start on a morale-building speech when the news anchor cut in.

'In another development, the National Intelligence Agency has issued photos and electronic photo-fits for the following people whom they wish to interview urgently…' A parade of mug shots and E-fit pictures of all the jihadis except for Martin followed. At the end of the list was the photo of Sayeed and the mention of the Million Rand ransom. The anchorman went on to state that these men were all armed and dangerous and not to be approached, but if seen then their presence should be reported at once to the police.

Sayeed banged off the TV. The room was silent. Finally Sayeed spoke.

'Well, the enemy knows our faces and they tremble. We have lit a fire that will consume them all.'

There followed cheers, but Sayeed silenced them with a wave.

'We have 24 hours to get through before the attack. We must use our time wisely to prepare for the battle ahead and for the sacrifices demanded. Nobody leaves the house until the battle is called. Keep the curtains drawn, no lights, nothing to draw attention to our house. We will spend the day in devotional prayer and in preparation. Our operation will be as slick and as polished as 9/11, Insha'Allah, and the glory of our deeds will ring around the world.'

Chapter 71

Tau and Gerry sat with their spouses in the Okapi Room eating breakfast. A muted TV hung discreetly on the wall, a banner subtitle relaying the news. Tau and Gerry watched with one eye as the mug shots flashed up, and grunted with satisfaction.

Joyce was relaxed and happy and enjoying a slice of paw-paw. 'If this is how the rich live, I can see the attraction,' she said.

'I don't know why people need to go abroad for their holidays,' said Aletta. 'A week here would be all the holiday I need.'

'I don't know,' muttered Gerry. 'All that jacket and tie stuff – I think I'd rather have a *braai* on the beach with fish fresh out of the sea.'

'Come on,' said Aletta, 'it's nice to get dressed up once in a while. And you both looked so smart.'

'Mmm,' said Tau, 'if I wanted to see penguins I could go to Boulders Beach.'

'Clothes maketh the man,' said Joyce.

'Yes,' said Aletta, turning to Gerry, 'why've you come down to breakfast in those old jeans. Haven't you got a good pair of slacks?'

Gerry choked. 'What? Are you trying to kill me, woman? *Slacks?* The chairman of my Dad's bowls club wears *slacks*. I'm not a *slacks* kinds of a guy. When I buy some *slacks* you can shoot me! *Slacks*?! Jeez.'

'All right, don't go off on one,' she said. 'Luckly I didn't mention cardigans.'

'Ja right. And you can wear a Crimplene sack dress just like your *Tannie* Wilma,' said Gerry, laughing.

'This *is* a pleasant way to start the day,' said Tau, attacking his herb omelette.

'I have to admit that their *boerewors* is the best, and their steak and eggs is pretty damn fine,' muttered Gerry through full mouth.

'Better than the Heifer?' asked Tau.

Gerry thought for a long moment. 'Now you're asking,' he said.

'I've got a lecture at 8.30AM,' said Joyce dabbing her lips. 'Got to run,' she prepared to leave.

'Will you be back here tonight?' asked Tau.

'There's a welcome dinner for a research fellow from Kenya,' said Joyce as Tau's face fell. 'But I could come by afterwards…'

'You know where our suite is,' he said warmly and kissed her.

'See you later,' she said and left. Aletta finished up too.

'I'm going home to check on the cat,' she said, 'and then work. But I'll see you back here tonight, Ger,' she said, kissing him on the top of the head and leaving.

'They seem chipper,' said Gerry.

'Ja,' said Tau. 'The good life, eh. Shame we can't afford it every day.'

'Never mind, Superman, we've got the world to save.'

The conference sessions were under way and the various seminar rooms were being policed by a variety of security people, all heavily armed and all deadly serious. In the lobby Tau and Gerry bumped into Hennessy who was wearing a blazer and flannels, with a red silk hankie flopped out of his top pocket.

'Ah, Agents Molepe and Viljoen. Are you happy with the security arrangements?'

'Good,' said Gerry curtly. 'If someone walks in carrying a bomb I'm sure they'll have him before he gets too far.'

Hennessy looked at Gerry, unsure as to whether or not he was joking.

'Uhm, nobody's actually likely to walk in with a bomb are they?' He asked.

'No,' said Tau. 'We're expecting an airborne attack.'

'Or possibly hand-held missiles,' said Gerry. 'In which case these guys would be about as much use as nipples on a mamba. Have a nice day now.'

When they reached the operations room Zwelakhe handed Tau a sheaf of papers.

'That information on missing persons,' he said.

'Thanks,' said Tau. 'Anything new from SigInt?'

'Nada,' said Sturgis taking off a pair of headphones. 'It's all chatter. Those fellers have gone to ground. You think maybe all the publicity will cause them to abort?'

'Nah,' said Gerry. 'The chance to take a pop at the Big Satan or whatever he's called will be irresistible. And worst comes to worst they get wiped out – so what? They become martyrs. It's a win-win game for these fuckers.'

Tau and Gerry exited the hotel and stood on the lawns, watching a car crawl slowly through the security barrier at the front gates.

'You call Sipho, I'll get an update from Jez,' said Gerry.

They spoke to their team in hushed tones for a couple of minutes.

'Let's grab a coffee and debrief,' said Tau.

'It's hard to think straight without the Heifer,' said Gerry.

They had coffee delivered on a tray with an assortment of tiny *petit fours* out by the pool.

'Jez and JoJo are making some progress at the estate agent's place. They've worked out a number of possible safe houses that they reckon fit the profile. Now they're checking them out one by one, but it's likely to take a while as they're spread all over the peninsula.'

'Time's the one thing we don't have much of,' said Tau. 'Sipho and Fix have split up and are checking all the flying schools – it'll also take a bit.'

'What's that material that Zwelakhe gave you?' asked Gerry.

Tau took out the file and slid it across. 'It's the dossier on the Missing Persons from Oliver – it doesn't sound too promising.'

Gerry flicked through it briefly and shut it. He was just pouring another coffee when he opened the file again.

'This white kid, Chisholm, his Ma reported him missing. Said there was girlfriend trouble but that he'd changed a lot lately. That's always worth a look.'

'How old is he?'

'Twenty four. Went missing two days ago. Got a phone call at work and just buggered off.'

'Just a sec,' said Tau. 'What did you say the name was?'

'Martin Chisholm,' said Gerry.

'Oh Jesus – he's the one! Remember that idiot Leon Wessels said he had a new trainee pilot?'

'THAT's where I've heard the name,' said Gerry, snapping his fingers. 'Hang on, there's a number here somewhere…'

Gerry waited while the phone rang and rang. Finally it was picked up.

'Hello,' said Gerry, 'Mrs Chisholm? This is Agent Gerrit Viljoen, I'm calling about the Missing Persons you filed. Is your son back yet? OK, you mentioned in your report that he had changed recently – what kind of changes?' Gerry listened grimly, then nodded at Tau. 'And where did he attend mosque? Uh-huh. Thank you very much. Look, I'll send an officer around to get a photo of your son and the details of his address and any vehicles he might own. He'll be with you within the hour. Thank you.'

Gerry hung up.

'He's the fifth member of the cell,' he said to Tau.

'A white boy?'

'Ja. Martin was brought up a Methodist but converted to Islam in the past six months. Guess where?'

'The 11th Street Mosque,' said Tau.

'Give the man a cigar,' said Gerry. 'Let's get someone to speak with his ma straight away.'

'You do that. I'll alert Leon and the commandos at the flying school.'

Just then Chitepo came lumbering out of the hotel and sat heavily in a chair.

'This isn't a holiday camp,' he growled. 'Give me a coffee.'

Gerry poured a coffee while Tau brought him up to speed on the latest developments.

'We might get some leads from Chisholm,' said Gerry. 'Reason being that these other guys are all hard-core criminals and used to ducking and diving, but this kid seems to have been a vulnerable youngster. Perhaps he's left some clues.'

'Get onto it,' said Chitepo popping the last of the *petit fours* into his mouth. 'I don't know what the hell you said to Miss Naidoo, but when the American investigator went in she wouldn't stop talking. Apparently thought for some reason that she was about to be deported to Riyadh. Know anything about that?'

Tau and Gerry looked at each other and shrugged. Chitepo ploughed on. 'She doesn't actually know that much because they work in such a tight cell structure, but her information is fed to our old friend Iqbal Jem in Pollsmoor who still runs things, even though he's inside. The courier is some low level grunt whom she's never met, but there are a few more bits and pieces. It's just being typed up and you can collect a copy from Zwelakhe.' Chitepo finished his coffee and checked his watch. 'Come,' he said. 'The most powerful man in the world is about to descend from on high.'

As they walked up the side of the hotel they became aware of a heavy thudding drone. Looking up they saw two Chinook helicopters flying in close formation in from the sea. On the side of each was written AIRFORCE ONE and the Stars and Stripes. As they rounded the front of the hotel they saw that an honour guard of US Marines was standing on the lawn, creating a gangway from the landing pad to the front of the hotel. Men in black with sunglasses and walkie-talkies were on hand, and standing near the front of the line was Stanton Fitzwarren. The two helicopters touched down in perfect unison and the doors opened together and several people emerged from each to be swallowed up behind the honour guard.

'Which one was he?' asked Gerry.

'Damned if I know,' said Chitepo. 'They always use two choppers so that the bad guys never know which one the President is flying on.'

'Maybe they'll give the reception to the guy who presses his suits,' said Gerry.

The honour guard quickly closed ranks and the doors to the hotel banged shut. Tau waved at Fitzwarren who strode over, looking ten feet tall.

'That sight always moves me,' he said. 'Well boys, so far so good. The President got here without being shot out of the sky, so I reckon we can breathe easy for at least – I don't know – say, five minutes.'

'Can we come and take a look at your ops room on the Alabama,' asked Gerry.

'Sure,' said Fitzwarren. 'We can fly back on the other chopper when the President returns to the carrier.' He turned abruptly and walked inside.

'Anything else, sir?' asked Gerry.

'Yes,' said Chitepo. 'Go and catch these bastards and make us all proud.' And he stamped off to join the party in the hotel.

Chapter 72

Jez and JoJo had been to two addresses, one in Noordhoek, the other near Muizenberg, and were heading back towards town when Jez's phone rang.

'Yes, Gerry?' he said. Gerry spoke quickly, bringing him up to speed.

'The mother's in Mowbray, you say. It'll take us about 20 minutes to get there, then we have to go to the kid's place. We were just going through the safe houses – two down, eight to go.'

'You have to put it on hold,' said Gerry. 'This is more important. This guy is the fifth man and we need to go through his life with a fine-tooth comb.'

'I understand,' said Jez, 'but if we find the safe house we find all of them together. Isn't that more important?'

'I know a good guy in CID. I'll see if he can link up with you and get the files. But right now I want you to go to Mowbray and see Mrs Chisholm.'

'Hit the siren,' said Jez.

Gerry and Tau had climbed onto the roof of the hotel, a position that gave them a strategic advantage. They were linked by walkie-talkie with the operations room in the basement, the gatehouse security, the AK-AK guns front and back and by cell phone with everyone else. They had discussed having weapons up on the roof, but Tau had thought it redundant. Gerry, on the other hand, had spoken to Chitepo who authorised two high-velocity heavy calibre rifles, a grenade launcher and a Protecta military shotgun that could shoot heavy solid slugs as well as buck shot. In addition, Gerry had insisted that they both wear flak jackets. He had spread their arsenal out on the roof and was checking that it was all functioning when Tau flipped open his phone.

'Oliver? Tau Moelepe. Listen, we need some help.'

'From *moi*? A humble detective? Surely not!' said Oliver.

'Cut the crap. You know Jez and JoJo, right? Well, they've got a list of possible safe houses that they were working through, but they've just been reassigned. We need someone smart and reliable to follow up…'

Gerry snatched the phone away. 'We couldn't find anyone like that so we thought of you.'

Tau took back his phone. 'We're guarding the President of the United States, and my fuckwit colleague chooses now to make funny. Call Jez and get the co-ordinates and you and one other please check out these houses ASAP. Needless to say, if you find anything remotely iffy, call in the cavalry. These guys play for keeps, OK.'

'Roger that,' said Oliver. 'Get Chitepo to square things with my boss here and I'm onto it.'

'Already done,' said Tau. 'Thanks.' He shut the phone and looked at Gerry who was holding one of the high velocity rifles to his shoulder and squinting through the scope, following an imaginary target. Tau shook his head, feeling the hopelessness of their task. Gerry took the rifle from his eye.

'I don't know if I can spend the next 48 hours here on the rooftop without going stir crazy,' he said.

'I think once the US President goes back to the cruiser we can move about a bit more. We can run it any way we want,' said Tau.

'I know, but I feel we should be looking at Chisholm and trying to find the safe house, rather than being bloody gatekeepers.'

Just then, a formation of Egyptian Geese flew over, honking loudly. Gerry instantly swung up his rifle and drew a bead on the lead bird.

'Don't,' said Tau.

Gerry gave him a dark look and brought the gun down.

'Has the hotel got a gym?'

'Of course,' said Tau.

'Let's go and work out for an hour. Get rid of some of the tension.'

'Good idea,' said Tau. 'Better than shooting geese off the roof, anyway.'

Chapter 73

Oliver Chang's partner of six years, Spark Marachera, had just been transferred to Jo'burg Murder and Robbery Squad, and Oliver was breaking in his new partner, Hester Hofmeyer, a solid farmer's daughter from Ottosdal in North West Province. Ottosdal was a small farming *dorp* and Hester explained that the week's highlight was the visit of the fertilizer rep from Pretoria. If the world ever needed an enema, Ottosdal would be the place of insertion. "*Dal* by name and *dal* by nature,' she quipped.

Everyone assumed that her short blonde hair, spray of freckles and bluff manner identified her as a lesbian until she seduced the head of the police rugby team on the dance floor at the Christmas party, and had worn him out within a week. It transpired that she had learned her loving from watching the farm animals, and what she lacked in finesse she more than made up for in enthusiasm.

Oliver picked up Hester from HQ then raced to meet Jez at an Engen Garage on the highway to Mowbray. He handed over the files and explained how they were trawling the list of possible safe houses, and had then had driven off at speed to go and see Mrs Chisholm.

'Where to?' she asked brightly, flicking her fringe out of her eyes.

Oliver passed her the file. 'Those ones first. We'll work our way through town and then do Sea Point, Clifton and Hout Bay last.'

She nodded and let fly a high-pitched tremulous fart.

'Jesus,' muttered Oliver, looking appalled as he quickly cranked down his window.

'Oops! Better out than in,' she said with a smile.

'Says who?'

'I can tell I'm going to enjoy working with you,' she said, slapping the top of his thigh with her large paddle hand.

Oliver set his jaw. 'First one – where is it?'

'Here,' she said, stabbing the map with a sausage finger. 'Observatory.'

Meanwhile Jez and JoJo had just pulled up outside Mrs Chisholm's modest little house in Mowbray. They marched up to the door and rang the bell. The faint strains of *Lara's Theme*, circa 1965, drifted to them then the door opened and a short woman with a bun of white hair peered at them through her spectacles.

'Mrs Chisholm? We're from the Police,' said Jez.

'Have you found Martin?' she asked, hope rising in her voice.

'Not yet,' said JoJo. 'But anything you can give us will help.'

'Is he in some kind of trouble?' she asked nervously. Jez and JoJo shared a look. 'You'd better come in,' she said. 'The kettle's just boiled.'

'Do you have a recent photo?' asked JoJo, at which point she burst into tears.

Oliver and Hester spent the rest of the afternoon checking four possible safe houses. One, in Green Point, had caused them some consternation because they found signs of activity at the house, and after kicking down the door discovered a couple of terrified winos inside. The situation had cost valuable hours and night was falling and so they decided to resume at first light.

After interviewing Mrs Chisholm, Jez and JoJo had gone to Martin's employer at Aeon, where they gained an impression of a somewhat unmotivated young man, generally moody and morose, who had recently caused eyebrows to be raised at work by taking breaks for prayers. The manager felt that his departure was no great loss to the organization and was in fact happy to be shot of him.

They had then spent an hour with Cheryl who took the arrival of the police as a very bad sign, and she had haltingly explained that she and Martin had been rock solid and were looking forward to a life together, when suddenly something had made him change. He became angry and irritable; finally breaking off their relationship with no real explanation other than romance wasn't something he wanted to think about right now. So when she had heard his phone message – which she had kept and replayed to the officers – she felt a surge of hope that they would get back together again, but after he dropped out of sight she was becoming more fearful by the day that something terrible had happened to him.

Tau and Gerry were frustrated by the lack of progress and felt all around them the eddying currents of tension. Snippets of information would yield a brief flare of hope only to see it extinguished moments later. Tempers were fraying and one of the diplomatic protection units had pounced on some poor tourist who had somehow managed to wander through the gates, asking if he could see the president.

Finally Gerry had pulled Tau away and they had spent some time in the gym, wearing out the running machine and then taking a scalding hot shower. Aletta had arrived in time for dinner and she and Gerry had slipped away for an hour of privacy while Tau ate alone and then went down to the ops room where Gerry joined him. At midnight they decided to turn in, with wake up calls every two and a half hours. After a fitful night's sleep they were pleased to finally see the dawn and banish those nameless fears that lurked in the darkness.

Chapter 74

Sayeed woke when it was still dark. He glanced at his watch – 4.43 AM. He quickly woke the others but forbade them to turn on any lights. They went through a ritual cleansing and shaved off all of their body hair, then prayed together, fervent and devoted, soldiers going into a battle which they knew would result not only in their own deaths, but also the deaths of the infidels. They were fortified by their faith and prepared for *shaeed*, the martyrdom of the total believer.

They ate a hearty breakfast and discussed in hushed tones their final arrangements. They decided that Martin's *bakkie* was probably known to the police, and so opted to use Rashid's Land Cruiser and Yussuf's Corolla which were both bearing false plates and registered to people who did not exist. Sayeed gave Martin, Yussuf and Hamidullah back their cell phones, for strict emergencies only. They synchronised their watches and went through the timings once more. The press conference was due at 6PM on the terrace of the hotel, which is when Sayeed would swoop down from the sky and crash into the gathering, detonating his explosives. Five minutes later, when the chaos was peaking, Yussuf would launch his missiles as Hamidullah swept in from the sea, torpedoing the mighty warship.

The time for preparation was over and there was nothing more to be said. Sayeed handed out the black battle scarves, giving each man a warm embrace. He sent Rashid into the grey dawn to fetch Land Cruiser, and moments later it pulled up outside the house. Sayeed quickly carried out the fire extinguisher packed with Semtex and slipped into the back of the car. Hamidullah and Yussuf quickly followed and Martin took the front seat beside Rashid, and without another word they drove off.

At the end of the block Sayeed dropped the videotape into a post box and they drove quickly away. Two blocks later they stopped beside Yussuf's Corolla and Rashid, Martin and Sayeed got into the smaller car, pausing briefly to say 'Allahu Akbar' before accelerating away. Hamidullah and Yussuf stared at the departing car, trying to fix in their minds the image of their comrades and leader, for the last time. Hamidullah swung into the driving seat of the Land Cruiser and he and Yussuf drove off in the opposite direction, making for the Waterfront where the ski boat waited.

It was ten minutes to six on Friday morning, the 28th of March.

Tau and Gerry were eating in silence in the Okapi Room. Gerry was attacking a small filet steak and hash browns while Tau sipped some granadilla juice. The TV news had yet to come on and they were the only people eating in the dining room, except for four of the Canadian contingent who seemed never to sleep.

'So,' said Tau. 'The big day.'

'Yup,' growled Gerry. 'You're not quite as perky as yesterday, eh?'

'Joyce came in at midnight when I was sleeping, then when I got up for the three am review she started complaining that I was disturbing her as she had a busy day today. Like I don't have a busy day! Perhaps it's better to be on one's own rather than nagged to death.'

'Letta was fine,' said Gerry. 'As a matter of fact...'

Tau held up his hand, silencing Gerry 'Thanks, but she's still on probation. Or rather, you are. But I think it's all academic if we're turned into *braaivleis.*'

'Let's start with the grounds,' said Gerry.

The crisp dawn air swept away the last vestiges of sleep, and the examination of all the security measures was swiftly accomplished. While walking around the perimeter fence they came across a group of three soldiers resetting a section of the electric fence.

'What happened?' asked Gerry.

One of the soldiers held up a peacock feather for Gerry.

'Peacock landed on the wire. Tripped the alarm and must've given him a helluva kick.'

'Dead?'

'Couldn't find him,' said the soldier with a shrug. 'You want it?' He asked, offering Gerry the iridescent feather.

Gerry shuddered. 'No. Get it out of here! It's bad luck.'

Tau sucked his teeth noisily and raised an eyebrow, but Gerry simply set his jaw and walked off.

The feather was, for Gerry, a bad omen. Instantly he saw the catastrophic cost of failure – the governments of the Western world devastated by the mass assassination of their leaders, the sword of militant Islam bloody and victorious over his beloved Cape. And on a personal note, Gerry himself would have failed, just as he failed his brother so many years before. The fear made him curl his fists, angry at his weakness, determined to prevail.

But also daunting was the option of success – if he managed to avert catastrophe, then what did the future hold? Not for the West or for the larger world, but for him, a white Afrikaner, part of a shrinking minority, teetering on the tip of Africa with nowhere else to go, and nothing ahead but thousands of kilometres of empty sea and the icy wastes of Antarctica.

They walked round the rest of the fence in silence.

'I'm going up to the roof,' said Gerry.

'Don't you want to update with the ops room first?' said Tau.

'If there's any news, they'll call.'

'I think I'll stop by and check it out anyway. See you up there,' Tau said gesturing at the roof.

'Doing everything by the book, eh?' said Gerry.

'What?' said Tau, wheeling around.

'Going to double-check. Make sure the paperwork all adds up. Neat and tidy.'

'What?' said Tau, puzzled.

'Good training for the top job.'

Tau stepped up to Gerry and stood nose to nose. 'What's your problem, man?'

'Come on,' said Gerry. 'We all know this is as far as I'm ever going to get. But you, you can go all the way. Fill Chitepo's boots when he steps down.'

'Whoa! Back up there. What's this all about?'

'I've got as far in the service as I'll get,' said Gerry savagely. 'I get to be the arsehole and you can still come up smelling of roses.'

'This is stupid. Why shouldn't you go for top office?'

'Because I'm a whitey!' snapped Gerry. 'Wake up, bra! No Black Economic Empowerment for Gerrit Viljoen. I'll end my days as a mercenary in Iraq or a security consultant in Australia or sitting in some fucken bank in Mowbray with a uniform on my back and a can of Mace to chase off the bad boys!'

Tau opened his mouth to say something but was momentarily struck dumb. He put a hand on Gerry's shoulder.

'Listen, I don't know where this is coming from, but when you want to talk, we can talk, but right now we got bigger shit to think about than career advancement. If we fuck up now we won't have a career, even if I am black! Now get up on that fucking roof while I go and check if there's anything those geniuses in SigIntel may have missed overnight.'

Tau shook his head and strode into the building. Gerry blinked a couple of times then turned and stalked off. Five minutes later Gerry was sitting on the roof, a grenade launcher across his knees, watching the sunrise over the Twelve Apostles. He looked down at his hands and realised that they were shaking.

Hamidullah stopped the Land Cruiser on the Green Point Road, a short walk from the Waterfront. He got out of the cab and Yussuf slid across the seat.

'I will meet you at the jetty in Kalk Bay at 11 sharp,' said Hamidullah. 'If there are any problems, come back every half hour. Go well, my friend. Allahu Akbar.'

Yussuf nodded and threaded into the early morning traffic that was starting to build.

Hamidullah made his way down to the yacht basin. It was deserted except for a lone ski boat that was heading steadily out through the breakwater towards the open sea. Hamidullah walked along the jetty looking as purposeful as possible until he reached the *Schadenfreude*, when he glanced quickly around and hopped on board. He opened the hatch and went into the cabin where a large overall was laid out on the bunk, with SA Marine Services embroidered on the pocket. Hamidullah smiled to himself and quickly slipped into the overalls and was making his way to the bulkhead when he felt the boat rock. He reached for his pistol.

'You! Come out!'

Hamidullah held his pistol loosely behind his back as he stepped up to the open hatch. A watchman was standing there with a torch and a *knobkerrie*.

'Who are you?' He asked.

Hamidullah pointed to the patch on his pocket. 'Maintenance. We've just put in a rebored engine and the boss wanted me to take her out for sea trials.'

'Who's your boss?' asked the watchman.

'Jamal. If you've got a problem take it up with him. I was supposed to have her out on the water 20 minutes ago, so if you don't mind…'

'I haven't seen you here before,' said the watchman. Hamidullah's grip on his pistol tightened.

'I work for Evinrude there in the Paarden Island workshops. That's why you haven't seen me. But give Jamal a bell, he'll sort you out.'

The watchman was just about to start arguing when his phone rang and he became engrossed in a chat with his sweetheart and moved away down the quay, Hamidullah already forgotten.

Hamidullah hopped ashore and cast off then went down to the bulkhead praying that the key would be there. It was. He churned the engine a couple of times then it took with a slow rumble. He carefully eased the boat away from the dock and took a course slowly towards the breakwater. There was a large notice prominently posted on the stone entrance to the harbour, saying WARNING! TWO KILOMETRE EXCLUSION ZONE AROUND USS ALABAMA. INFRINGEMENT WILL BE MET WITH EXTREME FORCE.

Hamidullah grinned to himself – he would show them exactly what extreme force meant. He opened the throttle and the back of the boat sank down and she took off for the open water. The salt spray was splashing onto his face and he felt the thrill of exhilaration. He could smell victory.

Tau stuck his head cautiously over the parapet.

'Hey. Arsehole. Are we cool?' he asked Gerry.

'Ja, we're fucken beautiful,' said Gerry. 'Sorry I went off on one, I just hate feeling so bladdy useless! We're sitting here like pumpkins waiting for the jihadis to attack when we should be out there!' He said, waving generally at the city laid out below their rooftop.

'Where exactly?' said Tau. 'Isn't it better to have our teams doing the field work?'

'Is there a vehicle alert on Chisholm's car?'

'Yes. Instead of picking at scabs why don't you take a look at the report that was compiled on Miss Naidoo. It makes for interesting if depressing reading.' Tau passed the file across to Gerry who started skimming it but couldn't concentrate.

'The fact that we haven't got the buggers means we've failed,' he said.

'Not quite yet,' said Tau. 'If they blow us all to hell, THEN we'll have failed. And then we'll be beyond caring anyway.'

'Right,' snapped Gerry.

'Go and work yourself into a pulp in the gym,' said Tau. 'I can cover for an hour.'

'It's OK,' said Gerry, breathing slowly and forcing his pulse rate down. 'It's just these bastards are always one step ahead, but unless we can ace them at the end it's Goodnight Irene.'

'Lousy choice of music to end the world,' said Chitepo heaving himself up onto the roof beside them. 'Actually, it's all going quite well. The American President gave his spiel and is preparing to go back to the safety of his ship. He'll come back for the summation and final address this afternoon.'

'If he's going back to the ship we should go and check the ops room.'

'That's fine,' said Chitepo. 'I don't see them attacking us while the President is having coffee in his floating fortress.'

'You go,' said Tau to Gerry. 'I'll stay here and keep in radio contact with you.'

'You sure? Possibly your only chance to see this stuff up close.'

'Personally, I'd rather sit up here and watch the geese. It helps my karma,' said Tau.

'Karma-shmarma,' said Gerry. 'If we're under attack I want to hit these fuckers with everything we have.'

'He'll be out in two minutes precisely,' said Chitepo. 'If you're going, go now.'

Gerry nodded and disappeared through the hatch. Chitepo sat down beside Tau and neither spoke for a moment, then Chitepo said, 'Are you scared?'

Tau gave him a long look. 'Hell yes.'

'Me too,' said Chitepo. He gazed at the vista. 'It's beautiful, isn't it?'

Tau looked around at the sugar loaf mountain rising up behind the hotel with its cap of clouds streaming over the top. In the distance the sea looked green with little flecks of white ruffling its surface. Tau inhaled the scent from the pines that bordered the property and felt the sun warming his bones.

'I'm not letting them destroy this,' he said.

Chapter 75

Martin was driving along small back roads knifing through the vineyards with Rashid beside him and in the back, Sayeed. They only encountered one other vehicle, a *bakkie* going fast the other way, but the driver was too preoccupied to notice anything. Finally they joined a larger dirt road which Martin recognised from his earlier trip with Rashid, who said 'Pull over here. Get behind those bushes.'

Martin bumped his car off the road and parked behind a stand of trees. They checked their inventory - weapons, a length of nylon rope and a fistful of cable ties, and started hiking up the small hillock in front of them. After 20 minutes they emerged from the tree line onto the ridge and saw below the small bungalow where Leon Wessels lived.

'His car's still there,' grunted Sayeed. 'I'll wait for him down by the gate.' Sayeed embraced his fellow jihadis and started creeping slowly under cover of the rocks and shrubs towards the lower end of the property, where the track to the house stopped at a barbed wire gate, before travelling down to meet the main road a kilometre away. As Sayeed passed the bungalow he glimpsed Leon and his wife sitting in the kitchen having breakfast, their small son sitting between them. Sayeed moved silently past, looking for cover from which to stage his ambush. Rashid and Martin hunkered down out of sight, waiting for Leon to leave his house.

In Kalk Bay Yussuf was turning into the road where their safe house lay when he saw an unmarked police car stopped opposite the house. He calmly turned into a driveway then reversed out and drove slowly away. He drove around Kalk Bay for half an hour with a growing sense of unease, and when he took the high road he saw with relief that the unmarked had moved away. He drove swiftly down to the house and parked in the garage and shut the doors.

He set a hand grenade in a vise on a workbench, with a string going from the pin to the garage door so that if the doors were opened from the outside, there would be a four second delay before the grenade blew. He went into the house and climbed the ladder into the loft and carefully unpacked the two Igla rockets from their case and laid them side-by-side next to their launching tubes. He carried some supplies into the loft space so that he wouldn't get hungry in the intervening hours, and settled down to wait. He ventured a peep through the skylight and saw the bulk of the great cruiser lying in the sea road. He noticed that the unmarked police car had come back – he must have missed the cops by a matter of minutes. He giggled to himself at his narrow escape, confidant in the knowledge that if the cops attacked the hideout they would be blown into a million tiny fragments. He unwrapped a cheese sandwich and washed it down with a Coke. After a few minutes the cops drove away again. Yussuf reflected once more on the power of the Almighty.

Hamidullah drove the ski boat carefully past the exclusion zone, barely glancing at the huge warship that loomed out of the water, high as a skyscraper. Once he faced open water he opened up the throttle and the boat lifted its nose and raced out to sea. He was about fifteen kilometres from the shore when he throttled back and cut the engines. The ocean was suddenly quiet aside from the hiss and suck of the water as it slapped against the hull. The swell was fairly strong and although he had spent several years on the fishing boats, Hamidullah still felt a touch of nausea as the boat rolled.

He spent some time examining the boat and working out the best place to put the gas bottle bombs, and trailed a lead from the batteries to the bulkhead where he would be holding the switch that would activate the detonators. He found a deep-sea rod in one of the lockers and attached a spinner and started the engines again and was slowly trawling as he went along, to all intents a fisherman out for a day's sport.

Leon Wessels emerged from his house, wearing combat pants and khaki vest, a camo hunting jacket across his shoulders. From where Sayeed was hiding he could see the pistol on Leon's waist and the rifle in his hand. The alarm on the Nissan Patrol blipped and Leon got inside and started driving slowly down to the gate. He got out, leaving the engine running, and opened the gate. As he got back into the car, Sayeed rose up out of the backseat, a gun to Leon's head. Leon squealed in fright.

'Give me your pistol. Now,' said Sayeed.

Leon was looking in his mirror, transfixed. Sayeed hit him with the gun barrel and Leon suddenly 'came to' and fumblingly undid his gun and handed it to Sayeed.

'Jeez, you didn't have to bladdy hit me, hey,' mumbled Leon.

'Drive,' said Sayeed.

'Where?' asked Leon shakily.

'That way,' said Sayeed indicating the main road. After a couple of kilometres Sayeed indicated that Leon should pull up next to the Corolla. Sayeed made Leon open the car's boot and take out the fire extinguisher filled with Semtex and transfer it to the Nissan. Leon got back into his vehicle sweating.

'Now what?' he asked.

'You once flew me low over a farm where there was a landing strip cut between the vineyards.'

'The Du Toit place?' asked Leon.

'That's the one. About half an hour from here.'

'What do you want there?' asked Leon.

'Just drive,' said Sayeed.

'You know the cops are looking for you, Farouk. Why don't you just give it all up, hey?'

'Why don't you shut your stupid mouth and drive, or do you want some more of this?' He said, brandishing his pistol.

'OK! Jeez,' grumbled Leon as he bumped onto the main dirt road. 'You know there's soldiers all over my flight school, hey. All looking for you.'

'Don't speak to me again. Understood?'

Leon glanced in the rear view mirror and the icy stare that met his gaze caused sweat to pop on his forehead. He tried to think clearly but his mind was a fog of conflicting thought and emotion.

Rashid and Martin had watched Sayeed slip into the Nissan then overpower Leon and force him to drive away. When the car was out of sight Rashid gave Martin a gentle shove. Martin put his gun in his pocket and walked towards the homestead until he was about 20 metres from the back door, when he stopped and shouted.

'Mrs Wessels! Come quick! There's been an accident!'

A moment later the back door opened and a puzzled Thespina Wessels looked out, drying her hands on a dishcloth. Martin jogged towards her.

'There's been an accident. Your husband…'

She squinted at him for a moment, then realised that something was amiss and took a step back and tried to close the kitchen door, but Martin was already there. He grabbed her by her wrist as Rashid charged out from behind a bush, gun drawn. They forced her into the kitchen in a second and bound her hands with a nylon cable tie. Her two-year-old son looked on perplexed, and then started to cry.

'Where's Leon?' asked Thespina.

'He's safe,' said Rashid. 'But you will call him now.'

'What about my baby?' she demanded.

Rashid cocked his pistol and pointed at the toddler.

'He'd better be a good boy,' he said. 'Now call him.'

She held up her hands showing that she couldn't work the phone. Rashid picked up the phone. 'Number?'

She called out Leon's cell phone number and moments later Rashid heard a trill.

Inside the car Leon was squirming as his phone rang in his jacket pocket.

'Answer it,' said Sayeed.

Leon snapped the phone out of his pocket and glanced at the called ID.

'Doll? Are you OK?'

Rashid held the phone to Thespina's ear. She suddenly started weeping.

'Leon! These men came and they've got the baby and me! I don't know what they want…'

Rashid snapped off the phone.

Leon bellowed into the mouthpiece. 'THESPINA!' Then he looked at Sayeed who winked at him.

'Now you listen to me. We have your wife and child and will not hesitate to kill them and then kill you if you do not do exactly as I say.'

Leon was trembling as he held the steering wheel, his brain frozen. He glanced in the mirror and saw that Sayeed was expecting a reply. He nodded.

'Good. Are we near the Du Toit farm yet?'

'Five Ks around the bend,' said Leon.

'Good. Pull over. Now here's what you will do if you ever want to see your family alive again.'

Leon nodded so violently that his teeth clattered together. Sayeed grabbed his hair and pulled his head back over the seat. 'ARE. YOU. CLEAR. SO. FAR?'

'Yes,' said Leon through gritted teeth. 'Clear as fucken crystal.'

'Very good,' said Sayeed, 'this is how it's going to work…'

Chapter 76

Gerry was sitting inside the Chinook flanked by US Marines, their uniforms starched and ironed and their weapons gleaming. Despite his reservations about some of the more gung-ho aspects of American foreign policy, Gerry had to admit that this elite corps of Presidential Guards looked pretty damn sharp.

The flying time to the carrier was seven minutes and when the door opened Gerry's breath was taken away. The deck was vast and any sensation of being on board a ship disappeared at once. Fitzwarren bellowed over the scud of the chopper blades for Gerry to follow him. He made his way down one companionway, then another, then along a series of corridors until they were deep within the bowels of the ship. Finally Fitzwarren stopped outside a heavy armoured door and swiped a card in the slot and pushed the door open. He walked inside, followed by Gerry.

Immediately a Marine stepped up to Gerry.

'Your ID, sir,' he said. Gerry frowned and offered up his ID for scrutiny.

'Wait here, sir,' commanded the Marine.

'I'm with him,' said Gerry pointing at Fitzwarren.

'Remain stationary and do not move,' said the Marine. He held the ID under a UV scanner then punched some data into a computer. Gerry, although exasperated, took the time to examine his surroundings. The space was an open plan work area, like an office except that there were no windows and the ceilings were lower, and everyone was in uniform. There were over 20 workstations plus a large electronic map of the Cape Peninsula and a big screen showing the circling AWAC's radar scan.

The Marine returned and handed Gerry back his ID. Fitzwarren grinned at him.

'Didn't mean to bust your balls there Gerry,' he said.

'I would do the same,' said Gerry. 'Can you show me what your AWAC is seeing.'

Fitzwarren led him to the luminous green platen where a young officer was staring hard at the screen.

'What are we observing?' asked Gerry. The officer did not look away from the screen.

'The AWAC is flying up and down in a grid pattern, showing us anything that moves within a 150 mile zone. We have in place a five mile no-fly zone around the hotel and our own cruiser.'

'Can she pick up a small single-engined crop-duster? Flying very low, say 20 metres off the ground.'

'We would hope so, sir,' said the officer.

'Hope?,' said Gerry. 'Is that No Hope or Bob Hope?'

'The footprint for such a small aircraft is normally very hard to detect. Especially flying so close to the earth where there may be interference from road traffic, for example.'

'And what is your scramble time?' asked Gerry.

'That information is restricted, sir,' said the officer staring at the screen.

'Can I ask what you can put in the air if you see a threat?'

'That information is restricted, sir,' said the officer with all the expression of an automaton.

'It's my job to protect your president while he's in my country. This is no time to be cute,' said Gerry.

'Take it up with my Commanding Officer,' said the man.

'Thanks,' said Gerry. 'You know what, I think I'd better get to the hotel where I can sit on the bladdy roof with a rifle. Can I hitch a ride back?'

Fitzwarren nodded and indicated that Gerry be taken to the flight deck by another officer who said not a word during the five minute walk through the labyrinthine maze of passages until they suddenly emerged onto the flight deck once more. He was the only passenger on the Chinook and felt for some reason both vaguely offended and disappointed, but his ruminations didn't last long because just after he landed at the Mount Nelson his cell phone rang.

'Oliver? What's up?'

'Listen Gerry, my partner and me are sitting outside a bungalow in Hout Bay. Something's not right here. We've checked off most of the other houses on the list and nothing, but this place has its curtains drawn and there's some garbage in the outside bin. It's supposed to be empty.'

'Excellent work! Don't go near the place. Get bomb squad there. I'll join you in 15 minutes.'

Gerry looked up. Tau was staring at him from the roof parapet.

'Get your arse down here! Oliver's found the safe house!'

Tau was holding onto the dashboard of the BMW as Gerry ripped through town, over Kloof Nek and down through Camps Bay, narrowly missing an old man who was doddering across the road on his way to get a piece of snoek and a bagel and didn't hear the siren or see the orange streak until it was almost on top of him.

'Where's the bomb squad?' bawled Gerry over the siren.

'Five minutes away!' yelled Tau as they swooped through the pass and shot into Hout Bay at over 160 KPH. Gerry slowed down and swerved into a side road and came to a halt beside Oliver's nondescript Toyota. Gerry and Tau leaped out. Oliver opened his door as Gerry bounded up.

'If you want anything done right get a proper copper,' said Oliver.

'How did you find it?' asked Tau.

Oliver gestured with his thumb at Hester who waved shyly from the passenger seat.

'My partner, Hester, had a bright idea – she thought that they would have a safe house near water because that would increase their options of escape rather than being stuck downtown.'

'They could have had a boat at the marina,' said Hester brightly.

'Good thinking,' said Gerry looking up as a siren yelped and a bright yellow car with black chevrons on the side roared up. The bomb squad had arrived.

Oliver got out of his car. Hester swung her legs to get out, her short skirt riding up revealing that she wasn't wearing panties. Gerry gaped in disbelief – she caught his eye and winked.

'Sometimes I like to go commando. It's nice to feel the breeze in the trees,' she said getting out and straightening herself primly.

The bomb squad guys got out of their vehicle, wearing heavy flak jackets. They put on steel helmets with plexiglass visors. The taller of the two, Kloppers, walked up to Tau.

'Who's in charge here?' he barked. Gerry gestured with his thumb at Tau, who turned to Oliver. 'Which is the house?' he asked. Oliver gestured at the bungalow opposite.

'Do we know if there's any munitions in there?' asked Kloppers.

'The last house this guy used had a Claymore rigged that took out three firemen when they tried to get in,' said Gerry.

'The Deep River op?' asked the shorter of the bomb men, Lenz. Gerry nodded.

'We should evacuate the surrounding houses,' said Kloppers.

'No time,' said Tau.

'You'll take responsibility if it all goes banzai?' asked the tall man. Tau nodded. 'Just get to it, OK. Every second lost increases the danger.'

The bomb men looked at each other and advanced gingerly on the house. They made their way to the garage attached to the side of the house. Kloppers made a stirrup with his hands for the shorter to stand in and boosted his colleague to look in the window.

'There's a blue Mazda 323 inside,' said Lenz. 'I can't see any evidence of trip wires going to the door.'

'Then open it,' said Gerry.

'I can't do that,' said the taller man. 'There could be hair-fine wires or electronic sensors or even laser beams. We have to do a full electronic sweep before we put foot in there.'

'Balls,' said Gerry. 'Lend me your hat,' he gestured to Lenz who looked hesitant, then handed it over, saying 'Be it on your head.'

Gerry shook his head, 'Everyone's a bladdy comedian,' he growled, lowering the visor. 'Get those guys to keep the muppets away,' he said, gesturing at the onlookers who had started to emerge from their houses.

'Take cover behind your vehicles,' said Kloppers. Everyone hunkered down.

'Maybe we should get the electronic surveillance done first,' said Tau. 'Just in case.'

'I think these guys were dossing down here. I don't think they set it up as a killing house.'

'The Deep River place was pretty lethal,' said Tau.

'That was because they didn't want to get caught. By now it's all over.'

'Che serra serra,' said Tau.

Gerry walked up to the garage door, took out his Glock and fired one shot point blank straight into the lock. Everyone jumped at the sudden loud detonation. The force of the shot punched the lock straight through the thin sheet metal door, but nothing else happened. Gerry turned the handle and swung the garage door up and dived aside out of the possible blast zone. He picked himself up off the ground and entered the garage with Tau, also with gun drawn.

'That's his car,' said Tau gesturing at the Mazda.

Gerry nodded. He stepped out and waved at the bomb squad guys.

'Hey! Come check out this door,' he said pointing at the door leading from the garage to the main house.

Kloppers and Lenz entered the garage.

'You should get back to a safe distance,' said the tall man. 'If this door is wired then it will take you all out.'

Gerry and Tau pulled back to where Hester and Oliver were watching with interest. The bomb squad officers drilled a hole through the door and inserted a fibre optic probe to get a good look around.

'See anything?' asked Gerry.

'Looks clear,' said Kloppers, 'but there could be a remotely-activated device.'

Hester marched up to the front door.

'Get back!' yelled Oliver.

'Don't be such a big baby,' said Hester, turning the front door knob. It opened and she turned and made a small curtsy at the watching policemen.

'Jesus, she's got some balls,' muttered Oliver.

'That's one thing I guarantee she hasn't got,' growled Gerry as he and Tau entered the house.

Once the bomb squad had determined that there were no devices hidden in the house, Gerry and Tau snapped on their latex gloves and did a quick search that revealed nothing except for a back room where the green Islamist flag was still draped and the camcorder stood in its tripod.

They were too late – the war had started.

Chapter 77

It was early afternoon when a pale and sweaty Leon finally arrived at his office at the flight school. The commander, a great bull of a man called Mhlope, strode out of the office to greet him.

'What's up, Leon? You're normally here by 8:30.'

'Bad morning,' said Leon averting his eyes. 'The kiddie is sick. Me and Thessie were up all night with him.'

'He OK now?'

'Ja, Thespina took him into town. Now I've got some work,' he said abruptly. He knelt down and opened the office safe and took out the Piper's keys.

'Can one of your guys give me a hand getting the plane out,' he asked.

'Sure. You going up?'

'Ja. She needs to go to the main dealer for a service.'

Mhlope gestured at Leon's empty holster.

'You forgot your gun today,' he said.

Leon looked down at the empty holster.

'Thanks for reminding me. Can't be too careful,' he said reaching into the back of the safe and taking out a short-barrelled Colt .32 that he dropped on the ground in his nervousness. Mhlope picked it up and handed it to Leon, staring into his eyes.

'Are you sure everything's OK?' he asked.

'Of course I'm bladdy sure,' said Leon. 'Now I just need to find the service logs…' He started rummaging through the filing cabinet. Mhlope shrugged and exited the office. Leon picked up an unused Kevlar vest which one of the squaddies had discarded because a shoulder strap had ruptured, and carefully cut out a bullet-proof panel which he slipped under his T-shirt and fastened his camo jacket over it. He strode out of the office a moment later and saw Mhlope talking to one of his men.

'Are you guys going to help me or what?'

Mhlope told one of his men to open the hangar and swing the prop on Leon's plane. He was concerned that something was amiss – today was the day of the expected attack and Leon was behaving in a markedly strange manner. Finally the engine caught and Mhlope watched as the yellow plane roared along the landing strip and took off but remained low as it slowly turned and headed towards the blue mountains. Mhlope picked up his phone and dialled the number of his contact in the NIA.

Gerry was pacing furiously outside the safe house while forensics worked slowly through the minutiae left behind. Charlie Brits was still in hospital but making good progress, and in the interim Katja was in charge and running everything with cool efficiency. Gerry felt that if only he and Tau had checked out every address the previous day then they would have caught the entire cell, ready for action. As it was, and had been throughout the investigation, they were too late. His phone rang.

'Gerry Viljoen… When? OK. Thanks, commander.'

He hung up and turned to Tau. 'Leon arrived at work looking very distressed and took off a few minutes ago. Flying low. The commander thinks there's something wrong.'

'Let's raise him in his plane,' said Tau, dialling their operational centre in the Mount Nelson. 'Zwelakhe? I need you to patch me through to someone who can contact a private plane in the air. Right now. I'll wait…'

Tau covered the mouthpiece, 'Do we know Leon's registration?'

'Ja,' muttered Gerry flipping quickly through his notebook. 'Here it is – a Piper Pawnee registered to Bluebird Flying School registration CA – 966 Y.'

Tau recited the registration to Zwelakhe and a few moments later he heard a static hiss as the connection was made.

Leon was holding the controls with white knuckles, keeping the plane low as ordered, when his radio blipped. At first he had ignored it because nobody should have known that he was aloft and he was certain that he was flying beneath national radar. When the radio blipped again he picked up the hand piece.

'Hello?' he said cautiously.

'Leon? It's Tau Molepe. Where are you?'

'I'm in the plane,' said Leon, panicking.

'I realise that,' said Tau. 'What is your current location and where are you going?'

'Uh…I'm taking the plane in for a service at the Piper agent,' he said.

'And where is this guy?' asked Tau.

'Uh…Near George.'

'So why are you flying low?'

'I can't hear you,' said Leon, changing the channel and cutting Tau off.

Leon started hiccupping with fear. He was five minutes from the Du Toit farm and he knew that when he touched down Sayeed would kill him. The promise was that if Leon co-operated then his wife and children would be spared, but as Leon sifted the issue over and over in his mind, he came to the slow and inevitable conclusion that even if he did co-operate they would die. The thought made him want to take the plane up to 10,000 metres then dive bomb the filthy bastard.

In his mind's eye he could see Sayeed churned into pink froth in the blades of the prop, but realised that the slim hope of sparing his family would make him deliver the plane safely, and then take whatever Sayeed dealt out. He ground his teeth and howled at the anger of it, then made a decision. Sayeed had warned him of lethal consequences if Leon contacted the authorities, but Leon turned the dial on his radio and called back on the previous frequency. Tau answered.

'Listen to me,' said Leon, 'they've got my wife and child…'

'Where?' said Tau.

'My house. Just shaddup and listen because I don't have much time. This Farouk or Sayeed or whatever the fuck his name is, his thugs have got my family and I have to deliver the plane to him. I think he'll kill me, but you must save my family, hey! You've got to do that!'

'OK,' said Tau. 'Keep it together. Where do you have to meet Sayeed?'

'At a farm. Belongs to a bloke called Manie Du Toit who does a spot of flying. It's got a small grass landing strip. He's waiting there for me. He's gonna kill me!' wailed Leon.

'Keep calm,' said Tau. 'You've done a brave thing by calling, Leon. I need co-ordinates for this farm. What are they?'

Leon suddenly became the detached flight instructor and he read the compass bearings to Tau.

'I'm signing off now. I'll be landing in two minutes. Listen, if I don't get out of this tell Thespina I love her. And my boy, Anthony. Don't forget, hey…' He clicked off the intercom, tears running down his face. He pulled back the controls to take the plane up over a low hillock then came down the other side and saw the grass landing strip below him. He thought briefly of crashing the plane so that Sayeed could not take off but knew that would mean certain death. He landed beautifully and brought the plane to a stop under a spreading oak. Sayeed emerged from the bushes, smiling, lugging a heavy red fire extinguisher. One shot, thought Leon, and blow this fucker to Kingdom Come. He slipped the little Colt down into the side of his boot and opened the door.

'Leave it running,' said Sayeed as he passed him the fire extinguisher cannister for Leon to stash inside the cockpit, then he clambered out of the plane and jumped onto the grass.

'There,' said Leon. 'Now will you let my family go?'

'You know all those children in Lebanon who got bombed. What choice did they have?' asked Sayeed. 'And in Palestine, and Iraq? Did they have a choice, huh?'

'You said you'd free them, you piece of shit!' yelled Leon, rushing at Sayeed. Sayeed fired once. The bullet caught Leon high in the chest and spun him around. He dropped onto the ground and lay there. Sayeed climbed into the cockpit and shut the door. He methodically checked the instruments, then slowly eased the throttle forwards and turned the plane around. He stopped briefly to tie his black battle scarf around his head, then faced into the wind and pushed forward on the throttle and started moving slowly.

Leon managed to half-turn himself over, propped up on one elbow, the blood spreading warm and sticky across his chest. He sighted the Colt at the departing plane and fired off a shot as Sayeed accelerated down the strip and lifted into the late afternoon sun.

Even on a good day Leon couldn't hit the side of a barn. And today wasn't a good day. He fired again, more in desperation than hope, then everything went black.

Chapter 78

Yussuf had waited until the unmarked police car had driven away. He had missed Hamidullah's first deadline but knew him to be reliable and when he had finally driven onto the dock at Kalk Bay the *Schadenfreude* was waiting at the quay. Yussuf had quickly handed Hamidullah the four gas bottles packed with fertilizer and aluminium powder and then had driven away. Hamidullah cast off and slowly took his boat out to open water, out of sight of land.

He spent an hour arranging the gas bottles. Too far forward and the boat's nose was dipping towards the sea. Too far back and some of the explosive force would be lost. Eventually he had placed two bottles in a forward hold and then strung back the detonator wires to two more which he packed on either side of the engine, hoping that the blast would detonate the fuel tanks as well as hurling steel shrapnel into the cruiser. He took the boat on a high-speed run to check the balance and found that on half throttle it lifted its nose and started to gain speed. He throttled back and cut the engines, happy to drift until the appointed hour. The cruiser lay 20 minutes away, a symbol of American might, soon to be humbled.

Yussuf was driving back to the safe house when he became aware that the unmarked police car was behind him. He glanced into the mirror and saw that the car contained one man who was speaking into his police radio. Yussuf turned off the main road and the unmarked followed at a distance. Yussuf sped up and swung onto a small track that led directly into the grass and scrub on the side of the mountain. He engaged four-wheel drive and bounced away across the tussocks, speeding around a bend behind a low kopje. He jumped out of the car and crouched down, his pistol raised. A minute later he heard the unmarked car approaching, going slowly, the driver hoping to avoid holing his sump on a rock. The car rounded the bend and stopped. In panic the driver tried to find reverse but his windscreen starred as the heavy slugs smashed it apart and the third shot took off the top of the cop's head.

Yussuf got back into his car and drove away, easing back onto the main road and making his way to the safe house. He reset the grenade booby trap on the door then rushed up to the attic. He tied on his battle scarf and loaded the two Iglas into their tubes then sat back to wait, his Koran in his hand.

Gerry and Tau had spent an hour at the safe house before concluding that there was nothing to be learned and were racing back towards the Mount Nelson. Gerry had made contact with the elite SWAT team and outlined the kidnapping of Leon's wife and child, and stressed the need to bring them out safely. The house was to be approached with the greatest stealth – any sign of a rescue attempt and the hostages would die, if they weren't already dead.

'Do you think we should pull the final press conference forward?' asked Tau. There were two hours before the 6PM deadline and it would be a relatively simple matter to bring things forward by an hour and have everyone safe in their beds by the time Sayeed struck, if they weren't able to intercept him in time.

'Or we could relocate,' said Gerry. 'Go for plan B.' This involved taking all of the foreign dignitaries to the press centre at the National Police HQ.

'We need to bring Chitepo up to speed and let them take the decision,' said Tau, flipping open his phone.

'Wait,' said Gerry, 'there's still one ace we have. Get me Fitzwarren.'

Tau dialled Fitzwarren and a moment later the caramel tones of the CIA chief came through.

'What is it, Tau?'

'I'm putting you on speaker,' said Tau, 'I'm driving with Gerry and we need to debrief urgently.'

'Here's the thing,' said Gerry. 'Write down these co-ordinates – this is where we believe Sayeed will be taking his plane up in the next few minutes. Your AWAC should be able to pick him up then your Tomcats or Apaches can shoot the fucker out of the sky. The map reference is…'

'Whoa! Hold up a minute, son. Our AWAC is currently down.'

'WHAT?!' yelled Gerry.

'She'd been up for 14 hours straight and needed to refuel. She'll be up again in an hour tops.'

'In an hour your dipshit president will be spam!' yelled Gerry. 'How can you have your fucken plane go down NOW?!'

'Just hold on a minute right there, boy,' said Fitzwarren, his bonhomie gone in an instant. 'First, I don't give a rat's ass how upset you are, you do not refer to my commander-in-chief in those terms. Are we clear? ARE WE CLEAR?'

'Sir,' mumbled Gerry.

'Second, if you guys had done *your* work we wouldn't be here now with our dicks in our hands waiting for the Goddamn world to end!'

'Here's the thing, sir,' said Tau. 'We know that this guy has his plane and his Semtex. God knows where the missiles are but we can assume that they are also being readied for an assault. There are three choices. One, evacuate everyone to the Police HQ for the press conference. Two, call the conference an hour early. Three, go ahead as planned and hope to hell we get these guys first.'

'The President is currently in the air and will be arriving in four minutes to give the closing address. I'll review with my fellow security chiefs and with the president himself and get back to you shortly.'

The line went dead. Tau looked at Gerry.

'Haven't lost any of your silver-tongued charm, eh.'

'Christ, I could do with a Heiferlump and whisky chaser right now,' said Gerry.

'Something occurs,' said Tau. 'No sign of the hand-held rockets. I doubt that Sayeed would be carrying them on his plane. No point. No way to launch and no likely target. So they must be somewhere else.'

'The second cell.' said Gerry.

'Think target,' said Tau. 'What would make a good target?'

'A plane. A 747 loaded with foreign tourists. Bang! One for the Prophet.'

'Could be. But the airport perimeter is pretty secure and it's too random. These boys are here for the big party. What else?'

'Well, if it were me the obvious bladdy target would be those monster Chinooks carrying Big Bubba Satan.'

'Correct. Except they have so much electronic jamming that you can't even watch TV within 10 kilometres of the things.'

'Do our jihadis know that?'

'It seems like they know a lot,' said Tau. 'What else?'

'The Alabama!' cried Gerry. 'They attacked a US carrier off Aden once before. A bladdy speedboat loaded with home-made bombs nearly sank the damn thing.'

'Correct,' said Tau. 'And where would you launch such an attack?'

'From the sea?'

'Could be. Or, if you could get up high then why not a land-based attack from the middle of civilian housing?'

'The Kalk Bay safe house! You're a genius, but still ugly!' cried Gerry. 'We've had plainclothes watching that place on and off ever since Achmad died. So far, nada.'

'They stick out like sore thumbs,' said Tau. 'Our jihadis only need to wait until the coast is clear then slip inside. Who's running that surveillance?'

'Some CID guy name of Drinkwater.'

Tau hit speed dial again. 'Zwelakhe get me the CID commander in charge of the covert surveillance on the Kalk Bay house. Name's Drinkwater.'

'There's something coming in right now on the Kalk Bay house,' said Zwelakhe. 'Reports aren't clear but the cop on plainclothes duty was found murdered ten minutes ago.'

'Get a team of special ops guys assembled outside the house. Extreme caution to be used. Notify me when they're in place. Nobody to move without the 'go' word. Please confirm.'

Zwelakahe repeated the instruction then rang off.

Gerry swung his car into the gatehouse of the Mount Nelson. The armed soldiers held up their hands indicating that they should stop. After the document check the car was making its way slowly through the zigzag concrete-filled barrels when they heard the thud of helicopter rotors. The two Chinooks came in low from the sea. The Marine guard was lined up at the helipad. Just as Gerry engaged gear a Jeep came roaring along the road towards them from the hotel, its headlights on bright. It blocked their path and four Marines leaped out and aimed their weapons straight at Gerry and Tau.

'Step out of the vehicle sir,' said the front Marine.

Gerry held up his ID.

'Stand aside, officer. This is NIA business,' said Gerry.

'I said step out of the vehicle with your hands raised,' said the Marine, his finger starting to curl around the trigger.

'Here's the thing,' said Tau. 'You are in my country aiming a gun at two senior officers of the National Intelligence Agency. Call Fitzwarren and confirm. Now!'

The Marine did not waver.

'Our orders stand, sir. Nobody is to enter the grounds while the president is landing or taking off.'

In the background Tau and Gerry saw the Chinooks touch down and the huddle of men swarm into the hotel. Without glancing behind them the Marines lifted their weapons and stood aside.

'You may now proceed sir.'

'What's your name?' asked Gerry.

'Captain Pidulsky US Rangers sir.'

Gerry nodded and accelerated hard down the drive, cursing all the way to the front door where he did a handbrake turn leaving two black skid marks on the pristine cement driveway.

Tau and Gerry found Chitepo in the banqueting suite and brought him quickly up to speed. Moments later Fitzwarren walked in.

'Jonas, I've just had a word with the President, and he wants to stay put.'

'He won't reschedule or move to another venue?' asked Chitepo.

'No sir. He believes that it will show weakness to our enemies.'

'Can we at least move the venue from the front press suite to something more secure? We've identified a space in the heart of the hotel that will be less vulnerable to outside attack.'

'It stays where it is,' said Fitzwarren. 'Any news on your side?'

'Well, the failure of the AWAC means that we've put a South African Airforce attack helicopter into the air and it's heading for the landing site, but may be too late.'

Fitzwarren set his jaw and looked furious. 'Correction. The AWAC hasn't failed. It's refuelling and will be airborne in 45 minutes. It's temporary.'

'Do our fellow G8 presidents know that their air umbrella has evaporated?' asked Chitepo. 'Temporarily?'

'Nobody knows,' said Fitzwarren, 'and that's how it will remain.'

'So they can all be blown to hell just to save face?' asked Chitepo.

'I don't need you tugging my chain, Jonas. There are good operational reasons for keeping this information private. Namely that, if we leaked it, those lily-livered sons of bitches would hightail it out of here so fast you wouldn't see them for dust. It wouldn't look good for you guys, nor would it look that good if my president was forced to run for cover either.'

Fitzwarren turned abruptly on heel and stamped out.

Tau and Gerry looked at Chitepo.

'Let me know when the SWAT team are at the Kalk Bay house,' he said, and walked out of the room.

'Let's go down to ops,' said Gerry. 'I need to find out what's happening with Leon's people.'

Chapter 79

For the first hour Rashid and Martin said nothing. Although Thespina was kept tied up they let her comfort the boy, Anthony. After her initial panic, Thespina had tried to carefully work out her options. She was second generation Greek South African, her father having come from Athens straight after the Second World War during which he had joined the partisans and made it to England where he trained as a mechanic in the RAF.

George Antoniou had set up a small workshop and engineering works on the outskirts of Cape Town, and had slowly built up his business. He decided early on to specialise in aircraft maintenance, and carved a niche for himself rebuilding engines at a highly competitive rate. Which is why when young Leon Wessels arrived one day with his old crop duster engine on a trailer, it had been the start of a long relationship.

Thespina, George's oldest daughter, used to help out in the office, and slowly she and Leon fell in love. Initially George wanted his daughter to marry a Greek and shunned Leon, but after several disastrous attempts to fix her up with local Greek boys, George had bowed to the inevitable and Leon and Thespina had become engaged, and after a two-year courtship, married. Now, five years down the line, they had a young son, Anthony, a prosperous business and a bright future, until the Jihad had come knocking on their door.

She glanced at Rashid and saw in his face neither pity nor compassion, just a simple dedication to a single goal and a single idea. She saw too that he was fearless and prepared to die, and it was that above all which chilled her to the core. The younger one, Martin, looked less certain. She decided that he was the one to work on if she was to stand any chance of escape.

'How long are you going to keep us?' she asked. Martin looked at Rashid for an answer.

'If your husband does what he is told you will be set free, after our work is done,' said Rashid.

'What work is that? Scaring women and children?'

'You will see on the news. A great work.'

'And my husband?'

Rashid shrugged in a way that sent fear coursing through her.

'I need the toilet,' she said. Neither man moved.

'I said, I need the toilet.'

Rashid gestured at Martin. 'Go with her.'

'What? Inside?'

'No. Check the windows are secure then wait outside. She will not try anything or else her little boy will die. Now go.'

Rashid picked up Anthony in one arm while Thespina got to her feet, her aching limbs numb. She held out her hands for them to be untied.

'I can't untie you,' said Martin.

'I've got my period,' said Thespina, and Rashid flinched. 'I need to clean myself. I thought you men respected women. It seems not.'

Rashid muttered a curse under his breath and cut the nylon cable ties. Martin followed her to the toilet and checked that the window was barred and then let himself out while she locked the door. She sat on the edge of the bath and tried to massage life back into her hands as she racked her brains for a solution. The next time she came to the bathroom she would need to try and bring her cell phone, but as she desperately looked around she saw nothing which could help her prevail against the two men holding her and Anthony hostage. As for Leon, the thought of what may have happened to him was too painful.

Martin was standing outside the bathroom door, staring at Rashid.

'What?' growled Rashid.

'I'm thinking,' said Martin, 'Sayeed is on his way but we don't have any way out ourselves.'

'Our job is to wait here until the bombs are delivered and the mission succeeds,' said Rashid sternly.

'We're not meant to get out of here, are we?' asked Martin with a sudden realization.

'This is Jihad, not your bloody Sunday school,' said Rashid. 'If you want to go to Paradise right now just say the word, neh?' He pointed his gun straight at Martin's head. Martin mumbled something and looked away, his eyes brimming.

'What's that?' demanded Rashid looking murderous.

'I will wait,' said Martin. Rashid hammered on the bathroom door and Thespina flushed the toilet and emerged. He tied her hands again and she sat down beside her son who was now crying.

On the other side of the hill the specialist team of five men found the Corolla parked in the undergrowth, and had swiftly climbed the up to the ridge behind the house. They were watching with high-powered field glasses, but their view of the action inside the house was limited. The marksman had set up his rifle with scope and was waiting only for a clear shot, but the concern was that even if one of the kidnappers could be taken out, the lack of a clear sightline meant that the other would be able to kill the hostages before the house could be stormed. It was then that one of the officers saw a bottled water van heading along the road towards the Wessels place.

Meanwhile a *Rooivalk* attack helicopter was scudding low over the vine lands until it reached the Du Toit farm. A quick search revealed the deserted landing strip, and the helicopter was about to depart when one of the pilots saw a body under a tree. The chopper landed and the pilot sprinted out and turned Leon Wessels over. Leon opened one eye, groaned and then blinked a couple of times.

'Jeez, took you bladdy long enough,' he said. 'I'm dead here.'

'Be still,' said the pilot.

'Argh! My fucken chest hurts, hey,' he said. 'Where's my wife?'

'Don't speak,' said pilot ripping away the camo jacket. Blood had soaked the T-shirt but the pilot felt a hard plate beneath the fabric and slid out a slab of Kevlar, punctured near its edge by a bullet hole. The pilot ripped the T-shirt open revealing a dark purple hole just under Leon's shoulder.

'Wait here,' he said and sprinted back to his aircraft. Moments later the co-pilot emerged and rushed a medical kit to Leon.

'How's my wife and son?' he croaked.

The co-pilot took a hypo of morphine and shot it straight into Leon's arm, knocking him out before the plunger was fully depressed. They loaded him into the chopper and took off for a nearby cottage hospital.

Rashid had allowed Thespina to feed her son lunch and the little boy sat fearfully at the table, having to be coaxed to through each mouthful.

'You got a family?' asked Thespina of Martin. Martin looked to Rashid.

'What's wrong? Doesn't he let you speak?' said Thespina.

'You're lucky you are still alive,' said Rashid. 'When we made this plan I said it would be simpler if we shot you all right at the beginning.'

'So he's the brains – what are you, the muscle?' she laughed contemptuously.

Just then they heard the slow drone of an approaching car. Rashid rushed to the window.

'Who's that?' he demanded. Thespina looked out of the window and saw the Ice Cool water van slowing down at the gate. She inwardly gave a prayer of thanks.

'It's the water man,' she said, pointing to a water cooler that bubbled in one corner.

'Get rid of him,' said Rashid. 'I mean it. Don't try and signal or send a message or your little boy will die.'

Thespina nodded, realising in a flood of despair that her situation was hopeless. She watched as the driver emerged from the van and opened the gate, then drove through and got out of the van again to shut the gate behind him. Thespina saw at once that the driver wasn't Willem, the usual delivery man. Her heart beat faster as the van crawled up the final slope and stopped near the back door of the house.

'Get ready,' said Rashid to Martin. 'The first sign of anything, open fire. Keep a bead on her from there…' he pointed at the living room. 'I'll have the boy.' He took Anthony from his mother's grasp. The boy started howling but Rashid clamped his hand over the child's mouth and dragged him out of sight into the living room.

Martin nodded, his mouth dry, sweat trickling down the small of his back. He raised his gun and aimed straight at Thespina while Rashid held his aim on the small boy.

The van driver was wearing a long brown dust-jacket with Ice Cool written on the back. He opened the back of his truck and took out a 15 litre clear plastic bottle of water and carried it with both hands towards the back door. Moments later he knocked on the door.

'Open it,' said Rashid from the doorway of the living room. 'Get out of sight, Martin.'

Thespina opened the door. The man was holding the water bottle in his hands and smiling brightly.

'Good day, Mrs Wessels. Nice weather for this time of the year, isn't it?'

'Hullo Willem,' she said, holding his eye. The man nodded slightly.

'Got your water. Put it inside?' Said the delivery man, cheerfully pushing his way into the kitchen as Rashid took a step back to get out of view. The man dropped the water bottle and fired three times straight into Rashid's chest. Rashid jerked back, then slowly toppled forward as Martin rushed through from the other room, his eyes wide with fright, his pistol aimed at Thespina, squeezing the trigger. The pane of glass in the back window shattered as a high-powered round passed through it and took Martin under the arm. He stumbled and fell onto Rashid who lay on the slate floor, blinking slowly, trying to say something as blood trickled out of his mouth. Thespina screamed and rushed through to pick up Anthony who she scooped up in her arms and ran out of the house as the rest of the police swarmed down the slope towards her.

In Kalk Bay the first intimation of trouble came when squad cars blocked off both ends of the road and police started running from house to house, evacuating the locals to the safety of the cordon. Yussuf primed his handgun and put a spare fully loaded clip nearby next to a yellow box of hollow points. Yussuf clambered down from the loft and ran into the kitchen where he turned on all the gas rings and heard the gas hiss into the room, then made his way back up into the loft and sealed the edges of the loft door with some paper towels to prevent being overcome. When he saw an armoured vehicle trundle slowly up the street he tied the black scarf over his head and pulled up a chair next to the skylight so that he would have a clear field of fire, then took out his cell phone and dialled Hamidullah.

'Why are you calling?' demanded Hamidullah angrily.

'They're all here,' said Yussuf calmly. 'Must be 20 bloody cops and the SWAT team are taking up positions opposite the house. It won't be long now. I just wanted to say if they rush the house then I'm going to fire the missiles. So if I have to attack early, I just want you to know it's Allah's will.'

Hamidullah was silent for a long moment. Then said, 'Goodbye brother.'

'Thank you,' said Yussuf. 'I didn't want to die alone without the word of a friend in my ear. Allahu Akbar.'

'Allahu Akbar,' said Hamidullah, terminating the conversation.

The *Rooivalk* dropped Leon at Oak Glen Cottage Hospital, the first time an attack helicopter had ever landed in the parking lot. The medics swept him through to the emergency room and within minutes were operating to remove the bullet that had lodged within a centimetre of his right lung. The helicopter roared into the air and found its ceiling of 5000 metres and turned towards Cape Town, its radar prescribing great sweeping arcs as it sought the rogue plane.

There wasn't much room in the tight cockpit as Sayeed had the fire extinguisher packed with Semtex between his knees with the detonator button taped to the plane's control handle. He had been flying at treetop height all the way from Stellenbosch, and apart from lifting to clear the high tension wires, the flight itself had presented no major problems.

However, looming ahead of him was the vast bulk of Table Mountain, with its 'tablecoth' spilling over the summit. He knew that there were dangerous thermals running up the sides of the mountain and that he could easily become disorientated in the cloud layer. His initial plan was fly up over the summit then race down at full speed into the hotel, moving so fast that nobody would even be aware of his presence until it was too late.

But now he had second thoughts. If he flew around the mountain it would add another ten minutes to his flying time and he would coming at the hotel from the East. The advantage of this approach was that the anti-aircraft weapons were facing directly due south at the front of the hotel, and north, covering the back of the hotel and the slopes of the mountain. In other words, the eastern flank of the hotel was vulnerable.

There was a stand of dense natural forest at the eastern perimeter, so he would have to gain some height to get over the trees then drop down in a dive into the building, swerving to zero in on the front rooms at the last moment. He swung out towards the sea until he found the coast road leading in from Llandudno. He would follow the road up over the Nek and down the other side. He started singing – soon he would be seated beside the Prophet, the blessings of Paradise forever his.

Chapter 80

Gerry and Tau were wearing their flak jackets as they strode across the roof of the Mount Nelson. Gerry had loaded the Protecta assault shotgun with solid slugs and held it in one hand while across his shoulders was the grenade launcher. Tau had his service pistol strapped to his waist, for form rather than because he had any belief in his ability to bring down a plane with a handgun. The anti-aircraft gunners had been put on heightened alert and the American Marines had taken up key positions around the hotel. They were interspersed with South African troops and members of the elite diplomatic protection corps of the G8. The gates to the hotel had been chained shut and an armoured car blocked the driveway. The two Chinooks sat on the landing pad, their rotors turning slowly.

The press corps had all been assembled in the Eland suite in the front of the hotel, waiting for the G8 leaders to file in. There was a small dais with a microphone and lectern, behind which sat the President of the USA, the UN representative on AIDS and the South African President, a strong advocate of AIDS awareness and a champion of cheaper drugs for the developing world, who would make the closing address. He was patiently listening to the US delegate's wordy summation. The other Presidents sat in the front row of chairs, and behind them, separated by a rope, were the journalists.

Chitepo and Fitzwarren were downstairs in the ops room. A loudspeaker link was carrying the intelligence from the *Rooivalk* pilot. Gerry and Tau were getting a live feed from the ops room in their earpieces.

'The conference has just ended,' said Fitzwarren, broadcasting on open channel to all the security officers. 'In the next five minutes our leaders will take their places in the press briefing room. We are on red alert, so if anything moves, whack it.'

'This is Captain Drinkwater in Kalk Bay. The SWAT team are in place. Waiting for your green light.'

Gerry looked at Tau who nodded.

'This is Gerry Viljoen. Go! Go! Go!'

Yussuf saw the door of the armoured car open. He leaped up onto the chair and aimed through the skylight window at the great cruiser. He suddenly realised that despite having a colossal target, he hadn't actually decided on a specific target zone, and so aimed for the deck where an Apache Helicopter was just starting its rotors.

He fired. The missile burst through the window, corkscrewed as it found stability, and then streaked towards the battleship. Yussuf gave a cheer as he saw the white smoke trail making for the helicopter deck. The chopper had activated its electronic jamming, designed to divert any surface-to-air missiles to pass harmlessly below the aircraft. The missile swerved low, hitting the aircraft carrier at the top of the hull, where it exploded against the double skin armour-plate. Yussuf fired the second missile that performed an almost identical flight path, but this time it burst on the deck, taking out a small grey radar dome and scattering personnel.

'Jesus! He's firing fucking rockets!' yelled Drinkwater over the radio.

'Take the leaders to the secure room immediately,' said Tau on his secure channel. Twenty security officers appeared at the edge of the dais and quickly led the dignitaries out of the suite and rushed them down a corridor, just as a bemused Silas Maponya was about to climb onto the podium. Within 30 seconds, all of the G8 leaders were safe in an armoured storeroom under the hotel that had been built in the 1890s to store gold bullion before it was shipped to Europe. The journalists had all been rushed to the food store at the back of the hotel, wondering what scoop they had just missed out on, but were soon distracted by the cans of *pâté de foie gras* and bottles of vintage champagne.

In Kalk Bay the police were firing up at the skylight and Yussuf was snapping back with his handgun, yelling with glee. Finally a team of men made the front door and started battering it down while a second team attacked the garage door. A bullet tore into Yussuf's stomach and he collapsed onto the ground, gasping for air. Yussuf smiled to himself as he heard the garage door give way and he slowly counted to four, when the grenade detonated and blew the gas-filled house into the air.

Fitzwarren came on line. 'Our carrier is under attack from shore-based missiles! Repeat, our carrier is under attack.'

The scene on the flight deck was one of chaos. The first Igla had made a two foot hole in the outer armour of the carrier's hull, too far above the water line to pose any threat, but the second missile had smashed into the small radar dome that was manned by two sailors, one of whom was critically hurt, while the other escaped with light burns. The radar dome was crippled and the fire had been quickly extinguished, but the sirens were still blaring and men were scrambling to action stations. F-14 Tomcats were being readied for flight as the Apaches were tugged out of their hangars, but none was permitted to take off until the radar dome had been by-passed and the back-up system patched in.

'Drinkwater here! The whole bloody place has gone up! Nobody could have survived that blast. My men are going through the debris. We have found one body, the main attacker in the attic. No other bodies except for three of my men who were badly hurt and are on their way to hospital as we speak. The area is now secure.'

'Please repeat,' said Gerry. 'Only ONE body found at the site.'

'Correct,' said Drinkwater. 'Badly burned but preliminary ID makes him as Yussuf Anwar.'

'Thank you, Captain,' said Chitepo, coming on the line. 'Take care of your injured men and we'll keep you posted.'

'We have taken out the attacker,' said Tau feeding his transmission to Fitzwarren. 'Repeat, deal with the situation on board ship. We have contained the land threat, but you need to be vigilant in case there is a simultaneous attack from the water.'

'We believe,' said Gerry speaking into the security feed, 'that there is still one member out there, believed to be Hamidullah Hamid aka Six Moreno. Extremely dangerous and not to be approached.'

'Not to mention Sayeed Dhatri,' growled Chitepo, coming on line.

'Correct,' said Tau. 'But we have a good idea of where Sayeed is and what he's doing. The other guy, Moreno, could be anywhere.'

In fact, after Yussuf's disturbing call, Hamidullah had started his boat and was moving closer to the exclusion zone around the carrier when suddenly he had seen a massive plume of smoke rising up from the back of the hill where he knew the Kalk Bay house to be, followed moments later by a hollow BOOM! He tied his black battle scarf on his head and stood with his feet firmly planted as he pushed the engines to maximum revs. He shouted 'Allahu Akbar!' into the wind as he raced in from the setting sun. He tore around the headland saw before him the great bulk of the warship, smoke coming from the flight deck. He yelled a prayer of thanks and asked Allah to guide his hand as he shoved the twin throttle controls forward. His ski boat was pushing 50 knots and still accelerating – smacking the waves at that speed was like hitting concrete. The gas turbine V6 was howling and the wind and spray made it hard to focus but the ship was getting closer by the second.

He was one and a half kilometres out when he was spotted. A swarm of men rushed to the Alabama's deck pointing at the boat racing towards them out of a scarlet sun. Two machine-gunners opened up on the incoming boat, the tracers they used to help find their target also helped Hamidullah, who swerved one way then the other, zig-zagging his way ever-closer to the ship. He was yelling with wild exuberance as he dodged the streaming bursts of tracer fire, closing the distance to his target by the second. Eight hundred metres, 700, 600, then at 500 metres a canon opened up, shooting huge plumes of spray into the air, 450 metres and closing. The mighty steel side of the warship loomed above him. He could see individual faces of the sailors lining the deck as he pushed the throttles hard against the stop. The boat turbine engine was screaming and the boat was literally flying from wave to wave. Three hundred metres. Hamidullah reached for the trigger mechanism as a single tracer round finally found its target, ripping through the hull and smashing into the primed bomb in the forward locker.

A massive fireball lit up the ocean, throwing debris hundreds of feet into the air. The air was heavy with the smell of ammonia, and all that was left of the *Schdenfreude* was an oily slick on the water.

Hamidullah Hamid had entered Paradise.

Moments later Fitzwarren came on line. 'Just to let y'all know that our cruiser has fought off a seaborne attack. If you want to find Six Moreno, I would say that he's probably feeding the fish. Oh, by the way, our AWAC will be airborne in five minutes.'

Just then the *Rooivalk* pilot crackled on line.

'This is *Rooivalk One*. We're still 40Ks from target but we've just picked up what could be a light plane at low altitude following the coast road past Llandudno. He's sweeping into Camps Bay right now…'

'He's in the Exclusion Zone,' said Gerry. 'Take him.'

'Cannot comply,' said the pilot. 'I need to be 25Ks to lock on. Am proceeding with maximum speed towards the target.'

Sayeed was flying at 20 metres above the road. Cars were swerving as the drivers rubber-necked the bright yellow plane virtually skimming their roofs. Sayeed grinned to himself – they would have stories to tell their grandchildren about how the bomber had buzzed their cars. Sayeed swung away from the coast and followed the road up towards Kloof Nek.

In a matter of seconds, he swooped over the Nek and there below him in the setting sun like a child's model was the

Mount Nelson. The hotel looked pink in the soft evening light with its neo-classical facade and manicured gardens. And out in the bay the huge bulk of the USS Alabama had a column of smoke rising from the deck, and even from this distance Sayeed could make out the hundreds of men skittering about in a frenzy of activity. He wondered briefly about why the attack had preceded his own but events were colliding too swiftly to regroup and his only option now was to achieve his main goal.

Sayeed pulled back on the controls to lift the plane over the dense stand of forest between him and the hotel. He checked that the battery terminals were secured and that the slim detonators were pushed deep into the Semtex. His thumb was poised over the detonation button.

'Do you think the *Rooivalk* will be able to get the bastard in time?' asked Gerry. Tau shrugged just as their joint operational line crackled into life.

'*Rooivalk One* here. The plane has gone over the crest of the mountain and we've lost our radar lock. He should be visible to you within 2 minutes.'

'Well there's our answer,' said Gerry angrily. 'Anti-aircraft gunners stand by…'

Tau was the first to hear the drone of the engine. He swung around. The noise was coming from the East. Down on the ground the gunnery crews frantically tried to swing their guns around but their field of fire was too constrained. The portable anti-aircraft units at the back of the hotel quickly tried to manoeuvre themselves into position.

Then Gerry saw it. The tiny yellow plane came buzzing up from the treetops, climbing steeply then dropping down and racing straight towards the hotel, its engine screaming.

Sayeed was fixed on his target. From the edge of his vision he saw people running around on the ground and a heavy gun trying to turn towards him, but he could see from the panic that there was nothing to stop him. Then he noticed two small figures on the roof of the hotel. One was swinging a stubby shotgun towards him while the other was standing aiming his pistol with both hands like he was at a shooting competition. He knew that from this distance the pistol would be useless but the calm way the shotgunner took aim then fired caused him to throw the controls to one side. The plane lurched violently then recovered and came on. He saw that the tall African was still coolly standing and firing pot-shots, but the other man threw his shotgun angrily to one side and brought up a grenade launcher.

Gerry was sweating and furious with himself. He had missed seven straight shots with the Protecta and he knew this was his last opportunity to save not only himself but all the people in his charge. Even from a thousand metres he could see Sayeed's face in the cockpit as he swung the RPG up. Gerry remembered hunting with his father when he was 15 years old, and shooting a Muscovy Duck out of the air as it flew low and fast along the river. He suddenly entered the zone and heard his instructor, Vladek, whispering in his ear, explaining how everything had to come together for the perfect kill shot.

Sayeed was 300 metres from the hotel and had just started his turn to bring the plane towards the front, when Gerry squeezed the trigger. Everything went into slow motion. He saw the dumpy grenade shoot from the muzzle of the rifle and felt the recoil, then watched as the grenade wobbled a bit then stabilised. It looked as if Sayeed's plane would turn out of the trajectory, but then at the last moment the two seemed to fuse on an inexorable collision course.

Gerry saw Sayeed trying to respond but it was too late. The grenade hit just behind the engine and Gerry swore that he saw Sayeed's eyes widen in disbelief as the front of the plane disintegrated in an enormous explosion that tore the aircraft in two. The tail plane cart-wheeled out of the sky and tumbled down onto the front lawn of the hotel in a blizzard of flaming debris. The heat and shock blast nearly blew Tau and Gerry off the roof, and, as Gerry started to exhale, a huge punch in the back knocked him face forward onto the tiled roof, then the lights went out.

Just then the radio link crackled into life. Fitzwarren said 'Good news, our AWAC has just reached operational height and should start feeding back any minute now…'

Chapter 81

When Gerry came round he was in hospital. He could see De Waal Drive through the window and so reasoned that he must be in Groote Schuur. His back was strapped up and in great pain. He cautiously waggled his toes and was relieved to see the foot of the bed move. Then he tried his hands – all present and accounted for. He reached under the sheet and felt around his crotch just as Letta came in with Tau. Gerry hurriedly pulled his hands out of the bed.

'Awake two bloody minutes and already playing with yourself,' said Tau with a grin, plopping down a bunch of grapes beside Gerry. Aletta threw her arms around Gerry's neck and started crying.

'What happened?' asked Gerry.

'You nailed him,' said Tau. '*The shot of the century*, as the Argus is calling it.'

'Any casualties?'

'The hotel had every window on its eastern side blown out, but the leaders are all safe.'

Gerry sank back with relief. Then sat forward again.

'I remember all that. But then something punched me in the back…'

'You were shot,' said Tau.

'SHOT?! Am I all right?'

'No,' said Tau. 'You're dead and I'm here to tell you that you're being reincarnated as a chameleon.'

'You just can't let it go, can you?' Grumbled Gerry. 'Seriously, what happened?'

'The Kevlar vest took the impact. You were knocked out when you fell on your face,' said Tau. 'The vest took 90% of the hit but the bullet came through by two centimetres and went in to your back just above your kidney. It made a small hole but nothing else. You were very lucky.'

'But who on God's green earth shot me?' Demanded Gerry.

Just then Chitepo entered with Fitzwarren.

'It was a friendly fire incident,' said Chitepo.

'I bladdy KNEW it!' cried Gerry.

'One of our Marines saw the plane above your head and tried to draw a bead on the guy. I guess his aim was a little out,' said Fitzwarren with an apologetic shrug.

'Lucky the stupid prick didn't shoot my head off! Who was it?'

'The name doesn't matter,' said Fitzwarren. 'He's been dealt with.'

'It was Pidulsky, wasn't it?' said Gerry wearily.

'How did you know?' Asked Fitzwarren.

'Cos he's exactly the type of gung-ho arsehole who would do such a thing. Where is he? I want a word.'

'Well you'll have to speak pretty loudly. He's on his way to Alaska. They needed someone to feed the huskies. But moving swiftly along, I am here to bring good news. The President of the United States has asked me to convey to you his warmest thanks for preventing a major catastrophe, and will be recommending you boys for the highest award for valour.'

Letta squeezed Gerry's hand.

'Thank you,' said Gerry.

'There is one other thing,' said Fitzwarren reaching into his jacket pocket and producing a long slim envelope. 'Strictly off the record, a small token of our esteem and thanks.' He handed the envelope to Gerry. 'An all expenses paid first class round trip to any destination in the States for you and your partner.'

'I don't want to go on holiday with Tau,' said Gerry.

'*Partner* as in your charming fiancée,' said Fitzwarren, nodding at Aletta.

'What about Tau then?' demanded Gerry.

Tau grinned and produced his own envelope. 'Joyce and I are going to the Everglades,' he said.

'Another bladdy swamp. What is it with you guys? Where should we go, sweetheart? Hawaii?'

Aletta nodded, smiling.

'One thing,' said Gerry, 'are these five-star hotels?'

'Uh…Four-star,' said Fitzwarren.

'Saving the pres doesn't merit five stars?' asked Gerry.

'I'll see to the upgrade personally,' said Fitzwarren, 'now I've got to be going before you guys cost us any more. Thank you, Jonas, you and your people put on a great show.'

Fitzwarren shook hands and exited.

Chitepo sat heavily on the bed and ate Gerry's grapes. 'There were a few operational issues that can be reviewed and tightened up, but overall you did well. This arrived on a BBC reporter's desk this morning,' he passed a DVD to Gerry.

'What is it?'

'It's their final video message to the world. Mad bad western powers, spawn of Satan, the usual mix of bombast and bigotry. Take a good look,' he said. 'These are our enemies. Home-grown. From now on we need to change our game. Thank you.' He shook hands with Tau and Gerry then got to his feet and left.

'Not exactly loquacious,' said Tau. 'But it'll do. I've also got something for you.' He looked around furtively and produced a brown paper bag from under his jacket. He handed the grease-spotted bag to Gerry who sniffed it a couple of times then slowly opened it. He reached in his hand and took out a Double Cheese Chilli Heiferlump. Tears sprang into Gerry's eyes.

'I'll leave you to your two great loves,' said Tau, and slipped out. A moment later Gerry saw Tau and Chitepo in the car park, speaking animatedly. Finally Chitepo clapped Tau on the shoulder and gave him a warm, two-handed African handshake, then got into his car. Tau remained standing for a moment, lost in thought, then glanced up briefly at Gerry's room. A frown crossed Gerry's face, then he turned and saw Aletta looking at him, her face glowing in the late morning sun as she smiled at him. Aletta helped Gerry sit up and tucked a paper napkin under his chin and watched the pleasure suffuse his face as he ate the burger.

It didn't get much better than this.

Post Scriptum

Aletta had one final surprise. She helped Gerry into a wheelchair although he insisted that he could walk, and pushed him out onto a small balcony where another person sat in a wheelchair, his back to them. Gerry knew immediately who it was because Katja was kneeling down beside the wheelchair holding Charlie's hand. She stood up abruptly and let Charlie's hand drop when Gerry appeared, suddenly embarrassed.

'Charlie Brits. How are you, man?' Said Gerry pumping his hand enthusiastically.

'Jeez, you were pretty insufferable before, but now your head must be so big you can't get through the door.'

'Are you ready to go surfing yet?' asked Gerry.

'Not surfing. The doc said it was too strenuous. I'm going to do hang-gliding instead.'

'Nice one,' said Gerry. 'Katja has done such a good job of running the place that when you fly into the ground and finally kill yourself it'll give her career the lift it deserves.'

'We've all got to crash sometime, my friend. What makes it worthwhile is the lift you get before your wings melt,' said Charlie. 'That's a reference to Icarus, by the way.'

'I got it,' said Gerry. 'Go fly the good flight, Charlie.'

'Wheel me to the garden, my sweet,' Charlie said to Katja, patting her hand. Katja smiled and turned Charlie's wheelchair around.

'Sheesh, it's like bladdy rush hour here, hey,' said Leon.

Gerry groaned and half-turned to see Thespina pushing Leon in a wheelchair, their little boy holding shyly onto his father's hand. Leon looked pale in his hospital gown and was heavily bandaged around the shoulder and upper chest.

He shook Gerry's hand. 'I just want to say thanks, hey, for everything. This is Thespina and this big boy is Anthony.'

Gerry grinned. 'Hi. Are you OK, Leon?'

'Better than OK. You know, when he shot me, I didn't see my life flash before my eyes, or any of that baloney. What I saw was Jesus standing on a drum, waving to me.'

'A drum? Like a bongo drum?' asked Gerry, incredulous.

'No, man! A 44 gallon drum of avgas. I can even see the red Caltex star on the side. What he was doing standing on a bladdy drum I don't know. And I said to him, *Lord, I'm not ready to come yet, if that's OK with you*. And you know what he said to me?'

'No,' said Gerry, certain that he would be told anyway.

'He said to me *Leon Balthazar Wessels, you have a job to do. You have crops to spray and a wife and child to look after. Go back now.* What do you think of that, hey? The Big Boss,' Leon pointed upwards 'was telling me that I was too early, so he sent me back.'

'That's great, Leon,' said Gerry, wincing. He turned to Aletta. 'You know sweetheart, I'm still feeling a bit weak. Perhaps you could take me back to my room.'

Aletta nodded and smiled at Leon and Thespina.

'You take care now,' said Leon. 'And if you ever want a flying lesson, it's on the house!'

'Thanks Leon. Take care,' said Gerry as he wheeled away.

Gerry allowed Aletta to push him down the corridor.

'I just said Hawaii without even asking you,' said Gerry. 'Where do you want to go?'

'Hawaii's good. But I would like to see San Francisco as well.'

'OK, we'll do 'Frisco THEN Hawaii. How does that sound?'

'Just perfect,' she said, kissing him.

Glossary

Asseblief	please
Bakkie	pick-up truck
Big Bok	big shot
Biltong	dried meat
Bliksem	bastard
Boerenasie	SA Ku Klux Klan
Boet	brother
Borrie	turmeric
Braai – braaivleis	barbecue
Bredie	Cape speciality dish
China	mate, pal
Dagga	marijuana
Dorp	small town
Fynbos	small bushes
IDB	Illicit Diamond Buying
Kabeljou	Cod
Klaar	finished
Klippies	Klipdrif brandy
Kloof	cliff
Koeksusters	syrupy deep-fried plaited cakes
Madrassa	Islamic school
Manne	police
Melktert	milk tart
Mielies	corn
Miggie	midge
Moered	murdered
Moffies	gay men

My bra	my brother
Ouma's Kombuis	grandma's kitchen
Oupa	grandfather
Perlemoen	abalone
Poisons	Durban Poison - marijuana
Poephol	arsehole
Poes	cunt
Predikant	priest
Rondavels	round thatched huts
Skelm	criminal
Skollies	criminals
Snork	gobble
Stoep	veranda
Stokkies	short sticks of biltong
Stompie	cigarette end
Shaheed	martyr
Takkies	canvas shoes
Tassies	Tassenberg – cheap wine
Voetsek	Bugger off
Volk	The Afrikaans people
Vrot	rotten, drunk